The Last Sage

By Chris Rathburn

THE LAST SAGE

Edited by Patrick

A Thurston Howl Publications Book
Published by Thurston Howl Publications
Lansing, Michigan

jonathan.thurstonhowlpub@gmail.com

Cover photo by Aryan Safabakhsh; cover design by Pia Pulido

Printed in the United States of America

Chapter 1:

THE CAR WAS GOING too fast, and Alice couldn't carry a tune anywhere. She picked it up during the parts she knew, dialing up the radio to outmatch the pounding raindrops splashing hammer falls against the roof. Timothy took a hand off the wheel and laid it over hers.

Their hands, hers and his, rested in her lap, warming her bare legs. Timothy sang with her, his ear for pitch and his smooth voice pulling hers toward something closer to the melody. He didn't know the words any better than she did, but they both loved the music.

Warbling unabashedly, Alice felt the car sliding in the deep puddles along the road, their surfaces an arrhythmic staccato of little collisions. She stopped singing when he pulled his hand away to speed up the wipers. Turned up all the way, their manic tempo cleared the glass for an instant, and then their work was washed away.

As the radio station shifted to its obligatory round of advertisements, he spared her a glance and asked, "Did you talk to them yet?"

Alice rolled her eyes, and he added, "I'm not trying to

be a nag, Al. Now that we've got a date set, I just thought we should start figuring out who we're inviting. I've already talked to *mine.*"

Timothy cringed as soon as those last words left his lips. Alice looked at him evenly and said, "Good for *you.*"

"I just meant..."

"I know," said Alice, "I *know.* It's just hard, alright?"

Timothy took his most reassuring tone; it sounded suspiciously like the one he used with clients. "I'm sure they'd be happy to hear from you. News or not, it's been what, five years?"

"Six," she said automatically. "It's not easy, like it is with your parents, Tim. You get to tell them things like how you passed the bar and got engaged. What do I say? Hey, Mom! Hey, Dad! Long time no see! Great news! I didn't get accepted into law school, but I stopped dealing dope! I racked up six figures of debt getting around to graduating with my now useless bachelor's in criminal justice, but it's cool. I'm getting married in six months, so it'll be like it's half his!"

Timothy winced as she spoke, taking his eyes off the road to meet hers. "I'm sorry, Al. I know it's a big deal. Sorry to bug you with things. Maybe I'm nervous, too?"

"You're nervous?!" she asked, incredulous. "Must be rough."

Then, she clutched at her armrest and braced her palm against the door as she felt the rear wheels start to slide out of line. He put his eyes back on the road and carefully turned to ease into the skid. There was a stomach-dropping lurch, and then all the wheels were in agreement once more, speeding them smoothly over the slick pavement.

Timothy reached for her hands again, and she took his gratefully. He pulled a face but said nothing. Alice looked at him apologetically when she realized how tight she was gripping him and relaxed. He didn't look back; eyes on the road but smiled and nodded when she eased up.

He took a breath, then asked slowly, "Do you want to change the date?"

Alice looked over sharply. "Are you *nuts?!* You already talked to your folks!"

He shrugged and said, "It's not set in stone. They won't mind. If you need time, that's ok."

Alice frowned, brooding. Half-grateful, half-guilty, she considered breaking it off right there. Though she cared for Timothy, maybe really loved him in a way, she knew this was just another face of the same pattern. All her life, it was as though she just went through the motions, waiting for something important to happen.

She'd finished high school because it had been easy enough to scrape by with C's and there wasn't much else to do. When college came, she'd already been dealing for a year; it was simpler than working, and she'd never been caught. The years had fled by while she switched majors, hiding in lecture halls while student loans mounted. It seemed like no time had passed before she was the oldest girl at the party, every party. Disheartened at the ever-increasing sense of alienation and old lady jokes, she'd been about ready to drop out and start thinking about a day job when Timothy came along and plucked her from her stale life.

Again and again, glimpses of the world outside their car flashed past. Alice felt it when they hit a long stretch of puddle and the wheels leapt free of the pavement entirely. The sedan turned as it glided over the water and, all at once, they were pointed the wrong way; hydroplaning. The hood ornament, a circled three-pointed star, became a chrome crosshair pointed straight for the shoulder and beyond.

"Ah, shit!" Timothy cried.

He yanked his hand away from hers and clamped it down on the wheel. She watched the ditch coming, everything moving so slowly while her mind raced along. They'd passed several cars and one truck on the side of the road on their way home. One of the cars had been on its side, a covered stretcher being loaded onto an ambulance. Apparently, there was no one that needed to breathe.

Timothy kept cool and quiet while they headed toward an accident of their own. Alice was too startled to scream as she watched him save them. Pump the brake, don't mash it down. Turn the wheel into the skid but don't overcorrect. Alice felt the tires touch down again, and her fiancé guided the Mercedes to a stop on the shoulder.

Breathing hard on the adrenaline pumping through his blood, Timothy looked at Alice and reached for her. "You ok?"

Alice was breathing heavily herself, her body saturating its cells with oxygen to prepare to fight or run away. It didn't know the difference between a car accident and a predator. She took his hand in her own. It was shaking. So was hers.

"I think so," she told him, taking yet another steady breath while her stomach muscles grudgingly unclenched. "but what I really want to know is who put all this shit in my pants?!"

Timothy blinked, and then they were laughing. It was good to laugh. It meant they weren't dying. He let her go again to turn down the radio, but she reached out and stopped him.

"It's ok," she told him, her laughter melting into a lasting smile. "We're fine. Let's go."

He looked unsure. "I should probably check and see if the car's alright."

Alice's lips twitched, then parted as her laughter was reborn. "What are you going to do? Request a motion for an appeal?"

Timothy frowned, but his eyes were smiling. "I'm not *completely* useless with my hands, Al."

She let her hands drop to her lap and shrugged. "Fine, go get soaked if you want."

He looked out the window then down at his dark suit. He was wearing his favorite tie; royal blue, fine silk. She could almost hear his toes curling inside his patent leather shoes. He looked in the rearview, running fingertips across a fresh haircut. He was looking for grays unconsciously, especially at the temples. His dad's had started there when he was thirty. Timothy was years past that and knew his time was coming.

"You know what?" he said, finally. "I think you're right. We're fine."

Alice peered at the sky. She thought it was getting lighter. She couldn't tell if the rain was slowing or if it just seemed that way when they were sitting still. Intuition suggested the former.

Seeming to hear her thoughts, he told her, "I think it's letting up. Let's get home."

"Let's get tacos!" she countered. "I'm starving."

He quirked an eyebrow. "Brushes with death make you hungry?"

"I was already hungry," she told him. "Facing death just reminded me. Please?"

The corner of his mouth twitched toward smiling. "Let's make a run for the border?"

"I said I want tacos, not diarrhea."

Timothy laughed. "Alright, La Fuente then."

Alice flipped down the visor and inspected herself in the little mirror; platinum blonde hair that looked good enough, most assumed it came from a bottle, pretty in an ethnically ambiguous arrangement of sharp, thin features and a year-round tan, still closer to thirty than forty. Too old to try for law school again, and too old to go back to selling dime bags to college students. Her thoughts came back to his question about the wedding while she reached for her purse and fished for lip gloss.

Meeting Timothy had turned her life in a good way, but now it was just as stale as any of the other years before him.

She imagined they'd probably have kids. Maybe she'd work, but it was more likely she'd just stay at home to be a mom and let him keep paying the bills. She'd never been interested, but Timothy wanted children, and she had no idea what else she'd do with herself.

Alice tried to see herself like that, slowly shriveling as the procession of gray seasons picked her over in turn. Getting married; it was a step to take, a box to check, and not for the first time, in her quiet, secret moments, she wondered if she'd be better off dead. Nothing else fit.

"You look great, Al," he told her. Both hands were on the wheel, the Mercedes back up to highway speed. She tucked away the gloss, smiling at him as she rolled her lips around to distribute the fresh layer of pink. She checked her work in the little mirror, put a hand on her stomach, and leaned back in her seat. She imagined a life in there and pulled her hand away to rest on her leg.

Inwardly, she chastised herself with a half-hearted variation of the little speech she kept for when her mind went this way. *Hell, I thought I'd be dead or in jail by now anyway, so I guess I'm doing pretty good. Tim's a good man. I should feel lucky.*

The guilt rose up in her then, and she met her own gaze in the mirror. *But I don't. I'm not sure I ever did. I can't keep doing this. It's not fair to him. I should tell him I'm not ready. I have to . . .*

Alice flipped the visor back up and steeled herself for what had to come next. She opened her mouth to speak but caught sight of something moving in her peripheral. She turned to look and saw an eagle flying through the rain. It was headed across the freeway on a vector that would take it in front of them. Curious, she glanced past the steering wheel to check their speed; seventy-ish. The great bird was keeping up with them, powerful wings pummeling the air with lazy strength. *Damn! How fast do those things fly?!*

Unsure, she turned and asked, "Tim?"

"Hm?"

"Do eagles fly when it's raining?"

"I'm a lawyer, Al. Ornithology isn't my thing. Why?"

Alice looked back, but the bird was gone. "Nothing, I guess. Just thought I saw something weird."

Timothy shrugged. "Maybe it's got an egg waiting for it back at the nest or something?"

She laughed it off, her doubts distracted for the moment, and brightened when a classic from her adolescence started up on the radio. "Oh hey! I love this song!"

Timothy listened, smiling as Alice crooned out something vaguely approximating the melody. He told her, "You know it's actually about the birth of his daughter, right? The lead singer."

"Yeah?"

He nodded. "Search it."

Alice nodded back while she looked in her purse again, trading her lip gloss for her smart phone. *I can tell him tonight, after we get home,* she decided, relieved to put off the inevitable a little longer. She thumbed her phone to life and grinned as he joined her in song. "I know who I want to take me home! I know who I . . ."

"Ah, shit!" Timothy shouted, hauling the wheel to the right. Alice jerked her head up, eyes wide, looking up from her purse in time to see him veer them away from a dark, hooded figure standing in the middle of the highway. She went from singing to screaming as they headed toward death for the second time in ten minutes.

Timothy mashed down the brake, locking up the tires and sending them into a broadside skid. He twisted the wheel under his white knuckled grip, turning until it could go no farther. They slipped sideways like that, a great fan of water splashing up to shine dully against the gray sky.

The wheels sank down through the sheets of water as the

Mercedes slowed, then caught abruptly at the pavement. The angle was all wrong. Centripetal force sent her head through the passenger side window as the car spun out in the opposite direction. Even as the glass exploded outward into the wet gloom, her scream carried on unbroken. It was a strange sound, as howls of mortal terror go, precisely the same note she'd been singing.

"I know who I want to take me home. I know who IIIiii . . . !"

Her scream wailed on as the sedan skidded across the shoulder and onto the slick turf. The slope of the ditch angled the car up and over, sending them into a roll. Alice's cry swelled to an impossible volume as the ground rose up to peer through her window. For a bizarre moment, she felt her cheek come to rest against cool, wet grass.

It felt just the way it did when she'd play in her yard on cool mornings as a girl. Sometimes, she'd lay in the dew long enough, she'd start to shiver with cold. That meant it was time to run inside to huddle under a towel, warming herself while mom made lunch.

Then the feel of the grass was gone, and Alice felt herself turning upside down. Timothy was shouting to her left and somehow above her. She turned to see her fiancé gripping the wheel, his soft lawyer's hands pushing out from locked arms, trying to somehow control what was happening. The steering wheel actually bent under the pressure. She watched the sky pan by through the driver side window as the Mercedes rolled and felt it when momentum lifted it wholly into the air.

The car twisted in the empty space in a barrel roll. It seemed to play out in slow motion. Timothy had time to look back at her, his teeth bared in a wide mouthed, terrified bellow. Somehow, she didn't hear him.

Instead, Alice heard the patter of raindrops against the underside of the Mercedes. It sounded cheerful, like a good day to sit inside and read with a mug of tea. Faintly, she could hear herself screaming on and on that one note. "IIIiii . . . !"

They were looking each other directly in the eye when the roof of the car slammed down against the ground. The sedan landed on the driver's side first. The windshield and Timothy's side windows shattered explosively, little sparkling daggers shooting in every direction. Alice watched helplessly as they rolled and the roof collapsed inward with crushing force.

Timothy's body tried to find a place to be as the car's frame wrapped around him. His face shoved forward until it was pressed against the steering wheel. He was wearing his seatbelt; he always did, but it didn't matter. The car's frame twisted so, the restraint was mashed right down with him.

Alice watched as her fiancé's head sandwiched between the steering wheel and the crumpled roof of their car. She watched his head crack and lose its shape, his skull fractured. She watched his scalp tear, blood and brains actually squirting out through the spreading fissures of his skin.

She felt herself lifting into the air until she was hanging over Timothy's mangled body, looking down at torn metal, torn grass, torn flesh. Still she screamed, holding that one note for an interminable stretch of time. She wailed in perfect clarity and pitch as her side of the car hammered back toward the ground.

Within herself, there was a strange sensation of opening. Alice felt as if something, some *things,* inside of her were somehow dilating along the length of her body. She could feel an exchange between them, like lightning traveling up and down her nerves.

Absurdly, the feeling of it didn't stop within her. Through the top of her head, she could feel another opening there, also. It was as if her spine extended up past her skull to connect with another sensation of self, outside her physical form yet somehow fully a part of her.

Alice could feel herself, her wide-open *somethings*, vibrating in tune with her scream. Then, the wheels of the Mercedes came down, connecting solidly with the ground. She lifted out of her seat, the inertia squeezing her through the passenger side window. She heard her seatbelt creak and groan and then give way, shards of glass and twisted bits of plastic and metal flying in every direction. She joined them in their mad dance, sailing up and out of the wreck in a graceful arc like the head of a shrapnel comet.

She didn't know if she was screaming anymore. Through the wind and the rain and the flying glass, Alice could only feel the throbbing power building inside her body. That feeling like electricity centered on a line through her like a live wire, passing through those dilated passages within her in steady waves. The sensation gathered intensity as the vibration rose up past her head, like each of those *things* was an amplifier passing on the signal toward something greater. When it reached that place beyond the top of her head, that uppermost place that was somehow still her, it was almost like the vibration was a part of herself, a *song* of herself singing out into the world in all directions.

It was louder than anything she could imagine, yet distinctly there was the percussion of raindrops as they pattered against her body. She could hear the notes of the wind whistling. As she struck the ground and slid over the wet grass, the hissing susurrus of her dress and skin against the little green blades blended with the symphony of her flight.

Alice slid farther than she would have believed. It was an unsettling sensation, feeling the ordinary ground offering no resistance, like the basic laws of physics had broken down. When she finally stopped, she could see their car was a warped and twisted heap. It seemed so distant, plumes of thickening smoke rising from the wreck, perforated by the rain. She was too weak to weep for Timothy, for herself, but slow tears slid down her cheek in memoriam of that sensation, that vibration she couldn't feel inside herself anymore.

An eagle swept down and paused in midair. *No,* she thought, *the same eagle!* It beat its wings furiously beside the remains of their car, their Mercedes, the first major purchase of their coupling. She remembered when they bought it, the two of them, if only for a little while, had seemed like something that could work, like their separate lives could somehow be joined by the tangibility of the cool, glossy paint under her fingertips. When she'd first leaned her hip against its smooth frame, feeling the car shift only a little to shoulder her weight, she'd felt hope something might finally change for her. It had been so material, so real; something to help them make a life together.

Now, she understood. *Things change; nothing lasts.* The car, their relationship, their lives were just as impermanent as anything else. Alice felt herself blinking slowly, the gray world of the rainstorm becoming fuzzy and indistinct at the edges of her vision. Quickly, quietly, impossibly, the eagle became the hooded figure. There was nothing ostentatious about it at all, one thing simply became another.

The hooded figure stepped past the car, thin flames now licking up into the smoke. Alice tried to sit up, but her body responded only weakly. She tried again, and the result was less. She gave up and looked past the man toward the sedan, trying to get a glimpse of Timothy. *It has to be a man,* she decided, *He moves like one.* She ignored him as he stepped carefully but nimbly down the slope to the bottom of the shallow ditch where she lay.

The fires were brighter now, even in the clearing light of the passing storm. *Do cars really blow up? Is that only in movies? Oh, God . . . Tim . . .*

The man knelt beside her and looked her over. He was indistinct in a dark gray hoodie and a black, billed cap. He wore black track pants, the ones with snaps running up the side so they could be torn off in an instant. His feet were bare, long toes curled firmly in the mud.

How did he miss all the glass? Alice thought dully, her vision fading, the world contracting down until the man's dark, unharmed feet were all she could see. The man stayed there with Alice as her eyes slipped shut, keeping vigil until the sirens called a distant howl. He was gone again, carried away by the beat of powerful wings, before the police and the paramedics could find her body, bleeding but still breathing.

Chapter 2:

ALICE OPENED HER EYES. The room was dark. She kept quiet, kept still, and tried to figure out where she was.

There was a large window to her left. A faint light was strengthening. *Dawn.* There was a small, blue sofa under the window. A little, round end table stood to its side, in the corner. The lamp sitting on top looked like something she'd find in a hotel.

She panned her gaze. There was a framed print of a deer, partially hidden behind a close up of a flowering bush. It was unmistakably corporate art, but she liked how the prongs of its antlers blended with the branches. Beside it, there was a white board divided into sections. It was covered in the scrawl of several hands, but it was too dim to make out what anything said.

Alice kept looking right and found her feet, poking up underneath a thin, beige blanket. She was laying in an uncomfortable bed. The foot of it was a slab of beige plastic. She'd never needed one before, but Alice had lived long enough to recognize where she was. *Holy shit, what hospital is this? Tim . . .*

She noticed a little device on her finger. It pinched but didn't hurt. She didn't know the terminology, but she knew it connected to a machine that was tracking her heart rate and probably her oxygen levels. Weaker than she'd ever been, she patted about for some kind of call button. It would be good to see a nurse, maybe someone with some information.

Finding nothing, she made to pull the sensor from her finger. It would probably set off some annoying alarm, but it would get someone in her room. She brought her hands together to pull it loose, but a large, dark hand reached out and laid gently over them.

Alice's eyes widened in surprise. *No one was over there before . . . I think?* She felt like she'd been sleeping for days but was still too tired to scream. Instead, she looked to her left to see the man from the accident standing over her. Still frames of the crash played through her mind; his bare feet as they stepped down the glass-strewn hill toward her.

He was silhouetted against the rising light of dawn through the window, but she could make out he wore a set of blue, short sleeved scrubs. His face was shadowed and indistinct but for his eyes. Those were unmistakable. The man's eyes were a swirling storm of fire, casting light like flickering candles in the dim.

"Please, be still," he said. "You were out all night. How are you feeling?"

His voice was sonorous; the deep richness of it filled the room, though he barely spoke above a whisper. She felt the ripples of the man's words against her skin and relaxed into a sense of familiarity. It was soothing, perfect, like being an infant stirring in recognition at the sound of her mother. There was no way to understand it, but she knew by the stranger's voice she loved him.

"Oh," she murmured, snuggling against her pillow. "It's you."

"Are you in any pain?" he asked her.

Alice shook her head slightly. "No, I'm fine."

"Good," he said. "We have much to discuss, and there is little time."

The man reached past her and turned on a light. She squinted at the sudden brightness, then looked toward the source of it as her eyes adjusted. The light came from another lamp standing on a countertop with a built-in sink. There was a box of latex gloves, a box of disposable masks, and other less identifiable items.

He'd only leaned over her a little, but the lamp sat beyond her own reach. *What the hell?* she puzzled. Alice looked back at the man, her brow furrowed in confusion. In the light, she saw then his deep, brown eyes were only eyes. He was fine featured, handsome, and swarthy. Waves of thick, dark hair were gathered and bound in a neat ponytail. His bare arms were hairless with deep cut musculature, like a professional bodybuilder.

"Who are you?" she asked him. It was dissonant, feeling so familiar with a complete stranger.

"I am Altair," he answered, "and I am here to help you."

"Help me with what?"

He smiled, warm and a little mischievous. "To reclaim your birthright. Alice, you are the eighth sage of earth, and you are needed."

"I'm what now?"

The sense of secure familiarity vanished in an instant. Grunting with effort, she propped up on her elbows and then forced herself to sit up. It was easier than she expected.

"That feeling of opening at the accident," said Altair, "those were your loci, your centers. In the face of death, you found your magic and saved yourself. Without it, you would be dead, and all would be lost."

Alice blinked. "Lost? Centers? What are you talking about?!"

Altair spread his hands. "I'm sorry, but I don't know exactly. That's why I came to find you and help you wake up. Whatever is happening, the world needs your music to find its way."

Images of the crash played through her mind's eye. *The eagle and the man. They were the same thing. He was right in the middle of the road...*

"You caused the accident."

It wasn't a question. He said nothing, and Alice knew she was talking with the man who'd killed Timothy. Maybe Altair hadn't done it directly, but he was the reason her fiancé was dead and she was laying in this bed. She wanted him gone, wanted him dead, wanted to kill him, but sitting up was the limit of her strength. Instead, she satisfied her urge to action with another question.

"What are you?" she said. "Your eyes..."

"I am a jinn," he answered without hesitation; his earnest, quiet voice pulsed against her body. She could feel that extension of her being, that thing she'd felt in the accident, above her head again. It stirred, blinking open like a sleepy eye. *My center,* she thought, trying the concept. It felt right.

"In this life," he continued, "I am to be your guide and your guardian."

"This life?"

"Your eighth," Altair confirmed, as if that explained everything.

"But why?" she asked, emotion rising in her to clench at her throat and choke her voice, "Guide me to what? Why the accident?"

"Because you asked me to."

Alice couldn't believe what she'd heard. "I asked for *this*?! I *asked* you to kill Tim?"

The jinn shook his head sadly. "That was not intentional. I am sorry for your loss, but the sign you foretold came to pass. You told me if I did not find you immediately, if I did not awaken you at once, it would be the end."

"The end of what? What *sign?!* What are you talking about?!"

"The end of everything, Alice." Altair held up his hands and patted the air with his palms. "Of all of creation as we know it. The other sages have all gone, disappeared as you said they would. *That* was the sign you spoke of, and now you are the last. You have been long in hiding, and you have much to learn."

She shook her head, scanning around for the call light. "This is crazy! You're fucking crazy! You need to get the fuck out of here! I'm calling a goddamn nurse!"

Altair remained calm, maddeningly reassuring despite herself. Smoothly, he reached out and plucked something from her bedsheets and held it out to her. Alice blinked and saw he held a device with a red button, a thick cord reaching from it back behind her bed. He passed the call button to her without hesitation.

"I will go," he said amiably. "I will be waiting. You will be ready enough soon, but don't take long. Danger is coming."

Alice snatched the call button from the jinn's hand and jammed it repeatedly with her thumb. She was afraid and didn't fully understand why. This man, this jinn had admitted to murdering her fiancé. She'd also seen him turn into an eagle. She felt something within herself stirring at the thought of Altair. *My centers,* she thought, *my loci.* It was as though there were a series of spinning vortexes wheeling along her spine. Somehow, she could feel them widening like the iris around a pupil.

As they did, she felt her sense of the world expand. Suddenly, she saw the man seated by her side was not a man at all. Seen clearly, Altair was a being formed of swirling fire. There was no smoke, and his touch burned nothing, but he blazed. She kept pushing the button, feeling the pulse of electricity traveling through the wire as she completed the circuit.

Alice felt her senses extend even further. She could discern vibrations she knew intuitively; the other people outside her room, healers and the sick, the electricity coursing through the building, giving life to its purpose. She squinched her eyes shut and tried not to feel any of it. She needed to block out the sensation. It felt like she was stretching out, spreading out through the world until she disappeared into it.

"Don't go too far," she spat, opening her eyes again to glare at the jinn. Anger and grief leant clarity, helped her focus before she lost herself. "You're going to fucking jail, Altair!"

The jinn smiled and rose to his feet. He slipped around the foot of the bed and headed for the door. He looked over his shoulder as he placed his hand on the knob. "Call for me when you are ready, Alice."

"How?" she blurted. She meant to be furious, imagining him in handcuffs, loaded into a police car, showing up at court in a gray suit, disappearing forever from her life into a little cell packed with more criminals. Instead, she felt panic rising in her as he turned his back, like she would be lost without him. She lay back, suddenly weak. "How do I call for you?"

"The music," he told her. "That's the key to your magic. You can always find me through your music."

He smiled. "You'll see."

With that, Altair turned the knob and opened the door. At exactly that moment, a nurse walked into the room. She pushed a cart laden with little boxes of cereal, disposable bowls and plastic tableware, single serving cartons of milk and juice, and pieces of fruit. Though there was hardly space to do so, Altair stepped around her. The nurse paid him no mind, didn't seem to notice the jinn at all. As he left the room, Alice's memories of him slipped away like smoke until she wasn't certain he'd ever been there.

"Good morning, hon!" The nurse beamed. Alice couldn't tell if she really was that cheerful or if it was simply a flawless bedside manner. She didn't care. At the sight of the food, her mind went strangely blank. She forgot all about centers and magic and jinn, about death and past lives. Her world was her growling stomach, and she needed to fill it.

Eagerly, she selected a banana, oatmeal, sausages, a doughnut, two little cartons of milk, and a tuna sandwich. The nurse smiled down at her warmly. Her badge read: Cathy. Middle aged, mostly in shape, soft and firm at the same time; the name matched her perfectly. Nurse Cathy handed over the banana, the oatmeal, and a milk.

"We'll see how you're feeling after that," she said, stepping over to a laptop console attached to the wall. "Don't want you making yourself sick."

Alice ate while nurse Cathy logged into the computer with a swipe of her badge. She clicked and tapped through a series of menus. Sometimes, she typed something; otherwise, it looked like box checking work. The nurse glanced over her shoulder and smiled. "I'll be out of your hair in just a minute. If you're not documenting something, it's not healthcare, right? How would you rate your pain?"

There was a handy chart on the wall to Cathy's right, numbered on a scale of simple cartoon faces; smiling to resting bitch face to uncontrollable sobbing. Alice mentally checked through her body. She felt tired and weak but was surprised to find her pain was minimal.

"About a two? Three, maybe?" she said, unsure. The corresponding cartoon faces still smiled at three, but only a little. Cathy nodded as she opened more menus and clicked more boxes. Alice finished her banana and started on her oatmeal when something stirred in her mind.

She pondered on the strange feeling around a mouthful of banana, like there was something she needed to remember, but couldn't quite manage it. Then, all at once, she felt the loci at her forehead pulse, and she gasped, her eyes opening so wide they bulged. Memories flooded back in a rush, as if they'd been held back by some invisible barrier within her that had abruptly given way. *Wait! He was here! Altair! He killed Timothy!*

Astonished at how she could have forgotten the jinn, she called out to the nurse, "You need to call the police!"

Cathy paused in her work. She turned to face her patient fully and asked, "Yes?"

"That man!" Alice shouted, flecks of banana flying out onto her chin. "The one that was in my room just now. He caused the accident! He killed Timothy! You need to call the police! Now! Before he gets out of the hospital!"

The nurse stood patiently, saying nothing while she ranted. When Alice stopped, Cathy turned back to her computer and logged out with another swipe of her badge. In that warm manner she had, Cathy told her, "I'll go and let the doctor know right now, Alice. We'll make sure everything gets taken care of. Okay?"

Alice looked the other woman over. She didn't understand it, but her senses were still something beyond anything she'd ever experienced. She felt as much as saw some kind of energy that surrounded the woman. It entered and left her body at certain points, centers much like her own, but they pulsed in a rhythm distinct from anything else she could perceive. *It's like her frequency,* Alice decided.

She looked closer and saw something meaningful in the play of the woman's aura; a sense of the nurse's mind. *She thinks I'm not firing on all cylinders because I'm recovering from the wreck. Delirious, hallucinating maybe. She'll make a note of it so the doctors can decide if I'll need a psychiatric referral.*

Outwardly, she said in her calmest tone, "Thanks, Cathy."

Alice gave her most disarming smile and lied, "Sorry about that. I guess I'm still feeling a little fuzzy from the drugs. I think I got confused for a second there, but I'm okay. Just needed to wake up a little more, you know?"

Cathy gave her patient an appraising look, her smile a practiced mask. It was an admixture of warmth and professional detachment. Alice could tell, could *see*, the woman was still checking boxes, screen or no. Arriving at an end of a mental decision tree, the nurse passed Alice a second container of milk and a tuna sandwich. She headed for the door, calling, "I'll check on you later, sweetie. Call if you need anything sooner."

Alice watched her go. When the door was closed, she unwrapped her sandwich and nibbled pensively. Beneath her confusion and her hunger, she ached with guilt for Timothy. If not for her, he'd still be alive. *It's not fair!* she thought. *He should have been somewhere else! He should have been with some*one *else! I should have told him how I felt, how I really felt a long time ago, but he pulled out a ring and I didn't know what else to do! I'm so sorry, Tim! I'm sorry!*

She wept as she worked at her sandwich, shedding tears silently so she wouldn't attract nurses. For the time being, she needed to be alone to feel her way into her grief. After a few mouthfuls, Alice put aside the sodden remnants of her sandwich on her sheet and hugged her knees to her chest.

Eventually, fatigue overcame desolation, and she slept again. She dreamt of fire walking toward her, holding out a hand beneath a handsome smile. Somewhere, she heard Timothy screaming as he burned.

Chapter 3:

LONG, WHITE FINGERS TREMBLED with nervous energy as they fumbled for the lump of dark crystal in his pocket. The stone wasn't big enough for Travis to see his father, but, once he got it working, they could hear each other fine. They'd spoken rarely in his life. Each time, he'd never wanted to touch the seer stone again.

Sitting in a shabby studio apartment fashioned from the basement of an old, creaky house, the heavyset man pulled out an unlined notebook and a pen and started scrawling out the ritual sigil, the only *true* magic he knew. His foster family, the Pothasts, had taught it to him when he was young. It went with his clairvoyance.

Travis couldn't control his second sight consistently, but it was the reason his father had gone through the trouble of transporting him to this world. It was his purpose here. The reluctant oracle worked feverishly at his drawing, squinting at the lines as he pulled the cheap, plastic ballpoint as slow as he needed to keep them straight. He knew the angles of the vertices had to be correct or, at best, it wouldn't work.

The intensity of what he'd felt gnawed at his mind, but

Chris Rathburn

his hand was steady. Through the snarl of images that shifted through his mind's eye, he traced out the one thing that
would help him untangle his thoughts again. He'd been drawing that same diagram every day since he was old enough to
hold a pen. Travis was homeschooled and kept offline, but
the Pothasts had let him read about mandalas. The diagram,
his special diagram, was like that; an image that left him feeling centered, if not at peace.

Beyond that small comfort, Travis had no way to cope
with what was happening to him, not in the long term, other
than to talk with his father. He could leave the Pothasts any
time he wanted to, but that way only led to madness. The
visions didn't come often, sometimes not for years, but he
knew another one was inevitable.

Without a way of divining his visions, of making sense
of them, he would dwell on them until they broke him. It
was a dark truth of his life, and it was for that reason he'd
been forbidden from learning anything about it. The penal-
ty if he disobeyed was exile, and Travis couldn't be sure he'd
find some way to know what he needed to know before it
happened again. He didn't even know whether he *could* do
it himself. Divination was the key that made his life into its
own cage.

Pausing his work, Travis tucked a lock of straggly, brown
hair behind an ear and looked down at his plump forearm.
He ran a pale, thin fingertip over a long scar, and then over
another one.

The oracle knew enough to understand death wasn't an
ending, only a way to something else, and he didn't know for
sure whether his father would simply meet him there. Travis was trapped in this life, or at least lured into docility by
its stability, and it galled him. His family provided for his
bare personal needs. *Not my family*, he told himself again, the
voice of a small, stubborn sanity ringing out faintly beneath
the thunderous rush of his work.

Travis shook his head and tried not to pay attention to the visions. He knew to keep his eyes open. If he shut them, they were all he could see. He kept his eyes on the paper and tried not to blink. He watched his hand seem to draw of its own volition. *Ted and Judy are just my keepers,* that small voice called out within him. *My handlers. They never loved me. They just keep me. Make sure my gifts are useful.*

He knew they didn't understand him, that they couldn't understand him. The Pothasts were human and, though he looked it, he wasn't. At least, not entirely. No one had ever deemed it important enough he should be told any more than that.

As the diagram took shape, his hand moved ever faster. Thoughts and anxiety dropped away. A handful of times in his life, purpose, his *true* purpose, had shown itself. The oracle knew none of the things he hated about his existence, even the fear of his father, were the real reasons he couldn't end it. Trying to blame anyone or anything else was just a denial of his true self, the one beneath the depressed coward he told himself he was.

The truth beneath it all was that there was simply too much to look forward to. Though he hated and feared his visions and the life they'd brought him, they were his calling, what he was meant for. Though he didn't often admit it, even within his own mind, Travis had long since decided the suffering was worth it. To know, to *really* know something the way he could made him feel like a god.

He held up the drawing against the weak light hazing through a dingy window. It was one of the narrow kind, up close toward the ceiling, rather than an egress window. His was not a legal bedroom. If something disastrous happened to the house, most likely Travis would die within it.

Sometimes, he wondered if the Pothasts would leave him in an emergency, but he doubted it. No matter how far they went, eventually his father would come for an accounting.

Travis knew he was a special enough asset he couldn't imagine what they could possibly tell *him* to save themselves.

The drawing ready, Travis carefully tore it loose from the notebook and laid the paper on the floor. There were rugs here and there, tattered things pinned beneath a bed, a dresser, a desk, and a chair. The oracle laid the paper on an expanse of cold, water-sealed concrete in the middle of the room.

He pulled a cushion from beneath the bent frame of the twin sized bed and grimaced as he lowered himself to the floor. Travis didn't care he was overweight and out of shape. The Pothasts were the only people he talked to, and they didn't care, either. Sugar and grease were simple comforts, brief friendships to pass the long stretches of time between when he could do *this*.

Settling himself into position, coughing up phlegm and curses, Travis spat into an old, paper cup that had once held a medium soda. Now there was only the black mildew that grew after the last of the melted ice had evaporated. Replacing it among a collection of old fast food containers, Travis felt for the lump of quartz again and pulled it from the kangaroo pocket of his faded hoodie.

The excitement mounted as he laid eyes on his treasure. Travis held the seer stone sometimes but tried not to. Without the visions, there was desire but no release. It only made him crave those fleeting times when he could scratch that deep itch, when he could finally open himself up and know again what he could really do. His hands were steady as he reverently placed the seer stone at the center of his diagram.

Leaning over to reach under the bed again, Travis fumbled around until he found a little box. It was made of polished, black stone. He hesitated a breath, then opened it. He pulled out something wrapped in a soft cloth and set the box aside.

Travis unwrapped a small pipe and hesitated again. It looked unremarkable, fashioned from the same kind of stone as its box and as plainly made. There wasn't much to the little implement, but, in his hand, the squat shape of it felt heavier than it should be.

He hated it, but he knew the pipe was part of the ritual just as much as the stone and the diagram. Every time after, he told himself he would never use it again. He'd tell himself his power wasn't worth what that little bit of stone did to him, but within a week, the cravings returned as they always did, and then he was back to looking forward to the next time, telling himself it wasn't so bad. The oracle licked his lips and squinted his eyes shut tight as he put the stem in his mouth and drew.

It felt like the pipe was drawing from him rather than the other way around, and he supposed that was the truth of it. The harder he pulled, the harder the pipe pulled back. Soon, he was puffing out little clouds of black smoke. They drifted toward the drawing and the stone, all the while Travis feeling like he was being hollowed out a breath at a time.

The billows reached out like they were alive, stretching for each other as they floated over the diagram. The smoke settled in place over the complicated lines and angles, tracing them in the air in a perfect match of what the oracle had drawn. Travis watched it, feeling weaker and weaker, already wishing he could slump over and pass out, but the need to have his visions *divined* overrode all else.

Soon, the smoky lines were complete. Fed from the oracle's own being, the ritual came to life. The seer stone flashed, and the lines of black smoke began to contract, slowly pulled into its facets. To Travis, the sensation of what was happening made him think of the quartz as something like a needle. The diagram pointed it, and the pipe took from him what the ritual needed to push it. Together, they probed until they made an opening.

The oracle felt it when it happened. The magic popped a tiny puncture in the smooth skin of reality. Through that pinhole, he sensed something he thought of as the narrowest bridge there could be, like a single thread of spider's silk. On the other side, there was another space. He didn't know how he knew it, but that other place wasn't anywhere on earth. Travis believed it was another world, maybe another universe, where his father dwelled.

The air felt charged. His skin tingled as the oracle felt something on the other side respond. He distinctly felt a sense of sentient presence, extending a power of its own back across to him. Suddenly, a voice boomed within his mind, drowning out all thought. A bizarre species of pressure made him feel as if his eyes were being pushed from their sockets. *What have you brought me, my child? What have you seen?*

Travis gasped in relief as he felt the visions shift toward the seer stone. Now that the magic was working, it looked after itself. Even without the pipe, the stone drew more of the black smoke from him. It seeped from his eyes, his mouth, his nostrils. He felt the visions, *his* visions, travel through the smoke, using it as a conduit.

They extended out into the little clouds whirling around the seer stone. As they started to stretch across to the other side, the oracle called out in rapture. The things he had seen became more than a chaotic jumble of images. Suddenly, everything made *sense*!

"An awakening, father!" Travis called. "A great power has risen!"

The oracle felt it as his mind was sifted. He didn't bother to ask questions. He wasn't in the habit of it. No one told him anything, but it didn't matter. Understanding was irrelevant if only he could keep *seeing!* He was a lens from which nothing could be hidden. Travis felt as though he saw with the eyes of a god again, and it was his greatest joy.

Father looked for a long time, longer than he'd ever done before. Travis felt more and more of the smoke leaving his body, but it didn't matter. He saw a car accident, an eagle that was a man, an ambulance, a hospital. There was a body, a man crushed, but his father wasted no time on it.

Then, he saw a woman and felt his heart stop. At some level apart from rational thought, he understood what he was looking at, what she was. Tears started from his eyes, evaporating into smoke and drawn away before they could slide down his cheeks.

Still, his father looked. His attention shifted to center on the hospital. Travis could feel his frustration. The oracle's second sight revealed much, but not all. After a point, the harder the otherworldly force pushed for finer detail, the more the visions sought to break apart, to be released. With each smoky black breath fed into the magic, Travis paid the price for his father's persistence. His vision grayed at the edges, and his neck went as slack as a rope, dangling his weakly bobbing head as he fought to stay conscious, to keep the divining from ending.

Finally, his father shoved aside the images. Travis moaned in despair, a long, throaty sound, as he felt them go, felt his visions disperse back to wherever such things came from. *You have done well, my son*, his father's voice rang out in his mind. *Rest in peace.*

With that, the connection was broken. The seer stone went dark as the power left it, becoming nothing more than an interesting bit of rock. The ritual ended, some of the black smoke began making its way back to Travis, but much of it dispersed, leaving the basement hazy and acrid.

The oracle slumped onto his back, hitting his head on the ground hard enough to bounce, but he was silent. He couldn't see at all anymore, and his body was numb. Distantly, he understood whatever it was inside him that let the magic happen, there wasn't enough left to maintain cohesion. His blind eyes stared blankly, mouth open, the dark smoke leaking out slowly as his skin crumpled and became translucent.

For Travis, it didn't matter. His fading consciousness was

still awash with the ecstasy of the vision, and, for him, it was enough. Even when his heart stopped, when he drew his last breath, it was enough.

Judy stumbled down the basement stairs to Travis' room. She carried a tray laden with provisions. Cans of pop, chips, candy, and microwavable things. *The kid doesn't care what he's eating, so why should I?* she thought. She smiled to herself, amused that, at his age, she still thought of him as a kid.

She knocked at his door. "Travis?"

She rapped again, then once more. She listened but heard nothing. Then, she smelled smoke.

The scent didn't leave her frightened or concerned. It was the smell of the father and his children. To Judy, it smelled like purpose, and it filled her with reverence.

For a moment, she feared she had interrupted something. She closed her eyes and concentrated, feeling with her mind. Though she was very much human and poor at such things, even for her kind, she'd come to associate magic with a tingling sensation, almost like her foot had fallen asleep, but behind her eyes. She frowned, sensing nothing.

As she looked at her watch and waited another full minute, Judy's frown deepened. She wished she wasn't so inept when it came to this sort of thing. Ted had more of a knack for it, but Ted wasn't home yet and wouldn't be for some time. She was, and so this was her responsibility. Pushing aside uncertainty, the woman opened the door.

Oily, black smoke filled the room. It trickled out sluggishly around her. On the ground, she saw Travis's most important things. The stone was there, resting on a piece of paper so badly smudged, the drawing beneath was unrecognizable. She thought the smudges looked something like fingerprints, but they were too big to be human. The pipe was there, too, and Travis's clothes, a collection of cheap, black cotton-polyester, lay empty in the shape of a man.

Judy stepped back and pulled the door closed gently until she heard the catch click. She didn't fear what she saw. Instead, her frown melted into a serene smile. The boy's death was no fault of her own. The father took what he needed from his children. Sometimes, he took all. For her, it didn't matter much. There were always more children, and she was happy to care for them.

"Thy will be done," she said in quiet reverence as she turned away.

The woman hummed something very much like a hymn to herself as she carried the tray back upstairs to their kitchen. She'd tell Tom when he returned. With Travis gone, there was work to be done, but it wasn't urgent; no need to call him now. There was nothing for it but to trim their lamps and be prepared. Though they could not know the day or the hour, the father would come around again, and, when he did, he would find them ready.

Chapter 4:

I T WAS NEARLY LUNCHTIME. Nurse Cathy checked in on her regularly. Alice kept calm and smiled as often as she could remember, reassuring the nurse she was doing well, her pain was managed, and she was having no further bouts of confusion.

No one had said anything to her about Timothy. She supposed they were waiting for her to be ready enough to ask. She decided it was a reasonable thing for the staff to do; no sense rattling her more than she'd already been.

She had been asked if there was anyone they should contact for her, but she told them there was no one. It was true enough. Other than Timothy, she didn't really have any close friends. Even as she was, Alice found she had no desire to bring her parents into her situation. *Maybe after I know a little more about what's going on,* she told herself, knowing full well it was a lie.

Strangely, she found the isolation of her hospital room to be the greatest comfort she had. As often as she was left alone, Alice was thinking hard. It was the last thing she wanted to do, but it was either that or else watch her mind replay

Timothy's death again and again.

Whatever had started up inside her didn't seem like it was going to stop. She could feel energy entering and exiting the centers of her body. She wished she knew what to call it. *Chi, maybe? Mojo?*

The strangest thing was it was happening to everyone and nobody knew it. The flow of this invisible energy seemed to be a completely normal thing people were completely unaware of. They didn't even seem to notice it when there was a direct exchange between their bodies.

No, she decided. *That's not quite right.* Looking out into the common area of her hospital unit, she saw another patient watching a nurse. He was a decent-looking guy beneath the stitches on his arms and stubbled scalp. The nurse was a pretty, young thing, trimmed with the vigor of youth and being made to keep on her feet for twelve hours a day. Alice could see he wanted her, could see a pooling of energy in his lower abdomen.

Some of it, his *mojo,* left his body and drifted toward the nurse. Her back was to him, but, the moment the man's energy touched her, she turned and looked directly at him. Alice smiled and closed the door to her patient's quarters as the man smiled and waved at the nurse, pretending he had some care issue that needed attention. *People* do *notice it. They just don't know they know. Why?*

Frowning thoughtfully, Alice retreated into her personal bathroom, a tidy study in wall-mounted handrails, easily cleaned surfaces, and quietly ominous pull alarms that could be reached from the floor. She didn't bother to close its door. Even if the door to the main room of her quarters were opened, there was no angle from the common area where someone could see in there. It was the most private place for her in the entire hospital, and it let Alice study her reflection in the large mirror over the sink at length without feeling self-conscious.

There seemed to be eight centers. Alice had seen no one, including herself, with more or less. The key difference seemed to lie in the one that floated over everyone's head. With her, it was open and active. With others, it was quiet.

She noted the seven centers running through their bodies waxed and waned, ebbed and flowed, but that weird, floaty one seemed to do next to nothing in most people she observed. Alone in her bathroom, Alice stared at the center hovering over her head and pondered what this meant. *The man,* she thought, *Altair. He said my music was the key to my magic. Shows what he knows.*

Alice smiled at her own joke. She'd never shown any aptitude for music at any age. *Whistling doesn't count, does it?* The only interest it held for her was the simple pleasure it brought most anyone. *So, I'm the chosen one,* she thought, *music is the key to this, and I can hardly sing a note.*

"That was deliberate, I think."

"Je-SUS!" she cried, whirling away from the mirror. A giant shadow of a man stood in her bathroom doorway. *No, not a shadow . . . what is . . . ?*

The being looked as if it were made of dark smoke. It appeared solid enough, but little whorls and plumes of its substance rippled and drifted about its body before reabsorbing. It spoke again. "You've been in hiding. Keeping away from music has kept your power dormant. Any other sage would have mastered their magic while their bodies were still those of children."

Alice wanted nothing more than to run, but the smoke man had her completely blocked in. It smiled and seemed to sense her thoughts in the same way she was learning to see them in others. It stretched languidly. Broad wings unfurled from its back, spanning the length of the main room of her quarters before retracting to hang like a cloak around its shoulders.

"Altair didn't send you."

The smoke man smirked, turned its head, and spat. A little jet of black smoke shot from its lips, struck the floor, and curled up into the air until it dissipated. With its voice like whispers from a child's nightmare, it replied, "Piece of shit jinn. No, Alice. I come on behalf of someone much greater. Someone who has used considerable resources to find you."

"Who? Why?" Alice said. The bathroom suddenly seemed very small. There were no windows, only tile and fixtures and a few towels. She was trapped.

"Now." The creature ignored the questions and reached for her. "Give me your hands."

"W-what?"

She fought the useless urge to hide her hands behind her back. She stepped backward from the creature, but there was nowhere to go. She nearly tripped over the toilet, catching herself with the chromed railing bars that lined the walls.

The smoke man was too big to fit through the doorframe without contorting, but, as it stepped over the threshold, its body simply dispersed where it touched a solid surface. The dark smoke reformed into its body where there was space. The creature easily took up half the bathroom, stooping to avoid the ceiling.

"Give me your hands," the creature repeated, its long arms stretching out for her.

"Fuckfuckfuckfuckfuck!" Alice shouted, trying to keep her distance. Desperate, she half fell, half dove to the floor. She crawled on her belly and tried to get between its legs and out the door. She had no idea what she'd do after that. Every instinct in her body simply screamed at her to act. *RUN!*

It caught her effortlessly, stooping down and catching her by the wrists. Hauled roughly to her feet, Alice threw herself from side to side and tried to wrench herself loose. The creature ignored her efforts. Its smoky fists clenched her wrists with strength that threatened to break bone.

It drew back out of the bathroom, pulling her hands

across the threshold. Alice gritted her teeth and pulled back. Her bare feet slid across the smooth tiles. As if from another world, Alice heard nurse Cathy knock and call at her door.

"You alright, sweetie?"

The main door to her hospital room creaked open. In the bathroom, Alice imagined Cathy's eyes widening in shocked terror at the sight of the smoke man. Casually, the creature extended a wing and slammed it closed again. Alice heard the sickening crack of the woman's skull as the door struck the nurse in the face with breathtaking force. The smoke man smirked, a thin spray of the nurse's blood reaching all the way to its ankle, then turned its attention back to Alice.

"No! Let go! Stop! Fuck! Please!" Alice cursed and begged as the creature transferred her hands so that it gripped both wrists in the curl of one massive fist. Taking hold of the bathroom door, it slammed it with that same crushing power it had brought to bear against poor Cathy.

Alice heard so many bones in her hands break under the force. She was too stunned by what was happening to feel the pain, to scream. Distantly, she was surprised her hands weren't severed outright. She found her voice again and wailed when the smoke man slammed the door again, then again.

It was completely unfair; the man's body dispersed where it would have interfered with the door. It reformed instantly as it pushed the door back open; its great fist somehow never lost the strength of its grip no matter the state of its flesh. The creature slammed the door one more time, then let her go.

Alice fell to the ground, landing heavily on her tailbone. She looked at her hands in horror. All thought of escape evaporated away. From the wrists forward, her hands were a red, wet pulp of torn skin and shattered bone. They didn't even look like hands, just broken meat.

The creature smiled as it stepped back into the bathroom; stray wisps of its being wafted through the doorframe.

Alice didn't look up. There was no reason to. She knew what it wanted, and she knew there was no reasoning with it. Whatever it was, this thing had come to kill her. Her hands were only foreplay to what was coming next.

In her final moments, she imagined the jinn's deep, rich voice. *The music. That's the key to your magic. You can always find me through your music.* With no hope and nothing else remaining to try, Alice closed her eyes, pursed her lips, and did the only musical thing she'd ever learned; she whistled.

It was a simple tune, the first thing that came to mind, something brought up from the depths of childhood memory. *A, B, C, D, E, F, G* . . . For all her pain, the notes were clear and bright on her lips, evoking the innocence of her early years. The creature's dark eyes widened, and it tensed as if she'd pulled out a loaded gun.

Alice thought of Altair as the tune left her lips. It was easy to do. Everything about him was so familiar. Thinking of the jinn was like reminiscing on the feel of her childhood home, memories so old and worn, they were more sensory impression than anything else, an instinctual imprinting on something deep and vital.

As the notes filled the air, she felt her centers twist within her, opening so the transfer of energy between her body and the world became a flood. She felt that strangest wheel of energy, the one above her head, yawn wide. It stretched like something left to slumber for far too long. The monster seemed to sense what was happening and pushed aside its trepidation.

The creature lunged for Alice. Long, thick fingers reached for her throat. Before they could touch her, a shaft of blinding, white light pierced through the smoke man's chest. Alice was startled at the sudden brilliance, the whistled notes of the child's song seeming to hang in the air about her. Vaguely, it registered the smoke man was being impaled by a magical sword through its back. Dizzy with shock, she amused herself with the thought that, not so long ago, such a thing would have surprised her. *Was that yesterday? How long have I been here, anyway?*

The smoke man opened its mouth to scream, but no sound came. Instead, great billows of black smog burst from its lips. Its body collapsed as the monster vomited itself apart. In moments, it was nothing more than a heavy fog smelling of burnt things, drifting thick and oily against the ceiling tiles.

Altair stood in the bathroom doorway, chest heaving, his eyes filled with a mixture of fear and exultation. The sword in his hands looked like a bolt of forged lightning. Assaulting the smoke man seemed to have taken a measure of the weapon's strength. It popped and snapped like a frayed wire; its light flickered and guttered as the jinn slid it under his coat.

The scrubs were replaced by a hooded, long coat and dark trousers. His feet were bare. Alice asked, "What's the deal with you and shoes?"

The jinn took one look at her hands, and his eyes widened. "Oh, sweet Jesus!"

Just then, the billowing remains of the monster triggered the building's fire alarms. The sound of klaxons, strobing lights, and a torrent of brackish water from the sprinkler system drowned out everything else. Sparing no further words, Altair swept Alice into his arms like she was a child and headed straight for the windows of her room.

He ran flat out the few strides he needed to cross the distance, his footing sure in the sudden deluge. At the last moment, the jinn leapt and kicked out with both feet, shattering the window. Glass exploded outward, and Alice found herself gripped in the talons of a great eagle. Her rational mind patiently fed her the knowledge there were no birds of that size anywhere in all the world. Some other part of her responded tolerantly what was impossible and what wasn't didn't seem to matter anymore.

She squinted toward the dawn, smiling at the brilliance

of another day. Distantly, there was pain, but it didn't matter. Alice slipped into numb stupor, strangely comforted by the sound of rustling feathers and the beat of Altair's wings.

Chapter 5:

ALICE NOTICED THE SHARP, cracking sounds and the feel of her own bones writhing beneath her skin. Then, she noticed she was awake again. She opened her eyes, wondering why her hands didn't hurt.

"Keep still," Altair told her, "the magic isn't finished."

She didn't move but gathered what information she could from where she lay. They were in a van, one of those creepy ones with no rear windows. It was adorned and equipped with all manner of tools, gear, and unidentifiables ranging from the mundane to the esoteric to the outright otherworldly. Most prominently, the van's interior light source held a complete disregard for reality.

Hovering overhead, a ball of smokeless fire burned steadily. There was no flickering. It gave off no heat. The flame was unmistakably magic, and it was being used for a simple task that could have been managed just as well by a conventional light.

"It's jinn light," Altair told her. "You can move now."

He reached out a hand to help her sit up, and she reached up without thinking about it. She stopped cold when she saw her hands. They weren't pulped anymore, but they weren't whole either. The twisted lumps of scar tissue at the ends of her wrists were scarcely more dexterous than having hooks for hands.

"Oh, god . . ." Alice murmured. Gently, Altair took her ruined hands in his. It stung, but she could take it. She let herself be sat up and then carefully laid them in her lap.

She found she was surrounded by a ring of smaller jinn lights. Incense burned. Strange glyphs were marked between the lights. She couldn't read it but recognized them at once.

"Those are jinn words," Alice said, uncertain how she knew it. "I almost remember what they mean, but I can't quite think of it."

Altair nodded and handed her a granola bar. He'd opened the wrapper for her. She needed all her warped fingers working together to keep from dropping it. As casual as flipping a light switch, Altair held out his hand, and the little balls of fire surrounding her leapt to him, disappearing into his palm. Alice was too hungry to be startled, surprised instead to find herself starting to adjust to her new reality.

"You've known the language of my people since your first life," the jinn told her, "and in every life since."

She shook her head and mumbled through a mouthful of sweet oats and raisins. "Everything about you is déjà vu."

Altair smiled and touched her face. The gesture was gentle, intimate, and Alice recoiled as if his hand were a viper. She dropped the bar and managed to kick it across the van as she grabbed for it.

"Shit."

"Would you like another?"

"No thanks," Alice told him, her appetite lost among the strange feelings that clashed within her. "Just don't do that. You don't *know* me, understand?"

Images of Timothy flashed across her mind's eye; how he looked when they met, when he proposed, when they made love, when he died. *He was there for me, all the way,* she thought, crushed with sudden guilt, *and I never meant any of it.* Tears started up, and she turned away, swiping at them with her sleeve.

Altair looked mournful but held up his hands and patted the air. "I am sorry. I should have known, especially after what happened to your Timothy."

Alice spat, "After *you* happened to him! I don't care what your special mission is. It doesn't change you're a goddamn murderer!"

The crestfallen jinn said nothing, and she eyed her sleeves. "When the hell did I get dressed?"

She wore a gray, long sleeved t-shirt and matching yoga pants with a pair of white sneakers. It was all her size. None of it was hers. She asked him, "You just keep my size in your van here?"

Alice shuddered, feeling so exposed, so vulnerable with a stranger she somehow knew better than anyone else she'd ever known. "Fucking stalker."

Altair accepted her anger calmly, patiently. "SamsMart while you were passed out. I wasn't sure on your size, so I picked out a few things."

He gestured to a collection of plastic shopping bags. Alice couldn't help but grin at the sight of them as she tried to imagine the man before her doing something so normal. Then, Alice thought of the jinn dressing her like a doll while she slept and shuddered again.

"I'm sorry," he said, sensing her thoughts. "Your hospital gowns were bloody."

"You know," Alice said, "I'm getting really tired of having my mind read."

Altair said, "Understandable. I can teach you how to mute yourself, if you like?"

Somehow, she understood his meaning at once. "Mute... Like how you walked past that nurse and she had no idea?"

Alice shook her head, bemused. "After you left, it took me a minute to remember you even *existed*!"

The jinn nodded, his dismayed countenance giving way to a broad grin. "Very good, Alice. That's exactly right. By now, you've seen that all things have their own vibration, yes?"

Alice bobbed her head, sniffing and wiping her face with her sleeve. He added, "All things also have their own intensity."

"Like volume," she answered, feeling as though she'd already known these things but had needed him to say them for her mind to set in motion.

"Essentially," he acknowledged. "Once you know how to turn yours down, you won't have to worry about someone overhearing your thoughts."

Alice thought of the smoke man, wondering how long the thing had stood there, listening in on her inner world. She felt ashamed she'd done it herself with the hospital staff and their patients, then blushed furiously as she remembered Altair could perceive her stream of consciousness. *Ok, fine,* she thought. *I guess I'm a bit of a peeping Tom, myself. Happy?*

Altair smiled but said nothing. Aloud, she asked, "What *was* that thing, anyway?"

"An ifrit," he told her. "They are cousins to the jinn."

"A related species?"

He nodded. "They are the smoke, and we are the fire."

"And you don't get along with each other."

He shook his head. "Not often. There are, ah, cultural differences."

"Did you kill it?"

"Hard to say," he answered. "Ifrit are tough. Nothing short of magic can truly harm them. Dead or not, we won't have to worry about that one again."

Alice held up her hands. "Because if he's not dead, then, in his own way, he's probably like me now. Crippled."

Altair was silent, so she asked, "Can you make them better? Work on them some more?"

The jinn shook his head. "If I were a sila, I might be able to do a little more, but I am afraid they are beyond medicine and magic."

"Sila?"

"Jinn inclined toward working magic," he supplied. "I am a ghul."

"A ghoul?" she asked. "Isn't that like a zombie or something?"

"Ghul," Altair pronounced the word carefully. "A jinn shapeshifter."

Alice gestured about the van. "What about the ball of magic fire over there? What about the healing spell you apparently did to me?"

Altair waved a hand dismissively. "Thank you, Alice, but as magic goes, it's pretty rudimentary stuff."

She blinked, at a loss. The jinn considered, then explained, "Think of it like basketball. Just about everyone can dribble or shoot a layup. Some are good enough to hold their own in a pickup game, and so on. Then, there are the pros."

Alice nodded, and he added, "If you need a giant eagle, a shark, a swarm of locusts, that kind of thing, I hold my own just fine. When it comes to spells and incantations and such, to stretch the analogy, I can occasionally win a game of horse."

She worked to digest the information. "So, magic lights and helping along healing is the easy stuff. Got it. How about when you magically appeared back at the hospital when I called for you?"

Altair spread his hands. "I am a genie, after all. You summoned me."

Alice raised her eyebrows, eyes wide. "No shit?! Like you have an actual lamp or a ring that you live in or something?"

He laughed. "No, I'm just messing with you. I wasn't far

off. I was just waiting and listening."

Alice laughed with him, surprising herself. She couldn't help it. It felt like home.

"Fucking stalker."

The laughter died away, leaving the jinn feeling like a stranger again. "So now what? I'm assuming more of those *ifrit* will be looking for me?"

"Possibly." Altair considered. "Probably. The enemy will have many resources at their disposal. They'll kill you if they can."

"Because I'm a *sage*."

"The last one," Altair agreed.

She considered. "So, how many sages are there? Where did they go?"

Alice hesitated, reluctant to ask the biggest question. "What am I?"

"There have always been eight sages," Altair told her. "They have been the guardians of your realm since your kind was exiled from Eden. Short of the gods, they are the most powerful beings known."

Alice raised her mangled hands. "But they're mortal, and someone killed the others."

Altair shook his head. "Impossible. The sages die and are reborn, or else the mantle passes on to a young soul. Somehow, the other seven have all gone missing. Something has to be keeping them. For some, it's been decades. If they had died, another would have come along by now."

Alice nodded. "The ifrit said I've been in hiding."

"Since your last life, yes," Altair confirmed. "You told me to come for you when the others were all gone."

"Why?"

The jinn shrugged. "You kept that to yourself, but I would guess it has something to do with the other sages. Whatever is going on, it's powerful enough to capture them all."

She considered. "And in my last, uhm, incarnation, I

knew enough of what was happening, I checked out early so I wouldn't be taken along with the rest of them."

"So it seems."

"And I didn't tell you what was going down?"

The jinn shook his head. "I asked you many times to let me help, but you only told me the less I knew, the less I was involved, the easier it would be for me to lay low and wait."

Her eyebrows furrowed, unsure if she wanted to know. "What happened to me in my last life?"

Altair shrugged, dropping his gaze and swallowing back sadness. "The same thing that happens to everyone. You died."

Alice frowned. The man was obviously trying to help. She could tell there had been something real between them. For Altair, their talk reopened old wounds, memories of the sacrifice of the love of his life, but for her, discussing something as abstract as a past life was like talking about any random stranger.

Despite that, the mix of emotions the jinn stirred in her was frustrating. She wanted to hate Altair, wanted to call the police and see him rot in a cell. She wanted to hold him and tell him she loved him.

The ambivalence left her feeling as though she was betraying Timothy, but that was only a deflection from a deeper shame. She could scarcely admit it to herself, but she was guilty at how grateful she was to the jinn. Whatever Altair had done, a sense of freedom was growing within her like nothing she'd ever known.

Confused and frustrated, Alice pushed the feelings down and changed the subject to something that might have answers. "So, how did you find me?"

"I've been watching over you."

"How long?" she asked, uneasy.

"Since you were a baby." He inclined his head toward her and winked. "Stalker."

"What about *them*? How long were they watching before they decided to come and . . ."

Alice's voice broke, and she looked away. She wrung her ruined hands and rubbed her fingertips over the twisted masses of fresh scars. Altair frowned. "I don't know yet."

She thought of the smoke man, the *ifrit*, smashing her hands again and again. She felt its grip on her wrists, impossibly strong. She imagined trying to get away from something like that on her own, its body melting like a ghost whenever it pleased while she ran on foot.

There was no turning back. It was plain the jinn told the truth. There was no way left to live a normal life. Alice knew unless she saw this out, she would die horribly at the hands of something she didn't even understand.

Strangely, she was excited. All her life, Alice had never belonged anywhere. She'd done what she needed to get by, to live a life, but had never invested in any of it. Now, it was like she was emerging from a chrysalis. For all its strangeness, she had gotten a taste of her true self. There was no going back.

"Altair?" she asked as she looked at her hands thoughtfully.

"Yes?"

"Why am I ok with this?"

The jinn chuckled. "Are you?"

She frowned and flexed twisted fingers. "Not really, but this should be traumatizing, shouldn't it?"

"Should it?"

"Well," said Alice, "I've just gone through some pretty big shit. My fiancé is dead. I'm crippled. Either one of those things should have wrecked me, right?"

The jinn's chuckle lingered on, reborn as a wide grin. "For others, maybe. You, on the other hand, have *no* idea what you're capable of."

She quirked her lips. "No pun intended?"

Altair laughed again, full and throaty. "Give yourself

time, Alice. This will make sense before you know it, and I will pray for your enemies when it does."

Alice went still and digested that. She couldn't ignore the sense of camaraderie between them. It was as if he had always been her best friend; she simply hadn't met him before today. Then, it struck her. "Wait. Why would someone be trying to just kill me outright when they kidnapped the other sages? Wouldn't they be worried about me reincarnating?"

Altair nodded, his face grave. "You wouldn't be reborn. This is your eighth life; the last humankind is given. When you die, you will go on, and your mantle will be passed to a new soul in its first life."

Alice thought it over. "Ok, but even if it's not me, that still leaves a loose sage. Isn't that still a problem?"

"Even if they were a quick study," said Altair, "a new sage would take years to assume their full power. My guess is the enemy wants you dead for two reasons."

The jinn held up a finger. "First, you are the only one who knows what's really going on, meaning you're the only player in the game that has a chance to stop it."

He held up a second finger. "Second, whatever is happening, it's endgame. The enemy believes they will achieve their goals before a new sage can mature."

"And then?" Alice asked.

Altair shrugged. "And then, my guess is the sages will be irrelevant."

She thought of what he'd told her before. "The end of everything."

The jinn said nothing, his eyes downcast. She asked, "So now what?"

He considered, then said, "It seems we have to teach you how to *be* you."

"Alright," she said, then tried to tuck her hands into her pockets before she realized she didn't have any and laid them awkwardly on her lap instead. "Where do we start?"

"Well," said Altair. "There's really only one place to start. Your power comes through music. It's how sages are able to do what they do."

"Why?" Alice wondered aloud. "Why not magic wands or something?"

"Everything has its own vibration," he told her.

"Like a frequency," she said.

He nodded. "Some can hear the music of all things. Some can sing along. Sages can write the songs. Like the gods, sages can remake the world in their image."

It was a lot to take in, but that was the new normal. Alice understood and said, "And that's why it wrecked my hands first. No music, no magic."

The jinn nodded. "Not with your voice."

He blinked as he realized he'd spoken that aloud. "Sorry."

"It's ok," she said. "I'm aware I sound like shit."

Altair smiled, his words sincere. "The whistling was a good idea. I don't know if I've seen that trick before."

"Will it be enough?" Alice asked, a cold vice of anxiety clamping down on her stomach, waiting for this man, this *being*, to tell her if she was truly and royally fucked.

The jinn shook his head, and she swallowed back her gorge, nauseated. "It won't. We need to get those hands fixed so we can get you up and running."

She cocked her head, confused. "But you said magic and medicine couldn't do it."

"I did," Altair agreed. "We are going to need a miracle."

Alice searched his face. He wasn't kidding. She managed, "Like literally?"

He nodded. "If the other sages were around, they could do it. Things being as they are, we are going to need help from someone else."

Her first steps into the larger world so far had amounted to little more than blind stumbling, but she was catching on. Alice had always been sharp. She didn't consider how she thought about things as guessing, just able to extrapolate from incomplete information.

That quick mind and keen intuition had allowed her to prosper before in treacherous places where others had not. The drug world did not suffer long those without guile, much less let them leave it. In this new life, she already understood something of what was unfolding and was afraid.

"You're saying . . ."

Altair nodded. "We're going to ask a god."

Chapter 6:

ALICE TRIED NOT TO make a mess of herself while the jinn prepared. Without her hands, nothing was easy anymore. She bit back tears as she dropped chips, a gas station sandwich, and a microwave burrito into her lap. Her right breast stung where she'd dribbled hot cheese beans immediately before scorching her tongue.

Altair politely ignored her difficulties as he marked out a ring of glyphs on the thin, stained carpet of the ratty roadside motel room. He'd chosen the place at random after they'd stopped for fuel and supplies. Alice had expected the trappings of magic to be something more like the way movies and books made them out; wands, chalices, ritual daggers. Instead, the jinn tapped a stack of white printer paper against his thigh, laid the straightened sheaf on the phone book balanced on his knees, and took up his cheap pen.

The paper was from the motel lobby. Muted, the jinn had simply walked around the counter, sidled past the clerk, and took some from the printer. While he was back there, he'd helped himself to a roll of scotch tape and a brace of pens.

Alice couldn't help but gawk while he did it. At one

point, the clerk followed her gaze and looked directly at the jinn. Altair only waved at him and kept rooting around in drawers. The clerk waved back and got back to work, forgetting the jinn completely while he took Alice's money and pretended not to notice her hands.

Cross-legged on the bed, she gave up on eating and cleaned up with a box of wet wipes he'd picked up with the food. It was frustrating, needing both hands to pluck one of the sodden, lemon-scented sheets. *Think of it as practice,* she encouraged herself. *You're going to have to relearn a lot of things, and there's no sense throwing a tantrum every time things get hard.* She rolled her eyes as she recognized the sound of her mother's voice between her ears and looked for something else to do to keep occupied and out of Altair's way.

She picked up his wad of cash from the bedside table where he'd left it and bounced the roll of bills in her palms. The bills were random, denominations large and small, new, clean edges and tattered rags of hard worn currency. She wanted to count it but didn't think she had the motor skills to keep from dropping it again. The clerk politely had helped her pick up before while he smiled and made small talk and looked anywhere but at her hands.

Embarrassed at the memory, Alice set the rubberbanded bills down and looked to the jinn. Altair knelt on the carpet while he taped the sheets of paper with their pen-drawn glyphs in a wide circle. Without looking up, he said, "If you're getting bored, I can give you something to work on."

Alice's face lit up. *Magic!* As strange as the idea of it was to her, it would be nice to feel like she knew what she was doing again. Setting aside his tape and papers, Altair turned to face her.

"Muting is going to come in handy," he said.

She nodded. "So I can keep a low profile."

"So I can concentrate." He smiled. "Remember, I'm piss poor at magic, and it's hard to work while you're blaring out everything you're thinking."

Alice felt her face flush. She wanted to tell him off for eavesdropping but accepted he probably couldn't help it when she was essentially babbling like a psychic toddler. She tried to clear her mind, picturing an apple to focus her thoughts.

"You're *not* a toddler," he said, "and it's really not that bad. Honestly, it's nice to have the company. It's just distracting."

"Sorry," she replied. "You're alone a lot?"

Altair waved his hand in dismissal, ignoring her question. "It's nothing we can't square away. Now, forget about the apple and listen."

Alice blinked, tried not to wonder if he knew *exactly* what apple she'd pictured, and listened.

"It's simpler than you think," he said, "but it's like tying your shoes. It's an incomprehensible, tangled mess until you know what to do and have tried it a few times. Now, grab a pillow and come over here."

Altair took a pillow for himself and walked to the unused part of the room. It wasn't much space, and he was obliged to squeeze a rickety, stained chair into a corner to make it work. He sat down on his pillow, folded his legs so they both rested on the carpet, and overlaid his hands, palm upward, in his lap. He touched the tips of his thumbs together so his hands described a neat oval and waited for her to follow suit.

When she was on the floor, he corrected her posture and position. "Keep your back straight, place your hands like so, and don't cross your legs."

"But yours are . . ."

Altair looked down. "This is called the Burmese position. You're sitting Indian style."

Alice looked carefully and copied him, then the jinn folded his legs into something like a pretzel, feet on top of his thighs, "This is a lotus position. It's also acceptable, but I don't like it because it's hard on the knees."

He adjusted, placing one foot on the floor, "This is the half lotus, so it's only half fucking awful."

The jinn returned to the Burmese position. "That's better. Anyway, take your pick of those and don't use the pillow as a seat. It's mostly there to prop you up so your knees help you balance."

When Alice was adjusted to his satisfaction, he said, "Now you're going to meditate on your centers. Just breathe and focus on how they feel as they open and close. If you get distracted, just start over."

"Ok," she said. Alice wriggled her butt until the pillow felt right. "Then what?"

The jinn shrugged and smoothly slid to his feet. "That's it."

Alice frowned, and Altair obliged. "Fine. Once you get a feel for it, you can start working on contracting your centers."

He pointed above her head. "Especially that little guy. That one draws the most attention. You've noticed by now basically everyone else's soul center isn't doing much?"

She nodded, noting while Altair had eight of the energetic loci, the same as humans, his were hardly noticeable. Altair smiled. "It's because I know how to keep quiet. Eight is the standard, by the way. Humans, cats, ifrit, dragons, it's how we're set up. Don't bother asking why. It's a God thing."

Alice caught the inflection. "Wait, you mean *God* God?"

The jinn swept his hand to the side; end of discussion. "Later. I need to keep working. For now, practice your meditation. Get a feel for your centers. Shrink them down, and you can blend in just fine."

"Ok," she said and wriggled a little more for good measure. "But how do I . . . ?"

Altair obliged patiently. "You know how to do your Kegel exercises?"

Alice felt herself blush. She was by no means prudish, but it was an intimate question; something a doctor or a family member or a *lover* might ask.

"I'll take that as a 'yes,'" said the jinn, giving her a thumb's up and a cheesy smile, and went back to his work.

The new connection with her body was intoxicating. Alice was astonished she'd never felt it before. *It's been here the whole time,* she mused. She dilated and contracted the swirling loci in time with her breathing, wondering at the flow of energy within her, the exchange of it between her body and the world.

Her eyes were closed, but, all at once, she knew Altair was looking at her. She'd always had that sense for when she was being stared at. As near as she could tell, most people did to some degree. That time, she felt it as an exchange of energy at the nexus on her forehead, between her eyes.

He was smiling when she opened her eyes and looked back at him. "Very good, Alice. Getting the feel of it?"

She beamed at him. "This is amazing!"

The jinn laughed at that, and it was everything she could do not to fall in love with him then and there. It was a deep sound, rich with emotion. Alice breathed in and contracted the locus at the center of her chest. Within it, within her heart, she held onto the image of Timothy and the guilt that went with it. No matter how handsome he was and no matter how much she felt herself longing to just give in to the strange, powerful emotions that welled up within her, she kept in mind the fact she was face to face with her fiancé's killer.

"I'm sorry, Alice," said Altair, sobering immediately. "I don't mean to confuse you. I *am* sorry for what happened. For what I did."

"Are you?" Alice replied bitterly.

"You were committed to him," said the jinn, "ready to give him an entire lifetime. I had to act to save your life, but I never meant to take that from you."

Alice glared. "It doesn't matter what you *meant* to do. You fucked up, Timothy is *dead*, and it doesn't matter how much is at stake here. You don't get a pass on something like that."

"I don't expect you to forgive me," said the jinn. Alice only glared at him, her hands clenched into weak fists, overcome by the push and pull of the competing drives within her. The silence stretched out between them, and he asked, "Do you need me to give you some time? I can leave until you're ready."

Alice wanted to tell Altair to go to hell. She wanted to tell him to leave and never come back. Then, she forced herself to think it through.

Without Altair, she'd be dead. No matter how she felt about him, something deep inside her was certain what he said was true, that if she died, it would mean the literal end of the world. Alice knew, despite what had happened, she had to act, and she needed Altair to do that. *I don't have have to forgive him, but I don't get a pass, either.*

She scrubbed at her face with her palms and made herself regroup. "No, you should stay. We need to keep moving. It's just a lot."

"It's everything, all at once," agreed the jinn. "It gets easier."

"Don't," Alice snapped then made herself get to her feet to look over his work. She put her mind on that and, when she trusted her voice to be steady, she said, "It looks like a spider web."

The sheets of paper were taped to the carpet, arranged meticulously in a concentric, octagonal pattern. Little orbs of jinn fire floated between the glyphs, creating a cat's cradle of crossing lines. She counted. "Sixty-four glyphs. Eight times eight, right?"

"That's right," said Altair. "Threes are usually important, too."

He pointed out the triangular aspects of the pattern. Vaguely, Alice noted the sun had gone down. The room was lit entirely by Altair's fire.

"Does that hurt you?" she asked. "Putting out little bits of yourself like that?"

"It's strenuous," he admitted. "It's the cost of doing business."

"Fair enough." She was concerned, but, at the same time, part of her didn't mind if he hurt. "And this takes us to see a god?"

"This takes us to Sayon," said the jinn. "We're going to my realm."

She cocked her head. "And this god lives there?"

He shook his head. "No, but I know someone there who can guide us to one."

"But if you can open a magic portal to jinn land, why not just open one up that takes us where we want to go?"

"It's Sayon," he said, "and moving between the realms is complicated. This spell is a sort of key; otherwise, I wouldn't be able to manage it. It opens a Way, a sort of door to a very specific place. You created it for me thousands of years ago, in your first life."

"Wait," she said. "You told me this is my eighth life."

"That's right."

"Well," she said, her brow furrowed, "you said *thousands* of years. That means, in each of my past lives, I would have lived for centuries. Is that normal for a sage?"

"No." Altair shook his head, then winked. "Most sages find ways to use their magic to extend their lives, but your first life was something extraordinary."

"More extraordinary than being one of the eight chosen guardians of all humanity?" she asked, incredulous.

"Later," he said. "I promise. Come stand with me."

Altair stepped carefully over the papers and the beaded lines of fire. She saw there was a place for each of them and delicately followed suit. She ignored his proffered hand. Touching the jinn was too confusing.

"I'm starting to think you like keeping me in the dark."

"It may not look like it," said Altair, "but we're in a hurry. The ifrit at the hospital didn't find you on his own. You're being tracked, and it's only a matter of time until something catches up to us again."

Alice's brow furrowed, and she rubbed her hands together. The bumps and ridges of her scars caught against each other strangely where before there had been smooth skin. She didn't like to think of what was happening to her like that; being *hunted*.

The jinn smiled impishly. "But it is interesting being the one with the answers, this time around."

Alice stuck out her tongue, her tension eased for the moment, and let it drop.

"Alright, when I tell you, I want you to whistle this tune."

The jinn pursed his lips and twittered out an odd, little melody. Alice closed her eyes as she listened. She'd never heard it before, but, somehow, she knew it by heart.

"Once you start, don't stop until we're there."

"Why not?"

Altair shrugged. "Like I said, I don't have the power to take us there myself. I can do some of it, but, mostly, I just know how to open the Way."

"Wait." Alice held up a finger. "Why would I give you a secret key between worlds that you can't use?"

"Because," he said, "I wouldn't be using it until after I had you with me again."

Alice nodded; it made sense. He had the key, but she had the strength to turn it. She considered how long Altair had been living in her world, waiting for her. *Was he trapped here all this time?* she thought. It was strange to think of the earth as a place distinct from some other place. *If he hadn't gotten to me, would he have been stuck here forever?*

"Also, it's old magic." The jinn obliged. "And it doesn't work the way it used to."

Before she could ask, he answered, "Your earth used to be a much more overtly magical place. The sages changed that, starting in your first life."

That impish grin again. "In fact, it was you that convinced the others to make the change."

"Why would I do that?"

The jinn shrugged and spread his hands. "Life's simpler that way, don't you think? Safer, at least."

Alice smirked and conceded the point. It was unreal that, last week, the biggest things in her life had consisted of senior finals and settling on a wedding date. . . . *and Tim . . .* Feeling strong emotions welling up again, she pushed aside the thoughts and focused on what was at hand. She felt she was starting to see the logic of it.

"And we can't call the god here," she surmised, "because of the change."

Altair raised a hand and teetered it from side to side. "Sort of. That's part of it. Earth is out of bounds for a few reasons."

Out of bounds from what, exactly? she thought. Aloud, she said, "But you're here, and an ifrit tried to kill me yesterday."

The jinn became solemn. "Yes. It seems times are changing. Are you ready?"

"I think so." Alice nodded, surprised at herself she believed it, and started whistling the tune. Beside her, Altair stopped muting himself. His centers flared open, and he breathed deeply. His relief was palpable as he burst into flame.

She gasped at the splendor of him, the burning master of the little flames that surrounded them. The jinn gave off no smoke and little heat. The carpet under his feet didn't catch fire, and the papers gathered around them didn't scorch. She wanted nothing more than to look at him, to tell him he was beautiful, and then her power took hold.

The world melted slowly at first, then ran like liquid as she repeated the tune. The earth rose up, and they were cocooned by the flowing contents of their hotel room. Soon, it was as if they were the centerpiece of a living, surrealist painting.

Beside her, the jinn was straining himself to the breaking point. Flames poured from his outstretched fingers, reinforcing the beaded lines of the ritual space. His body grew thin, almost skeletal, as he emptied more and more of himself into the magic.

Alice wanted to call out to him. She wanted to take the jinn in her arms and protect him. More than anything, she feared what would happen to them now if she stopped. She closed her eyes to block out the sight and whistled.

Each note was perfect. Alice felt her power reach out into the universe. The boundaries of space and time became meaningless. The sage breathed the last note of the eighth repetition of the key song, and, all at once, it was over.

Chapter 7:

Hours passed. Another morning came. The lights flickered on in a ratty motel room. There were no occupants, only a maid sent to clean.

There was something wrong with the custodian, but no one she passed seemed to notice. She was squat and plump, her body reminiscent of something between a frog and a rotting tree stump. She trundled down the long stretch of hallway, leaning on a cart stocked with all manner of cleaning supplies and paltry amenities.

The maid looked as though walking was difficult for her. It wasn't that she was crippled or worn by years. It was more she seemed unaccustomed to ambulating upright.

Once, she nearly fell when she paused to check the room numbers; garish pieces of tarnished, dented brass were affixed directly to the doors above their peepholes. A young couple, the sort that never had much cash but always an assortment of drugs, disheveled but not quite dirty, looked on with a passive concern. The maid could smell the blunt in the man's pocket. They were on their way out to wake and bake and find some breakfast, harmless stoners trying to look like concerned bystanders.

The maid sneered at them, showing a mouthful of teeth like needles. She gripped the cart, and ragged claws dragged furrows in the gray plastic as she pushed herself upright. She looked into their eyes and watched to see if they *saw* her. She waited for the fear to show in their eyes. When it did, she would spring at them and tear their necks.

The couple paused in the hallway, so close she could smell the salt of the old sweat in their clothing. She licked her lips, her dark tongue dragging a coating of mucous over their chapped skin. She'd been tracking the sage and her guardian since they escaped the hospital, and she was hungry.

They only smiled back at her, the maid's muting leaving them oblivious to the truth of what they saw. They were relieved she had kept her balance, that they could keep walking, that there would be no impediment to the pursuit of their hungers. She nearly leapt for them anyway.

"You alright?" said the man with the blunt, his hand going to his pocket in an unconscious, protective gesture. The girl smiled meekly, looking passably empathetic as she twined her arm through his. It was their chance to act concerned, now that the problem was past; uselessly helpful and pointlessly polite.

The man looked at her chest, but the maid didn't have a name tag. She shook her head and gave them a thumbs up. She bared her fangs at them again, and they smiled wider in kind.

"Just fine."

He bobbed his head and held up his own thumb. The three of them stood there like that for a beat, then two. Each waited for the other to move on. It was early enough it was quiet. There were televisions, and people talked and moved things, but it was all muffled and indistinct. The maid dragged her forearm across her nose and smeared thick, hanging snot from wide nostrils across her cheek.

The man and the woman moved only after the maid did, like they'd needed some sign of permission. The maid understood even if they didn't; predators lead the dance. They didn't acknowledge it, weren't consciously *aware* of it, but she could smell the blind, instinctual fear in the new sweat starting from their pores.

The woman pulled a smart phone from the back pocket of her shabby jeans and thumbed it to life. She looked it over, hands trembling only a little, never quite letting the maid out of her peripheral vision. The man looked over her shoulder and smiled at the little screen. They pretended to forget the maid, but then they really did.

The couple started walking again, seeing what they wanted to see. No one wanted to see the thing dressed as a maid. Seeing a maid was better. They could survive seeing a maid.

The man shot her one last glance as they gained inertia. He smiled and waved. "Thanks."

For letting us leave with our lives. She knew what he meant even if he didn't. "Welcome."

The maid kept on shambling down the hall. She sniffed the air with thick, goopy snorts. The jinn was more dangerous but easier to track. His scent was distinct because, in a way, he was like her, something else passing for human. She bent nearly double as she snuffled at the lock, a slit for a key card she left slathered in translucent, clinging scum.

She dug around in her apron pockets until she found her own. She'd simply walked around the counter at the front desk when she'd arrived and took it. So long as she kept muted, people let her do as she pleased. *Simple creatures,* she thought, cutting her lips with the needle-sharp points of her real smile. She shoved the door open with the supply cart as she slipped inside. She let it bang against the wall. A long scratch left by the cart's corner joined its faded kin in their crisscross across the cheap finish.

The moment the door was closed behind her, she dropped

to all fours. Her joints twisted and distended impossibly. The maid bent her head down to the thin, faded carpet and snuffled at it. Mucous dripped from wide nostrils that flared even wider. Scraggly locks of black hair dragged through the slime where she passed. She skittered along with uncanny dexterity; her awkwardness vanished once she could move naturally.

She kept searching until she found a scrap of paper. Crouching on her haunches with her skirt hiked up to her hips, the maid looked over the markings scratched onto it. There was too little to make out, but the edges were burnt in a neat border around the fragment. She peered about; nothing else was damaged. There was no smell of smoke.

The maid pulled the paper in close and sniffed at it. It stuck to her snot-soaked lip, and her eyes rolled back into her head as she scented the magic. *They* were *here! The sage and her jinn!* The maid clutched the scrap to her bosom. The yellowed flesh opened to make a pocket for her little prize. *The master must know! He will be pleased.*

Scents were one thing, but a tangible bit of spoor was so much more. The sage's trail ended here, but the maid knew that only meant they'd gone a Way she couldn't follow. In the right hands, she knew the bit of paper would be enough to find them again.

Despite her success, the maid was disappointed. It would have been better if she'd caught them herself. She could have ended things today and with a full stomach. She grunted out an empty belch, resigned to wait a little longer for such things, and set to giving the room a second pass, just in case there was something else she might have missed.

She'd nearly finished when there was a knock at the door and a woman's muffled voice called out, "Housekeeping! Hello? Housekeeping?"

The maid smiled and licked a long tongue over wet, flaking lips. *The master will know, but first . . . breakfast.* The creature scuttled silently across the room, up the wall and onto the ceiling. She positioned herself over the door, hanging by hooked toes. Snaggly claws wiggled in anticipation. She slavered. Thick drool drizzled down like syrup.

There was another knock. "Housekeeping! Hello?"

"Come in."

Chapter 8:

GAZING IN WIDE-EYED WONDER, the sage took her first steps into a new world and immediately fell into the bottomless abyss. "Shiiit!"

The hot winds of Sayon whipped her as she plummeted over the edge of a rocky ledge. Before her spread endless layers of shifting, autumnal-colored clouds. If there was a bottom to it, it was so far below, it seemed she would spend the rest of her life in freefall.

By the time Alice finished her second lungful of screaming, she realized that wouldn't be long at all. The deeper she fell, the hotter the buffeting winds became. Breathing took on a hot, thick quality on par with the hottest sauna she'd ever taken. She wondered how deep she'd go before it choked her.

All around, there were little islands of solid ground that floated impossibly amidst the russet clouds and the billowing ochre haze. Each was its own microcosm. Deserts and forests, meadows and pools, all hung in an ocean of sky. Alice wondered if she would be able to keep breathing long enough for her body to break against one of them.

On and around some of the islands, she saw all manner of alien creatures. Like the plants she glimpsed, though she could guess at their ecological niche, not a one of them was familiar. Like the animals of her earth, she saw feathers and scales, fur and quills; wings, legs, beaks, snouts. Some of the creatures were made of flesh and blood, others were born of fire.

A monkey with little suns for eyes chittered from its seat in the branches of a tree like a perpetually burning willow. It watched her drop as it nibbled the meat from the nut cradled in its lap, cracking away flakes of shell as it supped. A herd of wild horses galloped across the span between two islands. Their flaming hooves sparked against the clouds as they whinnied and tossed their smoldering manes.

Alice beheld what could only be a phoenix fold its blazing wings and dive into a river of lava. It emerged with a silvery fish in its claws. Its scales flashed white hot as it thrashed helplessly. Lava poured over the side of the floating island. The waterfall of molten rock cooled into smoking pebbles and steaming boulders that joined in her descent.

Far below, the layers of clouds built up into a depthless, blistering night. Dimly, she saw long bodies of serpents the size of trains writhing in the heavy, scathing clouds. Sayon's lesser creatures both great and small did not go to those unfathomable places. It seemed only the careless and the foolish delved so deep as to be swallowed up by those low leviathans of their bottomless world.

Alice wasn't screaming anymore. Her mind was numb to the terror of it. Her lungs were full of thick, soupy air that bubbled in her throat. She turned her head and looked for a horizon, something to see beyond the novel monotony of the countless, floating worldlets dotting ruddy cloudscapes before she died.

The vastness of Sayon defeated her eyes. If there was a skyline, the curvature of the world was beyond discernment.

Her body was nothing more than a speck of dust in a hurricane, unable to see beyond the next buffeting gust. Alice closed her eyes, accepted her fate, and waited for whatever death claimed her.

A hand reached through the burning darkness and caught her up. Alice was startled back into alertness and thrashed blindly, like any animal does when grabbed unexpectedly. Base instinct told her to go, get away, don't be eaten. Strong arms wrapped around her, passing beneath her own limbs, and bore her up. They were too strong to fight, but she bit and tore and kicked. Anything to get loose and be free.

A gentle palm pressed her head against a large chest. It was warm; the tide of breath beneath the firmly yielding muscles lulled her. Her neck and shoulders relaxed against the press of that strange, comforting body. Her arms and legs fell still and dragged furrows through the rusted, amber clouds as Alice drifted back into her aimless, shocked daze.

The next thing the sage registered was the press of a cup against her lips. It gently tipped a spicy nectar into her mouth, and she sucked at it greedily. It reminded her of jalapenos and mangos. The hot, sweet drink brought vigor back to her fear-worn body, and she opened her eyes.

A gathering of burning bodies circled her. They gave her space and did not threaten. Their ember eyes looked on her with keen interest. A jinn she recognized but did not know knelt beside her. It cradled her head in its lap as it fed her, speaking gentle words in a language she'd never heard but somehow recognized.

"You saved me." Alice smiled. "Thank you."

She made to sit up, and the jinn put a hand between her shoulder blades, supporting without pushing. The other jinn murmured as they watched, their language like the soft crackling of a well-banked hearth. She reached down and felt soft grass threading up between her fingers.

They stood in the shade of the single, giant tree that dominated that floating island. Its greatest boughs were like trees in their own right. Golden fruit weighed so thick and heavy she wondered if the tree would pull itself apart under its own bounty. Here and there, the fruits fell like rain into little pools around the great, twisted roots.

The jinn who sat with her turned to the pool beside them. Its waters were sweet with the amber juices of the fruits as they slowly pulled apart in their tranquil bath. The jinn dipped the cup into the nourishing, sweet waters and offered it to her again.

Alice took it gratefully and with both hands. The twisted ruin of her fingers could not be trusted to act without working all of them in unison. She drank in shameless gulps and filled herself until her stomach hurt with abundance. Sighing, she handed the cup back to the jinn and shook her head when it silently offered her more.

She let out a long, blissful belch and leaned back in the grass. "Thank you again."

The jinn laughed at that, the sound of it a merry crackling of a summer night's bonfire, and she laughed with them. Alice made to rise, and the jinn by her side rose with her, supporting her with a palm at her back and a hand beneath her wrist. When she had her balance, she looked about to take the measure of her succor.

Her rescuers had returned her from the depths to the upper reaches of Sayon. At this more tolerable altitude, the indigo sky was filled with stars and hung with dozens of moons. Some of them looked large enough to be worlds in their own right. Others were little more than rocky crumbs that tumbled across the velvet firmament.

Standing at the edge of the island, taking nourishment from his own cup, Altair saw her get up and rushed to her side. The pyre of jinn made way for him, and they spoke to each other. Alice couldn't understand a word of it, but all seemed amicable. Altair was thin, weaker than before. Bridging the worlds looked as if it had all but snuffed him out.

"Are you ok?" she asked.

"Am *I* ok?!" Altair said as he stepped to her side. "Holy shit, lady! I thought I lost you!"

He made to put his arms around her but stopped when she shrank away. The jinn remembered himself and dropped his hands to his sides. She could feel his love for her and wanted his touch despite herself, satisfying the yearning by putting her hand on his shoulder.

She turned her attention back to the other jinn. They stood in a rough circle around them. All of them looked on her with keen curiosity. A few gaped in open wonder.

"Altair?"

"Yes?"

"They're all looking at me."

"Of course." He smiled. "You're one of the eight sages. You're famous."

"How can they tell?" Alice asked. She puzzled a moment, then lowered her head and put her palm on her forehead as understanding dawned; the eighth center. "I forgot to mute myself."

"It's understandable," Altair said. "Your cage got rattled. Hey, even if you weren't a sage, they'd still be staring. You're the first human any of them have seen in a very long time. Some of them have never seen one of your kind at all.

"And, ah," said the jinn. His flaming body brightened around his cheeks. "You're a woman."

Did he just blush? Aloud, she said, "Yes?"

Altair actually shuffled his feet before he remembered himself and stood still. "You see, ah, human women are considered to be the most beautiful of all the peoples in existence."

Alice blinked. "Seriously?"

The jinn nodded. "It is believed humans were the last of the peoples made by God, but they were the first to be divided by sex."

"Wait," said Alice. "So, you're saying the book of Genesis is accurate?"

Altair snorted and burst out laughing. "God, no! I mean, there are some general ideas that fall more or less along the right lines, but it was a bunch of caveman jabber."

The jinn wiped fiery tears of mirth from his face. "That's true of all the human religions, though. A correct notion, here and there, mixed up in a pile of random crap people stuck in on God's *behalf*."

Alice was intrigued. "So, there's a jinn Bible?"

Altair teetered a hand back and forth. "Sort of. Jinn don't worry as much about religion. Faith comes easy when you know where Heaven actually is."

She arched an eyebrow, trying to gauge if it was just an empty boast. He told her, "We're not allowed in, mind you. No one is. We just know where it's kept."

Alice sighed. Asking Altair questions was like opening one of those Russian nesting dolls, except in reverse. Every time one was split apart, it led to a larger one.

"Matryoshkas," said Altair. "I think, anyway."

Alice blinked. "How . . . ?"

Before he could answer, she figured it out for herself. The sage concentrated and felt her centers contract within her. Reluctantly, the eighth followed suit. She held her focus for a few breaths until they stayed like that consistently.

"It really sucks being the ignorant one," she said, sighing. "I feel like I dropped out in the first grade."

"Don't let it get to you," said Altair. "We don't know it all, either. No one does. It's too big. Just keep paying attention."

Altair smiled and shrugged. "Besides, I think you're doing pretty well, so far, considering."

Alice cocked her head and asked, "How so?"

"Well," said the jinn, "you seem pretty at ease."

He waved his arm in a wide arc around them. "None of this is bothering you?"

Alice paused at that and took another look at their surroundings. "I guess not. It's all . . . hmm . . . alien, you know? But at the same time, I'm sure I've seen this stuff before. It's like I'm only a step away from *knowing* all this, but I can't get there, and I don't understand why."

"You'll get it," said the jinn, utterly certain.

"How can you know that?" she asked.

"Because I know you," he said, "and I've seen what you can do."

His confidence took her aback, but she smiled warmly. "Thanks. Can you, uhm, ask them to stop staring at me?"

"Ah, yes," Altair said, turning to the gathering. He spoke to them and apparently answered some questions. She noted his answers were brief. Soon enough, the other jinn said their goodbyes and took leave.

Some of them drifted away like embers on the breeze. Others transformed into any manner of forms suitable for flight. Wings beat and fluttered as some of them became birds. Others used patagia spread wide to catch updrafts like living kites, and Alice knew them to be like Altair. *Ghuls. The others must be sila.* Alice watched them go, envious of their effortless flight. She wondered if she had magic herself, that she might follow them.

As if in answer to her unspoken question, an old memory drifted up and caught the light of her mind's eye; something from another life that was herself before she'd been born. She saw Altair with her. They held hands as they passed through the great skies of Sayon together. She closed her eyes and somehow remembered a little of where she was now. When she opened them again, the jinn was there as he was so many lifetimes ago, his loving smile like the smoke of sweet incense.

Alice shook her head. "Phew. Déjà vu."

"That's good," said Altair. "We spent many years here. Would you like to see our house again?"

"I thought we needed to hurry?" she said.

The jinn nodded. "The agents of the enemy follow behind us. I think they found the motel."

He wrinkled his nose. "I felt something foul coming before we left, some kind of tracker, but we've put some distance behind us."

"Can't they cross over? We did."

Altair said, "A god or a sage, perhaps. Anything else would need to find a Way. If they managed to get through, they'd still need to travel in this world to reach us. We should be safe, for now.

"Besides." He smiled. "That's where we were going anyway."

"This guide lives in our old house?"

"Yes," Altair said, "but it's his now, you see. I gave it to him. The first time you died, I couldn't stay there anymore."

Something in his countenance tugged at her. "Will he be happy to see you?"

The jinn nodded, his eyes far away in the there and then of the millennia of his memories. "He will, I think. This reunion has been too long in coming."

Altair blinked away the past and turned his eyes back toward the future. "We need to keep moving."

"How do we do this?" she asked as she looked dubiously over the edge of their island. "I don't know how to fly, and you look so thin. Can you carry me?"

"I think it will be alright," he told her.

When Alice did not appear confident, he added, "Here. Let me teach you a song so you can fly with me if you need to."

With that, he began to sing a wordless melody. Alice listened as Altair's sonorous voice filled the air. Soon, she was whistling with him. As she did, she concentrated on the whirling energy hanging over her head. *The soul center*, Altair called it.

She didn't understand how these parts of her worked or their connection to music, but she could feel a well of power within herself. It was vast, its immensity leaving Alice feeling like who she was, her *self*, was nothing more than a thin layer over the surface of it. With Altair's melody, she found that, somehow, she could give a voice to that power.

Before long, she felt her toes part from the long grasses. She thrilled at the feel of it and waved her legs through the empty air. *OhmygodI'mflying!*

Immediately, Alice drifted sideways, buffeted by a sudden wind. The euphoria of being free from gravity's pull vanished. The edge loomed near, and she screamed. Arms and legs windmilled desperately to keep from falling.

"Aw, fuck!" she shouted. "No-no-no-no-no!"

The music lingered on the air for a beat, and then the magic ended. Alice dropped, landing on her bottom with a grunt. She threw herself on her back and clutched at the grass. There at the edge of the little island, the ground had an increasingly steep curvature. She was too close. Alice could feel herself scrape down the slope despite her efforts and shrieked as the abyss loomed beneath her.

Just then, Altair caught her by the wrist. She looked back in surprise and relief as he held out his other hand for hers. Together, they hauled her back onto level ground.

"I need-," Alice gasped breathlessly, "-I need to practice."

"That's wise," agreed the jinn. "In the meantime, where we're going isn't far. I can manage the both of us. Watch."

Altair closed his eyes and gathered his will. With effort, he became a large, winged serpent. As weak as he was, the change wasn't instantaneous like she'd seen it before. His body became a melting blur that was dizzying to look at before it resolved.

A giant snake curled where the jinn had been and extended a wing, one of four, for Alice to climb. She hesitated only a moment before she clambered as lightly as she could to the apparent seat between the two pairs of wings. Curious, she patted at the creature's feathers and slid her palm over its smooth scales.

All at once, she remembered who it was she was fondling and jerked her hands away. Altair the winged serpent gave no sign he'd noticed but simply kept still and waited as she arranged herself. Alice frowned, then, as casually as she could manage, she leaned forward and gripped at the serpent's back. *You've ridden bitch on a motorcycle*, she coached herself. *This is the same thing. Just hold on and keep my balance close to his.*

When she was settled, Altair the feathered serpent rose into the air with a lunge like a striking cobra. The lunge became a leap, then the great wings took over and turned their momentum into a glide.

Together, they left the soft shores of that little island hung in the Sayon sky. Altair beat his wings occasionally, but there were plenty of updrafts and thermals to lift them. Soon, they were in a rhythm, surfing the winds toward a place she'd never been that was her home.

Chapter 9:

THE SAGE WAS IMPRESSED to see home was a white castle of marbled stone, set on a great island at the center of a sprawling archipelago suspended in a sea of golden clouds. Alice could see on the grounds of the estate a set of neighboring buildings that could only be a university. The surrounding islands each held a share of their own structures and gardens. There were stands of statuary that made the old Greek masters seem like amateurs. Away from the islands with their great buildings hanging closer to the citadel, comfortable cottages housed the families of what Alice realized was a bonafide city of jinn.

"What *is* this place?" asked Alice as they landed.

"Shambhala," Altair told her. His lips formed a smile around the word. Alice was startled at his voice. She hadn't seen him change. The flight seemed to have been as restful to him as it had been for her.

"Shambhala," she repeated, tasting the sound of it on her tongue. Her eyes were greedy with curiosity. She couldn't see it all fast enough. So many jinn were coming and going and living their lives, it hardly made sense to her. In all the stories she'd ever read, faeries and monsters could usually be counted on one hand. Rarely, there could be dozens. This place, growing and growing as they traveled across Sayon's airy ocean, was *civilization*.

Throughout the city, multiple levels were the norm. As big as the islands were, there wasn't enough space to stretch out, so Shambhala had grown up. Some of the islands were built out all the way to their edges. Tall buildings of white stone shone in the bright sunlight.

A prevalent architectural feature was a lack of windows in favor of doorways. Sila came and went, flying in and out from any level. Their kindred, the ghul jinn, flew with all manner of wings, darting in and out of the doors. Those on foot typically traveled with enough cargo to make flying impractical. The rest, though an apparent minority, were a medley of beings like something out of a book of fairy tales.

Alice saw creatures she mentally matched against the pictures and movies accumulated in her memory. She saw what looked like elves and dwarves, devilish-looking goat men, and a centaur. The sage couldn't help but gape at that.

"Excuse me," an actual centaur said politely as he cantered past. Before she could remember to close her mouth and think to do anything, he'd gone on, lost in the flow of the city again. A heavy shadow passed overhead, and she squinted upward.

High above, she saw there were occasional large loads. These consisted of simple metal containers attended by teams of jinn. They worked together to manage the magic that supported their heavy cargo. She noted they kept mostly to routes that left as little of value as possible beneath them.

"How many are there?" She breathed.

"In Shambhala?" Altair asked, then took a moment to consider it. "The city is a bit bigger than your New York, I think."

Alice craned her neck to peer up at the tall buildings.

She smiled at the jinn floating and flying about their business overhead. When she saw a few of them look back, she caught herself and put her eyes back on where she was going. *Tourists do that,* she chided herself. *You need to blend in.* Already, her presence had attracted attention from passing jinn. Before the gawkers could form into a crowd, she concentrated on her centers.

The wheels of energy did nothing at first. She persisted and, slowly, they contracted. Feeling encouraged, she kept at it as they walked. Jinn still looked, but, as long as they kept moving, their eyes tended to slide off of her. A small few were undissuaded. Those trailed behind them and pointed her out to passerbies.

"Try whistling while you do it," Altair suggested.

"Easy for you to say," she replied, looking over his tidy bearing. Like the other jinn around them, he was not muting himself to the point where he became hidden, but thoughts and emotions were kept neatly out of view. She envied the unintentional display of precise control.

"Your magic will strengthen your will," he said encouragingly. "With the little things, it doesn't matter that you don't know what you're doing."

"Thanks," Alice replied dryly.

"I mean," the jinn added quickly, "with this, you don't have to worry as much about your skill. You're a sage. For now, you can get by on crude force."

She gave him a thumb-up. "The crudest."

"Just try."

Alice searched her memory for an appropriate tune. Her gut told her the music should match the magic. Drawing a blank, she fumed, pursed her lips, and whistled the first thing that came to mind; *Pop Goes the Weasel.*

A smile twitched the corners of Altair's mouth, but he said nothing. Soon after, his eyes slid off her, and he looked around blankly. For a moment, he looked quite worried, searching about before he managed to orient on her again. The jinn nodded approval and turned to head toward the great fortress of Shambhala.

Their progress was quick after that. No one else stopped to gape at the sage. Alice knew this was important and was glad of it. *Whoever wants me dead can get to earth,* she reasoned. *No reason they couldn't have some of their people here, too.*

For a time, she eyed the throngs of jinn all about them, but it was impossible. The endless mob of them walked, talked, and shopped, their city as alive as any major metropolis on earth. What's more, with the city of Shambhala designed with flight in mind, commerce and commiseration occurred in three dimensions. A spy or an assassin could be watching from literally any direction. Alice gave up, trusted in her magic and her guide, and put her eyes forward on the citadel.

When they arrived at the main gate, Altair approached one of the guards that stood to either side, ignoring the looks from the line of jinn waiting to be cleared for entry. They spoke in their strange but not unpleasant tongue. Altair became increasingly animate as they spoke, his body heating with his anger. When he became so intense that Alice had to step away, the guards shifted their grip on their spears. They didn't point them at Altair, but it was clear they meant to if he pressed the issue any further.

Alice stopped whistling. Her lips were tired, and it was a relief to stop repeating the simple tune. She asked him as they stepped away from the door, "What is it?"

"Fucking racists," he muttered. Alice looked at him blankly and glanced around. As near as she could tell, all the jinn were more or less the same. Some were taller or shorter, some broader, some slight, but they were all just anthropomorphic fire to her. It struck her she might have trouble picking Altair out of a crowd and suppressed a smile at the image of tying a balloon around his wrist for identification.

Despite her improving control, the jinn seemed to follow her thoughts. "I know, we all look alike to you, right?"

Alice raised a hand and made a little space between her thumb and index finger. He rolled his eyes and said, "It's a sila thing. Their sort are overrepresented in the cartographer's guild. When it comes to getting about the Realms and their Ways, they have a natural advantage. I am a ghul without proper documentation, so the assumption is I do not belong here."

"Don't they know you?" she asked. "You said this used to be our home."

"That was a long time ago," said the jinn, "and things change."

"Nothing lasts," agreed Alice. "But I thought you knew someone who works here?"

Altair looked at her sharply, then his eyes softened. "Yes, but we haven't spoken in a long time."

"How long?"

"Centuries," he said. "Since the first time you died."

She blinked. "That's a *long* time."

"Not so long," said the jinn.

"Could you, I don't know, send him a message or something?"

Altair nodded. "Yes, but it would take time we don't have. It won't be long until everyone knows a sage is in Shambhala."

"And we don't really know who's on our side."

"That's right," said the jinn. "You're paying attention."

Alice smirked. "I'm not stupid, is all. Once you get past the surface of it, people are people, and cities are cities."

She smiled, taking comfort at the thought of it. The concept made the ifrit that attacked her less frightening. It was still a threat, but it wasn't some unknowable horror from her nightmares. It had been a hitman hired to kill her and nothing more.

Alice looked at the main gate. The guards regulated the flow of traffic. That particular door appeared to be for guests and visitors. Regulars, employees and their bosses, looked to make use of portals overhead. She guessed they were the more direct routes. She considered the idea of jumping the system and going through one of the dozens of other passages available but thought better of it.

It could be assumed they would need some kind of identification or certification; some bureaucratic hoops and hurdles. Bucking the system that way also ran the risk of putting them at odds with the jinn that managed the place and possibly the specific people they were here to see. *Same shit, different day. Wait a second . . .* She snapped her fingers, the solution coming to her.

"Wait! I've got this!" she exclaimed and headed straight for the main gates. Trading secrecy for expediency, she made no effort to conceal herself other than to keep her thoughts tucked away. The guards gaped at the sight of the human woman. The line of jinn waiting to be passed through turned curiously.

Altair hurried after her. "What are you doing?!"

"Relax," she reached out to pat him on the arm. "I'm famous, remember? That means everyone will know I'm here by tomorrow no matter what we do, right?"

"Right," said the jinn reluctantly.

"But!" said Alice, "it also means I can do whatever the hell I want right now, so screw it. Let's go!"

"Hey there," she said and stepped past Altair before he could reply. She put on her prettiest smile as she stood before the guards. Their eyes strayed from her face to her chest down to her legs. Alice kept smiling as if she was used to the objectification. Then, one of them glanced over her head, and his eyes widened. He elbowed the other guard. The jinn's mouth dropped open.

"Do they speak English?" she asked.

"The center at your throat," he said, then pointed at the top of her head, "and the crown. Open them a little while you speak, and you should be plain enough to them."

Alice managed with effort. It was like patting her head while rubbing her stomach, but it became easier as she spoke. "I am Alice Olson, the . . ."

"Eighth," Altair prompted.

". . . the eighth sage of earth," said Alice, "and I need to see . . ."

"Ajdaha."

". . . Ajdaha immediately. It's extremely urgent," she said. "Please?"

The guards exchanged a look, then the nearest said, "Of course, Sage Alice. Please enter the great citadel of Shambhala."

The jinn's speech pushed uncomfortably at her mind, her understanding more psychic impression than true familiarity with the spoken word. Alice kept up her smile nonetheless and squared her shoulders as they opened the gate for them. Together, they passed through. Their footsteps rang on the polished stone of the capital.

Chapter 10:

ALICE STOOD BEFORE THE great dragon Ajdaha and quailed. Her head was level with its shoulder. Its long, supple body draped about the room in luxurious coils against velvet pillows. A haze of sweet-smelling smoke hung in the air, wafting slowly from hidden censers. The midday sunlight cut white corridors through it from the wide-open windows to the gleaming, pale marble floors.

Behind Alice and Altair, great doors were pulled closed by two exceptionally large jinn, the flames of their heavy muscles flashing with effort. The doors shut with a deep, echoing thud, and the three of them were alone. The dragon was sketching something in a large book on a low table. It held a long, thin pen among its supple claws, handling the instrument with dexterous care.

Every one of its scales was like polished gold. Some were as big as her palm, others so fine as to be nearly invisible. Its eyes were the colors of a midnight bonfire. When Ajdaha looked at her, Alice could see at once its intelligence and inquisitiveness.

The dragon finished its work with a few flourishing

strokes. It laid the pen down and closed the book gently. It folded its claws and rested its paws on the table. It drew back its lips, and Alice's cheeks blanched at the sight of its long, sharp teeth.

"Hello, mother," said the dragon.

"What?" said Alice, at a loss.

"What?!" The dragon looked at Altair. "You didn't tell her?"

The jinn shrugged his shoulders and smiled as he looked back and forth between the two of them. "Sorry, son. It's been hectic."

"Hectic?!" Alice blurted angrily. "Son?! Look, I know I've been learning on the job here, but you couldn't find a second to let me know I have a fucking dragon for a *son*?!"

She looked quickly to Ajdaha. "No offense."

The dragon nodded with lithe grace. "It's a lot to take in. It's good to see you, father. It's good to see both of you."

Alice looked to Altair. "Wait, *our* son is a dragon?!"

The jinn said, "We have several children, actually. Most were conceived in your first life. Ajdaha is our eldest."

Alice was reeling with the influx of new, extremely personal information. Ajdaha looked at her sympathetically. He said, "Well, it looks as though we have a lot to talk about. Refreshment?"

The dragon didn't wait for an answer but instead concentrated and sent out a kind of pulse from the center at his throat. Alice could feel the whisper of meaning as it passed but couldn't catch it fully. Soon after, the large guards pushed the door open again, and another jinn marched in.

It held its hand outstretched, and a platter heavily laden with fruits, meats, and cheeses levitated smoothly in front of it. *Sila,* Alice prompted herself. With a wave, the jinn placed the platter on the table. A smaller tray of fresh bread, a pitcher of wine, and two glasses followed. When they were seen to, the sila and the door jinn left quietly.

Alice hesitated, but Altair stepped forward and lowered himself onto a cushion next to the table. He immediately reached out for a skewer of meat while Ajdaha poured them each a glass of amber-colored wine. The bottle clicked in the delicate grip of his long claws. The dragon indicated other cushions scattered within easy reach of the table.

"Please, sit."

Alice sat and ate with the two of them. Tentative at first, she soon fell to with abandon, gorging unabashedly. Nothing was said between them at first. It was enough to eat together, as families do.

When they were finished, Alice leaned back and stroked her belly with pleasure. The jinn poured himself another glass of wine. Ajdaha nibbled at unfamiliar fruits; something like large, blue cherries. He crunched the stones of the fruit contentedly in his cheek.

"Can I ask you something?" said Alice.

The dragon spread his paws and nodded. "By all means."

"Why are you a dragon? I mean, he's a jinn, and I'm a human, so . . ."

Ajdaha gave a toothy grin. "I'm a nephilim."

When Alice looked back blankly, the dragon readily obliged. "A hybrid. Nephilim are the product of mixing the blood of one of the races; god, jinn, ifrit, or human with something else. All told, I'm half-jinn, a quarter human, and about a quarter god."

Alice blinked. "Wait, that means . . ."

". . . that I am a demi-god," the dragon finished for her, "though quite minor."

"And in my first life . . ."

Ajdaha nodded. "Yes, Alice. In your first life, you were a demigod, as well. Your mother was human. Your father was the god Marduk."

"Uh . . ." Alice managed, unsure.

Altair supplied, "It's his old, Babylonian name. The Norse

called him Odin. The Greeks knew her as Hekate."

"Her?" said Alice.

"Gods are weird," said the jinn. "Things like names and gender are mostly there for we lesser beings to wrap our heads around. Essentially, your parent is the deity most strongly associated with the same energy qualities as the soul center. The rest is trappings."

"So," said the dragon, "I am assuming you don't know anything of your previous lives?"

Alice shook her head. "I didn't know that was an option."

"You didn't teach her about the Akashic Record?" Ajdaha looked reproachfully at Altair.

The jinn blinked. "The what now?"

The dragon hesitated, eyeing his father, then said, "The mystical, collective sum of all human experience."

At Altair's blank look, Ajdaha shook his head and looked toward the ceiling. "You've been living on earth, among humans, *with a sage*, for centuries, dad. You're telling me it never came up?"

"Oh," said Altair, noncommittally adding, "it does sound familiar."

Ajdaha looked at the jinn and let out a long sigh before turning to Alice. "All sages have access to the Records. All you have to do is tap into it, and you can know anything your kind has ever known."

"Just like that?" Alice asked, incredulous.

The dragon said, "It's not *all* immediately available. Like any other knowledge, varying degrees of effort and sacrifice come into it. The easiest things to find are those directly relevant to yourself. That includes your past lives."

Alice was ecstatic. "Well shit! You're telling me there's a sage manual?! I can just access some metaphysical search engine?!"

"More or less," said the dragon.

"What the fuck, Altair?!" Alice spun to glare at him.

The jinn held up his hands defensively. "I'm sorry. I don't know these things."

"You've spent well over a *thousand* years with her," said Ajdaha. "Seriously, mother never mentioned it? Not once?"

Altair shrugged. "If I knew something, I would have said something. Alright?"

"Fine," said Ajdaha, letting the matter drop. "Here, mother. Let me help you?"

The dragon concentrated and sent out another pulse of energy. This one caught Alice square on, and she gasped as if plunged into ice water. All at once, she had the knowledge she needed. Her eyes dancing with delight, Alice pursed her lips and began the song the dragon sent her.

Alice felt the edges of her consciousness stretch out immediately as she searched for something she perceived as a massive, shadowed presence at the back of her mind. The center at the top of her head flared, then widened as she reached toward that sense of immensity. A few more measures of the melody, and she felt her mind join and merge with something far greater than herself.

In her mind's eye, a face emerged from the darkness. It was a woman, strong and beautiful. Her eyes were depthless, azure pools that seemed to contain whole oceans of memories. Across the centuries, they moved closer to each other, and Alice realized she was looking at the face of her original self. She reached out, and the woman reached back. A warm tingling passed through her body as the tips of their fingers brushed.

Without warning, that sense of connection broke away, replaced by a cold wave. It felt sharp, like a sea of broken glass, and Alice recoiled from it. The face disappeared back into the darkness, the sense of connection was gone, and she opened her eyes, gasping.

Altair and Ajdaha were looking at her concernedly. She looked back, feeling embarrassed. "I can't. I'm sorry."

The dragon narrowed his eyes. "It wasn't you. Something is blocking you from accessing the Records. Wait . . ."

Ajdaha reached out a paw, and a pan's flute leapt into his talons. Closing his eyes, he played the melody he had given to Alice. She could feel the power in it, could sense it taking hold as the dragon's mind sank deep within itself. All at once, his playing stopped on a last, screeching note from the pipes that made Alice jump.

"What is it?" Altair looked between them.

The dragon was solemn, the scales of his brow knitted in thought. "The Records. They are closed to me, as well. Somehow, something is blocking them."

"That's possible?" asked the jinn.

"It shouldn't be," the dragon answered. "It would take the power of a sage or a god."

"But the sages are gone, right?" Alice asked.

Altair nodded. "All but you."

The dragon stroked his chin with his taloned paw. "A god shouldn't be able to access the Records like that. Excepting the eternal God, the Akashic Records are meant for humans alone. With my mixed blood, even I can only access them with difficulty."

Alice fretted, wringing her hands unconsciously. "So, what does this mean?"

"It means," said the jinn, "that our enemy is more powerful than anything I've ever encountered."

She looked to the dragon. Her eyes pled for some sense of security, but he said, "This is beyond my own experience, as well."

Ajdaha looked squarely at his father. "Quickly, you must tell me everything you know."

Alice's head was swimming, and it felt as if the bottom had dropped out of her gut. All at once, it was too much. Ever since the accident, her world had been expanding so quickly, too fast to possibly keep up with. Her old life, only a few days gone, had been wiped away by the relentless press of jinn and dragons and magic and monsters and gods and . . .

Distantly, she registered Altair and Ajdaha had stopped talking. It seemed as though they'd been speaking animatedly for some time now, but she hadn't heard a word of it. Her head was laid down on the dragon's table. She clutched at herself and tried to stop from shaking as silent tears traced across her face toward her ear.

She noticed Altair was looking at her concernedly. His mouth was moving. She tried to force herself to concentrate through the panic.

". . . you alright?" Altair finished again.

Alice stared at him dumbly. Her heart was racing, her body bathed in a cold sweat. Her breath was coming in short hitches. She felt faint. She opened her mouth to speak but closed it again to swallow as nausea rose up to the back of her throat.

She felt another pair of hands come to rest lightly on her other shoulder. She looked, and kneeling beside her was a man unlike any she'd ever seen. He was bald. *No,* she thought, *hairless.* His skin was a rich, golden tone. He was large but thin, his body like a supple whip.

Alice saw the fiery eyes and recognized him instantly. "Ajdaha?"

The dragon nodded. "It's a lot. All of this. I understand. I thought this shape might be easier for you."

She leaned into him, her inhuman son of lifetimes ago. Her shoulders shook as more tears came. They were good tears, an emotional release she hadn't realized she needed.

"Th-tha . . ." was all she could manage through her weeping.

"It's alright," said Ajdaha, gently stroking her shoulder. "Father and I have much to discuss. Please, I will have a room prepared for you. A bath, rest, anything you need."

Alice nodded, grateful. She shrank away from their

touch. The sila jinn who'd brought them their repast returned to the room and exchanged a look with its master. Alice felt a pulse of energy pass between them, and the sila bowed.

"Salem will see to you," said Ajdaha. "We'll speak again when you're ready."

She got to her feet, shunning any assistance. Her head low, she murmured, "Thank you. I'm sorry."

Altair looked around sharply and opened his mouth to respond, but Ajdaha spoke first. "Think nothing of it. Rest now. Give yourself time. Thank you, Salem."

The jinn bowed deeply. "My lord."

"Now, wait just a damn minute!" Altair exclaimed. He planted his palms on the low table and pushed himself to his feet roughly enough to send his cushion sliding across the smooth floor. Ajdaha and Salem turned to regard him, and he glowered back, unwilling to relent.

"I've had my eye on her every day for more than thirty years!" he spat. "She's not going anywhere until I know where she's going and who's going to be there!"

Alice looked at the jinn numbly. Salem looked taken aback by the outburst and looked to his master for guidance. The golden man rose to his feet, motioned for his secretary to wait, and looked to his father, as patient as time itself.

"Father . . ." he began.

"Don't you 'father' me!" said Altair. "I want to know the plan here!"

Ajdaha stepped over to his father and put his hands on his shoulders. Reluctantly at first, Altair allowed himself to be pulled into an embrace. They stayed like that a moment, and then the demigod gave his father space.

Alice wasn't certain, but, before he turned away, she thought she saw Altair wipe a single ember of a tear from his eye. *No,* she thought, *you know what you saw. You just don't want to have seen it.*

"Father," Ajdaha started again, "the plan is for you and

mother to take the time you need to rest and prepare. You know as well as I do the walls of the citadel have not been breached in centuries. I know you've been gone a long time, but you must understand your home still stands as it always has."

The golden man gestured toward Salem. "You've known my chief secretary since he first came here. Salem keeps this place running smoother than I ever could. I trust his judgment completely. He will ensure mother is taken care of and as secure as you could want."

Altair looked uncertain, and Ajdaha beseeched him. "Please father, you need your rest as much as she does. Your long vigil has ended. You are home."

With that, Altair slumped a little, and Alice could see the fight was fading from him. She wondered at what his life must have been like for so long. She tried to imagine him as a literal fly on the wall of her childhood home, her silent guardian watching over her, alone for all that time.

Before the crash, she wondered how long it had been since he'd last spoken to anyone at all. Thoughts of Timothy rose up in defiance of the sympathy she felt for the jinn, but she pushed them down before they became overwhelming. As much as she hated the jinn, she loved him too. *Christ,* she thought. *I'm so sorry, Tim . . .*

"It's ok, Altair," she put her hand on his bicep, "We both need the rest. You brought me here so I'd be safe, right?"

Altair nodded wordlessly, and she told him, "Well, now we're here. Thank you. Whatever is happening, I never would have made it this far without you. We'll figure it out, ok?"

The jinn's stalwart defiance had persisted against his son's care. Against her, he had no defense. Looking as if the weight of the world were pressing on him, Altair lowered his head, then nodded in acceptance.

He looked between the sage and his son. "Y-you're right. It's just been so long."

Then, a smile touched his lips. "I guess I'm used to being on my own."

Ajdaha stepped in and rubbed his father's back between the shoulder blades. "I know, father. I've missed you. Let's have a drink?"

With a soft sigh of exhaustion and relief, Altair sank down onto a cushion. As if from nowhere, a decanter of amber liquid was in Ajdaha's hands. From it, he poured them both a drought. It smelled strongly alcoholic and faintly of mangos and jalapenos.

With that, Salem held out a hand toward the doors, and Alice allowed him to lead her from Ajdaha's hall. Her thoughts were sluggish and thick with the repeated stress. She didn't react when the sila worked his magic to carry them up a narrow shaft. Floors passed without her counting. All at once, their ascent stopped, and the jinn helped her into a foyer.

When she was well away from the circular portal between the floors, Salem opened a pair of doors for her. Within, there was a lavish suite. She passed through the rooms in a blur of silk curtains and soft cushions. Alice smiled at last when they stopped in front of a hot, perfumed bath.

She let Salem undress her without a hint of self-consciousness, too exhausted, too emotionally numb to be modest. She took his hand gratefully as he helped her down the short steps of the basin, large enough for several to use at once, into the steaming, bubbly water.

Once she was settled, he said something to her in the smoldering language of his people. Alice had let her centers return to their usual flow. She found flexing them tired her as much as physical activity and wondered if she would build fitness with use. She nodded politely as Salem gestured around her quarters. Her eyes slipped closed before he'd left her suite.

Drifting through a light doze, Alice's thoughts turned to

Timothy and the life he'd tried to build for her. It hurt that
she felt relieved all of that was over, that life that had never
been meant for her. The weighty guilt rose up as she opened
her eyes to watch the bubbles in her bath burst, one by one.

She'd done the best she could for Tim, but she knew it
would have been better if they'd never met. It was just she'd
felt so desperate for change, for something to happen in her
life, she'd clung to him as if she'd been drowning. *No,* she
thought, *like smothering slowly. I tried, but it was like I could
never get enough air.*

She'd changed for Tim the best she knew how, but now
he was gone. That was her fault, and she knew there was no
other way than to live with it. All that was left was to keep
changing, going on with this new life the best she could. *Or
until it kills me,* she thought. *The way it's been going, probably won't have to wait long.* It surprised her to realize the idea
didn't bother her, not when she finally had the chance to live
her real life, the one she'd always been meant for.

Alice stayed in the bath until her shivering bade her find
a warm, fluffy towel. Not bothering to dress, she slipped between the cool, silk sheets of a massive bed. It was like laying
in a cloud. The sage wept there until sleep rose up and swallowed her down into tawny and russet dreams of falling.

Chapter 11:

HIS OBLIGATIONS TO THE dragon satisfied for the night, Salem passed through the halls of the citadel of Shambhala like a ghost. It was easier in the evening, the castle's foot traffic reduced to the residential staff and an occasional guest. The sila made it a point to know who was working each day and where they needed to be to complete their duties. As one of Ajdaha's first secretaries, the information was at his fingertips.

As for the guests, the citadel was a three-dimensional maze he could navigate blind. It was nothing for the sila to mute himself and drift through the shafts and corridors without being observed. Alone, he made his way to the great yards, a series of meticulously maintained gardens and landscapes complete with ornate statues, topiaries, and sheltered areas for seating.

From there, he passed through one of the minor gatehouses. Simply flying away, even muted, was likely to draw notice, so Salem plodded along like some minor nephilim. Taking advantage of the bored indifference of the guards proved to be easier by far, and, soon, he was blended into the currents of the masses, a single drop in a branching river of jinn.

The sila's steps were cautious, nonetheless. They took him over the least used bridges spanning between several of the islands of Shambhala. Though it tested his patience, he didn't fly. Without freight to necessitate it, only the lowest of the jinn, the janni, made use of the low ways. Cripples and flawed half-breeds, Salem felt nothing but disdain for the dregs of the city. It galled him to walk among them, obliged to eschew the stature of his office, that he might be mistaken for one of their ilk.

Step by distasteful step, Salem made his way to an older village beyond the city proper. Like most towns falling outside Shambhala, it shared the name of its island: Thule. Thule had known its share of hard times and harder living. It fell in that shadowy area of being too far from the capital to be noticed but too close to be ignored. Constables made their rounds but infrequently and never alone. So long as the local gangs and powers of Shambhala's underworld kept quiet enough, none saw any reason to press for change.

The jinn passed the seedy and the desperate alike and with equal indifference. Few saw past his muting, and those that did knew well enough to leave him be. Salem wasn't looking for trouble, but, though alone, he was unafraid. His bearing was a clear message to those that could see it: make way.

His path led him to a simple tavern nestled like a cyst among the most disreputable streets of Thule: al-Siraj. The establishment lived up to its name, lights shining through its dirty windows at any hour. The sila passed through the doors like a wind, winding unseen through its patronage. Pyres of jinn clustered around tables, just as happy as he was to be overlooked in their quiet conversations.

Along the back wall, a rare solitary figure sat in a shadowed booth. Nothing could be seen of its features beneath a dark, hooded cloak. Clothing was not typical of jinn in their homelands, but it was not abnormal and certainly not worthy of notice itself. Salem slid into his own seat across the table, folded his hands, and waited for the other to speak. No one came by to serve them. The patrons of al-Siraj spoke for themselves if they needed anything.

"Sister," said the sila at last. He preferred to let others speak first in private meetings, feeling it conveyed that *they* needed *him* more than *he* needed *them*. That night, Salem needed to say what needed to be said and be on his way before he was missed at the citadel. As one of the dragon's first secretaries, his authority was double-edged; he could do as he pleased when he wasn't being called upon, but he was often called upon.

The figure returned the greeting by drawing back her cowl. The woman was nondescript. Her features suggested a poorly bred, mongrel nephilim of no account. Salem knew better. His half-sister Skadi was dangerous.

"You're looking well," he said. "Though much changed. Have you lost weight?"

The woman smirked and twitched her cloak. "A gift from the master. He said it would make me less obtrusive."

Salem shared his sister's smile. He kept the envy from his face with an effort. Their father was powerful, but Pazuzu served one who was greater still, and the sila was jealous of that one's favor. He wondered at the magic of Skadi's cloak, that it could contain something like her. When she said nothing further, he spoke into the silence. "Father wasted no time in getting you here."

"Another gift," said Skadi. "He opened a Way for me."

"The master is generous. I'm impressed," said Salem, his tone of voice uncharacteristically genuine, greedy for such signs of favor from the one whose regard he coveted most. "Events are moving quickly. The sage hasn't been at Shambhala so much as a day."

"She's a priority," said the woman. "It has been said the sage has tried already to access the Akashic Records."

The sila nodded. "It's true. She and the dragon were both unsuccessful. The sage is nothing!"

Salem spat the last sentence with more intensity than he'd meant to, clipping off each word with haughty precision, but the woman shook her head. "The returned sage forces the master to reveal himself at every turn. Already, she draws too much attention to his plan. As such, he has decided it is time for her mantle to be passed on."

"But why kill her now?!" pled Salem. Though he'd already made preparations for her, he was reluctant that his sister enter the citadel, bringing untold disruptions to the seat of his influence along with her. "Brother Za'eel took her hands. Without her consort and her progeny, she has no power!"

"Her magic is not gone," said Skadi. "Only her degree of access. Despite her ignorance and her hobbling, she is still a sage. Though they cannot rival the master's power, her followers are loyal. In time, the master believes, even crippled as she is, this sage would find a way back to her true strength."

"The master fears the sage then?" scoffed Salem. He rubbed his thumb against the tips of his fingers, the only tell of his deeper fear. The woman saw through her brother's façade and smirked.

Skadi's tone was dangerous. "Not fear, brother; prudence. The eighth sage has been our master's adversary since they learned of his plans. Somehow, this sage has evaded him, has escaped us all, where the others have fallen. To leave her now would be a foolish risk."

The sila slumped in his seat, defeated. "You speak the truth, sister. What is the will of the master for me?"

"Nothing at all," said Skadi, contempt in her eyes. "At least, you are called to do nothing directly. You have left her somewhere where she is vulnerable?"

He nodded wordlessly, and she said, "Then, you've done your part. You are to return to Shambhala and continue to be eyes for the master. For now, you may keep your place at the dragon's feet and grow fat on his scraps."

Salem glowered, his personal motives laid bare. The jinn was a worm, and he knew it, nestling into things greater than himself, growing patiently in strength until his host festered. The arrival of the sage at Shambhala had upset his routine. Now, he wanted nothing more than to wriggle out of the light, to resolve this business and burrow back deep within the bland soil of the citadel's bureaucracy.

He wanted to return her vitriol but thought better of it. Skadi could kill him in an instant, and they both knew it. Salem knew their shared lineage offered no protection. As useful as he was, their father favored strength over cunning. For the moment, his sister was in demand.

His courtier's mask slipped back into place; a warm smile lit up his face. "And you, sister. What is to be *your* role in this?"

"Obviously." Skadi ran a long tongue over pearly teeth. "I will return with you to Shambhala, and I will kill the sage."

Salem's eyes bulged. "You want me to *sneak* you into the citadel?!"

The woman spread her hands. "I am afraid I do not know the way, brother. I need your wise guidance if I am to be successful."

"And if I am found out?" Salem asked. "If we are seen together, what is my recourse?"

"There is nothing to save you, brother. There is no succor, no refuge," said Skadi. "As with all of Pazuzu's children, you will survive on your own merit. If it makes you feel better, if we fail in this, I doubt our father will spare any of us."

"And if I am captured?" asked the jinn. "What then?"

"Then," she said, leaning in and laying her hands flat against their table, "you will sacrifice yourself in honor of our father, Pazuzu, to keep his secrets and save him face in the eyes of the master."

Chapter 12:

SOMETHING WAS WRONG. ALICE opened her eyes and blinked away dreams; false memories of selling dime bags to her professors. She smiled at the juxtaposition of those two lives. She'd left the drug world as far behind as she could put it before she'd so much as filled out a college application.

It was quiet in the citadel, and dark. She was still tired, as if she'd only just closed her eyes. There it was again. It wasn't something she heard or saw, exactly, but she knew what it was that time. Someone was in her room with her.

Her first instinct was to call out. *Hello? Who's there?* With an effort of will, she kept quiet, let her eyes slip shut again, and pretended she was still asleep.

Alice took a mental inventory of her assets. *Butt naked in a strange place with no phone. Do they have phones here? Is there something I could use as a weapon?* Alice had no idea. Even if she trusted her hands to have the strength to hold onto anything heavy enough to be useful, beyond the bath and the bed, she couldn't have described her quarters with any accuracy if her life depended on it.

Her lip quirked at the irony; gallows humor. *Very funny,*

Alice. Fuck! How are they finding me?!

The sage's mind worked, and it struck her. *The magic! The ifrit trailed me to the hospital after I did . . . uhm, whatever I did to survive the accident. Altair said something was tracking us to the hotel. We opened a freaking dimensional portal there, so that fits. I must have showed up on someone's radar after I tried to get at that Akashic Record thing.*

But there's magic everywhere! Even on earth, apparently. Why should mine stick out?

"Because you're a sage."

Alice let out a frightened cry despite herself. It was a woman's voice, and it was between her and the door to the hall. *Unless I'm completely turned around,* she thought. *Shit! How do I get out of here?!* Taking hold of herself again, Alice concentrated on her centers and quieted them.

She clenched her fists in frustration as she did it, wanting to pound them against the wall until they ached, but didn't dare move again. She hated that others knew her thoughts, and not because they were snooping around in her mind, but because she broadcast them herself, babbling her stream of consciousness like a small child.

"The last of them," said the woman. "In all the Realms, there is nothing else like you."

Alice sat up and looked on her assassin. It was a hooded, cloaked figure. Nothing beneath the shadowed folds could be discerned. She could be looking at anyone.

"Sounds like I need to learn to be more discreet," she said. Alice listened, trying to gauge where the windows were by the sounds of open air. She didn't dare look, lest she betray her intent.

"Pity, then," said the woman, reaching up to her throat to unfasten the cloak's clasp, "that you won't have more time."

With that, the assassin cast aside the cloak. By the dim light, Alice could see the woman was quite average in appearance. Even without muting, she was the sort of female presence that could disappear into any context. Then, the woman began to grow, her simple garments tearing away.

The assassin's shoulders reached the high ceilings, and, for a moment, she stooped. The giantess looked as if she might fall, but then she straightened. She shrugged the thick stones aside like cobwebs, and Alice screamed. Her legs pistoned in panic and tangled her up in the smooth sheets as the room began to crash down around her.

Altair woke to the sound of stone smashing against stone. The sound was coming from directly overhead. *Alice!*

The jinn was out of bed and on his feet in an instant. The castle was shaking all around him. He felt the vibrations beneath his feet. Fine dust sifted down from the ceiling. Altair burst out of his room, slamming the door into a rushing guard.

The heavy door cracked with the impact, but Altair held his ground. A troop of the citadel's militia was rushing toward the main shaft between floors. The jinn were armed with spears. Most of them had light armor, chain-linked round plates that looked like eclipses against their fiery skin.

They wheeled on Altair as their fallen comrade cried out. He raised his hands in the face of a ring of spear tips and made no move. Just then, Ajdaha rounded the corner. He ducked to the side as another crash rang out and a section of ceiling collapsed above him.

The demigod was in human form, dressed in a loosely tied robe of red silk. He was headed for the shaft as well, the smaller body readily able to dodge past furniture and weave around uncertain bystanders as they trickled from their various quarters. Seeing his father, the lord of Shambhala waved his troops forward.

"The shaft!" he shouted. "We must protect the sage!"

The sight of the golden man catalyzed his guards back into action. Altair reached out a hand to the prone jinn as the spears tips of his comrades were lifted. He clapped him on the shoulder with an apologetic look, then turned to race with them toward the shaft. It was blocked.

Altair knew the citadel well enough that, even after centuries, he could navigate its halls blind. Each of the floors above could be partitioned with heavy doors that lay flush with the floor when they were shut. Normally, they were left open for ease of travel through the building. Tonight, the first of what he suspected would be many were closed tight.

There were other, smaller passages, but getting to them would take time. Also, they would have to decide between dividing their force among several routes versus having to thread the bulk of them through a single, smaller doorway. Either option meant more delay to get to the sage.

Without hesitation, Altair became a great bear and pushed his thick shoulders against the upper door. It didn't budge. He could feel additional weight on top. Someone had barricaded it.

Seeing his struggle, several of the guard shapeshifted with him. One became an elephant. Another became a great, horned lizard, its body armored in heavy plates of bone. A third simply expanded, becoming an ogre of a jinn. Ajdaha shed his human form. His robes tore to tatters as the great, golden dragon uncoiled. Together, they pushed against the upper door and felt it shift.

They'd moved it no more than an inch when Altair cried out, "Hold it there!"

The jinn became a dragonfly and buzzed through the gap. The moment he was through, he was the great bear again. He shoved at the next door up and confirmed his fears. It was barricaded, as well.

Taking on the shape of a jinn again, he shouted back down through the gap, "They're all blocked! We'll never make it this way!"

Ajdaha called up to him, "Just get to mother! We'll meet

you there!"

The portal door dropped shut. Random furniture was scattered around it, displaced from a haphazard pile that had been heaped onto it. Altair narrowed his eyes as he took stock of the situation. There were no scrapes and scuffs to show where things had been moved from. As below, sleepy and frightened faces were emerging from doorways. They looked upward nervously as another heavy thud shook the building.

Altair sighted the nearest exterior window at the end of the hall and took off at a dead sprint. He ignored the frightened jinn and nephilim, not bothering to tell them to evacuate; the more savvy had already sorted things for themselves and shouted warnings to the less adroit. Altair dove through the window and became a great eagle.

It's not too late! he told himself. *It's not too late! It's not too late!* He shouted her name as his powerful wings carried him upward in a tight spiral around the tower where the sage had been quartered, his voice coming out as a high-pitched raptor's scream.

Alice threw herself out of bed as the naked giant brought a great slab of stone down on top of it. She finally kicked free of her bedding as the massive woman tore out another section of the wall and raised it over her head. Half the roof was already gone; the giant simply slammed her makeshift weapons down through it as she sought to crush the sage.

In a panic, she looked around wildly and scrabbled on her hands and feet toward the nearest window. She felt the dust sift down to cling against her bare skin, felt the stones punch her back as they fell from the fractured ceiling. She'd just gotten her legs under her and was preparing to leap, quite possibly to her death, as the giant brought the hunk of wall down in front of her, barring escape.

It was a near thing. Alice slammed up against the sudden barrier with bruising force. Another step, and she'd have been crushed instead. She was grimly certain the monster had simply over led her target, narrowly missing her.

The giant roared, the sound of it oddly feminine for all its immensity, and swept a hand toward her. Alice dropped prone at the last moment. She wondered crazily whether the monster meant to catch her up or flatten her like a bug. The wind of its open palm buffeted her as it rushed past. She heard the impromptu barrier tip away from the window and forced herself up and into an awkward somersault as it crashed down behind her.

She made it two steps before she was lifted bodily into the air by another impact. She tumbled over to land on her back as a massive foot stomped down where she'd been an instant before. Alice felt herself come to rest against what could only be a manhole-sized toenail. Above her, thick fingers as big as she was reached down for her as the giantess awkwardly squatted down to seize her.

Alice rolled, headed for the monster's heel. It forced the assassin to have to reach between her own legs in pursuit. As she ran, heedless of the jagged stones that cut her feet, Alice pursed her lips and whistled. Instantly, she felt her centers flare wide along her body in response to the tune and then contract down until they were nearly nonexistent. She felt the notes wrap around her, the sound of them paradoxically woven into a blanket of quiet as the sage muted herself.

The giantess's fingers closed on nothing, and, for a moment, the hulking brute simply straightened and looked about. She actually scratched her head, looking exactly as Alice did when she lost her keys, went to another room to find them, then forgot what she was looking for when she got there. As quietly as she could, taking care to displace no stones, Alice stepped lightly to keep from scattering the dust while she crept toward the nearest open wall.

The reprieve was short lived. The monster shook her

head and blinked as if to cleanse a film from her eyes. The giantess looked about but did not see, could not see, the sage. Understanding dawned, and the giant held out her arms for balance. She raised up a leg until her knee was nearly level with her gargantuan breast. Then, with all her weight, the giant stamped.

Alice was thrown into the air from the force of it. The giantess's foot punched through the floor like a wrecking ball. She tried to keep whistling, but the shock of it tore the air from her lungs. Fortunately by then, the giant's back was to her, but that was a small advantage.

As soon as her great foot touched down on the floor below, the giantess' brought up her other leg and stamped again. Now knee deep between floors, the monster reached out, her arms nearly spanning the diameter of the tower. She pushed against the walls and what little was left of the ceiling, as much to keep herself balanced as to wreak arbitrary destruction.

The giantess crouched, and Alice knew what was coming next. The monster meant to jump up and crash down again, leveraging her full weight against the integrity of the already damaged structure. The sage climbed to her feet yet again. She was bleeding from countless cuts and scrapes all along her naked body, she but spun on her heel toward the open air and ran.

She still meant to jump. There was no other way out. Behind her, there was only death.

With a deafening shout, the giantess leapt into the air. At the apex of her jump, she raised her legs up to her chest and wrapped her arms around her knees. Alice risked a look over her shoulder as she hurtled toward the crumbling ledge of the tower. She leapt into the open air as the giantess slammed down. Her whole body acted as a balled fist to crush the entire structure into rubble.

Bits of stone and glass and wood flew all around her. The

sage licked her dusty lips, coughing and spitting for air. She
whistled again as the ground rushed up to meet her. Alice
called on her magic to save her, knowing it was too late. She
closed her eyes and placed all of her will into a single, shrill
tone.

"*IIIiii . . . !*"

Ajdaha watched as the tower fell. The naked giantess crashed
down through floor after floor. She kicked and flailed to max-
imize the damage. Jinn and nephilim sprinted out doorways
and leapt through windows in a mad rush for safety. Some of
them got clear; most didn't.

The dragon closed his eyes and listened to the shouts and
the screams of the wounded and the dying over the tumbling
cacophony of senseless ruin. One of the three great towers of
the citadel, it had stood for millennia. It was older than he
was. Now, it was gone, the fortress crippled.

His mother was somewhere in it all. He imagined her
body crushed until it was unrecognizable, her soul passed on
forever into the Eternal's heaven, never to be seen again. The
demigod was not a fighter by nature, but the thought of his
mother's death was more than enough to wake his wrath.

Ajdaha opened his eyes and looked again, seeing only the
giantess. Green flames jetted from his nostrils, curled from
his lips and twined around his long, flicking tongue. Wing-
less, the great serpent leapt into the air, roaring his hatred for
the monster.

Shaking the rubble from her shoulders, the giantess
stood tall against the rushing dragon. She held out her hands
as he came at her, seized his jaws in one fist, and took him by
the throat in the other. She was half his size, but she put her
weight behind her leverage and bore him to the ground as he
kicked and slashed with his fore and hind legs.

The giantess ignored the cuts and furrows he dug in her
flesh. She was already bruised and bleeding from her assault

on the citadel, but she paid no attention to the injuries, her teeth bared in a psychopathic grin. This was a monster who lived for destruction, even if it meant her own.

She might have had him there and then had Ajdaha not lashed out with his tail. He wrapped it around the back of her knee and heaved. The muscles of his stomach strained and tore with the effort of it. It was enough; the giantess released the dragon's muzzle as she put a hand out to steady herself. Her palm slapped against a thick, stone wall, and it buckled under the strain. Heavy bricks toppled down to leave shallow craters in the fortress grounds.

Ajdaha wanted nothing more than to breathe flame, to burn the giantess black so he could catch the scent of her death in his nostrils. With her hand around his throat, the dragon could not let out his fire. He did the next best thing and twisted around in her grip to catch at her clenched fist with his fangs.

The giantess roared in frustration as much as pain. Blood welled up where sharp teeth pierced, but her thick skin was like armor. Ajdaha knew fear then. *That should have taken her hand off by the wrist! Who are you?!*

Balanced again, the giantess lashed out to grip the dragon's neck in both fists. Ajdaha writhed but could not get loose. He glared up at her, and the two of them locked eyes. The dragon kept on biting. He shifted his grip to reach her thumb. He sought to take it with him as he concentrated and sent a pulse of magic from his brow to send a message. *You may kill me, but you'll never forget me!*

The giantess paused at that. Crushing his throat between her palms, she leaned in closer to smirk. Ajdaha let loose her hand and snapped at the monster's face. She let him close enough his steaming spittle flecked her cheek.

"And you will never forget me, dragon," said the giantess. She spoke in a whisper like rolling thunder. "I am Skadi, daughter of Pazuzu, and I am your death."

With that, she wrenched his neck. The assassin's fore-
arms bulged and strained with the effort. Skadi was loathed
to give any opportunity to a god, even a minor one such as
this. The giantess felt vertebrae pop and crush beneath her
fingers, felt the dragon's throat collapse. Ajdaha went rigid
for a moment, his eyes opened wide, and then he went slack
in her hands.

Skadi bellowed in triumph as she raised the dragon over
her head, then threw his body onto the rubble at her feet.

Altair searched and searched, but he could not find her. All
around were the screams of the frightened and the dying,
drummed out by the fall of stones that had set standing for
millennia. It was the work of ages, demolished in minutes,
and the jinn pushed it aside as he shouted her name.

"Alice!"

His form was a massive, flaming ape. His squat body
leant leverage to his long, powerful arms. He yelled and dug,
throwing boulders over his shoulder like crumpled balls of
paper as he searched for her.

Suddenly, there was a jinn at his side. Altair nearly swung,
wanting nothing else than to bat this distraction aside and
search for the sage. Tears stung his eyes; his heart felt as if it
would burst at his longing for her. He knew she might never
love him again, but he couldn't bear to exist where she did
not.

Altair controlled himself with an effort. It was Ajdaha's secretary, Salem. The sila was trailing a small crowd of
jinn, all of them setting immediately to aid his search. Altair
swelled with gratitude, and he paused when the sila raised a
hand to signal him.

"Father of the dragon!" shouted Salem. "We will find the
sage! I swear it! It is your son who needs you now!"

With that, he flung his arm to the side and pointed. Altair looked and saw the dragon in the clutches of the giant-

ess. He fought bravely, but the monster's strength was overwhelming. He noticed something pass between them, some communication from his son, then watched helplessly as the giantess leaned down to whisper her response before she crushed his neck.

The sound of Ajdaha's backbone snapping echoed off the shattered walls of the citadel. Altair bellowed his rage along with scores of fellow jinn. Like him, they had lost much to the monster that had come to their city. With him, they charged Skadi with vengeance in their eyes.

The jinn rose together, like embers that drifted up when a fresh log was thrown into the fire. Altair became a fiery griffin. He pawed the ground, his leonine form crouched low as he prepared to spring. He let loose an eagle's cry as he leapt, white feathers flashed around his wickedly hooked beak, great wings churned the air into a maelstrom. Altair threw himself bodily at the giantess, and the jinn of Shambhala followed with him.

The daughter of Pazuzu stepped over the fallen dragon and bellowed a challenge at the rallied jinn. She fought them as they came, caught them in her fists and dashed them against walls, rubble, and her own knees. She bit off heads and pulverized bodies with her swiping hands.

The sila brought their magic to bear, throwing lightning and fire from their hands. Others levitated boulders, hurling them at the monster with their minds. Ghuls came at her in all manner of shapes, the predatorial species of the Realms wreathed in flame, closing the distance on wing and on foot.

In the end, they were too many for her. The monster caught one of the boulders the jinn flung at her. Skadi used it like a hammer, bashing any that came within reach. More fell, screaming as their bodies were crushed, but the rest piled onto the giantess. They sought to weigh her down as much as injure her, using their mass to restrain her while they sought vulnerability.

At last, Altair saw his moment and took it. He alighted on Skadi's face and plunged his beak into her eye. The giantess howled and threw her head back. Instantly, a white-hot lance formed from a fallen flagpole speared into her exposed throat. A triumphant sila shouted in exultation as her magic drove it deep.

Skadi roared in pain as much as anger, the sound coming in a deafening, wet gurgle. The giantess staggered back and still the jinn pressed, never letting up for a moment. The monster flailed wildly, simply trying to prolong her life long enough to take another's, and another's.

The giantess was driven out past the citadel. She stumbled over groves of trees as old as myths. Their trunks cracked under her heels as she fought to keep her balance. Finally, she stepped over the edge of the floating island of the castle and toppled into the endless clouds of Sayon.

Altair, his form a jinn again, stood at the edge of the island and watched the giantess plummet. She struck a floating islet far below them. It spun her end over end as she tumbled down into the autumnal reaches. Skadi went still before she disappeared from view, her lifeblood spent in a rain of droplets that raced with her into the abyss. Her face was peaceful, a faithful martyr assured of her virtue.

The jinn spat over the edge and turned to see what needed to be done. He was startled, finding Ajdaha at his side, the dragon's eyes filled with hatred and pain. As the jinn watched, he saw his son's body regenerating itself. Scales pushed out from crushed flesh and became whole. The dragon rolled his head with a grimace. His neck popped and crackled as it reassembled itself.

"Son!" said the jinn, astonished. "Are you alright?!"

"Apparently," said the dragon, craning his neck until the last errant vertebrae clicked back into their proper places.

"I know demigods are hard to kill," said Altair, putting a hand on the great serpent's neck and patted the scales in wonderment and relief, "but I thought that giant bitch had finished you!"

"So did I," replied Ajdaha. "Live and learn."

His voice laced with quiet rage, Altair asked, "Where did she come from?"

"Pazuzu," said the dragon, the word a curse on his tongue, and turned back to his citadel. Altair looked back over the edge again and studied the layers of swirling clouds. He could still see the hole the giantess' body had torn through them as she fell. He watched until the clouds mended themselves. Soon, they drifted along as if the monster had never been. Still, the jinn stared after the child of Pazuzu, fear in his heart. His lips moved in a whispered prayer.

Alice didn't know why she was alive. She didn't think about it. She focused on keeping her eyes open. She feared she would slip away if she gave in to her exhaustion. Jinn surrounded her. Ajdaha's aide Salem knelt at her side. He held a cup of that nourishing, spicy nectar she'd first tasted when she came to Sayon. It gave her strength, and she smiled up at him.

"Thank you," she murmured.

Salem smiled down at the sage. It did not reach his cold, glaring eyes, but she didn't notice. None of the jinn gathered around them could see his face. They all peered down anxiously at her as they murmured among themselves, unaware that only their unceasing witness throughout the search had stayed Salem's hand. Though he knew even then he could end her, the immediacy of a murderous mob outweighed the fear of his father's wrath.

A cheer went up as Ajdaha and Altair approached. They made way for the dragon and his father and kept a respectful distance as they knelt by Alice's side. Salem passed the cup to Altair's hands and slid around to cradle her head in his lap.

"We found her there, lord," said Salem. He pointed to

a miraculously untouched clearing standing amid a field of rubble. "She is injured, but she will recover soon. The sage's magic is great, indeed!"

The sila kept his eyes from narrowing and held the venom from his voice as he met Ajdaha's eyes with forged sincerity. Filled with concern for his mother, the dragon paid the jinn little mind. He assumed human form and took her in his arms as Salem slid smoothly out of the way.

"Oh, hey guys," she said. Alice blinked up at the two of them through the dusty air. She smiled, then began to laugh. The dragon and the jinn looked at each other, puzzled.

"We're . . ." she snorted, "we're all naked!"

Wincing, she took their support as she sat up. She took the cup in her own hands and tried not to choke as she drank. Her abdomen kept spasming as she chuckled. "Th-that fucking giant's bare ass was the last thing I thought I'd ever see!"

She raised the cup of fiery nectar and drank deep. She drained the cup and let it drop, forgotten, and sat cross-legged with her hands in her lap. She stretched gingerly and grunted. "Ungh, shit! Can I get a blanket or something?"

Ajdaha looked to Salem, and the sila signaled a group of jinn to fetch supplies to care for the wounded. As the makings of a camp sprang up around them, Altair looked questioningly at his son. The dragon nodded in agreement.

"We can't stay here," he said. "Pazuzu's children are many. They know where she is. More will follow. Soon."

"We need to restore her hands," said Altair. "She has no other chance to survive."

Salem drifted near, his face a mask of concern. Ajdaha looked to his father. "We'll leave now, the three of us. I know the Way we need."

"My lord." The sila bowed deeply. "May I come as well? I would gladly lend my strength to avenge this insult."

Ajdaha considered, then shook his head. "You will act as seneschal in my absence, Salem. Begin preparations to repair the citadel immediately."

The sila hesitated only a moment, then bowed again. "As you wish, lord. Shambhala will rise stronger than ever before!"

Ajdaha dismissed his secretary with a wave of his hand. Salem swept away, a quiet shadow drifting through knots of jinn as they saw to their wounded and wept for their dead. The worm wriggled through the wreckage, relieved to burrow back into the safety of his station at the right hand of the dragon. He called out orders, and jinn rushed to obey his commands, thankful for the sense of security brought on by clear leadership. All the while, in the back of his mind, he twisted the skein of the story he would tell his father.

Chapter 13:

THE JINN, THE DRAGON, and the sage stood at the concealed mouth of a little cave. It was recessed among the rocky outcroppings of a barren, floating islet. They were deep down in the clouds of Sayon, the air thick and hot. The others seemed unaffected, but Alice was miserable, unsure if she was going to sweat herself to dehydration or drown in the smothering lower atmosphere of the gas giant.

Below them, the backs of gargantuan serpents crested above dense clouds. Alice couldn't tell if there were many of them or if she was seeing the same few emerging at various points as they slithered along through the bottomless skies. She took a sip of spicy nectar from her canteen and wiped her lips with her sleeve.

The jinn had dressed her in a full bodysuit. The material looked and felt like supple leather but moved and stretched like spandex. They gave her a small backpack that seemed to hold much more than it should. It was strange, being dressed like that. Losing her regular clothes was one more sign she'd been ripped out of the life she knew and she wouldn't be going back.

"What are those things, anyway?" Alice jerked her chin toward the massive snakes as she tucked away her canteen. She didn't know how it fit, the pack appearing to be filled to the capacity, but it slid into place easily. *This thing is handy,* she mused and slung it back over her shoulder.

"World serpents," Altair answered.

"Why don't they come up any higher?"

The jinn shrugged. "That's where they're comfortable, I suppose."

"Do they ever get *uncomfortable?*"

"Rarely," said Altair.

"Thankfully," said Ajdaha. "They are lazy at heart and slow to be provoked."

"Small blessings," said Alice, then she turned to face the cave.

"Okay, I get that we can't just bip between the Realms as we please," she said. "I just don't get why these Ways are here at all."

"What is there to get?" asked Altair.

She shrugged. "It just seems like life would be a lot simpler and safer without them. It's like an invasive species problem waiting to happen."

The others said nothing, a knowing look passing between them. Ignoring it, she added, "It's like that Asian snake head carp thing. A couple of them get loose, and, before you know it, they're in the Mississippi eating everything."

Ajdaha nodded. "There's some debate on it. Some think the Eternal god placed them between the Realms on purpose for lesser beings to use."

"Like maintenance tunnels," said Altair.

Alice smiled. "And we're the janitors coming to mop up."

The jinn grinned back. "That seems to be the way of things for us."

"I would say custodian is more accurate," said the dragon. "Others believe powerful beings used to tunnel between the Realms, when creation was new and there were fewer restrictions. For whatever reason, no one ever cleaned them up.

"Still, others think these Ways are flaws in creation, proving the Eternal god is finite at some level and couldn't eliminate some basic errors in how the Realms fit together."

"What do you think?" asked Alice.

"I think," said Ajdaha, "I have devoted my life to studying the Ways between the Realms. I've spent nearly a thousand years trying to lay it all out. As near as I can tell, the Ways are like gravity or the way light moves. They're a natural phenomenon in the universe with useful properties, surrounded, like everything else, by a lot of superstitions and maybes."

The sage nodded, finding the answer underwhelming. At the same time, it was comforting to know that, as much as her awareness of reality had expanded, she was not the only one confounded by it. Even dragons and gods couldn't surpass the infinite unknowns of creation.

The three of them entered the little cave, Ajdaha taking human form to negotiate its confines. Within, a cramped tunnel stretched and wound through the rock. Altair held up his hand and called up a flame from his palm to light their way.

Alice considered experimenting with her magic. *How hard could making a light be?* She pursed her lips to whistle, then thought better of it. She looked down at the twisted ruin of her hands and shuddered. She frowned as she ducked her head to avoid a low hanging rock. *What's the point of all this power if all I can do with it is paint a target on my back? Even if we can fix my hands, it's not as though I know how to play anything.*

A thought struck her, and she asked, "Hey, this god we're headed for. Is it my father?"

Ajdaha answered as they moved, "We're going to the lands of Ninhursag. Sometimes Brigid to the Celts. Sometimes Asclepius to the Greeks. Also, you should know that

Marduk isn't your father anymore."

Alice furrowed her brow, and Altair answered the unspoken questions. "In your first life, you were half-human, half-god. When your first life ended, your demigod nature was ended with it. Your soul that was human reincarnated and continued on as the second life of the eighth sage. Your soul that was a god went its own way."

The sage tried to wrap her head around it. "So, there's a me somewhere that's still a god?"

"Sort of," said the dragon. "There are only eight Baalim, the lesser gods. A piece of one was a part of you for a time. Now it's something else, but it is still from the god that fathered you. Understand?"

"I think so," said Alice, "like Marduk lent it to me?"

"Essentially," said Ajdaha. He stopped abruptly and held up a hand to signal a stop. "Ah, good! We're here! Step carefully now, it's a long way down."

Ajdaha became a dragon again as the tunnel opened out into a massive cavern. They stood on a small lip of rock overlooking a vertical column of empty space. Alice looked away, dizzied by a wave of vertigo. At least outside, there were the clouds to break up the distance. The Way looked like nothing less than a hole that led downward forever.

She looked up, puzzled there didn't seem to be a ceiling. As below, so above, the Way upward went on into the blackness without apparent end. Alice wondered at it; there was no way the bit of floating rock they'd entered could hold a fraction of what she was seeing. *I guess we're not in Sayon anymore . . .*

"So, we just fly down, right?" said Alice. "Easy peasy?"

Altair looked searchingly at his son, and Ajdaha shook his head. "The winds are unpredictably strong, and there are rock formations on the way down that may as well be swords. The climb is the first trial of this Way."

Alice thought it over and grimaced. "I get it. Three trials, right?"

The jinn beamed at her. "Hey! See? You're getting it!"

She smiled at that weakly, then held up her hands and feebly waggled her warped fingers. "So if flying is out, how do we do this?"

"Check your bag," said Ajdaha. "There should be some rope."

Alice slid her pack from her shoulders, and, sure enough, she rummaged up a long coil of rope. She started to dig for more climbing equipment. The sage wondered if what television had shown her as a child would be accurate, but Altair took the rope and shook his head.

"This is all we need."

She opened her mouth to protest, sure there must be more to it, then closed it as the jinn nimbly wove the length of rope into a clever harness. He bent down and held open a hole wide enough for her thigh. "Here, step into it, and we'll get you cinched up."

Alice laid her hands on the jinn's shoulders as he worked, and, soon enough, she was wearing the coils of a snug harness. She shrugged and stamped and waggled her pelvis experimentally. It was surprisingly comfortable.

Without a word, the dragon stepped into place, and Altair began to knot up the other end of the rope in loops around his son's neck and fore shoulders. Before long, she found herself neatly tethered to her son. Feeling her stomach lurch at what she knew was coming, Alice tugged variously at the rope.

"So, uhm, I'm going to ride you down, Ajdaha?"

The jinn and the dragon looked at each other, then back to her. Ajdaha shook his head, "No, you might slip and throw me off balance. We're going to lower you."

The sage shuffled over to the precipice, looked over the side, and wished she hadn't. She swallowed a lump in her throat and forced a smile. She gave a thumbs-up, did her best not to fear-vomit, and said, "Perfect."

Ajdaha regarded his mother. "Afraid of heights?"

Alice shook her head. "No. Just of dangling from a rope above an endless rift between worlds."

"Oh, it's not endless," said Ajdaha. "There's a bottom. It's just so far down there you can't see it."

"Excellent," Alice said weakly. Her mouth flooded with saliva as her nausea intensified.

The dragon blinked, then said, "Sorry."

"For God's sake, son," said Altair, shaking his head. "I'll go first."

The jinn passed his fire to Alice and became a massive, hairy spider. He clicked his mandibles together in an effort to speak but could only manage a chittering noise that made Alice's skin crawl.

The jinn spider paused and concentrated hard. She watched as his mouth parts gradually shifted to become a nightmarish hybrid between arachnid and humanoid. When he was capable of speech, he added, "We don't want any surprises."

As Altair slipped over the edge, Alice held the jinn's fire with awe. It was hot but not unbearably so. Somehow, it felt like him.

Aloud, she asked, "This is a piece of your soul, isn't it?"

The spider called back from over the ledge, "It's the same as your magic, only smaller. Sometimes, the power comes from the world; sometimes, it comes from within."

"Careful," called Altair as he began the descent. "Remember, some of these rock formations are razor sharp."

"It will be alright," said the dragon. The sage nodded, then let out a little yip as her shaking legs threatened to unbalance her. When she'd steadied, half-crouched at the edge with her arms out like a tightrope walker, he inclined his head toward her and asked, "Ready?"

"T-totes McGoats," said Alice. The dragon looked at her

expectantly but was polite enough not to badger. She took a deep breath, belched spontaneously as she all but puked, and bent to put her hands on her knees.

"Okay," she said and spat out the bilious saliva that flooded her mouth, not moving an inch closer to the edge. "Okay . . ."

A long beat passed. The dragon and the jinn watched patiently. Finally, Alice straightened and sidled to the edge. Carefully, she bent down and released the jinn light. The little ball of fire hovered amiably at her shoulder. She put her palms down flat, stuck one foot out into empty space, and lost her balance.

"Shiiiiit!" Alice screamed as she tumbled headlong into thin air. She reached the end of her line with a jerk that made her teeth click together. She twirled madly in empty space, eyes squinted shut, gripping the rope with what strength her crippled hands could muster. Then, she felt several long, hairy legs steady her.

"Easy," said Altair. "There you go."

Cautiously, Alice opened her eyes and looked down at the jinn. Eight compound eyes looked back up at her, the great spider somehow conveying he was looking on her with approval. She forced a smile back in return, all the while her imagination conjuring up crazy images of the jinn spider gobbling her up. Then, the rope lurched as the dragon began his descent, and the images dissolved in the greater fear of that endless pit with its walls like knives.

Alice abruptly vomited directly into the great spider's face, stringy remnants of her last meal dangling like tinsel down his hairy body. Altair the spider swiped his forelegs across his face, cleaning himself in that meticulous way arthropods have. The sage dry heaved and spat bile as she dangled and jerked, Ajdaha descending as smoothly as possible.

"Sorry," she said.

Chapter 14:

ALL SENSE OF TIME was lost in that climb. Everything was sharp rocks and jagged edges, narrow handholds and cautious scouting. Each erratic, pendulum swing left her wondering if that was going to be the time the rope broke and she fell forever. The best she could manage was to bite down on her screams to keep from distracting the dragon Ajdaha.

For all that, beneath her anxiety, Alice's trust in her son grew. It came on too gradually to notice, but, in time, her body relaxed into the steady rhythm of his descent. It took so long, it was simply impossible to keep up the fear. Though he was a stranger to her, each sure, careful placement of the dragon's paws spoke of his love for his mother. Helplessly surrounded by cutting dangers but safe in his care, Alice sank into a kind of trance as they descended.

It certainly wasn't out of boredom, the thought of a painful, plummeting death never leaving her entirely, but the monotony and gentle swaying were hypnotic. Altair's unfaltering light hovered over her shoulder. It made the shadows dance mysteriously in and out of the hollows and crevices in the rock. When she thought of their climb at all, she imagined this was how an infant must feel in its mother's arms, perfectly certain in its trust.

Alice only became aware the descent was finished when the swing of her harness lessened until she merely swayed. She blinked and realized she had no idea how long it had been since they'd started. She looked up at Ajdaha and found him smiling down at her, his long fangs and gold-irised eyes somehow looking natural, even familiar. She smiled back at her son of another life, the passage of the first trial stretching upward behind him into infinity.

The bottom of the Way was as smooth as freshly poured concrete. The column of sharp crags abruptly gave way. There was nothing left to grip for the last twenty feet. Altair reached the transition first, took the form of a great, fiery cat, and simply let himself drop the distance.

He landed in a neat crouch and then stood as he reassumed his jinn form. He called his light back from Alice, and she found she was disappointed to see it go. The jinn concentrated, fed more energy into the little fireball, and the flame expanded in size and intensity until it lit the entire base of the Way.

Carefully, Ajdaha crept to the lowest edge of the rocky face, Alice dangling from her rope. When he'd gotten her as far as he could, the jinn stepped forward to receive her. He became a flaming hulk of an elephant and took her by the waist with his trunk. Once relieved, the dragon took on his gold-skinned human form, his end of the rope slipping from his much smaller body as he dropped to the ground.

Standing together, Alice wriggled out of her harness and waggled her hips from side to side. Once her legs and bottom felt alive again, she knuckled the small of her back, closed her eyes, and grimaced in painful pleasure. When she opened them again, she found the jinn and the golden man looking on amusedly.

She quirked her lip. "Oh, what the hell ever. Not everyone has a timeless, immortal body, you know."

"I didn't say a thing," Altair said mildly.

Alice broke into a grin. "Yeah, well, stiff happens. Thirty-some isn't old, but it's not twenty, either."

Leaning a hand against the smooth wall of the Way, she bent her leg and caught her foot with her hand. Alice pulled to stretch a thigh. "So, now what?"

Ajdaha's smile faded. "The second trial."

As he said the words, a ragged slash of a wound opened across Altair's abdomen. Grunting, he dropped to one knee and put a hand to the floor to catch himself from falling. Looking about for the threat, Ajdaha became a dragon again. Alice tripped over her own feet as she lunged to his side. "What the fuck was that?!"

Altair didn't respond at first but probed at the torn skin gingerly, the brighter flame of his blood lighting up his fingers. His face had a faraway look, as though he were remembering something. When a slash opened on his cheek, as smooth as if it had been drawn with a razor, recognition dawned.

"Altair!" Alice cried. "What's doing this?! What's hurting you?!"

"Old wounds," he said and toppled as some unseen force hyperextended his knee. He cried out at the pain but seemed calmer as the injuries multiplied, as if he'd come to expect them. Ajdaha moved to curl protectively around them as Alice held her crippled hands out over the jinn, not quite daring to touch him.

"What do you mean?!" she asked him, unnerved as much by his reaction to them as she was the injuries themselves. "Altair, what's happening?!"

"The first . . ." He pointed to his belly. ". . . was from a troll. Skog was his name. Nasty bastard. Most of the hunters, I could lead away. He was the first to come close to finding you. I had to kill him."

The dragon cocked his head, still looking about for the source of the threat to his father. "What are you saying? I don't understand. You never told me about any troll by that name."

Desperate, Alice lunged for the jinn's sword of forged lightning. Altair didn't try to stop her from drawing it but only said, "It won't help. You cannot stop what's already been done."

Alice didn't know how to use the weapon, couldn't trust her hands to the task even if she did, but stood over the jinn with it anyway. She hated Altair for Timothy but at the same time knew she loved him more than she ever had her fiancé. She wished she could remember why. It would ease the guilt of knowing Timothy, though her feelings for him had been real, in a way, had only been a cover concealing her true self.

It occurred to her then everyone she'd known had been the same. For more than thirty years, she'd lived the mask of a makeshift life, patched with shallow relationships and thin friendships, and waited for it to be time for her true self to emerge. As she looked down at the man bleeding fire for her, she understood something of his suffering. Altair had been waiting for the same thing, watching and protecting her from a distance, hoping for the day he could reunite with his greatest love, only to find that, when the time came, she did not remember him.

She lowered the sword, dropping the hilt when the blade snapped into three pieces. A bright flash lit the bottom of the Way as the weapon shattered, and then it faded. Altair looked down at the broken hilt, the weapon's light guttering out as the magic left it.

"I lost one much like it when I fought Skog," he said. "Caught it in his teeth when I tried for his throat and bit it through."

"How old was I?" Alice asked. Understanding eased her

fright.

Altair smiled softly and looked distant as he remembered. "Two, I think. Maybe three."

She winced as his forehead lacerated and his right eye filled with blood until the lid swelled shut. "Thank you, but I never asked you to do any of that."

The jinn grinned through split, bloody lips and a mouthful of broken teeth. "No, you didn't. You made me promise."

Knowing he could see the guilt washing through her aura, too upset to mute it or care to try, she told him, "It's not fair. I don't remember it."

Altair shrugged, gasped as half his ribcage crushed inward, two jagged spurs of bone punching out of his skin, and whispered, "That's alright. I could never forget."

The dragon looked on as they spoke. He curled in closer as he realized there was nothing to protect his family from. "Father, let me help heal you."

The jinn shook his head weakly and gestured with his good hand at the useless, broken sword. The other hand now looked as though it had been crushed. Voice tight with pain, he told Ajdaha, "After. I think this needs to be seen through before we can go on."

The dragon flinched as another batch of cuts opened along his father's back and ran down across his side. "Can you survive all of it at once? How many times did you fight for her?"

"I don't know," replied Altair, answering both questions at once, then added, "I lost track after the first two decades."

Alice's brow furrowed. "How could it be so many? I thought you said I'd sealed the Earth away from all that magic shit. You said you were the only one that knew about me."

"You did," Ajdaha answered for his father, "and he was, but your wards have deteriorated in your absence. They still hold, but the strongest and the most cunning have been trickling through the cracks. It seems our enemy has been more influential in this than we knew and leveraged considerable resources searching for you."

Tears glistened on her cheeks as Alice sank down to her knees beside the jinn. Gingerly, she laid his head on her lap and stroked his fiery hair. "It's not fair. You've already been through this for me."

"I'd do it again," he answered. "As many times as I have to. I love you, Alice, and you're too important to die."

Alice knelt silently with the jinn. Her tears fell on her ruined hands and the fading fires of his skin. She wanted to tell him she loved him, too, but the way she felt was more complicated than that. The sage punched the bare stone until her knuckles bled, anything to vent the frustration at having no words to explain something that seemed so simple in her heart.

Then, a hole opened in Altair's stomach, just below his ribs. It was wide enough she could fit two fingers without brushing the sides and sank so deep, she feared whatever had punctured him so long ago had passed all the way through his body. Alongside the wounds already scoring down the length of him, she didn't know how he could possibly have the strength to endure it.

Gently, she put her arms around him, avoiding as many of his hurts as she could. "Just hold on, Altair. Please, don't leave me."

"I never will," he managed, then closed his eyes and didn't open them again. Alice and the dragon leaned in closer. The jinn's breath become so shallow, it seemed his chest wasn't moving at all. When she hadn't felt the jinn stir for what seemed like much too long, Alice looked into Ajdaha's eyes and found they were as bright with tears as her own.

"Is he?" she asked, unable to say the rest.

The dragon looked over his father, reaching out and gently probing with his magic. Alice waited, fearing she'd never have the chance to tell Altair how she felt. At last, Ajdaha answered, "He still burns. I think he has the strength to endure this."

"You think?" she asked. "But you're not sure?"

The dragon shook his head. "Of this? No one could be. It's too hard to say how much further he has to go."

Alice nodded. Her son's words were bitter, but they were the truth. Anguished, she asked him, "Is there anything we can do for him at all."

Ajdaha looked at her for a time, then his father. "Sing to him."

"But," she replied, "he said we couldn't use magic to help him until it was over. I wouldn't even know what to sing to help him, if I *could* sing at all."

The dragon laid a paw over her shoulder. For all their size, the claws felt as light as feathers. "It doesn't have to be magic. It doesn't have to be good. Just let him know what you feel so he can find his way back to us."

Alice hesitated, unsure what to do with that, then the first broken notes of some half-remembered melody warbled in her throat. Every note was flat, if it was the right one at all, but she sang them without words, somehow knowing the true shape of the song as she discovered it from moment to moment. Though she couldn't remember even all the time she'd lived just this one life, Alice knew it was a song she'd sung to Altair before she was born.

Distorted though it was, the melody felt old. More than old, it was ancient. She thought maybe it was something she'd sung for him many lifetimes ago, when they first met, when their love was new.

Alice wished she could, but she couldn't remember how she'd felt the day the song had first occurred to her to give to him, so she filled it with what was in her heart that day instead. She put her forgiveness in it. Altair had caused Timothy's death, but then, so had she. The jinn, at least, had been honest about it. Though she would have had no way of knowing why she'd done it, Alice had used the poor man for years.

Worse, Alice knew that, even if she could go back, she would do it again, if not to him, then to some other love-struck cat's paw. As strange as it seemed, Alice knew Altair had been right to do what he did, or at least that she had been complicit. Though she didn't know the nature of the enemy she'd hidden from all her life, she accepted then, as Altair had long ago, the last sage was too important to die. There was no justification for the innocent lives that had been spent in place of hers, but she could live with that knowing that, if she was lost, her entire world really would be lost with her.

The sage knelt in a spreading pool of burning blood and sang her broken song of love and forgiveness and acceptance. As the wounds kept opening, the merciless Way trying to tear the life from Altair's body, she sang of how much she needed him, now and forever, even if their changed love could never be what it had been. As the dragon wept beside them, Alice sang for the jinn to come back to them, to return to his family and be well again.

Chapter 15:

HOURS PASSED. WHEN THE last injury finally came, Aj-daha set to work on his father, using what magic he had to tend to the jinn's many wounds. The knee was of particular concern. It was straightened and set but could not bear his weight.

Alice opened her centers and let them expand as she watched the demigod work. She noticed her ability to see deeply into the world was associated with the nexus between and a little above her eyes. *My third eye, I guess?* In contrast, Ajdaha's healing magic involved the loci of power at the base of his spine and near his heart. For both, the center floating above his head seemed to amplify and focus the others.

In a way, she could hear the energy as much as see it as her son worked. She listened closely, noticing the dragon ac-tually was humming softly as he tended his father. The quali-ty of his magic was different from Altair's and her own. It was a hybrid, as much fire as it was song.

As he intoned and passed the flames that wreathed his hands over the jinn's wounds, the other pools of energy along his body became involved as well, but their influence was subtle. Something about the pattern of what he was doing pulled at her memory. She mulled it over and over, and, finally, it came to her; middle school music class.

It had been her last formal education on music theory, but she could still bring it to mind thanks to her teacher, Mr. Lars. He'd taught at the elementary level, as well, and, though she had little interest in music, his presence had been an enduring source of quiet joy among her class. Her favorite of his idiosyncrasies, the man never bothered to dust the chalk from his hands after he used the board, and the seat of his pants was always adorned with white handprints, like he'd been goosed by a ghost.

Chords! The word finally came to her. Individual notes added up together to make a more complex sound. Alice grinned, proud of putting it together herself. Finally, Ajdaha sat back, perspiring from the extended effort.

The jinn was not resentful of his knee but was grateful to his son. "Thank you, Aj. It will be right soon enough."

The dragon was in his human form. He rested a hand on his father's shoulder and said, "For that, you need your strength. You need to eat."

Altair grinned. "You look like you could use another log on the fire, yourself."

They looked to Alice expectantly, and she stared blankly before she remembered the backpack. She stripped it from her shoulders, rummaged, and found a small basket that emitted savory smells. Suddenly aware of her own gnawing hunger, she reached back into the little pack and raised her eyebrows when her arm reached in to the elbow before touching bottom. She looked questioningly at the two of them as she fished out an array of dried fruit, smoked meat, cheese, bread, and canteens of the spicy nectar she was quickly developing a taste for.

Altair spread his hands. "I don't know how it works, either."

Ajdaha shrugged. "I dabble in artifice. I know the principles, but I don't know how to make something this complicated."

Alice quirked an eyebrow, incredulous. "Seriously?"

Altair quipped. "How does a computer work? How do you make a car?"

"Good point," she acknowledged as she passed out their meal. They tucked in for a time in silence. Alice wolfed her food down with a voracity that drew a smile from Altair, unable to remember the last time she was so hungry.

"What?" she mumbled around a mouthful of delicious, unidentifiable meat.

"That's how you eat when you have something you really want to get to."

Alice blinked. Apart from close family, Timothy was the only one who'd ever noticed that particular tell. She wiped her mouth with the back of her wrist and looked appraisingly at the jinn. *How much of me is my genetics and how much is my soul?*

Aloud, she said, "I was thinking you're right. I need to learn to throw a punch."

Ajdaha raised up his hands. "I'm a cartographer. It seems I can take a hit better than I knew, but that's about all. Whenever I thought an exploration might get physical, I brought muscle to manage it."

Altair's lip quirked. "He's a pacifist is what he is. Never had the stomach for a good fight."

Ajdaha frowned; it was apparently an old sticking point between them. Alice said, "I don't, either. I just-"

Her words were drowned out by their laughter. Father and son leaned against each other, tears streaming from their cheeks. She looked between them, brow furrowed.

"What?"

Altair wiped at his eyes and composed himself with an effort. "You are responsible for driving nearly every non-native being from your earth. The nephilim, too."

"Didn't the other sages back me up?"

The jinn nodded. "They did their part, but it was on your initiative. To this day, anyone trespassing in your world keeps an eye out for *any* sign of you. You're the damned boogeyman!"

Alice digested the information while she gnawed at a crust of rich bread. That didn't sound like her. If it had been, it was literally lifetimes ago. *It doesn't matter who I was,* she thought. *I am who I am now.*

Full to the point of bursting, she set down what was left of a half loaf of bread and said, "So, can you show me something or not?"

The jinn dusted the crumbs from his own hands. "I can't show you how to do it. Beyond shapeshifting, my magic is pretty basic, at best. I *can* show you the principles."

Alice leaned in, listening intently as he said, "Eight centers, right?"

"Right."

Altair pointed at her crotch. "The one down there is your root. It's related closest to magic involving earth and survival."

"Like the planet Earth?" she asked.

The jinn shook his head. "Think more like the classical elements. Understand?"

When she nodded and gave a quiet thumbs up, he pointed at her stomach, below her bellybutton. "Sacral. Water. Sexuality. Connection."

Her upper abdomen. "Solar plexus. Fire. Power. Control."

Her heart. "Air. Love. Peace."

Her throat. "Communication. Expression."

The forehead between the eyes. "Third eye. Intuition. Light. Sensing."

"I got that one!" she exclaimed, pleased with herself.

"Good," said Altair, then pointed at the top of her head. "That's the crown. Thought and will. Knowledge."

Finally, he raised his finger to the spinning vortex hovering above her. "Soul. Magic."

The sage nodded and repeated the words to herself to commit them to memory. Altair went on. "Now, when you work magic, the centers combine in certain ways. It's like-"

"Notes," Alice cut in, "making chords. Or like blending colors, I think."

The jinn's pointing finger curled as he gave pause. "That's right. How did you . . . ?"

She inclined her head toward Ajdaha. "I watched him work on you. *His* centers. It took long enough I finally had a chance to get a good look."

Altair smiled and nodded, respectful. "That's my girl."

Alice flinched. "Don't make it weird."

"Sorry."

The sage got to her feet and looked around. "So, whoever is after me, whoever it is I'm trying to stop, they've been tracking me by my magic because it stands out."

Ajdaha said. "With the other sages gone, not counting the Eternal god, in terms of raw power, you're in the top ten of all known beings in creation."

Alice paused at that. It was strange to think of herself that way. It felt like they meant someone else and she was just standing in.

She pushed the thoughts aside and asked, "This place. Does it count as being somewhere?"

The dragon said, "Sort of. The Ways are not part of the Realms. They are the bridges between worlds. Why?"

"Could, the . . . uhm . . . the enemy track me here?"

Ajdaha raised a hand and teetered it back and forth. "Maybe. Just because we aren't anywhere right now doesn't mean we're off the maps entirely. That said, it's a royal pain in the ass to get here, and the enemy doesn't seem to be acting directly."

The jinn nodded and said, "They've got an impressive cadre of henchmen, but they should have the same problems we did getting here."

Ajdaha added, "*Plus* all the jinn in Shambhala stirred up and looking for someone to vent on."

Following her thoughts, Altair said, "So yes, you can practice your magic a little. With things as hectic as they've been, I don't know when you'll get another chance."

"Hectic . . ." Alice echoed. "That's a word for it, I guess."

"We're going to need you to open this end of the Way," said the dragon, "so a bit of magic can't be helped anyway."

Alice cocked her head. "Do all the Ways need someone like me to work?"

Ajdaha shook his head. "Not at all. Traveling with you just opens up more options. A lot more. Ways that others won't be using, if they know of them at all."

The sage nodded. *Fair enough; for once, there's time to breathe.* With that, she turned to face away from her companions to fix her eyes on the convex curve of the rock walls. Pursing her lips, Alice whistled while she concentrated on the feel of her energy, on those places where it collected along the length of her body. She experimented with tones until she felt her solar plexus stir.

Alice whistled a different tune, patiently varying it until she felt the place between her eyes tingle. Improvising though she was, it seemed a correct combination. *I want to be able to aim it, after all.* Then, she combined notes into a melody, and her soul center opened wide to facilitate the flow of energies. Her heart fluttered in excitement as she felt the power gather and focus within herself.

At the same time, it was frustrating. She felt fettered by her lack of musical ability and her crippled hands. Working the magic by whistling alone was like only being able to dip her toes in a pool when what she wanted to do was dive in.

Forcing herself to work with what she had, her cheeks beginning to burn from the tension of sustaining the melody, she willed the magic to come forward. Alice didn't understand fully how it was triggered. The sensation was reminiscent of a spasm; like sneezing, like coughing, like an orgasm. Her body just knew how to do it by reflex when properly stimulated.

She shouted, joyful as much as frightened as a torrent of flame exploded from her upper abdomen. The sage remembered herself as it started to gutter out and kept up her whistling. The streaming fire rebuilt itself in response, her body becoming a living flame thrower.

There was no skill or artistry to it. It was a crude dump of barely controlled power, but, soon, the jet of fire heated the air enough that it was difficult to endure. Alice didn't want to stop, she'd only begun, but felt like she would pass out from the heat if she didn't.

Reluctantly, Alice let the song end. Her flames died away almost immediately. Their absence left her blinking. Flickering afterimages ghosted across her retinas. When her vision cleared, her mouth dropped open in shock.

Alice found she'd bored a large hole in the wall. Several feet of solid rock looked as if it had been scooped out like ice cream. A pool of smoking lava glowed at the base of the hole. It cooled as it spread like honey across the smooth floor. Alice closed her eyes and relished the sensation of the power that coursed through her being. Released from its service to her will, the immense energies settled within her like the calm of a great sea after a storm as her centers irised down to their resting state. For the first time since the car accident, Alice felt like a sage.

Chapter 16:

ALICE SAT AT THE center of the bottom of the Way. Her legs were folded in the Burmese position, a small cushion beneath her tailbone. Her hands rested at her navel. The tips of her thumbs touched to form a smooth oval. The sage sat in meditation while her dragon son drew the glyphs around her.

The pattern was similar to the one Altair had formed in the hotel; sixty-four vertices connected by jinn fire. The configuration was different, as were the symbols. She wondered at their meaning.

"It's like sheet music," Ajdaha said as he sensed her thoughts. She'd improved at muting them, but, as she reached out with her magic, they stretched beyond her control. When it was just between the two of them, she found she didn't feel self-conscious about it. Alice smiled in contemplation. As strange as they were, it was good to have family again.

She couldn't remember what was said the last time she'd spoken to her parents, her sister. It bothered her from time to time, and yet she'd never had a strong urge to reconnect, not even when she'd become engaged. The path of her life had led hers too far from theirs to bridge. Though that road had been bitter at times, she didn't regret it as much as she thought she should. Strangely, sometimes, she had liked that life *because* it was bitter. Keeping her distance reduced the sense of alienation she felt around people.

Now, she found her heart was ready to change. She'd tried with Timothy, but it had been a mistake, one that had cost him his life. Though she didn't know if she'd ever be able to resolve that guilt, didn't know if she wanted to if she could, she knew this time was different. For all its strangeness and its dangers, this was a life she found she couldn't help but keep turning toward.

Feeling her concentration falter, Alice put the thoughts aside and breathed deeply. She felt the power within her come forward again. Her centers widened in anticipation. The longer she did it, the more the sage felt *charged*. The energy wanted a release just the way lightning seeks to ground.

"Good," said Ajdaha. "Your focus is improving."

He waved a hand at the ritual trappings. "In time, you won't need the support as much. You'll be able to play by ear."

Alice doubted that very much, but she let that pass along, as well. Even with Ajdaha's expertise, for all her efforts, this Way wasn't opening as Altair's had in the hotel. There was a trick to it, she could feel it, but it was dangling out of reach.

On intuition, she tried humming a note. She put her power behind it and felt the energy spread out around them. The effect was immediate. The crags above shook menacingly as dust drifted and pebbles pattered down.

Right idea, wrong note. Alice got the sense of what she was trying to do. If she could figure out the harmonic, the Way opened. If she couldn't, the Way would bury them.

Altair and Ajdaha squinted up nervously into the darkness. Together, they combined their jinn fire to form a protective shield around the three of them. Alice licked her lips and tried again.

The Way shook again in response. That time, rocks large enough to kill hammered down against the jinn barrier. Alice tried not to flinch as the protective film of fire above her flickered and wavered. Trial and error wasn't going to be good enough.

The sage refocused on her breath and kept still until the Way settled. She stretched out her senses again and looked for clues. She considered her companions. Each of them exhibited a different set of harmonics. It was as if each of them was their own song.

Curious, she examined the larger rocks that had fallen. They were much more similar to each other, but, like the jinn and the dragon, each had their own unique aura. Feeling encouraged, Alice reached out further. She listened to the stone shaft as it hummed its silent melodies. In time, it came to her entirely. The sage heard the song of the Way.

She smiled and chided herself for not noticing before. The problem had been the scale of it. When something was big enough, it stopped registering as a distinct thing. It was like noticing anything about the air she breathed. It was like a fish seeing the ocean, a worm realizing the soil.

Alice frowned, baffled by the emergence of a new problem; whistling wasn't sophisticated enough to capture the harmony of the Way. Even if her crippled hands could hold an instrument, even if she had one, she had no idea how to play it. The answer was there, right in front of her, but she didn't have the right tools to do anything about it.

"It doesn't have to be for long." The dragon could see her frustration. "Just enough for us to get through."

Altair concentrated and put more of himself into the barrier. "We can give you time."

Ajdaha shed his human form. His coils dominated the area around Alice's sigil. He threw his full power into the shield and let the raw strength of a demigod compensate for a lack of ability. His scales shone with a light that radiated from within, suffusing the air with his being. Neither of them looked as though they could keep it up for long.

Alice steeled herself, closed her eyes, felt the song of the Way, and whistled. It was a rough approximate at best, a symphony rendered down to its barest bones. The cavern trembled. It seemed unsure whether to keep listening or just bury them all.

Somehow reluctant, the ground beneath them changed as the first boulders fell. The smooth stone rippled, suddenly fluid, yet it still supported them. Its waves spread from a bright center directly beneath the sage. The light faded out as it ran toward the edges, the oscillating stone rebounded against the walls, and the little swells collided with each other into a pattern that wasn't chaos but was too complicated to be understood. Then, the ripples made their way back to the center, and the Way opened.

The three of them plunged through the suddenly permeable, fluid surface. Great boulders chased after them, racing them through the rift. The jinn shield glowed white. It flashed and flared where the stones struck. Alice had a strange sensation of falling but feeling as though she rose upward at the same time.

As they sank yet somehow soared, time stretched out until each moment was its own forever. The sage, the jinn, the dragon, and the avalanche they brought with them hung, poised within a twisting umbilical of blazing power. Nothing could be seen beyond it, and Alice was glad of it. She had the sense that, if she could look beyond the boundary of the Way, she would find only madness.

All at once, it was over. They burst through into the intense light of a blue sun. Alice gasped and sucked in her breath as though she'd nearly drowned yet had no sense for when she'd stopped breathing. The air was sweet perfume, and, as she drew it into her lungs, the sage felt herself relax into a peace unlike anything she'd ever known.

"Look out!" roared Ajdaha.

The jinn's barrier shattered as the avalanche caught up with them. Alice snapped back to attention and threw her arms up wordlessly in a useless gesture. Through her fingers, she saw the rock that was aimed to strike her down. A boulder the size of a prize-winning pumpkin tumbled toward her in that strange slowness the world takes on when the brain's survival mechanisms take hold.

The dragon threw himself around his family and wrapped them in his golden coils. Within, Alice felt his heartbeat and the sound of great stones as they pounded against his side. She heard his bones breaking underneath his skin, the sharp snaps and cracking soon replaced by the soft, wet sounds of muscles and organs being mashed together.

The cascading thunder of it seemed to go on and on, though she guessed in reality it was less than a minute. She waited a breath after the last impact, to see if there would be more, but there was nothing. The silence that followed was complete, no sound of the dragon's heart around them.

"Ajdaha?" Alice laid her hand on his scales. For a moment, nothing happened, and then the dragon convulsed. Ajdaha's heart beat again, spastic and weak at first, gaining strength with every pulse, his minor divinity defying what should have been a mortal wound.

Gingerly, the dragon stirred, careful that his impromptu cairn didn't collapse inward and crush them. Alice squinted as the sky reappeared, an expanse of alien violet. The crackling, popping sounds of bones reknitting blended with the crash of tumbling stones.

Once loose from the rubble of his would-be burial mound, Ajdaha spread out and waited for his body to heal completely. Altair stretched and breathed deeply as he squinted up into the sweet-scented brilliance. He was thinned out, as she'd seen him before when the jinn had overexerted himself, but he didn't seem troubled by it. The atmosphere was invigorating, his fiery form rapidly recovering its usual luminescence.

"You alright, Aj?" he asked his son.

"I think so," said the dragon, "but I don't like making a habit of it. Honestly, I don't know how you've kept up with her all this time."

Altair laughed, patted the dragon affectionately, then turned to catch Alice's eye. Grinning like a fool, he held out a hand and swept it over the horizon. They stood in a plain that reached to the horizon in all directions. Gentle winds stirred the tall, soft grasses. The vegetation rippled like water, a pleasant susurrus whispering around them.

"This is it," said Altair. "You've done it, Alice. Penglai, Olympus, the Lokas, Asgard, Kunlun. Call it what you want. This is the Realm of the Baalim."

Chapter 17:

Aworld away, Salem crouched in the thick, red clouds. The islet was nothing more than a speck in the stifling depths of Sayon. All around, world serpents slithered in great, ponderous undulations, at home in the shaded, sanguine reaches.

The nephilim hoped his muting would conceal him from the leviathans. Before such gargantua, his jinn magic was good for little else. Even with his ifrit heritage, he didn't know if he could survive if even one of the miles-long snakes took notice of him. Though he'd set the wards he'd been given with meticulous care, the little island could be crushed to dust if one of the leviathans so much as brushed it.

Though he had not the courage for it, nonetheless, the risk was necessary. To call on his father, Pazuzu, was to invite death. In Shambhala, especially then, it was an unforgiveable act. Any of the jinn that labored on their citadel high above would see him destroyed if they knew what he was. Of all the ancient enemies of the jinn, the children of Pazuzu were the most reviled.

Scarcely daring to breathe, the half-jinn reached into the

deep pockets of his robes and drew forth the seer stone. It resembled a lump of mottled, white quartz, larger than his fist. Concentrating, he drew the magic of his jinn fire to his palm until it glowed. He passed the faint light from his hand over the stone. At its center, a perfect sphere of magma flared to life. It shined like a miniature star.

It was a rare and precious bit of artifice, mined from the deepest passages of Tartarus, the Realm of the ifrit. Even with the fortitude of that race, Salem knew lives had been spent obtaining it. The idea of their sacrifice pleased him. His possessing such a thing as this lent a sense of security. Having it with him was a tangible sign that, in the eyes of their father, his life was worth far more than the sum of theirs.

Salem produced a small, black cushion from his robes. Like the seer stone, it came to him from the work of many hands. Those, he'd killed himself. Not directly, of course, but through the labor of an assassin, the winged sphinx Wamu-kota, herself long since fed to the world serpents, lured to her death with his empty promises of shared power at Pazuzu's right hand.

He alone held it now as he knelt on the same bit of ex-iled rock where he'd once watched that killer betrayed. The nephilim remembered the high, shrill sound of the sphinx's voice as it broke cursing his name. He remembered how dark smoke curled up from the twin ruins of Wamukota's burnt wings, blending into the orange and umber billows, ever fainter as it spread until any sign of her disappeared into the clouds. He'd lost sight of the assassin as she fell farther and farther until he was sure some great jaws must have snatched her up in the darkness.

Faintly, golden stitches glinted here and there, tracing out elaborate runework patterns. The nephilim passed his palm over the little cushion as well, its light calling up the en-chantment woven throughout its design. It would keep the seer stone safe, holding the artifact in place where he chose to set it, a warding enchantment ready to deflect anything that might try to strike it. Most valuably, it augmented his muting magic. Though his father had given no sign of acknowledgement of it, Salem was confident, though not fully certain, the enchantment concealed his location even from one with Pazuzu's resources.

He set the cushion on a smooth expanse of the floating bit of land and rested the seer stone upon it. He waited until he felt the enchantment take hold, the precious thing anchored in place, before he slowly drew his hands away.

Salem handled the stone with the reverence of a live bomb, which, in a way, it was. The nephilim knelt before the artifice and bent over it so his lips fell just short of grazing its cool facets. In a whisper softer than velvet, tracings of black smoke curled around his teeth as the traitor of Shambhala called for his father. The molten center of the stone flared at once, the magic leapt the expanse between the worlds in an instant, and Salem trembled at the voice of Pazuzu.

"The sage lives."

"Yes, father." Salam kept the astonishment from his voice with effort. He did not question how it was his father already knew it, but, instead, he added, "Your daughter Skadi fought bravely."

"What does it matter how she fought?" Pazuzu hissed from the depths of the seer stone, "My worthless daughter has failed, or you would not have contacted me."

Salem lowered his eyes, though his father could not see him. "Yes, father. I went in hiding to tell you as soon as I was able."

The nephilim relaxed as soon as the words left his lips. *It was only an educated guess. Pazuzu knows much, but he does not know all. The truth of Skadi's fall at Shambhala remains what I choose to make it.*

Pazuzu grunted, not angry, but only faintly resigned. "Tell me what happened then. Tell me everything."

The nephilim did as he was told and left out no details. Complete honesty rankled him. It was against his nature, but he knew his father would hear it in his voice if he lied. Pazuzu was too old to mistake truth from mere bald deception.

When he had finished, his father said, "You had a chance to kill the sage yourself."

Salem flinched despite himself and sifted quickly through the various responses he'd anticipated needing. "There were witnesses, father. My success was uncertain. If I would have tried, I would have been destroyed, and you would have lost another child, quite likely with nothing more to show for it than what you got for the first."

"A caitiff's shrewdness," spat Pazuzu. "The master would destroy us all if the sage is allowed to become a threat. What worth is your cowardice to you, then? Or to me?"

The nephilim stammered, not entirely deliberately. "The dragon Ajdaha discussed a Way. He journeys with his father to restore the sage's power. I-I think I know where they've gone, father."

Pazuzu sneered, "The Realm of the Baalim, obviously. I have already sent a host of your siblings to stop them."

Salem was silent, for once at a loss to respond to what he was hearing. He wondered at the power of their master that, at his word, his father would dare to invade the lands of the gods. He feared that even Pazuzu would not risk opposing the will of the master, even if it meant he himself would be a pawn and his spawn were to be fodder in a war on the Baalim.

"What do you want of me, father?" said the nephilim. "How may I best serve you?"

For a long pause, there was no response. Salem controlled the urge to speak again, inwardly soothing himself to keep still. Currying favor was always a path to safety to him, but, when Pazuzu said nothing, he wondered if it had been a mistake. He let out a long, slow breath and tried to imagine how the ancient one was gauging his worth, a single asset among legions, the value of each of their lives balanced against the cost of another's.

Finally, his father spoke, "Return to Shambhala. Help the jinn rebuild it. Make yourself useful and keep their trust in you. When the time is right, I will come for you."

Come for me?! The words echoed in his mind. Salem wanted to ask what that meant but didn't dare. Like his father, though it galled him, he understood that risks were simply another calculation to be factored into one's plans. Without accepting them, any goals worth reaching were unobtainable. The desire to be certain could only be satisfied to a point. After that, it became an obsession, weakening resolve and amplifying doubt into paranoia.

As the magma at the stone's center darkened, the nephilim's mind turned back to its web of deceit and manipulation. He dispelled the protective enchantments and gathered up the cushion and the stone. Salem called on his sila magic and lifted away from the islet, headed upward for the citadel.

He flew slowly, patiently scheming on how he might save himself from every threat he could imagine. At the same time, he accepted that, for all his guile, the game he played would remain obscured in riddles and shadows. It couldn't be won any other way; there was no precedent for what was really happening. Somehow, Pazuzu's master was steering all of creation toward its endgame.

And after that, he mused, *the possibilities are limitless.*

Chapter 18:

ALICE TURNED A SLOW circle as she looked out across the great plain. "So, where is everybody?"

"Everywhere," said Ajdaha. "Just not right here right now. This Realm is a little weird."

"This one in particular, huh?" said Alice. "*This* one's the weird one."

The dragon nodded. "The Realm of the Baalim is divided into eight Places."

She thought on it a moment. "Like apartments?"

Ajdaha looked at her blankly, then searchingly at Altair. The jinn nodded to Alice. "Essentially. Little worlds carved out of the big one."

To his son, he explained, "A cooperative dwelling."

"Ah." Ajdaha nodded understanding.

"Ok," she said, pleased with her guess. "Whose Place is this?"

"Nobody's," said the dragon. "This is the borderlands."

"So, wouldn't that be nine Places?" she asked.

Ajdaha raised a paw and teetered it side to side. "Technically, the borderlands aren't a Place. They are the baseline foundation of the Realm. It's neutral territory. Think of this as a common space, a foyer for a shared residence."

"Alright," Alice said. Altair looked equally curious. "Then how do we get off the front porch?"

"Pretty simple," said Ajdaha. "We just need to travel until we get to a Door."

At the look on her face, the dragon added quickly, "It's not as difficult as a Way. We're not trying to pass between Realms. We're looking for a connection point between two Places in the same Realm."

The dragon squinched up his face as he considered how to word the concept. "In the Baalim Realm, the borderlands are thought to be boundless. All the Places within it are set so far apart from each other, you could travel for years and still never make it from one to another. A Door is a spot where the Places touch, ignoring the distance."

"Oh!" Alice's face brightened. "You mean a wormhole!"

The dragon looked down at his long body, then cocked his head at her. "Is that a joke?"

The sage held up her hands, palms toward the dragon, and waved them side to side. "No, no! It's what they're called on earth. Scientists haven't actually discovered them yet, but they think they're out there. There're movies and shows where people find them or make them to get to other planets."

"Oh." Ajdaha pointed toward the horizon. "Well, they're real. In this Realm, anyway, and the closest one we need is about a day's travel that way."

"Sounds simple," said Alice. "Think we're going to meet anything on the way?"

Ajdaha shrugged. "It's possible. There's not much in the way of settlements out here. Mostly, it's bazaars near the Doors. The caravans between them are usually muted, the same as we'll be."

"Why's that?" asked Alice.

"Raiders," Altair said as he gazed into the distance.

"Are there a lot of them?" she asked.

"Hundreds," said the jinn, "maybe a thousand."

Ajdaha heard a change in his father's tone, followed his gaze, and said something in jinn. Alice couldn't understand a word, but it sounded distinctly like a curse. She frowned, looked as well, and echoed her son's sentiment. "Ah, shit."

The horde was distant, a black cloud among the drifting, silvery wisps of the violet Baalim sky. Here and there, clumps of stragglers, or else very large individuals, would break away from the greater mass. To the sage, it looked like a malevolent rot dragging itself across the plain, birthing and cannibalizing its children as it came.

Alice asked, "Who the hell are they?!"

Ajdaha said, "Children of Pazuzu. We need to move."

Altair held up a finger as Alice opened her mouth to silence her. He spoke quickly, "Pazuzu's a very old ifrit. Once, he was worshipped as a sort of god in ancient Mesopotamia."

At her tense, blank look, Ajdaha added, "The Middle East a long, long time ago. Pre-Judaic, and he wasn't a god. He was a demon. Now, get on my back!"

With that, Altair became a great eagle, and Alice did as she was told. They rose into the air and headed in the direction the dragon had indicated. The grasses rushed by, a great sea of vegetation. She could understand why there weren't people around. The borderlands were a green desert; abundant plant life, but nothing to eat or drink.

As they flew, the silvery clouds drawing closer, Ajdaha looked over his shoulder and said, "Demon didn't used to mean what it does now, by the way. The old use of the word just means he was a supernatural being, not necessarily good or evil."

"Alright, so which is Pazuzu?" she raised her voice to be heard over the rushing wind of their passage.

"Evil," Ajdaha said evenly, "but cooperative. He's essentially the head of a family of mercenaries. He has a Place in Tartarus where he, uhm, breeds them."

At her blank look, the dragon supplied, "It's the ifrit Realm. Pazuzu has slaves of many different species that he keeps there. Breeders. He, erm, keeps them pregnant to grow his army."

"Got it," said Alice, "ancient demon with his own private rape farm and a horde of monster babies. Sounds utterly terrible. He's the one who's after us?"

Ajdaha shook his head. "Pazuzu doesn't work that way. He's always been a contractor. He loans out his children, and there's enough people who pay him that he in turn is able to pay for others to ignore what goes on in his Place. His children coming here means someone has him on retainer."

The sage looked back at the horde and despaired. As quickly as they were moving, it wasn't dropping away entirely. The fastest of the demon spawn were breaking farther from the main group, eager to reach their prize. They were only a fraction of the gathered children, but even that little offshoot included dozens of beings.

"Who could afford a demon army?!" she asked.

"I don't know," the dragon admitted. "There's not many with the resources. Not for something on this scale. My guess would be whoever Pazuzu is working for is the same one who did away with the sages."

Alice frowned. "Do you think it was one of the gods?"

The dragon and Altair the great eagle exchanged a worried look. Alice looked back again. There was a noticeable gap between the horde and the swifter outrunners, and it was growing.

"It's possible," said Ajdaha. "One of the Baalim might be powerful enough."

"Then how do we know," asked the sage, "whether or not we're running straight toward the god responsible for it all? For all we know, we're stuck between being fucked and getting spit roasted."

The dragon looked back at her blankly, so she added, "Chinese fingercuffs?"

Ajdaha was uncomprehending, so she tried again. "Come on! Why do you not get any references?! Getting screwed from both ends?"

His golden eyes brightened as understanding dawned. "Ah! No, this should be fine. There wouldn't be any point in chasing us like this if we were already heading straight for our doom. A horde like this would be a spectacular waste if we were doing the work ourselves for free."

"Great." Alice peered over her shoulder. "That's a lot better than I was thinking. Do you think you can go faster?"

The outrunners were close enough by then, the black mass of their group could be seen as distinct entities. The swiftest of them all were of a kind in themselves. They were humanoid, their bodies black with leathery wings. They had the heads of dogs with a mass of writhing snakes for hair. In their hands, they held metal-studded scourges. Each of the whips had eight cords that twined and writhed like living things as they trailed in the monsters' wake.

The dragon shook his head. "If I could, I would. Sorry."

Altair screeched, his meaning clear. They would never outpace them at this rate. They needed more time. The jinn banked his wings and began to circle back.

"Wait!"

Alice shook her head and raised her hand toward him, fingers spread, telling him to stay where he was. She didn't know exactly what they were up against, but she understood, if the jinn turned back now, it would mean his death. Altair stayed where he was, keeping pace with Ajdaha. He shot her a look, and she knew he would only wait so long before he did what he had to.

Her heart swelled with emotion. She didn't want the jinn to die. Though she might never admit it, she was coming to accept a part of her did love Altair. The sage closed her eyes and breathed. She set the confusing, competing feelings aside so she could focus.

"What are those things?!" she called to the dragon.

"Erinyes." Ajdaha caught her uncomprehending look and clarified, "Furies."

When the sage only shook her head and shrugged, he said. "Nephilim. Usually, they chase down criminals. Today, it's us."

Alice didn't ask what would happen if they caught them. She imagined all of them being torn to pieces with whips and claws. *Ajdaha said the Door was a day away. Those things will be on us within an hour. We need more time . . .*

The sage pursed her lips and began to whistle. She thought of the melody she'd worked out at the bottom of the Way. She imagined solid stone melting before her and felt her centers open in response. The power gathered within and around her. Alice refined her melody until the air around her shook, visibly distorted by the intensity of it.

Alice turned and unleashed a blast of fire from her solar plexus. She launched it at the closest of the furies. The fireball burned through the air. A thick plume of black smoke trailed behind as it hurtled toward her targets. The furies kept on, impossibly swift, then, at the last moment, they veered off from each other. The spell passed harmlessly between them to curve off into the distance until it burnt itself out.

The sage frowned and glared at the baying, shrieking monsters as they bore down on them. She considered what she knew of magic that might be useful. Her body of knowledge was pitifully limited, but a solution came to mind quickly.

She thought of the sword Altair had used to slay the ifrit at the hospital, the bolt of forged lightning he'd lost against the troll of the Way. *Perhaps lightning is as good as fire,* she considered. *Now if I just had some lightning.*

Alice whistled again as she concentrated on her solar plexus and varied the tune until her body began to tingle. She continued to experiment with the melody and felt the fine hairs of her arms raise up as the air around her became charged.

She inhaled the sharp, sweet scent of ozone as she kept up the tune. The energy crackled and snapped around her as the power focused. When it felt like it was enough, Alice pointed where she wanted the spell to go. She felt that strange sort of spasm surge through her nerves, a sort of release, and whooped ecstatically as a bolt of lightning leapt from her twisted fingers.

The electricity covered the distance between them instantly, but, by luck, the lightning passed harmlessly between the furies. It crackled along, too fast to track by eye, and struck the figure of a more distant outrunner. The creature, whatever it was, froze in place as it was struck, then plummeted. Smoke trailed behind the burning body as it fell into the tall grasses below. Alice quickly whistled up another bolt before the furies could respond.

That time, the resulting fulmination caught one of the creatures squarely. It seized up immediately and fell. The monster caught fire on the way down. Across the distance, she heard the nephilim howl their rage.

Keeping up her music, Alice charged up another blast. The extended use of her magic was wearing on her, though not as she expected. The power within her was immense. It was like the pull of the moon creating the tides, like the shifting of tectonic plates; world shaping. At the same time, it was exhausting trying to push all that power through such a limited pathway. Being confined to whistling was like trying to pour out an ocean through a funnel.

She let loose another bolt and struck another fury. That time, it was a glancing blow. The torrent of electricity merely burnt one of its wings to cinders. The fury spiraled out of control, its body seizing, limbs spasming uselessly. The others spread out as their sibling fell to reduce the chance of another being hit.

Seeking to confound her further, the furies swooped and rose, rolled and twisted in the air to deny her any easy targets. Alice threw more lightning anyway. With everything she'd faced, everything actively trying to kill her, it felt good being able to *do* something about it.

Since childhood, she'd never been one to stand meekly and get pushed around. Alice was forgiving by nature and slow to anger. She preferred negotiation and compromise to direct conflict. Making friends, or at least amiable acquaintances, out of enemies was best, but, when provoked, she had never been one to turn the other cheek. Taking careful aim, Alice whistled up the lightning and burned the life from another of the furies.

She smiled as the monsters slowed, their efforts divided between pursuit and evasion. The space between them didn't widen, but it didn't shrink, either. Altair screeched in approval and dipped a wing toward her in a sort of avian bow. She inclined her head in return and whistled, electricity crackling between her fingers and arcing across the gap of her palms. Their crisscrossing scars tingled, not unpleasantly, as she chose her next target.

Another bolt of lightning crackled through the air, but the furies were dodging with stunning displays of aerial agility. The sight of them would have filled her with wonder if she weren't already bursting with a manic fear. She tried again and failed again. The monsters were ready for her. Their unpredictable movements made it impossible to anticipate a target.

After another handful of futile attempts, Alice realized the furies were no longer the tip of the horde's spear. They had become a feint. Behind them, she saw another of the faster figures had drawn closer.

It looked much like Altair, a powerful eagle. The jinn and the other bird appeared roughly the same size. She understood it was an optical illusion based on distance, the same way the sun and the moon were made into similar discs in the sky. The eagle behind them was gigantic in a way she had no previous reference for, massive enough that her mind struggled to understand it.

Clouds gathered around the titanic eagle. The beat of its great wings condensed them out of the air. They darkened from moment to moment, built higher and higher into towering thunderheads. Lightning played through their depths, striking the ground and crackling thunder through the eagle's feathers.

Alice called out to Ajdaha, "Is that a, uhm, a . . ."

"It's a thunderbird," said the dragon.

"I guess turnaround is fair play," the sage said ruefully.

Ajdaha agreed, "Payback's a bitch."

Alice eyed the gathering clouds. Already, it was shaping up into the greatest storm she'd ever seen. The thunderbird soared through the layers of clouds, and the rains began.

The endless plains below churned to mud as the thunderbird passed overhead. The deluge pooled off the creature's back and became waterfalls. Each beat of its wings sent up a spray so high it was lost in the heavens.

Nothing could be seen of the following horde anymore. The thunderbird's display eclipsed all else. The sage sat mesmerized, entranced by the raw power of the thing. The arcs of energy around the colossus reminded her of the plasma lamp she had in high school, illuminating its darkly shining plumage from any angle. For all her fear of it, the thunderbird was beautiful.

She had no time to react when the lightning came. The thunderbird let out a deafening screech, and electricity arced across its hooked beak. It reached out toward her with its talons. Energy gathered at each tip, then the claws clutched together to form twin orbs of power.

The thunderbird shrieked again and slammed the globes of lightning together. Light flashed out and blinded the sage. It took her a beat to understand she wasn't dead. She gasped as she realized the afterimage burned on her retina was that of the eagle Altair, throwing himself in the lightning's path.

Alice felt Ajdaha dive, unable to see anything but the jinn's sacrifice. Gripping with her legs, she blinked and rubbed at her eyes in a panic. She felt the scar tissue of her hands against her eyelids and wondered if she was doubly crippled. Ajdaha's roar drowned out all else as they plummeted.

Feeling her organs floating within her as they entered freefall, she wondered if the dragon had been struck as well. Desperate for information. Alice forced herself to breathe slowly, concentrated on her third eye center, and willed her senses to expand.

It wasn't the same as seeing, but it was enough for her to know what was going on. Ajdaha had caught up to Altair as the eagle fell. The dragon clutched his father in his foreclaws. The tall grasses of the plain hissed where his tail dragged through their tips. The jinn's body smoked, all but burnt out. Behind them, the furies gained as the storm raged behind them. The thunderbird towered over them all, reaching with its talons for more power as it approached.

Alice concentrated on the center at her root. Her energy flowed down into the base of her spine. Altair had told her the magic there was related to survival. As Ajdaha leveled out to race along just above the tops of the grasses, the sage hummed, feeling for the melody she needed.

The next lightning the thunderbird threw struck the dragon on the tail. Alice's jaw clenched shut, and she nearly bit off the tip of her tongue as her muscles seized. She should have been dead, she knew it, but her magic had protected her enough to save her. Just the same, she slid to the side and toppled from the dragon.

Ajdaha faltered as he was struck, but, with the fortitude of a demigod, he recovered quickly. The dragon rolled as Alice slipped and caught her up with one claw while carrying the jinn with the other. The ground passed below in a blur. The tall grasses whipped painfully at her body. Roaring with pain and exertion, the dragon reared up and strove for the sky.

Behind them, the storm grew and grew until it was a typhoon. The dark clouds spread out to overtake everything from horizon to horizon. They plunged the world into shadows broken into still images by the strobing forks of lightning. Beneath it, the children of Pazuzu were coming, visible only as snapshots of a black, monstrous mass of reaching claws, searching eyes, gnashing teeth.

The thunderbird drew its claws together again as it flew after them, shaping the energy with its talons. Dangling like a ragdoll in the dragon's grip, Alice willed herself to concentrate. She whistled as loudly and clearly as she could, thinking only of escape.

Don't die! Go faster! Don't die! Faster!

As the monstrous eagle threw another fulmination, the sage felt her soul center yawn wide above her head, exchanging power with her root in a feedback loop. It felt like the magic meant to twist her in half, to squeeze and crush her to death. All at once, the spell leapt from her lips, and time slowed to a crawl.

Alice saw the individual raindrops as they fell. They drifted lazily through the air to strike down into little, explosive splashes on the leaves of grass below. She could feel the individual droplets where they struck her clothing and skin, could see Ajdaha's golden scales reflected in them like a million tiny mirrors. There was time to witness each discharge of electricity among the clouds, the arcs of energy that played and danced among the wings of the thunderbird. The crashes of thunder became a deep, steady growl. Her body trembled in slow motion under the press of the purring sky.

The lightning bolt was coming, stretching out impossibly slowly from the thunderbird's claws, its wings pushing down so gradually it was nearly imperceptible. With only the one, stretched out instant remaining to her, the sage slapped her palms down on the base of the claw that held her. She willed the energy of the spell into her son, and then the lightning struck.

Alice felt her consciousness slip away as currents of electricity rocked through her body, and a sense of time returned to her fading awareness. The deluge pounded against her like a thousand little fists. Her eyes slipped closed. The constant, rolling thunder drowned out all other sounds as she blacked out, hurtling through the open air in the claws of a dragon.

Chapter 19:

ALICE AWOKE IN THE palm of a giant. Fingers like trees curled overhead. Above the looming digits, a mountainous countenance in profile paid her no more attention than if she were a bit of dust. Sucking in breath in an inverted scream, she flailed reflexively, reached out with both hands, and tried to find something to hang onto that wasn't the massive bed of warm, strangely stoney flesh that palmed her.

Finding nothing but the low rises of the monster's hand, she fell weakly onto her back. She turned her head at the sound of shallow breaths. Altair lay next to her, his thinned, still form like so many dull, red embers. Alice tried to scream, but all that came was a throaty rasp.

She could hear Ajdaha's voice distantly below her. There was pleading in it, and, though she couldn't understand anything he said, the sage was certain her son was begging for their lives. She tried to scream again as she stared up at the massive face that nearly blotted out the sky.

The sky! Recognition rekindled memory. There was that blue sun, the heavens an intense purple above the silver clouds. *The borderlands!*

Weakly, Alice tried to sit up. Her strength failed her, but she was able to roll to one side. Peering over the heel of a palm large enough to park a car on, she saw a town in the middle of a full-scale evacuation. It was the definition of a bazaar, a loose collection of dozens of temporary structures, simple paths wending organically between them. The smells of fried bread and roasting meat wafted up, incongruously delectable amid the fearful rush.

Relinquishing their wares, all manner of beings were surging toward a massive set of doors that stood alone in the endless plains. Alice could see jinn and far fewer ifrit. There were centaurs, satyrs, minotaurs, and dozens of other fusions of beasts and humans. Orcs, trolls, goblins, and creatures beyond anything she'd heard of were running, flying, and slithering for their lives.

The double doors looked as though they were forged from pure gold. They were tall enough for the giant to step through with hardly a stoop of its shoulders. Behind them, a bright light shone. It concealed everything that lay beyond. *Not just doors,* Alice realized, *those are the* Door!

The people of that town disappeared into the light in droves, clutching their possessions and bawling children. To the other side of the Door stood another giant. In one hand, he held a longsword, the weapon forged from the same aureate material as the Door. The being itself was like a mountain, its skin gray and rugged. Moss and even small trees were collected on its scalp and shoulders.

In the distance, a great storm was rising up to swallow the sky. It was larger than anything she'd ever seen on earth, dwarfing hurricanes. Below the tempest, a great, black horde swept toward them, eagerly devouring the scant miles that lay between. Alice wondered if it was the end of the world. The way the entire town was running, that seemed to be the way of it.

Refusing helplessness, Alice concentrated on her root

and soul centers and hummed softly. Her lips were too parched to whistle. The tune was poorly shaped, but she felt a small measure of strength return to her body, drawn from the very air as the magic worked. Soon, she was able to sit up and better see what was happening.

She saw the dragon staring up at her as she came to her senses. The sage concentrated again, that time focused on the vortices at her throat and the top of her head. All at once, their words became clear.

"But you have to let us through!" said the dragon. "We'll die out here!"

The giant grunted like rolling thunder and replied, "Serves you right for bringing trouble to our Door."

The other giant scratched his back with the tip of his golden sword and said, "For all we know, you're with them."

Ajdaha shouted up, "If we were with them, why would we be here now?!"

"Spies sent ahead to spread confusion, maybe," said the giant. His fingers flexed unconsciously. Alice cringed and waited to be pulped.

"Maybe buy time to keep the Doors open, eh?"

"Please," the dragon begged, "We did not mean to bring trouble to your Door. We have come with the last of the sages! A great enemy has taken all the others and has destroyed her hands! Without her magic, this sage will fall as well, and earth with her! We've come seeking the help of Ninhursag to restore her!"

The giant scoffed, lightly bouncing Alice and Altair on his palm. "What does Ninhursag care for earth? The sages' problems are their own."

The dragon flung his foreleg toward the approaching horde and called out, "Look at what's coming! Whoever this enemy is, they have the resources to call on all the children of Pazuzu! They are powerful enough to defeat the sages! When earth falls, who knows where the enemy of that world will turn their eye next!"

The other giant hefted his sword thoughtfully and stared into the distance. The horde was drawing ever closer, a collection of all the nightmares that had ever been. It was dizzying trying to make sense of the shapes of them; carapaces and tentacles, long claws and sharp horns, black ooze and too many eyes. The thunderbird loomed above them all, a force of nature incarnate. It screamed as the children of Pazuzu headed for the Door, a sound like the sky being torn in half. Lightning arced all about it, scorching the earth and starting grass fires that were immediately extinguished in the downpour.

Alice looked up at her captor and forced herself up onto her knees. Altair lay beside her inert, slowly dimming as the light of his life faded. She concentrated on the spinning locus of energy in the center of her chest and let her emotions spill out of her being. It wasn't music, exactly, but the sage spoke from her heart. Her words were forged from fear but tempered by love.

To her, the idea of the entire earth being conquered was too big to be anything other than an abstract concept. She understood the loss of the sages was immeasurable, but, in this life, they were strangers to her. When Alice spoke, it was for the love of her family. She had no children of her own, yet her son spoke for her now, born from lifetimes ago by her own soul. Her husband lay beside her, their marriage irrevocably broken before Alice's own parents had named her, but his love for her was undying.

"Please," she said, Altair's head cradled in her lap. "He's dying. Please help us."

The giant went still, glaring down at the sage, but moved by the spoken truth of her heart. Her magic drifted through the air, the rising sounds of Pazuzu's horde fading to a dull murmur. It didn't change his mind by force. Alice's magic only let the guardian of the Door know her in a way no words could match.

The giant looked down at the sage, the cliffs of his face unreadable. Finally, with a heavy sigh like the katabatic winds tumbling down from a mountaintop, the giant looked to the other guardian. They nodded to each other after a moment, their faces grave with the weight of their duty.

"You may pass." The second giant restlessly shifted the weight of his sword in his hand. "You must take her, Ephialtes. I will hold the Door."

His eyes bright with emotion, Alice's giant Ephialtes drew his own sword from its sheath at his side. "Take this, brother. I will tell Ninhursag it was Otos who held the Door for her when the children of Pazuzu came."

Otos grinned as he took the towering blade, his teeth like boulders. "I'll tell her myself at dinner, brother. Now hurry!"

With that, the giant Ephialtes stepped toward the massive, golden Door. By then, most of the people of the bazaar had made their way through. The few stragglers rushed to make way for him. Alice looked back toward the horde as they fled. The giant's hand shifted beneath her like a ship at sea. Ajdaha flew behind them, his eyes filled with worry as they came to rest on his father.

Otos stepped away from the Door alone to face the horde as it came. The thunderbird screeched again. The air split with the intensity of it. Lightning gathered in its claws, and it loosed a bolt at the giant.

He raised his massive swords as the electricity slammed into him. The golden blades glowed as they drew the lightning to them. The bolt struck them squarely. Arcing energy played all across their lengths. Laughing a mirthful thunder, the giant swept his swords out and downward.

The lightning scattered across the plains from the tips of the golden weapons. The drenching rain parted before the wave of energy for an instant, bringing a moment of surreal quiet to the world. Shouting challenge, the giant Otos took a lunging step forward and threw one of the colossal swords at the thunderbird.

The blade spun through the air, the length of it blurring until it looked like a miniature sun. It covered the distance in a heartbeat and buried itself in the thunderbird's chest. At once, the monster's booming cries melted into a gurgling crash like a great river flowing through rapids.

The children of Pazuzu parted around the great eagle as it weakened and fell, never breaking stride. Their eyes fixed on Alice, the horde screamed for her blood in a dozen languages through a thousand voices. The colossus dropped out of the sky, shaking the earth as it struck down. The hilt of the giant's golden sword snapped away from the blade as it came under the monster's weight.

The great weapon broke with a deafening crack that shook the plains. The thick grasses bent outward in a shockwave of sound that spread out in all directions. The giant Otos strode forward with his brother's sword and roared his defiance at the demonic brethren.

Ephialtes reached the Door, careful not to crush the citizenry below. The people of the bazaar flowed around the giant's feet like ants, looking fearfully in all directions as they passed over the threshold and disappeared into what lay beyond. Alice couldn't bear to look away from Otos, his sacrifice apparent as he reached the horde.

As the Door of the god slammed closed behind them, the last she saw of the guardian was his feet planted, soaked in black ichor up to his shins from the foul bodies crushed beneath his soles. The great, golden sword was a blur of light. Each sweep cut through scores of bodies, but, still, the children of Pazuzu came. Relentless, they alighted on the giant's chest and flowed up his legs.

The giant beat at the monsters on his body. He mashed them against his rocky skin and snatched at them, pulping them in his hand before throwing them back at the horde.

The golden sword never stopped moving, though Otos' aim became erratic. Accuracy didn't matter, the space around the giant so thick with horrors it was impossible to miss them entirely.

For all his ferocity, the horde soon covered the giant. They bore him to the ground in a wave of ripping claws and tearing teeth. Otos swung his sword even as he fell, kicking and thrashing, taking as many of the demon-spawned lives with him as he could. The children of Pazuzu kept coming. They waded toward the giant through a shallow lake their battle had made from the black ichor of their fallen brethren. In the light beyond the Door, his brother Ephialtes wept bitterly. Great tears crashed down his cheeks like a river pouring down a mountain.

Chapter 20:

Passing through the Door, Alice felt as if she were falling through a twisting passage without end. The giant Ephialtes, his eyes shining bright with tears like icy mountain pools, held them close. He cupped the sage and the jinn in one hand and sheltered them with the other. Ajdaha hovered close, peering between the great fingers with eyes only for his wounded father.

Ifrit and jinn and nephilim and creatures Alice had no words for tumbled along with them. All around, there was a transparent membrane of light, the defining border of the Door. Beyond, she could see stars blurring past.

Alice wondered at the immensity of it. *Are the Realms different places in the same universe? Are they in different dimensions? Is each Realm its own universe?!*

All at once, they were through. The light of the Door faded behind, and Alice looked down from the giant's palm on the home of a god. Ninhursag's Place was a paradise.

The world before her teemed with life the way she imagined the tropical rainforests on earth. Great trees reached to the heavens, filtering the sunlight. Everything below was well lit, but it was a soft, pleasantly warm shade.

Animals of all kinds made their homes among the giant boughs. Alice couldn't name any of them, but that didn't bother her. It was the same for her there as it was with most life from her own world. Raised in a city, she'd spent little time outside the lands of pavement and glass and Wi-Fi. Nonetheless, witnessing the sheer density of the life here left her awestruck.

Below the trees and their many layered biomes, there were fields and orchards and pastures, lush and abundant. Alice was no better at identifying the domesticated species than she was the wildlife. She blinked dizzily at the scope of it all. It didn't seem possible there could be so much life.

Ephialtes, outwardly calm and focused, walked between the massive trees with careful strides, mindful of the beings all around him. Though his steps couldn't help but wound and damage, there didn't seem to be a lasting effect. The crops and vegetation crushed in the giant's wake sprang back up again soon after, no worse for his passing.

Alice cast about for Ajdaha and found him drifting along close at hand. The dragon still looked worried for his father, but the vigor of the Place seemed to have set him at ease. She looked at the jinn beside her and smiled when she found his fire was brighter again. Altair remained unconscious and weak, but he wasn't fading as he was in the borderlands.

She called out to the dragon, "It's beautiful!"

"It is." Ajdaha panned his vision over it. "Wonders can be found in all the Realms, but the green lands of Elysium are a miracle like no other."

"Elysium," Alice said to herself, trying the unfamiliar word. "Where are we going now?" she asked.

"The world tree," said the dragon. "It's Ninhursag's seat of power in her Place."

"Is it far?"

Ajdaha spread his claws and shrugged his golden shoulders. "It's as near as she wants it to be. In their Places, the gods can arrange things as they please."

Alice tried to snap her fingers, but the gnarled tendons would not oblige her. She managed a dull thump of her fingertips against her palm and said, "Just like that?"

The dragon shook his head. "The Baalim are powerful, even more so than the sages. The only being above them is the Eternal god, but they have their limitations. From what I understand of them, I would think it's their equivalent of remodeling or redecorating."

She considered the information. "So, a manageable pain in the butt. Not something you'd want to do every day."

Ajdaha nodded. "Something like that, yes, but the Baalim are not well understood."

"You know," she mused, "I notice the big distinguishment between the gods and *the* God is that term, Eternal. Does that mean the Baalim can die?"

"In a way," said Ajdaha.

"What way?"

"Why do you ask?"

Alice said, "Because whatever it is we're fighting against is on their scale, right? It seems like an important detail."

"Fair enough," said the dragon "Yes, the gods can die."

"What happens when they do?"

"They are remade," he told her.

"Like reincarnated?"

Ajdaha shook his head. "It's different for them. When a human reincarnates, a sage in particular, they are born again; an old soul in a new body. When a god dies, they are a new soul in a new body, but their basic essence remains the same. It's like Jupiter and Zeus. They aren't precisely the same being, but they are functionally equivalent manifestations of the essence of that Baalim."

Alice quieted as she pondered his words. The more she knew, the more reality just kept opening wider and wider.

She wondered if she would ever reach the edge of it. Anymore, she didn't think she wanted to. The mystery of existence was a present ever in need of unwrapping, a gift whose surprise and delight could never fade.

The sage sat back, reclining on the palm of a giant. She watched the alien world as it passed along, each new thing a wonder. Allowed that rare handful of peace, Alice rested and took in the nourishment of discovery.

The world tree reached from the depths of Elysium to the stars and beyond. Communities rested in its boughs like fruit. The little lights of civilization sparkled among great leaves like sails that rustled in the soft breezes, so far above the ground, there shouldn't have been air at all.

The giant Ephialtes was obliged to step over roots like foothills as he made his way to the base of the tree. They became so massive he eventually had to place Alice on his shoulder so he could climb over them. Ajdaha took Altair in his claws and held him as delicately as glass. He offered to let Alice ride, but the sage could not resist the opportunity to stand tall on the shoulders of a giant.

She clung to an apple tree that stood above the giant's collarbone. Ephialtes moved with a silken grace belied by his size. It reminded her of a rocking boat on a gentle sea. She watched with wonder as the world tree drew closer, munching apples excitedly as the sight of it filled her vision.

When they arrived at its base, Alice stepped closer to the giant's ear that he might hear her clearly. "Thank you, Ephialtes!"

"It is nothing," said the giant. "Should they be worthy, to serve the needs of others is to serve oneself."

"I will do my best," she told him "What will you do now?"

"I will do as I have done for ages," said the giant. "I will stand guard at my Door."

Ephialtes's face fell; his eyes glistened with sudden tears. "But, first, I will mourn my brother."

The sage laid a hand against the giant's neck. "I'm sorry for what happened to Otos. I really am."

"Then," said Ephialtes, "if you really are a sage, you will put an end to Pazuzu. You will avenge the death of my brother."

"I will," said Alice, uncaring of the enormity of what he asked, "and all the other lives he is responsible for taking. I swear it."

The giant nodded once, stricken with grief but satisfied at the prospect of closure. "Then go, sage. I must return to my duties."

Ajdaha swept in and alighted on the giant's shoulder. Alice went to him and clambered to her place. As they lifted off, Ephialtes turned the way he had come. His long strides carried him swiftly into the distance.

"That was a good thing to do, Alice."

"Je-SUS!"

The sage jumped despite herself. The light, feminine voice had come from just behind her. She turned quickly, startled. No one was there before, but now, among the twining leaves and branches of the world tree, stood a god.

Ninhursag was unequivocal. She didn't do anything out of the ordinary. She didn't float or glow. There was no halo or heavenly chorus. She was simply and unmistakably a god.

She was tall and slender, long, dark hair draped smoothly over soft, milky shoulders. Deep brown eyes like rich soil gazed serenely, her long face tapered to full lips and a rounded chin. Ninhursag wore a simple, black slip of a dress that floated over feminine curves to brush at her bare feet.

Alice cocked her head, eyebrows furrowed. *Wait . . .branches? How can there be leaves? We're at the bottom.* The sage looked around and was astonished.

The four of them were standing close together on one of

the innumerable limbs of the world tree. Above, the foliage extended without apparent end into the heavens. Below, the lands of Elysium were obscured by layers of clouds.

Rocked by sudden vertigo, Alice carefully lowered herself to the ground. Instead, she found herself coming to rest in a comfortable chair. It seemed to be an extension of the tree itself, grown in that moment to support her.

Following suit, Ninhursag sat in a chair of her own, the furniture coming to be as it was needed. Altair lay between them, his breathing gentle and easy. He looked less like he was unconscious and more like he was in a deep sleep.

Ajdaha came to rest uneasily at Alice's right hand and laid his coils around his mother and father protectively. For all his worldliness, Alice could see even he was out of his depth here. The god smiled kindly, and the sage felt herself relax. Alice laid a hand on the dragon's back and felt his tension ease, also.

"I know why you have come, Alice," said Ninhursag, "and I am happy you are here."

"Thank you, uhm, Nine Hearse Sag . . ." she replied, weakly.

The god laughed. "It *is* a mouthful. Gaia is fine. Perhaps Isis."

"Thank you, Gaia," said Alice, and she focused on getting to business. She felt if she just sat there, she would be enthralled and stupefied by the being before her. "You said you know why we're here, so you know who it was that took the sages?"

Gaia shook her head. "I do not. This enemy's power is great. They have succeeded in concealing themselves as well as their intent, though I fear for the Realms if they are left unchecked."

Alice furrowed her brow in a silent question, and the god supplied, "The sages have protected your Realm since the Eternal gave life to your species at its beginning. They live, and they die as mortals, but they have never disappeared."

"What does it mean?" asked Alice.

"I believe the enemy has made a nest for itself in your Realm," said the god, "and took the other sages to eliminate threats to it."

"A Place on earth?" Alice asked.

"So, it would seem," said Gaia, "but even if I knew, I could not say where. The Baalim have influence in your world, but we are not permitted to act with impunity. It is an interesting problem for us. By taking the sages, this enemy has turned your Realm to their own purposes. Earth is being used as a ward against our involvement."

Alice and Ajdaha looked at each other searchingly, and the god said, "I do not know their goal for doing this thing, but you must have learned of their plans, at least in part, in your previous lives. Otherwise, I imagine you would have been taken, as well."

"I just died instead." Alice's lips twisted as if tasting something bitter.

"Everything dies, Alice," said the god. "What's important is your death nourished this opportunity. You planted yourself like a seed, that you might grow to face this enemy. Now, it is time for me to tend to you, that you might blossom. Come here."

Gaia rose smoothly. Her seat melted seamlessly back into the bark of the world tree. Alice followed suit. Her own chair faded away as its purpose ended. Ajdaha shifted, at hand to protect his father, but staying out of their way.

Slowly, cautiously, Alice walked along the bough. It was difficult to remember they were in a tree, the broad limb large enough to host a dance. As she neared, Gaia held out her hands for the sage's. Her dark eyes were filled with care and compassion. Alice felt compelled to go to her, like a small child toddling toward the warm safety of their mother.

"Let me see your hands," said the god.

Chapter 21:

ALICE WATCHED, TRANSFIXED AS Gaia took her hands in her own. The god's skin was flawless, smooth, and warm against her twisted, scarred flesh. She felt small, tainted, her touch a defilement of Gaia's purity. The god held the sage's hands with gentle compassion, like they were the most precious things ever.

Her hands enfolded, there was a pulse of magic that took Alice's breath away. There was no precursor to it. If the god had centers in the way mortals did, their presence was far too subtle for her to see it.

The energy traveled from her hands through her arms, spreading out until it suffused her being. There was no fire, and there was no music, but the essence of it was not unlike the feel of Altair's jinn magic or her own. The sensation of it moving through her made her feel as though literally anything was possible. The sage closed her eyes and relaxed into the wonder of a true miracle being bestowed on her.

When she opened them again, her hands were gone. There was no blood and no pain. Her wrists simply ended where the damaged parts of her would have been. She felt fear, but it was distant, blanketed by the dizzying warmth of Gaia's power.

The god knelt and laid the ruined hands down gently on the bough of the world tree. The dragon Ajdaha kept carefully to the side, coiled loosely around the still form of Altair. As they watched, Alice's hands melted into the world tree, fading to transparency as they did so until there was nothing but smooth bark.

Gaia reached for Alice again, the god's miraculous power saturating the air around them. The charge of her magic was somewhere between perfume and electricity, overwhelming to the senses but not unpleasant. Looking into the eyes of the god, Alice slowly realized, impossibly, that Gaia was holding her hands.

She looked down and saw her hands were whole again. *No,* she realized, *it's more than that. These are not my hands. They're . . . oh, God!* Alice held her palms before her face, open mouthed, and marveled at their perfection. They were the hands of a god.

Gaia smiled serenely and let her hands come to rest in her lap. Alice looked and saw that they were her own, mottled and twisted and scarred. She looked quickly where Gaia had set the ruined things only a moment before, but there was no denying what she was seeing. Somehow, there they were, as if they'd always been. The god's magic faded around them, and the sage came back to her senses.

Alice shook her head to clear away the euphoric dreaminess and cried out, "No, you can't! This is too much!"

The god spread her flawed, mortal hands and said, "It is already done."

"Don't you need these?!"

"I can manage," said Gaia, "and I trust you will return them to me when you have completed your task."

"But why?!" said Alice. "Couldn't you just have healed mine?"

Gaia said, "I could have, but it wouldn't have been enough for what you are trying to accomplish. With these, you should be able to play whatever you like on any instrument you take up. I understand your musical training up until this point has been limited."

Alice lowered her eyes and nodded. "Negligible to nonexistent."

"Then simply say, 'thank you,'" said the god, "and promise you will do something for me with them."

"Thank you!" Alice said quickly, feeling sheepish. "This is incredible! I never would have imagined anything like this! What do you need?"

"Destroy Pazuzu."

The sage blinked, surprised a being so wonderful could make a request like that so bluntly. "Wha . . . ?"

"That ifrit has had his way for long enough," said Gaia, "and now he has tried to trespass in my home here in Elysium. I was forced to close the Door that led you here to prevent his horde from following you."

Her lips twisted in bitterness. "Many died that others might live."

Alice felt her stomach lurch with guilt. "It's my fault. If I hadn't come, it wouldn't have happened. I'm sorry."

The god shook her head. "There's nothing to forgive. You were right to come here, but those are the things that happen, and will happen again if this evil is allowed to continue."

Alice looked to Ajdaha, but the dragon looked just as much at a loss. The god said, "This must be done, but I will not act directly, you see. Were I to travel to Tartarus, myself, it would upset the balance of creation even more than it already has."

Ajdaha's eyes lit up as understanding dawned. "If you start going around smiting things, the other Baalim may be more likely to do so, as well."

Gaia nodded, her smile sad. "Whether I am justified

in doing it or not, it could lead to a great war between the Realms. Such things have happened before. Each time, so much life is lost. I cannot permit that to happen again, and so I will restrict myself to this one miracle. No one would begrudge a host providing for a guest in their own home."

Alice thought it over. "Wouldn't the other gods be on our side with this? We're already facing an entire Realm being overthrown. Isn't that enough?"

"It is," said Gaia, "but not everyone has the same sense of balance."

Dread washed over Alice. "You mean there are gods that *want* what's happening?"

"I mean," said the god, "everyone is looking after their own best interests, as so should you be."

Though she wanted to press further, Alice didn't quite dare. Gaia's tone was clear. There was nothing more to be said on the matter. Instead, she turned her attention back to the miracle of her hands.

"So, you're telling me now I can go and murder a demon king?" said Alice, experimentally wiggling her fingers. "Just like that?"

"Now," said Gaia, holding up a crooked finger, "you can avenge yourself and countless others as an agent of balance and justice."

Alice winced at the sight of her ruined hands on something so otherwise flawless. She felt self-conscious, absently rubbing her new, perfect blessings together. She looked to Ajdaha, and the dragon said, "It *is* your purview as a sage. Your kind have always been the great paladins and prophets, the messiahs and heroes of the ages."

She remained uncertain, overwhelmed at the reality of what they were saying. Since Altair had first come to her, she had understood the idea of being a sage, but only abstractly. Learning how to use her magic had been an incredible experience, but now she felt as weak and helpless as she did when she woke in the hospital.

Sensing her distress, the god said, "It's better than you think. Why don't you try them out?"

Alice opened her mouth, unsure of what she would say, but Gaia was already reaching into the surface of the giant bough of the world tree. A moment later, she drew her hand back. She was holding an oblong, wooden instrument. Large enough to be held with both hands, it had dozens of holes and a projection off the main body that seemed to be a mouthpiece with three separate chambers. Smiling, Gaia passed the instrument to the sage.

Taking it gingerly, she asked, "Is this a flute or something?"

"An ocarina," said Gaia. "Give it a try."

Alice looked at it doubtfully. "It's got like thirty little holes. I wouldn't know where to begin."

The god smiled patiently. "Have a little faith."

The sage blushed at that and smiled. She looked to Ajdaha for reassurance, and he nodded to her in affirmation, clearly interested in what was going to happen next. Feeling awkward and unsure, Alice lifted the ocarina to her lips and blew.

Immediately, the air was filled with a haunting melody. Her supple fingers danced over the little holes as if she'd been born doing it. She considered the nature of her new hands. *I know how because* Gaia *knows how.* Alice soon found herself lost in the music. Her thoughts and fears drifted away as she improvised on the melody effortlessly. Alice's magic stirred, her centers pulsing and opening in anticipation.

Eventually, she became aware of the world around her again. The dragon and the god were watching her with interest, but it was the image of Altair's still form that brought her back to reality. Reluctantly, Alice let the melody fade and looked at the ocarina in awe. "Holy shit . . ."

Ajdaha was looking at her with a mixture of wonder

and approval. Gaia had the smugly satisfied look of a parent whose child figured out they should have just listened to them in the first place. Alice rose, paced over to Altair, and knelt at his side.

"What about him?" she asked. "Can you heal him too?"

"I could, but I don't need to," the god answered. "You're capable."

The sage hesitated until Gaia began twirling her hand in a circular gesture; get on with it. Alice's stomach hitched. She looked down at Altair, her worried thoughts jumbled together. *What if it doesn't work? I don't know what I'm doing! What if I hurt him?!*

Alice looked to Gaia again, but the god only sat and watched her. Her face was impassive but not unkind. Despite her fear, the sage understood why the jinn had been left to her; fledglings needed space to learn to stand on their own.

She took a deep breath, let it out slowly, and rolled her shoulders. Alice started to take another deep breath, realized she was procrastinating, and let it out in a huff. Suddenly irritated with herself for balking, she put the ocarina to her lips and played.

Her body responded immediately to the music. Energies traveled through her centers as they dilated then reached out into the world. Alice felt the magic find Altair and envelop him. She felt her power focus at the locus of her third eye as well as at the top of her head; the crown center. Curiously, she probed for the Akashic Record. She could sense it, but she could also sense an alien force barring her from getting too close to it. *The enemy,* she thought bitterly. *Son of a bitch. It'd be nice to know what I'm doing for once . . .*

Reluctantly, she backed off and turned her attention fully on Altair. Even without access to that fount of knowledge, Alice's consciousness expanded with her senses. It was as if she became an observer outside of reality. Her mind likened it to watching an aquarium. For the fish, it was the entire world. To her, it became increasingly clear there were only so many variables, and they interacted with each other in ways that, from the right vantage point, were readily observable.

As she played, it became increasingly obvious what was wrong with Altair. From moment to moment, her understanding of his injuries developed into something comprehensible, even simple. Better still, she could see what needed to change to restore him.

In a way, it was like looking at a jigsaw puzzle, sorting out the pieces by color and type, finding the corners and edges. In time, the pieces revealed their order and all that was required was a hand to assemble them. The sage hesitated, but only for a moment, and then she began to play the melody she needed to heal the jinn.

Altair's fiery skin brightened immediately. His breathing deepened. She could feel his heartbeat strengthen. The sage played patiently, letting the magic do its work in its own time. The urge to have the jinn on his feet again was there, but, hands of a Baalim or not, she didn't truly know what she was doing. The focus on healing him properly won out, and so she played as long and as slowly as she had to.

In time, Altair opened his eyes and looked at her. He smiled and sat up when he was ready. As the jinn stretched and examined his restored body, Alice lowered the ocarina and let the magic fade away.

"That's my boy," she said, giving Altair a thumbs-up.

Altair stretched and blinked as if he'd woken up from a long sleep. "Don't make it weird."

The jinn looked about as he yawned, orienting himself. He arched an eyebrow at the sight of the world tree. His brow furrowed when he saw how high up they were. His jaw dropped when he saw Gaia.

"Holy shit!" he exclaimed. "We made it!"

Altair gazed upon the god, awed. Alice smiled at him and felt better about how she'd been managing. As old as the jinn described himself as being, despite thousands of years of experience, including having been married to a demigod and raising a demigod dragon son together, waking up to face a Baalim was enough to give anyone pause.

The jinn panned his eyes over Gaia, taking in the sight of her. His gaze came to rest on Alice's old, ruined hands on the ends of the god's wrists. He whipped his head around to see Gaia's perfect hands attached to Alice.

"What the hell?!"

"Ta da," the sage raised them up to do her best spirit fingers. Gaia did a neat little bow and curtsey. Ajdaha quietly withdrew himself from around his father to coil to the side like a snake. He rested his forelegs atop the upmost curve of his body and laid his chin down on them, watching with interest.

"Ninhursag blessed you . . ." Altair narrowed his eyes. "What's the trade?"

The god laughed. "So cynical."

Alice said, "We have to kill Pazuzu."

Altair paled, his fires dimmed, then his face became resolute. "Fair enough. Bastard has it coming."

"And he seems to be the lieutenant of our enemy," said Ajdaha. "Destroying him will make things much easier for us. Besides, we were headed that way anyway."

Altair looked a question at his son, and the dragon supplied, "Alice already promised a giant she'd kill Pazuzu in exchange for being allowed into Elysium."

The jinn frowned and rubbed his head. "Damn. How long was I out?!"

Alice chuckled and felt herself relax, relieved her magic had restored the jinn and pleased they were readily in agreement with what had to come next. From her own experience, cutting off the head of an organization, especially one that operated outside the boundaries of law, was the quickest way to resolve the whole as a threat.

There might be a few, she thought. *The* really *loyal ones that come looking for revenge. The rest are going to be making power grabs, carving out territory, cutting throats and back-stabbing rivals, and generally doing everything they can to cover their own asses. It'll be months, maybe years, before the children of Pazuzu get their shit together, if they ever do at all.*

"It'll be nice being able to fart without a dozen demons bursting through the bathroom door." She shared a smile among them. "So, where do we find him?"

The sage looked to Gaia, but the god only raised her hands and shrugged. The Baalim began to sink into the bark of the massive bough. There was nothing ostentatious about it. The god slipped down, effortlessly casual, disappearing into the world tree like she was wading into a calm pool.

"This is as far as I go," said Gaia. "You have what you need to be successful, and I have other matters to which I must turn my attention."

Alice raised a hand to protest, caught sight of its perfection, and relented, deciding to count her blessings instead. "Thank you, Gaia. I couldn't have done this without you. I'll do what you've asked, and I'll return what's yours when I'm finished."

"I know you will," said the Baalim, and she passed out of sight. Alice's heart sank. Seeing the god go was worse than the last time she'd seen her parents. She felt alone, lost, and vulnerable.

Then, her eyes caught the glint of something left where Gaia had stood. She walked up and stooped to retrieve it. It looked like a coin but weighed almost nothing in her fingers. It was covered on both sides with fine writing in a language she did not understand.

She held it up for the others. "What's this thing?"

"A token," said Altair automatically. "It's like a favor."

"For what?" She squinted at the script.

The jinn looked with her. "I don't know. This is written

in Baal."

"Let me," said Ajdaha as he took human form. He stepped up to them and reached out a hand. Suddenly, Alice clutched the coin to her chest and glared. She felt silly doing it but, at the same time, genuinely felt loathe to let others handle it. The dragon waited patiently, and the sage forced herself to relax.

She took a breath and held out the coin with an effort. "Sorry. I'm not sure what happened."

"That's normal," he said. "Gifts from the gods are precious to mortals. I'll give it right back."

Instead of trying to pluck it from her fingers, Ajdaha held out his paw and waited for her to drop the coin in his palm. It felt as though she was giving away one of her own eyeballs, but Alice opened her fingers and let it drop. The dragon pulled his paw away before she could change her mind and held up the object to study it.

Alice watched him anxiously and rubbed her palm against her hip to scratch at an itch she could never reach. Even when trafficking was her sole income, she'd never been one for drugs, at least not the hard ones. As far as she was concerned, a couple drinks and a little weed never hurt anyone. That sort of work was a lifestyle as much as a trade, but she saw what happened to her best customers and steered clear.

She forced herself to keep still, irritated at her own weakness. *Touch one magic coin, and I'm a goddamn junkie*, she thought ruefully. She felt a hand on her arm and looked to find Altair at her side. He smiled at her, warm and supportive. She blushed and blinked rapidly to hold back the tears as she took his hand. Immediately, her restlessness eased.

"It's a writ," Ajdaha said at last as he turned the coin in his hands to reread both sides. "Basically, Gaia is calling in a favor with Enki."

"Who's N-Key?" asked Alice.

The jinn whistled appreciatively and offered, "Hephaestus."

When she stared blankly, he said, "Vulcan? Ptah? Hm, Volund perhaps?"

Alice sighed, let go of him, and let her hand fall back to her side. "I went to public school, ok?"

"Show off," Ajdaha admonished his father. and looked to Alice. "The Baalim most strongly associated with the crown center. The artisan god. Gaia is requesting he craft you an Instrument."

Alice blinked. "I get a super flute?"

Ajdaha grinned. "Basically. The Baalim and sometimes the sages have been able to create Artifacts. They are items of great power."

"Excalibur and shit?!"

He nodded. "Excalibur and shit. For the sages, it is always a musical instrument designed specifically to be able to play the eighth note."

Alice cocked her head and reached back in her memory to middle school. She counted on her fingers. "Every good boy does fine. F-A-C-E. I don't remember there being an eighth note. Only seven."

Altair shrugged. "Eight gods, eight Realms, eight centers, eight notes."

Ajdaha handed back the writ and said, "A musical instrument lets a sage unlock their magic. An Instrument enhances it. Even regular humans, the ones with *no* aptitude for magic at all, could access their soul centers with one. When it comes to this sort of thing, Artifacts, short of the Eternal, Enki has no rival."

Alice snatched it back and cupped the coin greedily against her chest. Then, she remembered herself and blushed. Reluctantly, she slipped it into a pocket. She was still wearing the tight-fitting bodysuit she'd been given when they left Shambhala, now filthy with travel, and it took some doing.

It was an act of will to let the writ drop into her pocket so it no longer touched her skin. The moment her hand was free, she automatically patted her leg so she could feel it. She deliberately pulled her hand away, just to be certain she could, then sniffed at her fingers.

She wrinkled her nose and flicked out her tongue as she made a sour face. "Do we have time to stop first? I need a fucking shower!"

Chapter 22:

THE SAGE SAT IN her room alone. Following the audience with Gaia, they had gone to Eik-Himinn. It was one of the countless communities among the branches of the world tree. Altair took the form of an elf, a form of nephilim common enough that its variations were essentially their own species. He'd rented a suite for them at the inn, The *Alfdanz*. Carefully muted, Alice and Ajdaha stole their way in after he was settled.

A shower, a hot meal, and sleep in a soft bed left her feeling human again. She wore only a loosely tied robe as she sat on a cushion and meditated as Altair had taught her. She held the ocarina in her godly hands, contemplative.

I have my full strength, she realized, *but not my full power.* Apart from the songs Altair and Ajdaha had taught her, every act of magic Alice had done, she'd played by ear. It worked, but it was inconsistent and slow.

We've been lucky so far, she thought, *but it will run out. I need to be faster, or, sooner or later, I'm dead.* The sage breathed and sat and turned the ocarina in her hands until an answer came to her.

The Akashic Records! Her eyes lit up at the prospect of it. *If the Records really contain everything everyone, every human, has ever known, including the sages, then every spell I could want is in there, I bet.*

Alice frowned. She'd contacted the Records twice now, and, each time, she'd been blocked. *That last time, though, I just poked at it a bit. I didn't really push the issue. I wonder . . .*

Uneasy, the sage licked her lips and lifted the ocarina. Using her magic risked drawing attention, and she had no way of knowing if Pazuzu or anything like the demon had influence in Gaia's Place. Images of being hurt, of running for her life, of seeing people die passed through her mind; Ajdaha crushed, Altair burnt by lightning, the giant Otos falling, dying beneath a swarm of demons.

Thoughts of Timothy floated up to her mind's eye. *No!* Alice's shoulders bunched, and she clamped down on the memories, pushing them down deep. She swallowed at her shame, but it kept rising up to distract her.

Alice lowered the ocarina back to her lap. Her hands shook. She wiped at her eyes, closed them, and breathed. She waited for herself to settle, let the images pass in their own time. Soon enough, she was thinking again, not just reacting.

I've already used my magic to heal Altair, she reminded herself. *If something's coming, it's probably already on its way. I need to know what I'm doing! There're no other sages to teach me, and there's no time to learn on my own.*

The sage lifted the ocarina to her mouth and muttered, "Fuck it."

She began to play, focused on her crown center. The dragon and the jinn were nearby in the suite. They were recuperating as well in their own rooms, but she knew they would be ready if something happened. She almost stopped as she considered whether she should let them know what she was doing before she went any farther.

I don't need permission, she told herself. *There's no one in*

the universe who can help me *with this but* me. *I don't need
the whole Record. I don't even need everything about the sages.
I just want to know* my *own life. Lives, I guess. My own memories. I'm the only one that knows what's going on, but even* I
don't know unless I can get inside my own head. I have *to do
this!*

Alice experimented with the melody, felt out what it was
she was looking for through intuition. Like healing Altair,
the pieces she needed slowly became clearer the longer she
played. The ocarina sang softly in her hands. Notes became
phrases. The phrases became sections.

Her consciousness reached out until she could sense the
presence of the Records. As she did, she could feel the resistance of the enemy, a layer of warding magic that pushed
her away from her goal. She pushed back, determined, slowly building toward the song she needed to get through; the
movement of the seventh life of the eighth sage within the
greater mellifluence of the Akashic Records.

As she played, at another level of awareness, Alice could
sense the others stir elsewhere in the suite; another factor
moving to work against her. She played on, determined to
know her own self. Then, all at once, the music was complete.

Reality dropped away, and her consciousness rose from
her body. She found her mind in a boundless void, a speck
of thought in a universe of nothingness. Then, there was a
feeling of rushing, her sense of self propelled across some immeasurable expanse until she reached some impossibly distant place. After a span beyond any sense of linear time, she
could see the Akashic Records appear before her. They shone
like a star; immense yet without any sense of a true boundary
to define them.

Distantly, she could sense the presence of other stars like
this. Intuition told her those were the Records of the other
sentient races of creation; the jinn, the ifrit, the Baalim, and
perhaps others more distant still. She ignored them as she

willed her mind toward the totality of knowledge of her entire species.

The star grew wider still until it was all she could see. Its immensity shut out all else. Alice continued on, feeling for a sense of herself within it. Faced with the Records, it seemed such an insignificant thing, the memories of a single being among so many.

Yet, she sought, and there it was. To Alice, within that brilliance, the little portion that reflected the total content of her lives was the brightest point of all. Joyously, the sage headed for that singularity. She entered the Record, and her reality, her experience of having a distinct self, faded into that flawless, white brilliance.

The air had the smell of winter. The sun was setting behind thick clouds, the ash pale light turning coal gray. Snow crunched under bare footsteps, the only crisp sound. All else was shrouded, muted beneath a clean blanket of snow. The empty world about the man looked like a pure vessel, ready to be filled with life. It didn't look like the grave of a dead city.

Gregor strummed his lyre as he walked. His fingers wove a song of protection and muting about himself. The long path of his seventh lifetime had led to this, what he expected to be his last day, at least in this body. His old bones ached with every step. The weight of years became so great, even *his* magic struggled to carry the burden. His robes, gray with long years as he was, floated gently around his thin body.

The sage's path had led him to the radioactive wastelands around the ruins of Chernobyl. The Door he sought was beneath the plant itself, beneath the center of that fount of poison and death. For all his power, Gregor could feel the radiation all about him, waiting. None but the most powerful beings on earth could stay there long, and those he could count on one hand.

Most of the other sages were gone. Including himself,

there were only two left for sure. Kwame, the first sage, of
the root center, kept in regular contact with him. Neither of
them had heard from Mateo in a long time. Neither of them
expected to hear from him again.

The enemy had taken the rest. Gregor feared for them.
They couldn't be dead, or else they would have been reborn.
He knew their fate was something far worse than mere death.
He'd come for them, come to save whom he could and re-
lease whom he couldn't. He'd come to put a stop to their en-
emy and his plan.

Gregor passed through the halls of the ruined nucle-
ar power plant. He paused; something was wrong. Despite
the empty, old building's hard floors and walls, the notes of
his melody didn't echo. The sounds of his lyre simply disappeared once they'd gone away from him. Somehow, he felt
encapsulated, like the world didn't exist beyond what was immediately around him.

The sage turned a slow circle, but there was nothing to
see but the drifting dust in his wake as it settled back onto
chipped paint and old concrete. Within himself, he had a
strange sense he knew why he was there and what he had
come for, but, when he tried, he couldn't think of it. It was
as if there was a curtain that separated his actions from his
memory.

Deep within Gregor's mind, Alice was frustrated. It was
a terrible feeling, relegated to being an outside observer to
what she knew to be one of her own lives. She could feel the
deeper memories, but they were indistinct, like they were se-
questered behind some translucent barrier; just out of sight,
just out of reach. She was angry, but she was also afraid. She'd
grown so much and come so far. What could be stopping her
now she was here, flowing through the light of her own Record?

Hardly aware they'd been walking, Gregor and Alice
reached the end of the hall. The sage hesitated at the top of

a rough staircase no man had dug into the earth beneath the building. They were unsure whether it was safe to keep going, if there was any chance of survival. She and Gregor looked through the same eyes back the way they had come. The dark tunnels of the dead building led to blocks of abandoned houses, corpses of trees, rusted cars. The bones of the city stared back at them, impassive. Nothing moved out there, save for the stirring currents of a radioactive breeze.

Gregor shook his head to clear the wave of disorientation. For a short time, it had felt like his consciousness was being shared. His fingers faltered on the strings of his lyre, but his magic held. Returning to the melody, his only lifeline, the sage took the first step down into the depths.

The bottom of the stairs hardly resembled his Realm at all. The landing opened on a crude cavern, an ugly cross between a basement and a lair of beasts. As he stepped into their den, creatures of the enemy sat all about him, engaged in all manner of foul acts. They came in all kinds, but all were beings of horror and filth. Each of them was descended from ifrit, the fortitude of their heritage protecting them from their toxic nest.

No, he thought. *Not of the enemy, but of his lieutenant, the ancient Pazuzu.*

The monsters fought and fed and fornicated while they waited for their next command. Heaps of bones were scattered in puddles of dark, thick fluid; someone had been feeding them there for a while. There were men and women who moaned weakly, praying the radiation would kill them before something worse could happen, but the creatures there defiled the world about them for the sake of pain itself. The children of Pazuzu felt better when others suffered more than they did.

To Gregor, the old ifrit's spawn were a pitiable lot, though he had no mercy for any of them. He would destroy any of them, all of them, without hesitation, should he be challenged. Their beginnings and upbringings were living nightmares, but the sage knew there was always a choice in how a life was led. When one of the children chose to be the cause of pain, on earth's Realm, Gregor chose to be the effect.

For now, he ignored them. None of the children could perceive him through his magic. They were only as much a threat to him as he wanted them to be.

Gregor knew the monsters and their atrocities in all their horror were a distraction, meant to divert him from his real goal. The sage let his senses take the measure of them. Selecting the strongest among the devils, he changed his tune.

The gorgon responded immediately. It was massive, even for its kind. Its lower half was the body of a snake, large enough to swallow a man whole. From the waist up, it was strangely beautiful, quite feminine and comely from a distance. Up close, the fine scales of its skin shone, betraying the semblance of humanity.

The daughter of Pazuzu kept her eyes closed as she turned to face the sage, lest she turn her siblings to stone. The mass of snakes that were her hair writhed and twisted, guiding her with hissing whispers into her ears. Black eyes looked in all directions while forked tongues tasted the air. Viperous heat pits felt the press of bodies all around as the gorgon slithered to his side.

The center at Gregor's heart opened in response to his music and fed its influence into his magic. He felt it as the monster's heart became his, her love for him exceeding even her bond with Pazuzu. The spinning vortex of his third eye pulsed, and his melody muted both of them, the rest of the children forgetting the gorgon had ever been there. The sage accessed his crown and throat centers and spoke directly to the monster's mind.

What is your name, child?

I am Jana, sage Gregor, the gorgon answered him in her thoughts. *What would you have of me?*

You are the greatest of the children here.

That is true, the gorgon agreed.

Do you know the secret of your master's Door?

The gorgon hissed within his thoughts, *Pazuzu is my master. I am a retainer to the lord of this Place . . .*

Gregor flinched and closed his eyes as a wave of nausea washed over him. Jana spoke the name of the enemy, but he could not hear it. Within his mind, Alice strained, replaying the memory again.

. . . this Place . . . this Place . . .

The sage doubled over, the ache in his gut becoming real pain. Alice could feel her hold on these memories of another life slip. The influence of the wards on the Records pried at her magic. Though it galled her to be denied, she let it go and focused on seeing what she could. She could feel the power of the enemy receding as she relented, hateful but unable to bar her completely.

Gregor straightened, the discomfort gone as if it never was. He realized his hand had fallen from the strings of his lyre, and he resumed his song. He looked about for the attack he was sure was coming, but the gorgon only stood at his side, her face and serpents serene. The children of Pazuzu fed and rutted as if nothing had happened, rending their prey as they wept and begged for death.

I am not interested in the details of your brokerage, child. What do you know of the Door?

Of course, sage, thought the gorgon. *I know many secrets. Would you like me to open it for you? I can take you there, if that is your wish.*

That would please me, Jana, thought the sage, *but I have a small task for you first.*

Anything, sage.

Gregor expanded the notes of his heart center and let them swell with his music until the room was filled with it. He let his muting fade out of the song, and the children of

Pazuzu and all the humans looked to the sage, their eyes filled with love. He met their gazes and was ashamed. The idea of what he was doing was revolting to him, but the people had suffered enough, and he did not know if he would be able to return to keep the monsters from roaming once his work was done. The sage consoled himself that their time of enthrallment to him would be as brief as possible.

Feeling as much a monster as Jana, Gregor loosed a pulse of magic. All eyes turned from him to the gorgon. Jana became visible to them, and they regarded her with faces of passive contentment. They were like toddlers passing into sleep, their stomachs filled with milk, their ears with lullabies.

Then, the gorgon opened her eyes, and the lot of them, man, woman, and monster, became stone. The humans had no time to scream; their bodies simply transitioned. Contented faces showed tranquility and peace come at last. The weakest of Pazuzu's children were much the same, satisfied with their deaths like a belly full of meat and a bed of bones.

The strongest of them resisted, but not long. Some threw their hands over their eyes as they tried to shield themselves from what was already done. Others turned away and tried to run even as their bodies hardened and died. Mouths and snouts and beaks opened to scream in fear and rage, realizing at the last the betrayal within their own minds. Their shrieks and bellows rattled like pebbles in their stony throats, and then there was only the music of the lyre to fill the air.

Disgusted and full of shame, Gregor plucked his strings, and the gorgon closed her eyes. *It ends today,* he thought, sick to his soul, *or all is lost. At any price, this ends.*

"Take me to the Door," said Gregor, unable to keep his voice from trembling. Tears rolled down his cheeks.

"As you wish," said Jana.

The gorgon slithered through the murk, the rough pit lit by patches of faintly glowing fungus. She clicked her nails and drug the pads of her fingers against her siblings. She let her touches linger as they passed. For all their evil, Pazuzu's children were a family in their own way. Gregor's shoulders slumped as her kind of sadness passed through his mind. For all her outer, enforced calm, Jana felt loss, and she suffered.

They came to another portal, little more than a hole in the ground. The gorgon slipped her coils in first, then turned to offer her hands to the sage. He ignored her and simply stepped out into the open air as his music made a path for him. He drifted down until his feet touched the cold, bare earth.

The gorgon drew a pattern in the air around them and on the stone lip of the depression. Her magic was ifrit at its root, lines of black smoke that trailed from her fingertips and stayed where she left them. Gregor watched until Jana inscribed the sixty-fourth vertex and nodded in satisfaction.

"Open it," he said.

"Of course," said Jana.

The gorgon poured more of herself into the magic. Even with her strength, the trick of it was nearly beyond her. Had she been of her own mind, she would have stopped short for fear of exhausting herself completely. The love she felt for the sage made the sacrifice trivial.

Gregor pushed aside his guilt and waited. At last, the gorgon collapsed. She caught herself with thin arms as the ground below them changed. Her gasps rattling in her throat, Jana's serpents looked up to him, her face that of pride and adoration as she wiped at the black ichor that bubbled to her lips. The sage shifted his shoulders to resettle the weight of his lyre and played on.

The ground below them flared brilliantly as it became a pool of white light. The monster fell through the opened Door. Jana screamed as the magic of the enemy tore her apart. Gregor suspected as much. No one should have been expected to open the Door but the enemy, and he had taken steps to ensure this was so.

With Pazuzu in his employ, it was a given at least one of his spawn would have the acumen to learn the way of it. The great ifrit would never miss even the smallest chance at seizing the prize that lay beyond the Door's light. Gregor gave thanks in silence for the sacrifice of Jana, the spare key to the lock on the end of days, and passed through the Door.

Reality twisted around the sage, and Alice wondered if it would settle out again. She could sense where it was in Gregor's memories he reached the other side of the Door, but what lay beyond was obscured. She considered the vague forms around her, the presence of the enemy's wards again pushing her consciousness one way and then another. This time, it felt less like she was being blocked from something. Instead, it felt like she was being led past something she wasn't meant to see.

Alice considered struggling against it but didn't dare. It had been difficult getting as far along in these memories of her past life as she had. She had no way of knowing if she would be able to return if the enemy's wards were able to expel her now. Resentfully, the sage allowed herself to be led forward until the memories became clear again.

Gregor stood at the elbow of the enemy. The sage watched as he worked within the Place he had made. It was a simple space, fields of energy demarcating a cube. Beyond its walls, a starlit void extended out to infinity in every direction.

At the center of the Place was another Door. *No,* thought Gregor, *a Way.* The sage knew it was the only Way in all of creation that truly mattered to the Eternal god. He knew it was the gateway to the most important secret there was. The enemy had striven for lifetimes to keep it hidden, but Gregor had learned the mystery as well. He'd spent lifetimes of his own on it, suspecting but never substantiating before these last years of his seventh life what it was the enemy truly sought.

The sage knew what it was the enemy was doing. He knew it would mean the destruction of all that was if he was allowed to succeed, but, try as he might, Gregor could not remember what it was he'd learned about all of this. He couldn't put a finger on why it was he'd worked as he had, why he'd sacrificed so much to prevent it. Deep within him, Alice shouted in anger. She hurled herself against the barriers to her own mind, only to be thrown away from her birthright.

Beyond the enemy, the pattern to the ultimate Way was incomplete. Gregor knew as well as the other did there were five hundred and twelve vertices. He was relieved to see their position and even the order of their assembly was still a mystery to them both. The greatest lock in creation had yet to be picked.

Gregor readied his magic. He would destroy the enemy, destroy them both, as he brought this Place crashing down around them. He knew the enemy would die today, but even that wouldn't be enough to stop him.

The sage knew the true end of all these machinations would come in his next life. His thoughts turned to Altair. Gregor's heart ached for their love of centuries, kept apart now to protect him. He knew his rebirth would be strange, keeping himself from his own power to remain hidden until the time was right. He accepted it, another of countless sacrifices made to protect his Realm. If Kwame failed, he would be the only sage left.

He had faith their love would guide the jinn. Altair would find him and lead him to what needed to be done. He said a silent prayer to the Eternal god. *Please. Forgive me for what I have done and for what I will do again. Watch over Altair. Guide him. Love him as I have loved him. Amen.* Then, the sage prepared to die.

Before he could begin the song that would destroy them

both, the enemy turned toward Gregor and smiled. Something was wrong. There was that dizzy, nauseous feeling again, and that sense his consciousness was being occupied by two minds.

Gregor knew this wasn't how it had happened, but that it was happening anyway. The sage stumbled as a wave of vertigo washed over him. He knew the face of the enemy, he'd seen it so many times before, but now it slipped away from his eyes and memory, just out of view. There was only a translucent blur before him that smirked disdainfully.

"Hello, Alice," said the figure, and it reached for her.

Chapter 23:

ALICE RECOILED FROM THE figure. As she fell back, she
had a strange sense of lifting up and out of her own body.
Too late, she realized she'd moved outside of the memories
of her predecessor. She could feel the wards of the enemy
press against her consciousness again. They pushed her ever
farther away from the echoes of Gregor's mind. She tried to
hold onto it, that sense of attunement with another person
who was at the same time herself, but then her control over
her Record slipped away entirely.

The sage found herself flat on her back. She was looking
at the back of the head of her seventh life. The figure's fingers
closed on the memory of Gregor and threw him aside with
a snarl. The old man pulled apart as he flew through the air,
tattering like his robe until he lost cohesion and disappeared.
Alice gaped as the being before her ceased to approximate
the enemy.

The figure's substance melted and reformed, denying her
so much as a glimpse of her enemy's true face. In moments,
her memory of the enemy was replaced by what looked something like a large teddy bear. It was covered in dark fur and

would have been downright *cuddly* if not for its long claws and sharp teeth.

The teddy stretched and drew itself to its full height. Alice was head and shoulders taller, but the creature was stocky, its heavy musculature apparent even beneath its thick pelt. It snarled as it lumbered toward her.

Alice scooted away from the creature on her backside, propelling herself with her palms and heels. She fetched up against the outer wall of force of the Place, cool and smooth like glass, yet leaving her skin tingling like a static charge. She pushed herself upright like that, desperate to make space between them. She would have kept going up until she hit the ceiling if she'd been able.

"These are just memories!" she shouted at it. "This isn't real!"

"No, it isn't," agreed the creature, "but I am. Don't worry, Alice. It will be over soon."

The sage slid sideways along the wall. Her fear grew as she began to understand. The monster stayed just out of arm's reach as it paced along with her awkward, sliding gait. She knew, if she kept going, all she would do was put herself in a corner, but all she could think to do was get away. It was nightmarish, finding something alive with her there, laying in wait within her own memories.

"What the hell are you?!" she cried. She prayed it answered. If she could get it talking, she could buy herself some time.

The monster grinned but did not answer. Its fangs gleamed in the starlight. It took a step closer and reached for her, slowly and gently.

"You were warned, Alice," it said at last. Its voice was low and deep. "Twice, you tried to enter the Records, and, twice, you were repelled. All you had to do was stay away, but I'm glad you were so persistent. The master has kept me here for a long time, in case you found your way. Adam keeps me hungry, but there was no need for it. I am happy to have the chance to taste a sage."

Alice's eyes went wide. *Adam!* The moment she heard it, Alice knew it at once as the name of her true enemy, the would-be destroyer of worlds. She still could not remember what Adam hoped to accomplish by such a thing, but he was this creature's master, and Pazuzu's also.

With that recognition came clarity. Alice gasped as a critical detail came to the glimpses she'd gotten of Gregor's memories. It had slipped away from her before, but now she knew Adam's face. *A name and a face,* she thought. *Not much, but it's something, if I live.*

Alice winced as her shoulder crashed against the next wall of the Place. She cringed as the creature rested its claws on her shoulder, but the thing had her boxed into the corner. There was nowhere left to go.

The monster stepped in closer still until she could feel its hot breath on her neck. It sniffed at her, inhaled the scent of her with pleasure, exactly the way she lingered on the smell of freshly baked bread. It hooked the claws of its other paw around her waist and drew her into a terrible caricature of an embrace.

The sage twisted and let herself drop straight down just as she felt the creature's soft fur against her belly. Its claws gouged her shoulder and side as she fell, but she didn't care. She'd do anything to get away from it.

Unfairly quick, the monster maneuvered with her. Quick as a snake, it reestablished its grip, pushed her down on her back, and wrapped its legs around her waist. Its prominent belly pressed down on her chest, and she tried to hold her breath as the creature leaned in. She strained under the pressure, its weight seeking to push the air from her.

The monster looked into her eyes as they struggled. They were big and brown, like a dog's. She batted at it, twined her fingers in its fur, tried to get leverage to roll it off her; anything so she could get clear and breathe.

Fingers like iron wrapped around her wrists. Sharp claws poked and pierced her skin. The sage was fighting for her life, but the monster simply let its weight do the work. Alice's shoulders and biceps were already burning from the strain of bearing its bulk.

The creature soon won out. It leaned farther and farther forward until it pressed her arms down to either side of her head. Its hips were locked against hers, preventing her from twisting out from under it. The field of force that was the floor of the Place felt incongruously pleasant, cool, and tingly against her skin.

This isn't real! She screamed within her mind, delirious with fear. *This isn't real! I'm not Gregor! I was never here! This isn't the enemy's Place! This is just a memory! I'm in some tree house hotel room, right? There're elves for staff, and my best friend's a genie! I think we had a kid together! A dragon? Fuck! What's going on?!*

The monster lay down on top of her, its face right up against her own. Alice wanted to close her eyes, to shut it out, to deny the reality of the thing, but she couldn't bear to do it. If she did, she knew she'd have surrendered entirely, and Alice didn't want to die.

The cool, tingling sensation of the floor gave way to nothing as the fields of force of the enemy's Place faded away. The two of them hung suspended among the stars, the Records and her memories gone entirely. Despite the void all about them, Alice could somehow still feel her back pressed against the floor, though there was nothing down there for her to push against. It was as if the laws of physics only agreed with the creature killing her. She couldn't even wiggle; the monster's belly crushed up against her ribs.

She kicked her legs uselessly while the creature waited for her to breathe. Alice's lungs burned, and she could feel herself growing faint. It was like drowning. The temptation mounted with every oxygen-starved heartbeat to part her lips and let her death in for want of just a little air to follow along with it. The furry beast licked at her lips in anticipation; planted a sloppy, little kiss on the end of her nose. She shook her head, and it nuzzled her like a cat, patient as a saint.

Finally, she couldn't take it anymore. She needed a breath, or she was going to pass out. Alice opened her mouth, and the air rushed out of her. The monster clamped down tighter, using its bulk to work her like a bellows, emptying her. Then, its mouth locked down on hers. Their teeth clicked together painfully. Its fangs pierced her lips and stabbed at her gums as it pressed its head down.

Blood welled up in her torn mouth and dribbled back into her throat until Alice thought she was going to choke on it. The monster stuck out its long tongue, the supple tip tickling at the roof of her mouth as it slithered by on the way back to her soft palate. She tried to shake her head loose, but the creature only leaned in deeper and clamped down harder. She was fighting for her life, and she knew it, but its teeth and its weight held her fast while it probed for her uvula.

She felt it as the monster's tongue plugged up her throat. Her ribs ached under its belly. She could see the stars fading away through its velvety soft fur and understood in stark clarity she was smothering. She felt herself convulse and lost control of her body at the last as her cells screamed for air. The little points of light disappeared, one by one, at the edges of her sight. The darkness worked toward the center of her vision until all that was left were a sparkling handful nestled among a dark shock of fleecy softness.

Then, even that was gone. Alice felt herself sink. She couldn't tell if the two of them were physically moving or if it were only within her own mind. Her vision faded, and all she could feel was the monster on top of her, tucked in like a warm, snuggly blanket. She could feel its tongue spread her jaws until they ached.

There was the scent of her childhood's favorite stuffed animal. Her mind was fading like a candle under a glass, but she knew it by instinct. It was the smell that went with a toy dog in a pair of red overalls; Snoopy. She was so small then, it was as big as she was. Snoopy smelled like cotton and faintly of her own sweat. Alice relaxed as she sank down into sleep with her toy doggy cuddled up against her. She wasn't afraid anymore. Then, she wasn't anything.

Chapter 24:

HANDS WERE SHAKING HER shoulders. She could hear voices, but they were muffled like she was under water. She tried to open her eyes, but it was so bright. She winced and kept them shut. Sleep was better.

She felt fingers at her neck, pressing, probing, searching for something. Alice tried to shrug them away, but she was too tired to move. It didn't make sense to make a fuss over such things when she was so tired. *Maybe if I just keep laying still, they'll give up and go away and let me rest.*

The hands weren't on her shoulders anymore. They were on her chest, pressing down hard and fast. Another pair of hands pinched her nose closed and lifted her chin. She felt a mouth clamp down over hers. Distantly, she was surprised she didn't taste blood. Her lips didn't hurt anymore.

The mouth blew hot air down her throat, forcing oxygen into her body. Nothing happened at first, but then it brought her another breath, then another. Slowly, Alice could feel her mind rising toward consciousness. She didn't want to wake up. She was so tired. She hadn't slept well; maybe had a nightmare.

The hands kept on pressing, pumping, pinching. The mouth kept lifting away and clamping down again, filling her full of someone else's breaths. She kept going up, her body heavy and still. It was like letting the air in her lungs float her back to the surface of a pool after a deep dive. It was strange, being made buoyant with someone else's air. It was gross, a little like unexpectedly being made to chew someone else's gum, but they wouldn't just let her spit it out so she could sink.

Alice opened her eyes and blinked slowly, unevenly up at the lights of her room. A man made of fire was cradling her head. Another man, a golden one, was pushing on her chest. She tried to lift her arms to shove the golden man away, but they were too heavy. She tried to tell them to leave her alone, but her tongue was too thick, her throat too tight.

"Her eyes!" The fiery man leaned his face over hers. "Look! There's something wrong with her eyes!"

The golden man leaned in beside him. His rapid breathing washed over her face. It smelled like flowers and cinnamon. His eyes widened. "There's something in her! Hold on!"

The fiery man backed out of the way, and the other man turned into a long dragon. It reminded her a little of those Chinese parade dragons, and she smiled. She could use a beer, and fair food was the best.

The dragon leaned in, his muzzle a hair's breadth from her mouth. He pursed his lips and inhaled. There was space between them, but it felt like he was sucking at her through a straw. For a moment, she thought he was trying to pull the air out of her entirely.

It made Alice remember a little of her bad dreams. She remembered soft fur and puppy dog eyes. *Oh, God! I'm still asleep. Snoopy's still here!* Then she felt something move in her chest. The dragon was trying to get something else out of her. She felt sharp points inside her body that prickled and scraped deep in her windpipe.

She started to cough. There was something thick and hairy in her throat, and it was scrabbling and straining fiercely to stay there. The dragon kept pulling with its breath, and she kept hacking and convulsing. Her body was racking so hard as it strained and spasmed, it felt like her stomach muscles were tearing, but together, they were working the fuzzy thing free.

It was at the top of her throat when she felt long claws reaching out of her mouth. They bent over her lips and tapped at her cheeks. She felt the talons start to grip at the soft flesh of her lips, threatening to tear them open as they'd been in her dreams, but then the fiery man leaned in again and grabbed at them.

The man of fire pulled. *Altair!* Alice looked down her nose and saw he had his fists wrapped around a pair of furry wrists. The dragon became a gleaming, golden man again and took one of them in both hands. *Ajdaha!* Altair shifted his grip so that he held the other wrist like a baseball bat.

Altair and Ajdaha heaved, straining to pull the fuzzy thing out of her. Alice shuddered and spasmed as she felt its body slide, inch by inch, out of her mouth. The creature's form grew as it passed her lips.

Her jaw strained until it felt like it would crack in two as the arms gave way to a head and shoulders. She clenched her throat again and again around the wet, fuzzy softness of it, her body trying to sick out a scream past its fluffy bulk. Finally, she felt its heavy stomach pull out of her mouth with a soft popping sound, and then the thing was sliding faster.

Her teeth rattled as sharp nails and kicking feet protested against the forcible eviction. Alice gasped as her friends pulled the monster free of her. The air was cool and good as it slipped down her throat. It was the greatest feeling of her life, drawing breath into her lungs, filling them again and again. She felt her heart beating; hadn't realized it had stopped. The shock of it kept sending adrenaline into her system, forcing her to stay conscious. She sat up, arms trembling, blinking and shaking her head to clear it.

The jinn and the demigod, a dragon again, had the creepy, cute monster on the ground. They stomped on it repeatedly and trampled its body until their heels tore through its skin. The thing growled and snapped all the while, trying to hurt them as much as get itself away. The thing's body was healing nearly as quickly as they were breaking it, but the two of them didn't let up.

Ajdaha flicked his tail and knocked something off the table by her bed. That something landed in her lap. Alice looked down and picked it up. It was her ocarina.

"Burn it up, Alice," shouted Altair. "Kill it!"

The sage raised the instrument to her lips but stopped. Though that thing was no longer in her, she felt herself growing weaker by the moment. She slipped back to the ground despite herself and fell on her side as her strength failed her. The ocarina tumbled away from weak fingers.

The dragon shouted something to the jinn and slipped clear of the struggle. Ajdaha whipped his head around and drew a deep breath. His mouth opened wide, like a snake readying to devour a meal. Light flickered at the back of his throat, as if he was lit by a fire from within. Everything seemed to pause at once, the moment stretching out, and then he was breathing a green, eldritch fire onto the jinn and the monster.

Altair crouched behind the creature while Ajdaha kept up his assault. He held it in a full nelson as it struggled, used it to shield himself as its body burned away in thick clumps of black ash. The monster tried to get its legs under its bulk, tried to leverage its center of gravity under the jinn's so, it could flip him and be free.

It was too late. It heaved against the jinn twice, and then the monster was too weak to go on. By then, half its body had burned away. The thing didn't seem to have bones or muscles or organs. Beneath the crumbled, blackened patches of hair burnt to ash, and a dark skin melted like rubber. The creature's insides looked to be made entirely of a uniform, tarry substance that bubbled and dripped thickly onto the hardwood floor.

Finally, enough of the creature was gone that Altair let go and jumped away. Jinn were made from fire, but even he seemed to have limits of how much dragon's breath he could take. Ajdaha kept on burning, belching out viridescent flames until there was nothing left of the monster but a smoking smudge burnt into the ruined floorboards.

The jinn looked about the room as his son did his work. Half of it was a wreckage of charred lumber. Thick smoke filled the space, curled under doorways and through windowsills.

"We need to get out of here," Altair said flatly. The jinn's skin was flecked with burnt patches where no light shone through. He'd been hurt by his son's fire, but he paid it no mind, the scabrous plaques already healing.

Ajdaha gave no reply but looked to Alice concernedly. Taking human form, he scooped up the ocarina and deposited it in a pocket in his golden robes. Slipping his arms under her shoulders and knees, the demigod bore her weight easily.

"I can get us back to Shambhala," said Ajdaha.

"Do you really think it's safe there?"

"No," the dragon admitted, "but it's the fastest way. We'll have access to all the maps and information we'll need to take a Way to Tartarus."

Altair cocked his head. "We're going after Pazuzu? Now?! Wouldn't it make more sense to get the Instrument first? It seems like we're passing up on an advantage."

"That ifrit has been on us at every turn," said Ajdaha. "He has too many resources for us to go on like this. Pazuzu will just keep throwing his pawns at us until he is successful. If we're going to survive, we need to put a stop to him."

"What about her?" asked Altair. Alice listened vaguely, her eyes slipping closed when all she meant to do was blink. Soon, she'd be asleep again. She prayed there'd be no dreams.

"That dab tsog hurt her." Ajdaha inclined his head toward the lumps of black ash on the floor. "Her mind more than anything else. For now, she's helpless."

"So, you want to go after Pazuzu while Alice is helpless?" Altair was incredulous. "What do you expect to do when we get there and it's just us?! The two of us can't stop Pazuzu! We *can't* do it without her!"

The golden skinned man smiled. "Don't worry about it. She'll be just fine. All she needs is time."

Altair looked uncertain. "I don't know. Maybe we should forget about Pazuzu *and* the Instrument for now. We should head back to Elysium. Maybe Gaia will help her again."

Ajdaha shook his head. "She already told us. Whatever we're working against, more miracles are only going to escalate it."

"What then?!" The jinn looked down on the sage, forlorn. All he wanted was for her not to hurt. Altair wanted Alice whole, and every moment he saw her like that was agonizing.

"Father," said Ajdaha, "I know how you feel about her. She's *my* mother, isn't she? I need you to trust me."

He smiled warmly when his father looked up to meet his eye and told him, "I know about being part god. Even if going after another miracle was the right answer, she won't need it. All we'd be doing is stirring up the Baalim instead of seeing after ourselves."

The jinn gave pause at that. He prayed sometimes. Most sentient creatures did, at least at some time in their life. The difference was, when he did it, unlike the greater part of humanity, he *knew* for a fact that something, some*things*, might hear him, and that he might not like their answer.

The ways of the gods were their own and sometimes cruel. Most times, it was better to be weighed down by one's own problems than pay the price of a miracle. A long silence passed; the words of an unspoken prayer dared the jinn to breathe life into them.

"What do you mean, part god?!" Altair finally said. "She hasn't been a demigod since her first life. She's only human and ... oh ..."

The jinn gave pause as he considered the sage's perfect hands. Ajdaha smiled knowingly as he paced to the nearest window. Propping it open, he turned and held his hands out for Alice.

"Pass her to me," he said.

Altair obliged him, the matter settled. He lifted Alice gently and carried her to the window. The jinn helped her onto his son's back after he stepped over the sill. Ajdaha became a dragon again. Alice clung to him unconsciously.

"We used that incantation you gave me to get back to Sayon from earth," cautioned Altair. "Unless you have another of those things, the children surely have the sense of it from that last time. If we use it again, they'll be on us before we can arrive. Are we going to find a Way?"

The dragon shook his head and waited while his father disappeared into their suite. Altair re-emerged quickly with their supplies. All they needed was handily contained within Alice's backpack. The jinn took the form of a winged centaur. He stamped his hooves and flapped feathered wings restlessly as he slung it over his shoulders.

"I have a few different means, Father" said the dragon patiently. "This *is* what I do for a living."

"I'm sorry." Altair lowered his eyes, "It's just that ..."

"Yes, I'm worried about her, too." Ajdaha followed his father's thoughts. "Even *knowing* she will be alright, it's hard seeing her like this."

Alice stirred a little. She was aware she was being talked

about but couldn't understand what was being said. She had the sense they were going somewhere. She soon lost interest and settled again. As long as she could breathe, anywhere would be fine with her.

Chapter 25:

EPHIALTES REGARDED THE THREE of them as the travelers waited patiently in the palm of his hand. The giant, golden doors stood strong, though not as they once were. They bore deep scars of countless claws and fists. They were noticeably warped, pulled toward Elysium as if they had been yanked shut by an immense power. Ajdaha spoke with the giant as Altair looked on worriedly.

"The Door is to remain closed," said the giant. "There is no telling what may remain of the nephilim horde beyond. I await the word of Ninhursag before I will open it again."

Ajdaha nodded. "I can't say I blame either of you for that. What Door should I take, then, to return to the borderlands?"

Ephialtes frowned. "All Doors to Elysium are closed for now. That is the will of Ninhursag, for already the children of Pazuzu have found their way into her dominion."

The three of them eyed each other, but the giant appeared confident. He told them, "The spawn of that demon *will* be rooted out and examples made of them. Then, the Doors will be opened again."

Altair raised his hands. "Well, as much as I'd like to see a few demon spawn drawn and quartered with silver ropes or the like, we are an exception to the rule. You must stand aside, or else open the Door for us."

The giant opened his mouth to argue, but the jinn had already moved to Alice's side. He reached into the pocket where she kept the writ and pulled it out to show him. Alice startled and batted weakly at the intrusion. The sense of loss at having the Artifact taken from her, even if it was only a minor object, was galling.

She flailed clumsily for the coin, but Altair was deft. Agitated, she forced herself to sit up. Ajdaha moved to her side and took human form to support her in his arms.

Altair held up the writ for the giant to inspect. It was too little for Ephialtes to hold himself, so the jinn raised his palm so it was level with the giant's nose. He squinted as he tried to make out what it was Altair was holding.

After a moment, the giant's eyes widened. They narrowed when he looked back at the jinn. Altair smiled smugly, flicked the coin toward Ajdaha, and put his hands on his hips imperiously.

The gold-skinned man caught the writ and handed it to Alice. She scrabbled at it weakly and nearly dropped it in her eagerness. Clutching it to her chest, the sage blew warm air on the bit of metal and polished it with her sleeve. Ajdaha smiled down at her, lovingly patient as she agonized over the object.

The jinn called out, "As you can see, Ephialtes, we have a writ from Ninhursag herself. We are to travel to Agarti, the Place of Enki. There, the sage will receive an Instrument. If you bar us here, we cannot fulfill her writ. You will be standing against the word of your Baalim master."

The giant sighed, nearly blowing the three of them over the side of his hand. Ephialtes considered his prospects, finding himself lodged between the presses of his duties. If he opened the Door, he was acting against Ninhursag's wishes. If he didn't open the Door, he was still acting in rebellion.

Altair watched closely, following the giant's thoughts. "Ninhursag doesn't give her favors out lightly. If the sage has this coin, then she is among the Baalim's higher priorities."

The giant's brow creased, but he said, "Then it seems my path is clear. I will open the Door for you. From there, I will accompany you, of course, to ensure the Door is kept clear and there are no further intruders by that route. Once you are on the other side, will you need direction to find a Door to Enki's Place?"

"No need," said Altair. "Once we're out, we're headed for Shambhala on Sayon."

Ephialtes glowered. "If you are not headed directly to fulfill this writ, then why not simply wait until Ninhursag gives the word that the Doors be reopened?"

The jinn grinned. "Because we're going to gather our strength there. Then, we are going to head into Tartarus. We are going to find Pazuzu and destroy him. From there, we'll see about the Instrument. I agree with you that it's counter-intuitive, but, in the end, it's a bit of a shortcut, you see?"

"That's quite a shortcut." The giant looked thoughtful. "Allow me to join you?"

Altair looked back to Ajdaha, and they exchanged a shrug, uncertain. Ephialtes added, "You are taking quite a loose interpretation of Ninhursag's writ. I think there may be some leeway in my commands, as well."

"I am stationed here," said the giant, "to guard this Door against hostility and invasion. Right now, Pazuzu is the main source of aggression against us. If I venture out a little, I may be able to strike the head from the serpent before it has a chance to slither up to the gate again, yes?"

The jinn and the dragon looked at each other again. Altair said, "I wouldn't ask you to risk yourself for us. You have already sacrificed much for your duties."

"It's nothing," said Ephialtes immediately. "My brother Otos sacrificed much more."

Altair nodded solemnly at that. "We will accept your company, if that is what you're set on. I am curious, however. How do you plan to travel with us? Some of the places we need to go will have, hm, ceilings."

The giant smiled impishly and stooped smoothly to lower them to the ground. Ajdaha stepped off with Alice in his arms. Altair leapt to the ground and looked up at the giant curiously. Reaching into a weathered pouch at his side, the giant pulled forth a square of cloth. Unfolded, it was large enough to be a blanket. To the giant, it was less than a handkerchief.

Ephialtes carefully took the cloth by the corners and then shook it out. Immediately, it expanded out beyond the scope of reason, each of the giant's shakes folding loose another corner. Soon, the giant had an immense, ruddy, brown cloak which he swept up and around his shoulders.

The cloth turned in the air like a massive sail as it caught the wind and shadowed the ground below. As the giant fastened it at his neck, he began to shrink. Within a minute, the living mountain of a man had become something scaled for travel in small confines.

The giant's skin was still gray and rugged. He looked more like a walking, talking boulder than anything else, but he was small enough to pass through a doorway if he stooped. As she watched the proceedings with dull detachment, Alice supposed his looks didn't matter. *We're headed for Shambhala, not Chicago. Ephialtes should fit in fine,* she considered, *and we could use the muscle.*

Altair's lip quirked. He reached up to dust a bit of stray lichen from the giant's shoulder. "Quite convenient you had something like that in your pocket, isn't it?"

Looming a head taller than the jinn, Ephialtes returned the mischievous grin. "Ninhursag left it with me after Otos died. She said it was the least she could do for his sacrifice. Told me it might help if I needed to step away from my Door for a bit. She said she was relying on me solely until she could find a new guardian."

The giant winked. "And then she said she trusted me to keep things secure here at my own discretion in the meantime."

The jinn laughed. "Seems we're both taking some interesting shortcuts to get where we need to go."

The giant nodded and adjusted the cloak to rest neatly on his shoulders. Alice noticed beneath the shifting cloth, opposite the giant's pack, a metal ring that hung from his narrow belt of finely woven chains. His golden sword had hung there before he'd given it to his brother; now, it was empty.

"It's a little out of the way, but since you're headed there anyway, leaving Pazuzu's head on a spike outside the gate should give any other would be invaders pause, I should think?" said Ephialtes.

Ajdaha smiled. "At the cartographer's guild at Shambhala, we say the wisest path is not always the quickest, the shortest, nor the straightest."

The three of them laughed. Alice smiled confusedly to be polite. She felt like she needed a cup of coffee, a couple days' worth of sleep, maybe some uppers. She couldn't understand why she felt so fuzzy and sluggish, but it *did* seem to be improving. The changes were gradual, however, and she wasn't certain if she was actually gaining in functioning or if she was merely hopeful as she became accustomed to living with a damaged mind.

With the sage in tow over the shoulders of the dragon, the giant fell in step with the jinn. The great Door opened with a wave of Ephialtes' hand. Altair noted a glint of metal and saw there was a ring on his finger, a simple band with a square of gold as its centerpiece. It looked to be made of the same material as the Door itself.

Ephialtes waved his hand again as they passed over the threshold. As they slipped into the rushing space between Ninhursag's Place and the borderlands beyond, the great doors slammed shut behind them. Far away and high above, nestled within the twining boughs of the world tree, Gaia the Baalim nodded in satisfaction and turned her attention to other affairs.

Chapter 26:

ALICE FELT A LITTLE more herself as Ajdaha carried her through the Door and back into the bright, blue light of the borderlands. *The borderlands?!* Her eyes widened as she finally registered the danger they were in by coming back here. She looked about, expecting something nasty to be heading for her, but saw nothing.

The bazaar and the surrounding community were rebuilding. There was still wreckage, but there were no fires, and there were work groups breaking materials down to be reused or discarded. The bodies looked to have been cleared away, but then Alice startled at the sight of a quartet of zombies hauling away a splintered beam.

The sage blinked, uncertain of what her eyes were telling her, then patted at Ajdaha's neck to alert him. The dragon paused and looked back at her. A smile spread across his snout.

"Feeling more alert, mother?" he asked.

Alice said nothing but pointed toward the walking corpses. She felt the dragon tense and fall still. Altair stopped short with them and followed Ajdaha's gaze. Ephialtes tsked and shook his head, he but didn't break stride.

As the giant looked out over the burnt settlement, his hand strayed to the empty ring on his belt. He held it in a loose fist as he panned his gaze out toward the near plains where his brother had fallen. All that was there now were the crushed and trampled grasses, solitary shoots standing here and there amid the torn soil.

Ephialtes eventually came to a grudging halt when he realized he was walking alone. He turned back to find them staring at him oddly. He looked about until he saw the zombies, and understanding dawned. The giant took his hand from the ring and twitched at his cloak until the cloth draped over it, then shrugged his shoulders and waved a hand dismissively.

"It's only a wight," he rumbled. Alice stared blankly, so he obliged. "Undead."

She thought over the giant's words, her thoughts thick and slow. "Wait, you said it's *a* wight. I see . . . uhm . . . four."

The giant nodded. "That's how they are. The wight can wake up dead bodies and add them to itself. It's one of those group creatures. Poly-something"

"A collective," suggested the dragon, his voice relieved. "A hive mind."

Ephialtes snapped his fingers with a sound like billiard balls cracking against each other. "That's right! Polycorporeal! That's the word for it! Mouthful, right?

Alice eyed the walking corpses. The longer she looked, the more she noted their uncanny degree of coordination as they worked. It wasn't like watching a collection of individuals, even ones who knew each other well. The bodies functioned together like they were the fingers of a single hand.

Alice cringed, unnerved by the sight of them. "What does that do to the dead person? Does it trap their soul or anything?"

The giant nodded, unbothered. "For a time. The wight

keeps the memories that were in the brain. They can make the bodies last awhile, sometimes for decades if they're not too hard on them. Sooner or later, the bodies wear out, and the person they were passes on."

"Doesn't that *bother* anyone?" Alice was aghast.

"Why should it?" The giant scratched at the lump of stone that made do for his ear.

"That . . ." Alice blinked and shuddered, then shook her head to clear the fogginess. "No one cares that this vampire thing is . . ."

"Wight," Ephialtes corrected. "Vampires are something else."

". . . this wight thing is going around snatching bodies?!"

"Just look," said the giant and pointed about the regenerating community. Alice looked and was surprised to see not all of the wight's bodies were engaged in manual labor. She saw an old, dead woman smiling and playing with a gaggle of grandchildren. The corpse of a baker was hard at work in their kitchen. The baker wore gloves and a long-sleeved shirt to avoid tainting his wares with any stray tatters of dried flesh. There were several zombie carpenters and masons among the other skilled workers, all of them going about their business to remake their town.

"Sooner or later, everyone dies," said Ephialtes. "Here, for a while, the bodies become part of Esu. That's his name."

Alice kept watching until her fear and revulsion faded to interest at the sight of the living existing seamlessly with the dead. The giant kept on, "There are bad wights out there, just as there are bad people of any kind. Esu is one of the good ones, and he's been here a long time. He *likes* living among people. If their friends and families are willing, those vessels mostly just keep on with their old lives. The less welcomed ones stay in Esu's home. If it gets too crowded, he sends a few through a Way."

"What happens to those?" asked Alice.

"It's their reproductive cycle, I guess," said Ephialtes. "If the stragglers get away and make a life for themselves, as it were, they eventually become their own wight and keep their own vessels."

Alice relented and let herself hang limp over the dragon's back. Ajdaha looked over his shoulder and told her, "Actually, come to think of it, there is a wight working at Shambhala. Eben. He's much like this Esu, but his duties are mostly janitorial."

The giant regarded the dragon, "Wouldn't you want a chance to keep your older staff around? Especially if they died unexpectedly. It would be an opportunity for them to finish their work."

The dragon smiled as his eyes took on a faraway look. "Mapping every inch of creation we can get a look at. There *have* been a few such vessels permitted to Eben. I think, in his way, the wight shares our passion for the work, but we have only rarely employed him in that capacity, and only when the loss of critical information was at stake."

"But still, only a few?" asked Ephialtes. "Seems a waste."

Ajdaha answered, "It is, but to be honest, I am afraid of the precedent it would set. I'm sure the practice of retaining our dead in order to document the last of their work would prove itself indispensable. Documentation is practically a religion in Shambhala, but, even so, I do not think it would outweigh the risk."

The giant looked another question at the dragon, and he elaborated, "Knowledge is a form of power. Concentrating power is always a danger. Better we do our work in the time our lives permit and let it end there. There are enough gods already in the Eternal's creation."

At that, the giant relented. Altair looked over the wight vessels at their work and considered. "Might be worth talking to this one on our way out. The way he fits in, he'll probably know more than anyone how things played out here."

Ephialtes and Ajdaha nodded assent, and they headed toward the closest construction site. The burnt ruins of a building were being pulled apart and carted off. Easily half the laborers were undead; the rest were jin or jinn-related nephilim.

Each of the wight's bodies worked in smooth unison. It was like watching a flock of birds in flight. None of them collided with each other, no matter how many turns there were. One of the wight's vessels stood with a clipboard and pen, scribbling notes while it gave verbal directions to the living workers.

That corpse looked something like a well-worn orc in tattered rags, but as they approached, it looked at them appraisingly. The wight's eyes widened as they came to rest on the giant. Beaming, it stuck out a hand as it strode toward him.

"Ephialtes!" said the wight. "It's good to see you again. We're sorry for your brother. He saved many lives. We will always be grateful to you, to pay for his sacrifice however we can."

The giant took the hand and shook it. "You saw to him?"

"Cremated," said Esu, "as he would have wanted. I didn't take him for a vessel. I knew it would have broken your heart to see him so."

Ephialtes looked over the reconstruction somberly. He kept calm, though strong emotions pulled at his face as they washed over him. Alice considered the two of them, her fuzzy thoughts slowly plodding along. An undead giant would have been a valuable asset to the community, but for the wight to use Otos' body against his wishes would have been to treat him as nothing more than a useful object. Instead, their community honored their guardian, though it meant for a while they would have to do without themselves. With that, the sage felt her view of the wight shift. A soft smile touched her lips as Esu and the giant embraced briefly.

"Thank you, Esu. You're a good friend," said Ephialtes.

The giant wiped his eyes and took hold of himself. "One more thing?"

The wight gave him a knowing look. "We never recovered either of the swords. The horde took them as spoils before they left."

Ephialtes nodded, as if that was the answer he'd expected to the question he hadn't needed to ask. His hand strayed toward the shadows beneath his cloak, toward the empty metal ring at his belt, but he stopped himself with an effort. Instead, he redirected the hand and brushed imaginary lint from the material where it draped on his shoulder, as if that was what he'd meant to do all along.

Letting his hand fall back to his waist, the giant visibly composed himself and resolved to keep going forward. "Well, we won't be staying here long. It wouldn't be safe for the rest of you, and there is much to be done. I'm sorry I can't stay here to help."

"Of course," said the wight. "We understand."

He glanced toward the sage, the dragon, and the demigod. "My guess is you will be doing more than laying bricks and shingles. We are grateful for that, and we are certainly capable of looking after ourselves while you are away."

Ephialtes smiled warmly. "I know you are. All of you. By the time I get back, I wouldn't be surprised if this place looked as if nothing had ever happened."

Then, the giant's smile faded and, somberly, he said, "Now, if you would, I'd like to hear what happened here after the evacuation."

Esu shrugged. "There's not much to tell. The children of Pazuzu captured every breeding female they could find. They killed and ate the rest, though not always in that order."

Ajdaha winced, then asked, "And they didn't stay? They left no one to watch the Door?"

The wight shrugged again. Nearby, two of his collective loaded broken bricks into a wheelbarrow. "The children were only after the sage. Is that her?"

Esu pointed at Alice, and Altair nodded. "It is. Alice. She's in bad shape, though. A dab tsog got at her."

"A dream demon?" asked Esu, clearly surprised. "*Inside* Elysium?!"

The dragon shook his head. "The Akashic Record. Near it, anyway. She hasn't said. This is the best she's done since we pulled it out of her."

Esu looked at the sage thoughtfully, then faced Altair. "At any rate, there was no way of knowing she'd be back this way, and there was no sense trying to lay siege at the doorstep of a god. Pazuzu is powerful, but even he can't win a war if it has to last as long as one of the Baalim can fight it.

"I would be surprised if there weren't a few spies left to watch out for her," the wight continued. "I doubt it was anyone in town. We're pretty tight knit. Hard to keep a boss like that a secret. Probably some nasty little worm watching from the shadows. We'll keep an eye out, but, like you said, you won't be here long."

Altair and Ajdaha looked at each other, seeming to speak in silence, then Ajdaha looked to Ephialtes and said, "We shouldn't stop here. Let's mute ourselves and keep moving. It shouldn't take long to get to a spot we can use as a temporary nexus point."

"Of course," said Ephialtes, then he turned back to Esu. "Goodbye, my friend."

The wight raised a hand in supplication. "May I have a look at the sage before you go? I have some memory of human magic. Perhaps I can help her?"

The jinn and the dragon looked to Ephialtes. The giant shrugged and said, "Esu has been here a long time. He wouldn't *still* be here if he caused trouble. He's on our side."

Altair relented. "Alright. We can stay awhile if you think there's something you can do."

Ajdaha added, "And thank you, Esu. We've been worried

about her."

The wight stepped over to the dragon and peered at Alice. "Don't blame you. A dream demon is no joke. It's good she's doing as well as she is."

Esu passed his hands over her body. The wight took a measure of her energies as much as he examined her physically. He stopped, wide-eyed, when he came to her hands. Not quite daring to touch them, he looked back searchingly at Altair. The jinn nodded in confirmation, and the wight let out a soft whistle.

While the orc vessel looked over Alice's ocarina, two more of the wight's collective, a pair of heavyset men, came forward to help the sage off Ajdaha's back. She slid down fluidly to lean against the dragon's side. His slow, deep breaths were soothing to her, and she quickly passed back into the half sleep that had come to dominate her existence.

Another of the collective came forward with a flute. It was the body of a satyr female. The corpse looked as if it had been lovely back when it drew breath. Without a word exchanged, the satyr wight lifted the flute to her lips and played a slow, repetitive melody.

One of the heavies who had helped Alice set off to work. The other carefully took the ocarina and helped Alice hold it. Esu spoke through his orc's body, "This should help with your recovery. An attack by a dab tsog is as much mental and spiritual as it is physical. It disrupts everything. This song can help your body regain balance."

Alice listened and found she enjoyed the tune. It was pleasantly languid; simple and sweet. None of the soul centers of the wight's vessels were exceptional, but they added together to create a communal pool of strength. The magic behind the song was weak, but she could feel its effect seeping into her.

Eventually, her hands found her ocarina, and she put it to her lips. Her fingers missed the melody at first but caught on with practice. She felt her own centers respond to it. Her root collected energy and filtered it before releasing it back in a loop with the others.

The magic of the wight's song wasn't quick, but it was persistent. At first, Alice would falter as her concentration broke. She would drift through her own mind for a time, but eventually she would hear Esu's melody and bring her attention back to her own playing.

In time, the periods of stupor shrank, and lucidity grew. Alice just kept at it. She stayed in rhythm with Esu as best she could, and, eventually, she realized she hadn't lapsed in some time. She looked up to see the wight smiling at her from three bodies, his flute idle in the satyr's hands.

Alice lowered her ocarina. She *did* feel better. Her thoughts were clearer, though still sluggish. Her body felt much the same, more coordinated, but still slow and easy to fatigue. By any measure, it was an appreciable start, and she was glad to have it.

"Thank you," she told the wight and held out a hand.

The orc body took the hand and shook it, then helped pull her to her feet. "It's nothing. Play it often, and I think you'll feel yourself again in time."

Alice stowed her ocarina and asked, "How can I repay you?"

Esu said, "If it's within your power, I want you to destroy Pazuzu."

The wight looked sadly at a number of his vessels. "Many of these were friends until the demon-spawned horde came. They continue on, as do we all, but I'd rather they would have died in their own good time. I wouldn't expect you to understand, but sometimes it's better to *know* someone than to *be* them."

Alice smiled, thinking she had the same problem but inverted. *Harder to be yourself when you don't know yourself,* she mused. Aloud, she said, "Thank you again, Esu. It's probably time we get moving."

She looked to her company and found they were already waiting. Ephialtes had a hand on his belt. The giant absently fingered the empty sword ring there as he stood stoically until it was time to move. Ajdaha preened, nibbling at the edges of his scales for errant bits of dirt. Altair looked over the town's reconstruction, his eyes straying unfocused into the distance. When he became aware of Alice's attention on him, he snapped back to attention and smiled at her warmly. For a moment, it didn't feel awkward when she smiled back.

Chapter 27:

SALEM SAT ACROSS FROM the wight. Eben had expanded significantly since Skadi's assault on Shambhala. Pure blooded jinn and ifrit didn't always leave a body when they died. Their remains were more inclined to simply extinguish in a puff of smoke. Even so, the half-breed bodies of nephilim were piled high that day.

Unused to such loss, Salem persuaded the people of Shambhala to have Eben absorb their lost ones, and they were happy. They found it was better their knowledge and skills be put to good use as they rebuilt the citadel. Some even asked that the vessels of their dead to remain in their family's homes. With their memories, Eben could approximate his vessels' old personalities well enough. For the families, it was a helpful transition, a way of saying goodbye to the ones who had been taken from them so abruptly.

The wight had brought three of his bodies to the tavern al-Siraj, on the island Thule, outside Shambhala. A looming ogre and a tattered troll stood to either side of a bouda, each of them a study in layered muscle. He found the show of strength off-putting, but Salem was confident he could get away from the wight if he had to. He hoped it wouldn't come to that. The sila meant to profit in the wake of the tragedy, and the creature before him could be instrumental.

Eben clearly preferred the bouda. The wight kept its lycanthropic form at the hybrid stage between hyena and human. Salem approved; it was delightfully intimidating. The vessel looked something like an Egyptian god.

He concentratedand gathered his magic to mute their meeting. Eben supported the muting as well, drawing power communally from his gathered vessels. Salem noted the preserved corpses of the ogre and troll becoming still as he did it; the wight's energy and attention narrowed as it focused on the bouda vessel and its contribution to the magic.

When he was sure they were hidden away from stray eyes and ears, the bouda said, "You should be destroyed for what you have done."

"If you were convinced of that." Salem smiled. "You wouldn't have bothered with coming here to talk. Tell me, what do you know?"

Eben said through the bouda, "I saw you leave Shambhala. I followed you here. I lost you for a time, but then you returned to the citadel. A woman came after you. It was the giant who attacked us. She came for the sage."

Salem spread his hands. "Sounds like an unfortunate coincidence."

The bouda's lip curled about its muzzle in a savage smile. "I've watched you since. You leave the citadel when you think no one is watching. You go down deep into the clouds. You think no one will follow you there."

"But you did?" Salem asked, impressed.

The three creatures shook their heads in unison, and the bouda said, "I didn't want to risk a vessel going that far down. Your muting makes it difficult, besides. I would be as likely to find a world serpent's stomach as whatever little spit of rock you go to hide on."

"So essentially," said Salem, "you've been following me around, and you've watched me go to what you feel are suspicious places."

"I think-" the bouda vessel jabbed a finger at the tabletop for emphasis. "-that you are the most suspicious person in Shambhala! I wouldn't doubt a thorough investigation would expose you for what you are!"

"And what is it," Salem asked, "that you think I am?"

"I think you're a child of Pazuzu," the bouda hissed, "or an ally to him, at least!"

Salem smiled broadly. "There *have* been rumors that old demon has been increasingly active over the past few years. It's not a bad guess."

"So, you admit it!" said the bouda vessel. Eben's ogre and troll took a step forward, the wight's attention suddenly shifted. Salem nearly faltered as he took on the full burden of maintaining their muting. He kept his face friendly and smiling, careful to show nothing of the strain.

"Well, of course, I am!" Salem ignored the heavies walking up on him and made a little flourish with his hands. "A sila-ifrit hybrid, born in Pazuzu's spawning pits. Lucky for me, my mother was the dominating influence on most of my traits, allowing me to pass for jinn.

"I've been at Shambhala a long time. I keep my father informed of what he needs to know, and I do good work for the cartographer's guild. I have learned much from both my father and the dragon. I have also amassed an embarrassment of resources by quietly keeping a finger in everyone's pies."

Salem leaned back in his chair. It felt surprisingly good to talk about his life, the real one beneath the roles he played. Up to that moment, he wasn't sure if there was anyone he'd ever been fully honest with. It had been a risk meeting with the wight directly, but experience had taught that, when a problem had a face, it was best to face that problem.

The sila said, "There's your answer, Eben. Speaking honestly, I'm impressed. You're the first to notice me in all the time I've lived at Shambhala, and *that* takes something special. The question I have now is, now that you know what I am, how are *you* going to profit from it?"

The wight gave pause at that. Eben had stopped advancing on him. Now, the ogre and troll vessels looked around suspiciously. No one returned their looks, the muting about them doing its work. The bouda vessel looked only at the sila, uncertain but calculating.

Salem beamed, his confidence growing as he saw the wight's resolve falter. "Come now. You came here suspecting I was some kind of monster, yet you came alone, and you've told no one of your guesses about me. Why a private meeting with the enemy if you are so dedicated to your master, Ajdaha?"

The three vessels of the wight grinned together. "And why would you accept a private meeting, *yourself*, if you are loyal to your own, true master?"

Salem spread his hands, then clapped them together. "And there you have it! My point exactly! We're just two little people who'd like to get bigger."

He spread his hands out, fingers blossoming wide, as he finished. Salem watched the wight think, his attention kept fixed on the bouda. Eben said nothing. His silence spoke for him. The ogre and troll vessels relaxed and pulled out chairs for themselves.

Salem sighed happily as they sat. "Ah, it's nice being able to talk about these things out loud for once."

His vessels shrugged in unison, and Eben said, "It's difficult, being among the living. I've leant my skills to Shambhala for two hundred years. No matter how long I work, how much I give of myself, there are always some who would keep me from advancing in the citadel's leadership. They use their fear of the undead to justify their mistrust."

"Those paranoid fools," Salem said dryly.

Eben's vessels blinked, then glowered. The bouda said, "You understand what I mean! I can never prove I wouldn't attempt to actively murder to multiply myself and attempt a coup. My level of access to Shambhala's records has always been, will ever be, capped to appease their ideas of safety and good sense."

Salem nodded. "It's difficult being outcast, even when you *do* make a home for yourself. I've feared my true nature being found out since I left Tartarus. There are many who would kill me just because of who my father is, regardless of anything I've accomplished in my own life."

The bouda vessel leaned back. The ogre and troll bodies did nothing more than occasionally pass their eyes over the other, oblivious patrons. Eben said, "It seems we *are* both a pair of misfits looking to make their lives a bit more secure."

"It's good to have friends," Salem agreed. He leaned forward suddenly. "Of course, you must be wondering at the particulars of what I can offer for you to justify your little betrayal. No point in killing off old friends unless the new ones bring something more to the table, yes?"

The wight said nothing, but three pairs of eyes looked back at him with hungry curiosity. Salem reached into the folds of his cloak, and, with a flourish, he produced the seer stone. He laid the artifact down gently on their table between them. Eben stared at the lump of white quartz. Pleonexia shone in his eyes.

"Is that what I think it is?" asked all three vessels in unison. The wight's precision of control faltered with the intensity of its emotions.

Salem noted the lapse and filed the information away. "It's exactly what you think it is. It's a seer stone, and, if you can help me, *show* me you're with me, then I won't be needing it anymore."

The wight's vessels stared at the seer stone, unabashedly greedy for it. The artifact was a hive mind's dream. With items like it, it was possible for him to have colonies in multiple places without splitting himself into separate entities. For a creature like a wight, such a thing was a movement toward true immortality. Even if an entire colony were destroyed, his continued existence elsewhere was almost certainly secured.

Eben looked at his new conspirator and extended a hand. Salem shook it without hesitation. When they parted, the wight had to restrain himself as the sila half-breed swept the seer stone out of view, secreting it on his person. The bouda took hold of himself with an effort, folded his hands on the table, and did his best to look friendly.

"And what is it you need?" asked the wight.

Salem's eyes were dancing. "The sage and her company are returning to Shambhala. My father's spies have whispered such things to me when they can, and I have seen it for myself."

"And when they arrive," said Eben, "we will destroy them."

The sila shook his head as he patted his robe where he kept the stone. "Not at all. When they arrive, *if* they've survived, I want you to help me help them. They will need every advantage if they are to be successful."

"Successful?! With what?" asked the wight. He was curious what the jinn meant about surviving, but the thought of the seer stone in his pocket outweighed all else.

His voice heavy with avarice, Salem told him, "When the sage leaves Shambhala, they go to slay Pazuzu!"

Chapter 28:

ALICE PAUSED HER SONG as the Way dematerialized around them. Something was wrong. Ajdaha had told her when they left the borderlands of the Baalim they'd arrive at a secure location, but it was the same island they'd arrived on when she first came to Sayon. She surmised the little bit of land likely served as a nexus point for many of these temporary Ways that were among Ajdaha's secrets, but it wasn't where they were supposed to be.

She concentrated and extended her senses, relieved to find the trick of it was coming back to her. Altair and Ajdaha were both weakened from the expenditure of power the Way required. She'd been able to lend a little of her strength to the effort, but the two of them had shouldered the brunt of the burden. Now, they lay in the grass, near senseless as they recovered themselves.

Unsatisfied, Alice reached further but faltered. The wight's song had helped her, continued to restore her, but she wasn't yet whole. She didn't understand fully what the dream creature, the dab tsog, had done to her, but she didn't know if she would ever recover from the wound fully.

"What is it?" Ephialtes looked about suspiciously. The giant's own magical acumen was negligible, but his survival instincts were keen. His cloak hung down the middle of his back, kept off both shoulders to minimize impediment. The jinn and the dragon looked up at his words, then turned to look at Alice. Ajdaha saw her expression and looked around himself. His eyes narrowed as he realized where they were.

"I don't know," said Alice. "I can't sense it well. There's something . . ."

At the center of the small, floating island, there was a pool of still water. Alice hadn't paid it much attention the last time she'd passed this way, having nearly thrown herself to her death within her first minute on Sayon. She studied it then, probing with her expanded senses. Curious, she walked toward it. She leaned in cautiously to peer deeper when a single ripple made its way from the center of the water and gently spread to the narrow shore. Suddenly, the giant leapt at her.

"Look out!" roared Ephialtes as he knocked her aside. Alice tumbled over, feeling like she'd been run over by a car. Out of the waters leapt the biggest rodent she'd ever seen. It was something like a rat but dripped with black sludge. The air around it was distorted by noxious vapors that wafted around its body.

"Don't breathe!" shouted the giant, half-choked on the fumes himself as he struggled to get a grip on the slippery vermin. His stony hands were actually smoking from coming into contact with it. He rasped out in a roughened voice, "Don't let it touch you!"

Alice held her breath as she panicked. She turned her tumble into a roll for the edge of the island. The rat creature thrashed, making thick, squelching noises until it slipped from the giant's grip and charged after her. The giant stepped quickly to interpose himself and caught its body against his chest as it leapt. The rat hissed and spat something gooey and vile into his face, but the giant lowered his head, eyes and mouth closed. The foul ichor hissed against his stony skin, radiating poison fumes.

Altair and Ajdaha were all but helpless. They would recover, but they needed time. Ephialtes was doing what he could but couldn't grow to his true size in such a small area without dooming them all. Her breath burning in her chest, Alice kept her lips sealed as she reached into her pack for her ocarina.

The instrument found her hand as if her bag knew she was looking for it. She concentrated on her heart center as she raised it to her lips. The spinning vortex, close to her lungs, felt correct for what she wanted.

Alice wondered about her experience of Gregor's memories. She hadn't had the opportunity to process what she'd witnessed, but, as she began to play, it seemed her time seeing through the mind of a fully developed sage had been more helpful than she'd realized.

The notes of her melody became a great wind that blew toward the giant and the rat creature. Its fumes wafted safely away as they rose from its reeking body. Any drops of ichor were blown to the far side of the island and down into the endless, autumnal clouds below.

The giant bent against the gale. His mass kept him rooted as he looked over his shoulder, gauged the distance, and then threw the rat up into the air. The wind caught it immediately, and the creature spun off with a shrill squeaking, tumbling end over end as it fell past the edge of the island.

Far below, a passing world serpent paused at the sound of it. A great maw emerged, ripping a blanket of crimson fog to tatters, large enough to swallow an elephant. The serpent rose up as the rat creature fell, and its jaws snapped shut when they met.

The leviathan sank back into the clouds and resumed its languid slithering through the skies. Soon, however, it paused, a great rumbling from its gut echoing all around. The world serpent began convulsing, rhythmic spasms passing into an all-out seizure. Its thrashing coils crushed several small islands into slowly sinking clusters of little meteorites.

The world serpent drifted down as it weakened, too. All around, more of the great beasts gathered to feast on their fallen kin. Alice stopped playing and jerked her eyes away. She looked to Ephialtes as he fell to his knees, his body wracked with heaving coughs.

The giant collapsed onto his side, and Alice was sure he was dying until he held up a hand and said, "It's ok. I will be alright, I think. There is a strong ifrit heritage in my family."

Images of Otos' death flashed through Alice's mind. She recalled Altair slaying the ifrit back in the hospital, a lifetime ago. *Death is a constant*, she thought. *It doesn't matter* what *you are. No one is an exception. Things change, nothing lasts.*

Aloud, she said, "I'd try to get that muck off yourself. You're still all steamy."

Ephialtes blinked, and he looked at his hands. Sure enough, the vitriol was sending up little plumes of white smoke as it ate away at his rocky skin. He looked to the pond, then expectantly to Ajdaha.

"It's alright," said the dragon. He didn't stir from his resting place. "Get yourself cleaned up. That lavellan already tainted the water. No one will drink from that pool again."

"It's weird you know what everything is," said Alice. "You're like some nature show host."

She grinned broadly, but Ajdaha ignored her, the reference lost on him. While she wondered if they had something like television on Sayon, he looked about the little island and frowned. "No one should have come back here at all. This island was set up to be an entrance point, a spot for Way spells to anchor onto. I suspected it might be compromised, so I used a variant spell to get us somewhere else."

"Right," said Alice. "I thought this was weird. You said

there was another island."

The dragon nodded. "That's where we should have been. I don't know exactly what happened, but either someone was able to modify the outcome of my spell so we'd end up here, or else they destroyed the other island."

"What's more likely?" asked Altair.

"If someone had interfered with the spell, they would have had to do it while we were in the Way to avoid our noticing. Destroying the secondary island would be much simpler and could have been done ahead of time without anyone the wiser."

Alice cocked her head. "If the other island was destroyed, wouldn't we have just appeared over nothing and fallen?"

Ajdaha shook his head. "This was a safety function. There were two arrival points, each able to serve as an alternate destination for the other."

"Do we need to destroy this one then?" asked Altair.

The dragon shook his head. "Waste of time. There're only a few people that have access to the guild's master works on Wayfinding. They just need to know that, for now, the Shambhala nexus is lost."

Alice considered what he was saying. "How many people even know something like this exists?"

The dragon glowered. "Not many."

The sage said, "But no matter what, now there's no more quick escapes?"

Ajdaha bobbed his head. "Not unless you can master the trick of doing it on your own. It will take the guild some time to find and develop another entrance point."

"We should be safe for now, at least," said Altair.

"Safe?!" the sage said, dubious. "Won't someone come along and try to kill us since their trap didn't work?"

The jinn shook his head, rolled onto his back, and closed his eyes. "Whoever left something like that doesn't want anyone to find out who they are. Rushing at us headlong wouldn't fit with wanting to maintain their anonymity."

Altair yawned, his voice slurred with exhaustion. "Besides, we need to rest before we can move. Any hordes of flying horrors out lurking in the clouds are just going to have to fucking wait."

Alice opened her mouth to argue further, but Ajdaha had lain down his head against the sparse grasses on the uncontaminated side of the island. His breath was already slow and heavy. The sage's hanging jaw gave way to a wide yawn at the sight of them. Grudgingly, she relented, took a seat, and lifted her ocarina to her lips.

Ephialtes washed himself in the pool while Alice played. The melody of Esu's healing song filled the air. It gently pulled energy from all around and concentrated it on her. Alice could feel the restorative effect of it and saw her friends relax. Even Ephialtes seemed to feel the weight of his pain lifted as he scrubbed and picked at the tacky substance the lavellan had smeared on him.

Far below, the bones of a world serpent drifted out of sight, picked clean by others of its kind. More leviathans swept away from the falling corpse. Many of them moved weakly, sickened by the tainted meal, headed for their secret homes in the airy depths of Sayon to rest and recover. Soon, there was nothing stirring around the little island except orange clouds and the high, woodwind notes of the sage's song.

Hours later, Shambala appeared before them in the clouds. Ajdaha carried Ephialtes. He shouldered the burden with only a little difficulty. Altair had taken the form of a griffon. Alice sat just behind his tawny wings.

Though the wreckage was readily apparent, repairs were well under way. Rubble had been cleaned away, and neat workstations were set up all around the damaged sections of the citadel. Repair crews were working steadily, drawing from continually supplied, temporary depots.

Around the reconstruction work, life in Shambhala was going on. Scientists and engineers and artisans applied themselves to their trades, slowly but steadily pushing back the veils of creation's truth. Alice eyed the most deeply damaged, sometimes burnt, areas and wondered what had been lost because of Pazuzu. *No,* she corrected herself, *lost because of the enemy. Pazuzu is only Adam's pawn.*

Maybe more of a rook, or perhaps a bishop, suggested a little voice in her mind. Alice puzzled at that. She'd never liked chess. *Why that analogy, then?*

She worried at it before she recognized the voice. *Gregor?! Holy shit! Tell me I've got a sweet ghost mentor now!* The sage looked around eagerly in the hope some apparition might materialize, like something out of a movie; the soul of a kind, old master ready to comfort her with their wisdom. She waited, but nothing happened.

Her shoulders slumped with disappointment. It was a silly dream, and brief, but the idea of someone to guide her was enchanting. Her friends knew a lot, much more than she did, and had already awoken a lifetime of questions within her. They'd even answered a few of them, but no one could tell her how to be a sage.

Instead, the more Alice knew, the lonelier she felt. *I'm the single most powerful person on earth and there's not so much as a pamphlet to look over. Everyone is dead if I slip up. People already* have *died because I have no idea what I'm doing.*

"Alice?"

At the sound of Ajdaha's voice, the sage blinked and shook herself from her reverie. She smiled at him reassuringly, but it didn't touch her eyes. She looked about as they touched down, never having noticed their descent onto a nearby airfield.

Salem stood at the edge of their landing zone, a neat rectangle of standing stones in the grass. The sila jinn smiled and burned brighter as he stepped over the threshold to meet

them. Attendants trailed behind. Most of them bore ledgers
and various documents.

The familiarity of seeing the functionary at his work
touched Alice. She'd been on both sides of the law. Over her
life, though she didn't always agree with it, the wheels of bureaucracy kept the world turning. It was comforting knowing there were people doing what they could to cultivate and
nurture civilization.

She noted Salem's attendants, though they were all manner of jinn-nephilim, were of a kind. All of them moved with
a slight shuffle. Their skin was dry and flaking. Their eyes
stared through graying film.

"My lord!" Salem called out joyously. "It's good to see you
again! After you've rested and eaten, I imagine you'll want a
briefing on the goings-on since you left. Was your journey
successful, I hope?"

"It was," said Ajdaha as the giant slid down his golden
scales. "The sage has been healed."

The dragon noted Salem's attendants. "I see there has
been some turnover since I've been away."

Salem's face fell, seeming to recall the recent deaths at the
citadel, but then brightened. "Yes, lord! This is our resident
wight, Eben. You are familiar with him?"

"I am," said Ajdaha. "You have worked as an aide and
seen to the daily care of Shambhala, yes?"

The attendants nodded in unison. "Yes, lord."

"Eben has been instrumental in our reconstruction," said
Salem. "Through him, we have been able to maintain much
of our organizational memory, as it were. Without his taking
their bodies as vessels, many great minds would have been
lost."

The dragon eyed the wight. "I would assume there are
plans to transcribe the useful contents of those minds to expand our archives?"

"Of course, lord," Eben spoke from an elf at Salem's right

hand. The elven vessel held a clipboard in the crook of one elbow. The arm ended in a stump just before the wrist. The wight said, "For now, most of my vessels are devoted to the practicalities of reconstruction. Bricks don't mortar themselves, but I assure you the project of gleaning what may be had from these beautiful minds has already begun."

Alice looked about as she reappraised the bustle of labor all about them. Sure enough, Eben's presence could be seen everywhere. There was nowhere she could look where she didn't see a shambling body, completing all manner of tasks with precision despite their apparent clumsiness.

She wondered exactly how many bodies Eben had claimed after the attack. Knowing each set of eyes, ears, and hands were connected to a singular mind set her on edge. If the wight wanted, it could double its ranks with a single, simultaneous assault. The mass murder would be distributed all about the citadel, an army of assassins seeded seamlessly among their choice of targets, each of them working with a habituated knowledge of the citadel's layout.

By her appraisal, against Ajdaha's policies, Salem had invested considerable trust in the wight. She hoped it was well founded. It would be nice to have solace, even briefly, in her son's home before they had to find their Way into Tartarus.

The sage felt tired to her bones, like she could sleep for a year and it wouldn't be enough to make her feel whole again. Ajdaha excused himself briefly and paired off with Salem. They spoke quickly as they walked away, and in low tones, about affairs of state. One of Eben's vessels took Ephialtes by the elbow and, with a few disarming words, led the giant toward the promise of an ichor cleansing scrub down and a hot meal. Another made to lead Altair to private quarters to refresh himself as well, but the jinn hesitated.

He looked to Alice. "Will you be alright?"

"You can't babysit me forever, Al." She smiled. "I'll be fine. I've got mojo of my own now, right?"

The jinn frowned and looked to the nearest of Eben's vessels. "I want the rooms directly neighboring hers."

"Of course," said the body of the elf. "I'll have them ready for you at once."

Altair said nothing more but nodded in satisfaction as the sage waggled her ocarina at him and then allowed herself to be led off. For all the changes that had come to the citadel, she'd noted Ajdaha didn't seem overly guarded. She didn't have the will left to be cautious for him, either, wearily thinking instead it would be nice to be able to finish a meal and take a shit, in either order, in peace without worrying about being murdered. Esu's healing song was a blessing, but it couldn't compare to the feel of real rest. The sage stumbled with a bleary smile toward the citadel on the arm of the wight, imagining the feel of silk sheets against her skin.

Chapter 29:

THE NEXT DAY, THE war room breathed with the flow of activity. Maps and charts covered tables and hung from the walls. Alice couldn't get over that most of the bustle was the collective work of a single entity. She didn't know what bothered her more: the concept of the undead as a tangible reality, or the sight of a telepathic hive mind working in eerily silent unison throughout the city.

Eben only spoke if he was interacting with a body outside of his collective. Otherwise, his vessels moved with a coordination that made ants, bees, and synchronized swimmers look like drunken mobs of club-footed oafs. Once or twice, to satisfy her curiosity, Alice stuck out a foot to trip one up, but the wight only stepped over the obstacle with a smile and a wink. She gave up once she'd cemented the concept she couldn't sneak up on a being who was looking in every direction. Even if one vessel couldn't see her, the eyes of another betrayed her every move.

As uncomfortable as the wight made her, she had to admit he was efficient. Eben looked to be organized into anchors, vessels who stood and talked with the singular, living beings, and runners. The runners broke down into short and long range, the closest facilitating the tasks at hand and the more remote carrying supplies to, and messages from, the room.

For the sake of space, Ajdaha was in his golden human form. Altair stood at his side, his brow furrowed as they spoke over maps and ledgers. Salem was in attendance, splitting his time between consultation and managing the citadel. Ephialtes looked about as lost as Alice, mostly staying quiet and out of the way. She was glad to see all of them looked refreshed. She was amused to see the giant had gone so far as to have himself polished, the angles of his stony flesh gently shining with a soft luster.

"So, Pazuzu's Place has an entrance point like Shambhala's?" asked Altair. "We can just head straight there?"

Ajdaha shook his head. "Nothing so easy. We need to take a Way to Tartarus. Once we're in the ifrit Realm, we should be able to get to a nexus point, work the ritual, and open the Door to Urugal."

"That's all?" said the jinn. "Just a quick trot into Tartarus before we smile, wave, and murder one of their heroes?"

"Pazuzu is not beloved by all," said Salem, his tone of voice carefully even. "Not all ifrit are like him."

Altair quirked his lip. "So, you would expect a warm reception?"

The sila smiled, spread his hands, and gave a little bow. "Of course not, sir. I just meant some, if not most, of the ifrit you're going to come across are simple civilians."

"Excellent." Ephialtes absently fiddled with the ring at his belt. "We'll just focus on the ones running at us with swords."

"Unfortunately," Ajdaha said, "that's sounding like our best bet. Based on the information at hand, the most straightforward strategy is a rush across the Way with a contingent of jinn. They hold the forward position long enough for us to perform the ritual and open the Door. Once we're through, they retreat back to Sayon."

Ephialtes was frowning. "And what's the plan for when it's time to leave?"

Altair pointed variously at another map set. "We have a decent understanding of the layout of Urugal. After the old demon goes down, Pazuzu's Place is going to collapse into chaos. During the pandemonium, we'll have a few options to choose from to get out of there. Once we're back in Tartarus proper, we'll get to a Way that will lead us out of the Realm."

They fell silent at that, no one quite agreeing, but no one having a better idea. Everyone there knew there would be risks. Alice felt the burden of it deeply. Everything on the table was to support her. Every life at hand was there to die to protect hers, including Altair and Ajdaha.

"It's funny," she said, shifting the subject to something that kept nagging at her. "You had all these maps the *whole* time?"

"Yes," said Ajdaha. "I doubt we would be able to field an attack this straightforward without them."

The gold-skinned man's eyes narrowed. "It *is* funny. I knew we had maps of Tartarus, but I didn't realize we had this level of detail on the important Places. Pazuzu does not share his home. Apart from his children, beyond its name, I doubt there are many that know anything about Urugal at all."

Alice said, "And here we are with more or less complete maps of his Place, the locations of the Doors to get there, and a keyring of rituals to open them."

Salem smiled and brushed his hand in a caress across one of the maps. "Our guild has worked diligently for centuries, but an unfortunate reality of our prosperity is we've grown large enough one hand doesn't always know what the other is doing."

Altair looked to his son, picking up on his suspicion. "And yet, it's fortunate we were able to dig up these partic-

ularly obscure bits of paper, and in such short order. It must
have been difficult with all the destruction and chaos."

Ephialtes peered over their shoulders. "It looks like we've
even got information on patrol routes, shift changes, and the
like. How in hell would some map maker have gotten that?!"

Salem's smile never faltered but only became oilier. "As
I've said, Eben has been instrumental with the recent up-
heavals. He honestly cannot be praised enough for the work
he's done. He's taken on enough of our dead, he's become a
walking index of the collected works of our association. Once
things have settled down, there's been talk of developing an
improved filing system based on his collective memory."

"It's good," said Altair, "that we happened to have Eben
on hand, then. It seems we have an embarrassment of happy
coincidences on our side."

One of Eben's endless procession of vessels, a pale dwarf
missing half his beard and most of his face, stepped forward
to address them. Alice watched quietly. She wasn't certain,
but she thought she saw another of the wight's vessels shoot
a reproachful look toward Salem. It was gone in a blink, then
the vessel moved on with its work. If the sila jinn saw it, he
didn't react, but only kept on with his toadying. The sage
pursed her lips as she recalled the things she *didn't* like about
bureaucrats. Behind the rules and the order they brought
about, there were always quiet meetings happening in back
rooms.

The dwarf vessel spoke, "If there are any concerns of my
conduct, I am happy to stand aside. I am well aware there is
a certain level of mistrust for my kind, and I do not wish to
create more trouble for Shambhala."

Ajdaha looked the dwarf vessel over, then, finally, he said,
"No, your work is valuable. After we have gone, you and Salem should continue as you have been."

He looked the sila in the eye, his voice icy. "It seems the
two of you have made yourself indispensable in the wake of

recent events."

"Thank you, lord!" Salem executed a graceful bow. "We do only what has been necessary to protect Shambhala."

"Of course." Ajdaha exchanged a look with Altair but said nothing further on the matter.

"Well," said Ephialtes, "if we've got our route, we should be talking about equipment."

"You'll want to see the armory," the wight spoke through a more-or-less human-looking vessel.

The giant grinned, coming into his own at last. "Yes, please."

The armory of Shambhala seemed implausibly well stocked. It was a basement the size of a small warehouse, carved from the rock beneath Shambhala. Alice was all but certain the dimensions of the space were bigger than the island could allow.

The gear available ranged from swords and bows, to shields and armor, to actual tanks and modern military gear. Each of them were scouting around for something suitable. Ephialtes and one of Eben's vessels were talking animatedly as they disappeared down a hall of shelves filled with increasingly sizable weaponry.

Curious, Alice lifted an assault rifle from a rack of dozens. She tested its weight and sighted down the barrel, then thought better of it. The sage replaced the firearm with a clatter and asked, "So, why all the swords and clubs and old timey shtick when you've got this stuff?"

Ajdaha stepped over to a tall rack, selected and drew a long, curved sword from its sheath, and swung it experimentally. "Enchantment, mostly."

He paced over to her and held up the sword, a katana, for her inspection. Along the spine of the blade, from hilt to tip, was a scrollwork of runes. He told her, "Many things the guild runs into are resistant to physical injury to some degree. Jinn, as you've seen, are resilient, but ifrit make any conventional weapon laughable."

Alice thought it over. "How is that possible? You said before Artifacts were mostly made by gods and sages."

"Mostly," Ajdaha agreed, "but we're not talking about Artifacts. We're talking about enchantment. Just as minor magics are available to certain ones of your species, the art of imbuing physical objects with mystical properties is an area of study the cartographer's guild has taken very seriously."

"Oh, of course." Alice quirked her lip. "What is this place about, really? Are you people map makers or arms dealers?"

Altair was looking over a nearby table covered with an arrangement of curved sabers. He and Ajdaha exchanged a grin at her question, then Altair told her, "There's a lot of existence out there. Not all of it is safe and friendly. A good field cartographer knows what they'll need to bring to ensure a successful expedition."

The sage considered the idea of it and tried to come up with a frame of reference that made sense to her. "I guess it's a little like the *Enterprise*."

They only stared blankly, so she said, "It's from a tv show about a spaceship full of explorers. They go where no one has gone before, and when they do, they bring a shitload of guns."

Ajdaha grinned. "Sounds about right. A formal armory was your idea, by the way."

Alice smiled back and stepped away from the assault rifles toward racks of pistols. "So, if I'm understanding correctly, you're telling me you *can* make weapons that are kind of magic. Enough to hurt an ifrit."

Ajdaha nodded, so she asked, "So, why not make magic bullets or arrows instead of a magic sword? Seems safer, for the one with the gun anyway."

Altair said, "Enchantments aren't durable like a real Artifact, but they usually last for a while. A few fights, anyway. Ammunition is gone after one use. Making these things is a difficult enough process that it's too much hassle to enchant each round."

"Okay, then why not enchant the gun?" she asked.

"Good question," the jinn looked to Ajdaha.

Ajdaha said, "An augmented gun might be able to shoot faster, quieter, etcetera, etcetera. The problem is the bullets are still normal bullets, no matter what the gun is like. It's the same with a bow or crossbow."

Alice was looking over a growing selection of pistols. She laid out her preferences on a nearby table. She ran a finger down the one that called to her: .22 caliber with a 30-round capacity magazine.

"That's too bad," she said as she sighted down the weapon.

Altair eyed her process. "I didn't realize you were this into guns."

"I'm not," replied Alice. "I'm just going with what I know."

She hefted the pistol, the weight of it similar to the one she'd carried during the early years of her adulthood. There was a time when she slept with something like it under her pillow. Toward the end, it had become something she didn't feel comfortable setting down even to use the bathroom. For all that, outside of a shooting range, she'd only fired a gun once. It was the same day she'd decided she'd had enough of the drug world.

"I'm going to want four of these, three magazines for each, and the easiest books you've got on enchanting," she said. "I've got some ideas."

Alice studied the bullet. Its surface was etched with runes. They weren't like those on the sword Ajdaha had shown her, but the ever-present wight insisted they were correct for their purpose.

"Then thank you, Eben," said Alice, "and you can make

more?"

The vessel before her had once been an attractive, mostly human woman. Alice noted the wight tended to use the prettiest corpses for its social interaction. Under a layer of makeup, the matter of the vessel's death was less noticeable.

"Yes," said Eben. "I have dedicated enough vessels to complete inscribing them by morning. You will have as many prepared as you need."

Alice looked down at the box of prototypes. Enough for a full magazine. She wondered what wasn't getting done because she thought what she was doing justified the resources.

She pushed the thought aside. *No sense feeling guilty. Not about this, anyway. I'm going to make sure Pazuzu doesn't hurt anyone else. I hope . . .* Alice replaced the bullet among its siblings and carried the box to the ritual space Ajdaha had helped prepare. Sixty-four vertices, not unlike a temporary Way though configured quite differently, she set the box of bullets at the center and pulled out her ocarina.

The soft whistle of her melody filled the air. Alice's centers flared as she played. She focused on her soul and solar plexus points, though she'd noticed, as she'd developed, she'd found the emphasis of her concentration was less necessary. Like peeing, reading, or riding a bicycle, the body remembered so it could automate, habituated so it could forget.

Energy gathered all around her. Some of it was pulled from the area. Most of it came from within. The music reached out through her crown center, realizing a connection between herself and the bullets. The ritual space channeled and augmented the magic, structuring her intent into reality.

The magic felt right just as the etchings on the bullets began to glow. The sage brought her song to a close, and the gathered power settled into the bullets. The graceful lines of their engravement grew brighter as the energy coalesced. On the last note, there was a blinding flash, and it was over.

She wasn't sure if she expected them to glow or twinkle,

but, when the afterimages faded from her vision, the box of bullets looked just as they had before her spell. The sage kept disappointment from her face as she leaned in and plucked one up.

Alice took a pistol from the tactical vest arrangement Altair had prepared for her and paced over to an impromptu shooting range. She chambered the bullet, cocked the gun, and sighted on a small statue of a dragon. Unsure, she looked to Ajdaha.

The dragon waved a paw. "Don't worry about it. We sell those at the gift shop."

She quirked an eyebrow. "We have a gift shop?"

"The wall is thick." The dragon ignored the question. "That little bullet can't get through."

Alice hesitated. "To be safe, is there anyone on the other side?"

Ajdaha looked to Eben. The wight hesitated a moment, then smiled. "Air traffic is being directed away. You have nothing to worry about."

The sage smiled, wished that were true, aimed, and fired. The pistol roared, but it hardly kicked in her hand. The statue disintegrated, along with a foot-wide hole in the wall behind it.

All of them hesitated at that, then Altair looked to Alice and said, "Good shot."

The sage trotted over and looked out the hole. The sides were nearly smooth, widening only a little as they exited the structure. The thin pedestal the statue had rested on was standing, but the top few inches were similarly obliterated.

Curious, she reached out to touch the place where the statue had been. She hesitated before she let her skin come into contact. Heat radiated like her hand was hovering over an oven. Thinking better of it, she headed back to the box of bullets and picked them up, then sat down at a long table and began loading a full magazine.

When it was ready, she slipped it into the butt of her pistol and slid the weapon down the waistband of her pants. It rested comfortably and familiarly in the small of her back. Alice knew her magic would improve in time and speed would come with proficiency. For now, it was good knowing she could protect herself at a moment's notice.

The others watched with interest. They were familiar with firearms but had never seen much use in them. Altair, in particular, was intrigued.

Catching his look, Alice pushed herself back to her feet and said, "What?"

"You're acting more like your old self again," he answered. "It's nice to see."

The sage shrugged and winked. "What, like some old German dude?"

Altair almost concealed a wince. Alice puzzled a moment, then understood. For her, Gregor was a patchy collection of memories. They were useful, and she drew comfort from them, but, for him, that old German had been the love of his life, seven times over. Now, his soul lived in her body, had *become* her, and the love she must have felt for the jinn over all those lives, though not extinguished, was changed.

But then, she thought, *there are a lot of things that are different this time around for both of us.* She pushed down the urge to apologize or comfort the jinn. She set aside her guilt, told herself she was her own person, that she felt how she felt, and that she didn't owe Altair anything, or Gregor for that matter. The sage reminded herself there was work to be done and there wasn't time yet to sort out the deeper things between them.

"I'm sorry, Al," she said at last, keeping her voice even. "I know things might've been different if I'd grown up with my magic. I get it. That's how it should have been, but that wasn't my life."

Altair nodded quietly. "It's alright. It's as you've said to me, many times before. Things change; nothing lasts."

Alice cleared her throat as they looked away from each other, waited a beat, and then changed the subject. "You want me to make you some, too?"

The jinn shook his head and blinked as he called his mind back to the present. "Hmm? Oh, no. I don't know my way around the things. Thanks. I'll stay with swords."

"Suit yourself," said Alice, focused now that the moment had passed. She noted Ajdaha had unobtrusively moved on to other tasks. Their relationship was more comfortable, but there was sorting to be done there, also. She sighed inwardly; none of it was easy.

"Now," the sage said to the wight, "do you have a music room or whatever it's called? Where you keep lots of instruments."

"Of course. This way," Eben's vessel said, then bowed and headed for the door. Alice grabbed her tactical vest and followed after. She smiled at its three siblings as she slipped the pistol back into its holster. *Peace of mind is redundancy.*

A pair of harmonicas, a spare ocarina, and a concertina joined her pistols. Standing in a vast room with shelves holding all manner of musical instruments, enough to provide for several full-scale orchestras, Alice looked over the tactical vest, amused at the contrast. She tried it on and examined herself in a floor-length mirror held by another of Eben's vessels.

Satisfied with the setup, she slid the backpack on as well and turned about. The weight was manageable and distributed well enough. As an afterthought, she stepped over to a table where she'd laid out her musical prospectives and selected two sets of castanets. Slipping them into little pockets on the vest, she turned to the wight's pretty mouthpiece.

"What do you think?"

Eben considered. "You look like a killer one-man band."

The sage rolled her eyes, and the wight said, "Sorry. No

one's ever asked me about accessibility issues with musical instruments in a combat situation before. Why the accordion?"

"It's not an accordion," said Alice. "It's a concertina. It's easier to schlep around."

"Yes, but why . . . ?" Eben closed his mouth around the question and decided on a different tack. "I suppose I think it looks like it will work?"

Alice took a last look in the mirror. "I'll take this stuff back to the armory and practice. We're still on track for dawn?"

The wight nodded. "I'm making excellent progress."

Chapter 30:

*T*HE WAY WAS A ten-foot vertical stone ring set into the center of a stepped dais. The floating island supporting the structure was hidden in plain sight. It was positioned so high above Shambhala as to be nothing more than a speck, even with a clear sky. The atmosphere at that height was thin enough, Alice felt woozy.

The score of jinn accompanying them, as well as Altair and Ajdaha, looked uncomfortable, too. Their fiery flesh was dulled to a red glow. It was only Ephialtes that looked at ease. The giant sat astride a jinn in the form of a gigantic raven, a hand set contentedly over the pommel of a new sword, his cloak fluttering about him in the constant winds of that world.

It was a longsword, not unlike the twinned blades he'd shared with his brother. This one was silver, however, not gold. Near the hilt, the name OTOS was engraved so that it ran down the blade, the letters oriented vertically. The single word was surrounded by ornate scrollwork, the sweeping lines of the design coming together to form a graceful braid that ended at its tip. The sage liked the look of it; somehow, it seemed to complete him.

Around the Way stood another contingent of jinn. Like those that accompanied Alice, they were a mix of sila magi and ghul shapeshifters. The sila carried eclectic and various equipment, though few were overtly armed or armored. The ghuls never had any more than their clothing, a spear, a shield, and perhaps a satchel.

Alice looked between the two sorts of jinn appraisingly. "You'd think the military types would have more gear."

Altair told her, "It's difficult to shapeshift with any more than that. Some can't bring anything with them at all."

"Sounds like a hassle," said the sage. "What about the mage-y ones?"

"Enchantments," he replied. "They work them into their clothing, sometimes their tools."

He pointed out the occasional wands and charms. "To augment and focus their magic."

Catching herself fiddling with her writ, Alice stopped herself from eyeing the jinn artifices and looked over the guardians of the Way. The jinn there stood at attention, their eyes on the dragon. They looked well accustomed to their post. Only the dullness of their skins betrayed their shared discomfort with the high altitude.

Ajdaha flew forward first to meet them. He held up a paw, and their group stopped short. Alice saw they were talking and strained to hear what they were saying. Then, she rolled her eyes as she remembered herself.

The sage extended her senses and listened. The dragon said, "Greetings, guardians. I hope all is well?"

Their leader, a large sila with wands hanging at his thighs, drifted up to face him. "Greetings, Lord! Much more peaceful at this station than down below, I've been sad to hear."

"It *has* been interesting of late," Ajdaha agreed, "but not only here."

The jinn nodded, somber. "Bad times always seem to find

a way to spread themselves out, eh?"

"That, they do," said the dragon.

The sila looked past his liege to study his accompaniment. He paused at one and asked, "Is that the sila that struck the killing blow to the giantess?"

"It is," Ajdaha looked back proudly. "Djamila. She was one of the first to volunteer for this mission."

"Brave," said the jinn approvingly. "Strong, too, the way I've heard it. Real potential, that one has."

"That, she does," said the dragon, then fell silent as he eyed the other pointedly. In the lull, Alice tried to sight the sila in question, but, if this Djamila knew she were being discussed, she gave no sign of it. Each of their guard looked fixedly forward and awaited their next order.

Reluctant, the jinn asked, "Master Ajdaha, do you mean to open this Way?"

"I do, Niall," said the dragon. "Things need to get worse before they get better, and this is the quickest path to getting it done. Please prepare to disable the wards."

Alice looked to Altair and asked, "Wards?"

The jinn blinked, then realization dawned on his face. "Listening in, eh?"

She shrugged and twirled a finger, urging him to answer. Altair said, "Once they open, Ways stay open. That can be a problem, but, fortunately, they tend to appear and disappear very slowly. Once you know where they are, with enough resources, it's possible to block the undesirable ones."

"Wait," she said. "*Ways* disappear?"

The jinn shrugged. "Everything disappears. The jinn and the ifrit used to be a lot warmer to each other. Once, this Way used to be a major route between Sayon and Tartarus. With things as they are, we each keep our side warded shut. Niall's been watching this end since the wards went up."

"That's why he's so bummed about it?"

Altair looked at her blankly, then ventured, "No, he has a

place for himself. He lives here when he's on duty, and he can make use of the barracks at Shambhala if need be."

Alice cocked her head, furrowed her brow, and tried again. "That's why he's so *sad* about it?"

The jinn's eyes lit up. "Ah! Yes, it's the end of an era for the fellow."

Alice nodded, understanding what it was like to be uprooted. She frowned as she considered. "If it's shut on the other side, how do we get through?"

"I can't explain the physics of it," he said, "but my understanding is you're going to push it open with a ridiculous display of raw power."

Alice's lip quirked as she turned her attention back to the dragon and the guardians. The keepers of the Way were already in motion. They took places on smaller stone daises surrounding the center. As they moved closer, Alice could see the stone ring was saturated with magical energy.

As she set foot on the floating island, Alice asked, "What powers it?"

Altair shrugged, but Ajdaha caught the question and told her, "The ward powers itself through the ring. The ring draws energy from all around and from the Way itself. The guardians perform rituals to maintain it and make sure it's doing what it's supposed to be doing."

She eyed the guardians. Niall was not alone in his displeasure. None of them looked enthusiastic with what was happening. Many looked frightened. The sage didn't blame them. She felt about the same.

"What happens on this side once we're through?" she asked.

"The guardians reestablish the wards," said Ajdaha. "It will take time before they are at full strength again, so they'll start as soon as we're in the Way."

"But I can open it up again from the inside if I need to?" she asked. "The same as how I'm going to open the Way up on the ifrit side?"

Ajdaha shook his head. "You could, but the explosion would kill the jinn guarding the ring."

Alice paled. "Wait, *that's* what's going to happen on the ifrit side?!"

"It's the chance we've been given to do this," he said. "Do you want to try to find something else?"

The sage hesitated as she thought of Gregor and the gorgon. The idea of killing a bunch of people in an ambush, even if she thought of them as monsters, didn't sit right with her. From what she'd been told, just as with humans, there were billions of jinn and ifrit. There were good odds none of the guards on the Tartarus side of the Way had anything to do with Pazuzu. *Not personally, anyway,* she thought. *They're like police, just doing the work they were given while the responsible people stay somewhere safe.*

Swallowing her guilt, she said, "No, this is the chance we've got. There's no time for anything else."

Ajdaha nodded solemnly, and she understood he took no pleasure in this, either. She turned to Altair and saw the sentiment mirrored there, too. When she looked the giant, he shrugged back at her.

"Anything could have come for me while I was guarding the Door for Gaia," said Ephialtes. "Eventually, something did. Shit happens."

Alice frowned, then realized there was something she needed to do before they went any farther. She looked between Altair and Ajdaha. "He's right. Listen, there's something I need to tell you, just in case. It's what I got from the Akashic Record. It's not much, but you'll need to pass it on to whoever comes after me, if I don't make it."

The jinn and his son looked at each other, then back to her. Altair said, "Alice, we will keep you safe."

She shook her head. "You can't know that. We have to plan for the worst. If I die, you'll have to find whoever takes on my mantle. I know there might not be time to get another sage ready, but if there's going to be any hope at all, they'll at least need to know as much as I do, right?"

Ajdaha frowned but nodded. "You're right. Please show us."

The sage concentrated on her hard-won glimpses of Gregor's memories. Putting the ocarina to her lips, she shaped them with her magic so she could share them with the others, making sure to emphasize the most important details. *This is Adam,* she told them. *Remember the face of our enemy.* Altair and Ajdaha closed their eyes as they received the memories, and, when they opened them again, both were bright with tears.

Alice paused at their reaction, then understanding dawned. For her, the memories were still just images from the life of a stranger. For them, Gregor was much more. He was the last face Altair's ancient love had worn that still knew him, the last face that had truly known their eldest son.

She wished there was something she could say to console them, that there was time for her to recover more of the person they knew her to be, but Alice took a breath and let it out slowly instead, "Alright, let's go."

Ajdaha turned and gave a signal to Niall, the guard captain of the Way. The jinn nodded and began ordering about his contingent, directing with a wand in each hand. The jinn guardians wasted no time in getting into their respective positions. As they began to pull at the magic of the wards, it was the sila jinn that took the greatest share of the work. The ghuls fell in beside them to do what they could to take on their share of the strain of the magic.

Solemnly, the dragon's guard lined up before the stone circle, side by side and ten deep. The ghuls went first. Enchantments crackled at the tips of their spears. The wards on their shields distorted the air in front of them. The following sila stood at the ready, orbs of force held ready in their hands.

Ephialtes had dismounted and strode toward the front of the column. The dragon made a faint sound as though he meant to argue it. The giant looked directly back at Alice in silent supplication.

The sage nodded without hesitation. *Ephialtes lost a brother to Pazuzu,* she thought, *he watched his family die for protecting Gaia's door. The monsters were only there because of me.* The giant looked grateful and took position at the head of the column.

Alice was at the rear, Altair and Ajdaha at her flanks. Afraid as she was, she envied Ephialtes. The giant got to face his anger head on while she had to hang back and watch people die for her. *More people,* she reminded herself. *People have been dying for me over this since before I was born.*

Memories from another life drifted at the edge of consciousness. *Gregor.* She knew he wasn't there, wasn't some spirit taking form to mentor her, but scattered images of his life experiences leant her bitter comfort. They told her the regret was normal and she would learn to live with it.

"Are you ready, Alice?"

Altair rested a hand on her shoulder. She let out a breath she hadn't realized she'd been holding as she reached up and took it. She looked over her vest one last time, then checked over her clothes.

Alice had been apportioned with a set of tight fitting, dark clothing that were supposed to be stab and slash resistant. They'd gone so far as to give her a matching balaclava and a pair of tactical goggles. The hooded face mask was tucked into a pocket with a pair of dark gloves. The goggles hung from their strap around her neck. Altair hadn't approved, but she had stubbornly stood her ground. She wouldn't try to play with gloves on, and the headgear seemed nearly as much an impediment.

The sage started to recheck to make sure her boots were tied and realized she was procrastinating. She straightened up and looked at the jinn with embarrassment. He smiled, patted her arm with his palm, and waited.

"I'm ready."

Altair grinned and dropped his hand down to the pommel of his own new sword. Like his son's, it was a long, curved saber. She wasn't sure if it was a katana, but it reminded her of something out of a kung fu movie.

Ajdaha called out commands, "Guardians, remove the wards. Ephialtes, go forward the moment the Way is open. I want us through as quickly as we can manage."

The jinn controlling the Way worked in unison, exuding orbs of energy and trails of fire. A pattern emerged quickly and grew brighter as the magi fed their power into it. Alice worriedly watched them dim, but there were enough to bear the burden.

When the pattern was ready, Niall lifted his wands and drew a sigil in flames that hung in the air. He pushed at the sigil with his palm, and it drifted over the ritual pattern toward the stone ring at the center. When it touched the Way, there was a flash of light as the spell activated.

Alice felt power rush past her. It flowed away from the emptying wards in a dizzying rush. Then, the energy levels in the area evened out. The tingling sensation, like the air was charged with electricity, faded, and the Way came to life.

The stone ring blazed white with power. The magical energy spun around its perimeter, steadily gaining in speed and intensity. It distinctly reminded Alice of one of her centers.

She sensed the harmonics of the Way. They changed as the energy shifted, and they moved toward some specific melody. Soon, the song of the Way became clear to her, and the spinning lightning flashed toward the center of the stone ring.

The Way opened with a rushing shift in pressure that made Alice's ears pop. Within its circumference, where before there had only been empty air, there was a pool of light that rippled like water. Alice realized then what she was look-ing at and laughed giddily. Altair looked at her with concern.

"Still alright?" he asked her.

She bobbed her head and wiped at her eyes. "It's a star gate!"

When he gave her a blank look, she elaborated, "It re-minds me of another tv show. More explorers with more guns."

The jinn smiled politely and began marching with the column through the Way. Alice followed closely. She resist-ed the urge to comfort herself by keeping a pistol in hand. She didn't want to risk accidentally firing it as they passed through. She noted her companions did the same. They nev-er took their hands from their weapons but kept them se-cured and safe for the moment.

Quickly, the column passed on to the next Realm. First, Ephialtes stooped carefully through the ring. The jinn passed through the rippling energy field behind him, leaving no sign behind them that they'd ever been. When her turn had come, despite herself, Alice held her breath and closed her eyes as she passed through the stone ring. The power of the Way washed over her like fluid electricity. When she opened them again, the world collapsed into a rush of motion and blurred lights.

Chapter 31:

WHEN REALITY TOOK SHAPE again, they were standing in a cylindrical hallway of white stone. Alice looked about for the first trial of the Way, but nothing was apparent. The hallway led into the distance, lit by the light of the assembled jinn.

As their company walked, Alice tugged at Altair's elbow and spoke softly, "I thought Ways had three trials to pass."

"They do," he answered and looked to his son.

"The trials change with the Ways," said the dragon. "For this one, the first trial has become getting through the wards on Sayon's side. The third, I expect, will be opening the wards on the Tartarus end."

"And the second?" asked Alice.

"Hard to say," said Ajdaha. "This Way hasn't been open in a long time. Wait."

Alice stopped short. "What?"

The dragon spread out his paws and concentrated. He looked to be feeling for something, then his eyes snapped open. He looked down the length of the passage fearfully, and then to Alice.

"We need to move!" he said. "Fast! Quick, get on!"

Ajdaha lowered himself to the ground so Alice could get on his back. Altair paused and looked back at them, then caught a look from his son. Looking about quickly, his eyes narrowed, then widened.

"Ah, shit!" said the jinn. "The tunnel is shrinking!"

Alice looked around and tried to see it. Other than the twisting vortex of energy at its entrance, there were no landmarks. The stone was smooth and unblemished. Finally, the dragon heaving beneath her as he charged down the path, she noticed the ceiling.

She was sure she hadn't seen it before, but the glow of the jinn was being reflected from above. Once she knew what she was looking for, the sage was sure the walls were brightening with their troop's luminescence. Her stomach lurched, and she squinted into the distance. She'd hoped to see the end to give herself some kind of perspective, but there was only darkness.

The shining gate receded behind them as the company ran full out down the length of the Way. Though she knew turning back to reopen it would mean the deaths of all the jinn on the other side, losing sight of their entrance point made her feel claustrophobic.

The jinn broke ranks as they ran, the fear of being crushed up against each other until their bodies broke outweighing their sense of discipline. The ghuls became a flock of birds that swept on ahead. The sila let the orbs of energy they held dissipate, instead focusing their will on speed. Some leapt into the air to glide along beside the birds. Others propelled themselves along the ground, skating across the smooth surface as crackling electricity leapt from their feet.

Still, the tunnel shrank with no end in sight. Altair became an eagle, and Ajdaha took flight, the undulations of his body in the air not quite brushing the walls of the tunnel as they fled. Ephialtes plodded along as best he could. He was tireless, and the hard soles of his feet ran steadily against the stone of their path, but, for all the giant's strength, he could not push himself along fast enough.

Soon, he was trailing behind the jinn. Altair swept past him with a dip of his wing and a warning cry. Alice ducked down as the dragon flew close to the ceiling to make a way around him. The corridor was tight enough now there was hardly room for the maneuver.

Seeing the giant fall farther and farther back, Alice made a decision. She reached for her ocarina, swept it up to her lips, and began to play. She concentrated on her root, the pool of energy most closely associated with earth. Her power built quickly as her senses extended out, getting a feel for the nature of the tunnel. *If it can contract, maybe I can make it expand . . .*

Alice gasped as her mind worked to comprehend what she was perceiving. The smooth, white stone of the Way was no more than a foot thick. It didn't seem to become denser or thicker as it shrank, but she didn't worry about the physics of it. Outside the tunnel, there was nothingness.

No, she thought, *it isn't nothing, exactly.* She tried to make sense of it, the nature of the spaces between the worlds, but it was a dizzying infinity of chaos. Shapes emerged and receded in that interdimensional space, always in transition.

It was primordial, the universe as it was before every creation story. It was what was before God divided the light from the darkness and the skies from the seas, before the land rose from the waters and the heavens were filled with stars. They were passing through a shrinking straw plunged through the uncast clay of reality itself.

"Forget the path!" cried the dragon. "Feel for the wards at the far end! I don't know if I'll have the chance to do any opening ritual properly. If we get there in time, it's going to be you or nothing."

For all her fear, Alice's heart was heavy as she took her

eyes off the giant. She changed her song and felt for the third trial of the Way. All around, the tunnel continued to shrink. There was hardly space for two people to stand side by side without being thrown off balance by the curve of the passage. The weaker, flightless sila were pressed together, torn between moving in single file and trying to stay spread apart so as not to be the last in line for salvation.

"Make way!" bellowed Ajdaha, flying as close to the ceiling as he could without knocking Alice from his back. The ghuls simply became a cluster of butterflies and moths. Their little bodies easily made way for the dragon. The sila grudgingly slowed, crouching and leaning as best they could. Ajdaha's lashing tail struck two of them as he passed, sending them tumbling with cries of despair. Behind them all, the stone-on-stone ring of Ephialte's heavy footsteps fell farther and farther away.

Gripping the dragon with tense, burning thighs, Alice kept up her melody. Not knowing what else to do, she let the magic build within her. It was more power than she'd ever handled before. The tissues of her body ached with it. Her cells cried out for release. She had no idea how much force she needed. She had no idea if what she could do would be enough. Alice played through her fears, sick with the weight of her magic. She let it build until she couldn't feel her doubt, until she couldn't feel anything else.

Suddenly, the far end of the Way came into view. It was a smooth, circular section of white stone. There were no apparent signs or symbols, but Alice could feel the magic of the wards. They layered over the energy of the Way, sealing it.

The tunnel was small enough, Ajdaha could hardly fit, let alone fly. He called back over his shoulder, "Get ready, I'm going to change!"

With that, the dragon took his gold-skinned, human form. Alice landed clumsily, stumbling off balanced and reeling, but she didn't dare let her melody falter. Before she went down entirely, Ajdaha and Altair were at her sides to keep her upright and urge her forward.

The ceiling was low enough by then, most of their company were running with their heads down and shoulders stooped. Distantly, Ephialtes could be seen moving in a low crouch. The awkward posture made him even slower. Before them, the flat wall capping the stone column shrank visibly with every moment.

Unsure of what else to do, Alice released her magic and willed the Way to open. The white stone groaned and shuddered all about them as the ifrit wards resisted her. Cracks appeared and spread. They split and ran in every direction.

Still, the sage poured as much energy as she could into her intent. The tunnel heaved, and the cracks became fissures that led into the distance, out of sight the way they'd come. Alice closed her eyes and kept playing, fully expecting their thin skin of stone to shatter with every note. In her mind's eye, she imagined them all cast out into the chaos, their bodies torn apart and lost between the Realms.

Finally, the fissures seemed to come to a consensus. The many cracks ran to converge at the center of the circular stone wall capping the Way. As the rock broke away and the cracks became holes, white light poured into the tunnel. There was a terrible sound like the entire world was ending in an avalanche, and then the end of the tunnel dissolved into a circular pool of rippling light.

Ocarina dangling in one hand, Alice pressed to the side of the tunnel to let the jinn pass. They looked at her gratefully as they poured through the ragged brilliance. Far behind, Ephialtes was still loping along. He helped his balance with his hands against the narrow walls. The dwindling space forced the giant to run nearly doubled over.

"He's not going to make it!" Alice shouted over the din of falling rock. The fissures were continuing to widen, radiating out from the doorway. The integrity of the tunnel was completely breaking down. It was just as likely Ephialtes would be thrown out into the void or crushed. *Maybe both,* Alice thought grimly.

"We can't go back for him!" Altair warded a fist-sized hunk of falling rock away from his head. He winced where it struck his forearm. "There's no time!"

"He's right!" shouted Ajdaha. "Come on, Alice! We have to go! Now!"

She knew they were right, but the sage ignored them anyway. Lifting her ocarina to her lips, she spun out a lively, rapid tune. They tried to take her by the arms to haul her through the exit, but she pushed them both away with a surge of force.

"Alice!" Altair leaned bodily against the will of the sage and grasped for her. "Don't do this! This is our chance!"

Ajdaha was trying to crawl to her on his belly, his fingers seeking holds in the crumbling floor. His legs drifted up in the air as if he were lifted up by a great wind. With pleading eyes, he held out a hand, not quite able to brush her ankle.

"Please, Alice," he said. "It's too late. Come with us."

The sage closed her eyes and concentrated. Her rapid breath left her feeling dizzy with hyperventilation. She loosed another press of energy and forced Altair and Ajdaha through the shining white light of their exit. They fought the magic, throwing themselves at her in a desperate bid to save her from herself.

Altair became a badger and tried to lodge his heavy claws in the cracks. He scrambled and scrabbled, but the stone crumbled like stale bread under his paws. There was no room for Ajdaha to become a dragon. Instead, he called on his own magic. Jinn fire leapt from his outspread hands, trailing lines from his fingertips. The demigod's flames caught in the white stone like barbed hooks, but he fared no better than his father as they guttered and broke apart.

The two of them tumbled in a shower of brittle flakes and pebbles through the blazing egress. They called out for her in despair as they disappeared, but the sage kept her eyes on the giant as the shouts of her family abruptly cut off behind her. It was impossible to stand anymore, so she let herself sink down to the floor, her legs folded into the Burmese position as her fingers flew over the ocarina's holes.

Ephialtes crawled. His back scraped against the ceiling. There was fear in his eyes, but, as he drew closer, Alice could see it was more for her than for himself. The giant lifted a hand and pushed the air with his palm as he clambered.

"Don't be a fool!" he shouted. "*Go!*"

Alice ignored him and played on. The cracks and holes in the tunnel were little windows. Each of them revealed a vista of unchecked chaos. The magic of the Way kept them safe within their shrinking sanctuary, but it was dying. She knew the tunnel would collapse at any moment.

And then, there was a cracking sound that shook Alice hard enough to throw her up from the ground. She struck the ceiling, and the world went gray and hazy at the edges. Hot blood trickled from her torn scalp down through her hair, but she kept the ocarina pressed to her lips and refused to miss a note. Her lips bruised from it as she played.

The tunnel snapped in half, and she distinctly felt their end spinning off in an uncontrolled tumble. Visions of primordial bedlam whirled from the jagged end of the Way. She couldn't be certain through the tumult of it all, but Alice thought she saw *things* moving out there.

Their bodies seemed to be mercurial, like kaleidoscopes, impossible configurations of both living and inanimate matter that changed from moment to moment. The barest sight of *them* threatened to tear her mind apart, but she played on, tasting the blood as it seeped from her mashed gums.

The light of their exit was fading. Tatters of white stone grew dark as they broke apart. She sensed the *presences* outside moving closer, curious and hungry. Through it all, Ephialtes never faltered. The giant pushed himself forward even as the floor broke away under his hands, the tunnel too small then for the giant to crawl without continuously dragging his back against the ceiling. His spine plowed a furrow of splintered white rocks that tumbled away, weightless, into formless infinity.

Finally, the sage felt the tunnel touch against the top of her head. Sandy pebbles stuck to her torn scalp and blood-matted hair. The giant was close, but he couldn't reach her. He was on his belly then, hauling himself forward with his elbows even as they tore through the stone, breaking it apart like thin ice.

Alice watched as his legs fell through the tunnel. Ephialtes scrabbled desperately and dug his fingers into the rock. In a moment, the sage knew he would fall away and that, soon after, she would join him in annihilation. Then, the last of the white stone shattered, and it was too late.

In the instant the Way ripped apart, Alice released her magic. She closed her eyes, her mind unable to accept the madness of raw, unformed reality all about her. It occurred to her then, at the last, to pray, but there was no time.

Chapter 32:

THE TUNNELS OF TARTARUS were shattered and broken. The Way was gone along with its wards. The shockwave of the broken enchantments echoed outward through the endless honeycomb of passages. The ruined corpses of ifrit and nephilim lay scattered all about, all of them destroyed in an instant. The bodies of the ifrit were dissipating into heavy, oily smoke that slowly rose to pool thickly against the ceiling. The blood of the nephilim spread across the floor, the puddles joining to form little pools among the wreckage.

Altair blinked through the haze. He'd forgotten how hot the Realm was. Here and there, little seams of magma dribbled. It was enough to light the ragged hole their entrance had torn in the underground.

It was hottest above them, and the jinn knew the surface of the ifrit world was near. *Doesn't matter*, he thought ruefully. *She's gone, and we're trapped.* Ajdaha stood at his side, drawing his katana from its sheath. Around them, the score of jinn were gathering up their weapons and forming into a defensive circle. Without the sage, there was nowhere to run, and the howls of enraged ifrit, still distant yet, were coming

Chris Rathburn

from every direction.

No one broke rank or spared a look toward their leadership, and Ajdaha felt a swell of pride at their courage. He caught his father's eye, and Altair said nothing, but only drew his sabre. The dragon told them, "We make our stand here! If the sage still lives, this is where she'll come. We need to hold this point for as long as we can."

The jinn shouted their reply as one. The ghuls stood staggered with the sila to provide cover with their shields and protection with their spears. The jinn mages formed orbs of energy in their hands and waited for something to throw them at. For what seemed a long time, they stood like that, peering at the shadowed tunnels. Then, they saw the darker forms of their enemies.

The first ifrit to emerge from the splintered tunnels were destroyed in a hail of fire and lightning. They flew forward, roaring vengeance for their dead and the wanton destruction of their home. Moments later, the smoke of their melting bodies was rising to join with the cloud of the ifrit who'd died before them.

A pause followed, but the reprieve was short lived. The sila had hardly summoned their power again before another mob of black, demonic figures were swarming from every hole and every passage. The jinn mages loosed another volley, and many of the ifrit fell, dead or wounded, but it wasn't enough. Dozens flew over the fallen, red eyes glowing from their sooty faces.

The ghuls closed ranks as the ifrit reached them, the sila stepping back for protection. The magic of the jinn shields pushed back against the press of ifrit, waves of force distorting the air as the black figures reached for them. Some of the ifrit became smoke and attempted to slip through, but the enchanted shields held them at bay.

Howling their rage, a number of the smoky figures swept toward the ceiling to launch an assault from above. The sila were waiting, jinn fire crackling between their fingers. The mages threw their burning, sparking orbs at the ifrit and shouted defiance as their wraithlike bodies ripped apart and their vaporous remains rose to join the mounting dark clouds of their dead.

Jinn crouched low as the enchantments on their shields began to fail. As one, they readied their spears, their rune-work glowing as their wielders fed their fire into them. It would augment their enchantments, but pushing the weapons' magic beyond their limits meant they would break down quickly. It didn't matter. All of them knew, if they fell, it wouldn't matter how long the enchantments lasted.

When the first shield failed, the soft aura of its white light extinguished with an audible snap and crackle, the ifrit around it howled in triumph and surged into the gap. The jinn thrust their spears into the charge together, those not facing the assault grimly eyeing the angry shadows before them. The ifrit lunged here and there, watching and waiting as the shields burned lower.

The ifrit tried to push further into the carnage while the spear jinn were bringing their weapons back to bear. The nearest sila loosed another barrage of destructive energy. Several fell and slowed the others, but the ifrit had breached the defensive barrier.

Altair and Ajdaha stepped past the sila, swords held high. They brought them down, cutting through smoky flesh, and down again, pushing back their assailants. Behind them, one by one, the shields of the ghuls were winking out.

The first jinn made no sound as he died. Smoggy claws ripped his head from his shoulders, and the body gently leaned forward into its killer. The ifrit victor laughed as the corpse, flames still gouting from its neck, sank to its knees before it. The creature died a second later as a pair of spears lanced into its throat and chest. A cry of dismay rang out as the first of the spears broke. The magic of its ruined enchantment dispersed into the air in a rippling burst, like oil in water.

Though the weapon itself was intact, without the enchantment, it was nothing to the ifrit. The jinn dropped it immediately and became an ox. He lowered his horns and charged the next closest of their enemy, but it was useless. The ox merely passed through the jeering monsters. The ifrit toppled him, smoky hands snatching at the ox jinn's legs until he fell. A moment later, the ox jinn bellowed out his last as the ifrit tore out his bowels.

More ifrit fell, but more spears failed with them. Few of the ghuls had a working shield or spear by then, and none of them possessed both. Sila hurled their magic where they could, but their formation was deteriorating into the chaos of battle. The jinn mages were visibly weakening besides. They dimmed as they drew again and again from their fiery souls. Their group had never been meant to hold a position indefinitely, only to create time for the sage. Without that purpose, they were doomed.

Ajdaha twirled like a dancer as he passed his katana through the bodies of the ifrit. The sword was not a true Artifact, but its enchantment was superbly made. It would not hold forever, but, in the time he had with it, the gold-skinned man laid waste all about him such that he could scarcely be seen behind the wreaths of oily smoke that rose from the bodies at his feet.

Holding his sabre in one hand, Altair snatched up a functioning shield from a downed ghul. The others of his sort took the forms of rhinoceroses and great tortoises, any creature that might resist the ifrit awhile longer by way of thick hides and hard shells. Altair vaulted up and then leapt from the back of one of the tortoise jinn. He landed on top of his shield on an ifrit and bore it to the ground as he sliced the arm from another.

The ghuls were all buried beneath billowing swarms of

ifrit when the sila began to fall. It was difficult to see through the thick smoke of the dissipating ifrit corpses, fitfully lit from beneath by the bodies of the jinn as they burned away. The living ifrit moved through the smog, using their fallen brethren as cover. They began taking the sila from behind where they could, the quickest, most desperate jinn detonating the orbs of energy in their own hands, doing as much damage as they could as they destroyed themselves.

Altair and Ajdaha stepped so they stood back to back as the last of their guard fell. Dozens of ifrit had died. The jinn had given much more than they had received, but, without the sage, the weight of numbers was the deciding factor. The eight remaining ifrit wiped the smoldering blood of jinn from their lips and spread out to circle the two.

Ajdaha's weapon was holding. The enchantments still blazed brightly from the scrolling runework down the spine of the katana. Altair's sabre was flickering. The damaged magic seeped out in flares of white light. It was still functional, but not much longer.

Though they could have been taken in the next rush, the ifrit did not advance. They kept just out of striking distance and waited. From an intact corridor leading from the burnt cavern the jinns' arrival had created, another ifrit flew forward.

This one was bigger than the others and moved with the confidence of a leader. Its command over its form was greater than its lessers. It appeared as the shadow of a well-groomed man in a suit. The ifrit looked pointedly at the others, and they followed his example, their smoky forms taking on coherence until they were entirely solid.

"Put those swords down," said their leader, "and let's have a conversation."

Altair shook his head. "Can't do it. Besides, there's only nine of you left."

"That you know of," said the ifrit.

The jinn shrugged, the tip of his sword never moving. "I'll take my chances."

"Look," said the ifrit, "be reasonable. Our end of this Way explodes, killing everybody in the room. Then, you and your henchmen come pouring through and start trying to kill everybody else. You *should* be dead on the ground now with the rest of them, but I'd be happy to discuss letting both of you go if I can get some answers."

"He's stalling." Ajdaha adjusted his grip on the katana. "Waiting for reinforcements."

Altair rolled his eyes. "No shit, son. What do you think *we're* doing?!"

The ifrit narrowed his eyes and looked about the cavern for some sign of help for them. Seeing nothing but burnt rock and black smoke, uncertain, he said, "What do you . . . ? Ah, hell with it! Kill them both!"

The eight ifrit leapt forward, wings spread wide. Faces like gargoyles leered triumphantly as they sought the flesh of the jinn. Altair and Ajdaha raised their swords in grim, futile defiance. They meant to kill as many as they could, but neither expected to survive. Nonetheless, they shouted bravely as the monsters came, each of them swinging for their nearest target.

Just before they met, a burst of brilliance threw them apart. Alice and Ephialtes appeared in front of Altair and Ajdaha. As the sage and the giant stepped through a ragged circle of white light, the jinn and the demigod were thrown on their backs, as astonished as the ifrit.

The portal began sealing itself immediately, revealing glimpses of boundless chaos. Moving quickly, Alice pulled a pistol from her vest, cocked it, and shot their leader twice. The bullets flashed as they punched overlapping holes through his chest, killing the ifrit instantly. Holding her ocarina in her left hand, the sage pivoted and double tapped the next ifrit closest to her. Its body dissolved into formless smoke almost before the second bullet could touch it.

Recovering their wits, the remaining ifrit howled and threw themselves forward. Ajdaha slid his sword to Altair and took his dragon form. His long body twisted around and righted itself as he blew green flames at two of the ifrit. In seconds, nothing of them remained but thin, black wisps of heavy smog.

Altair flipped to his feet in a neat kip-up. He hooked Ajdaha's katana by the hilt with his toes and kicked it up into his hand. In quick succession, he buried his sabre and the last of its magic in the chest of an astonished ifrit. As the blade's magic guttered out, he released it to take the katana in both hands. He raised it high, then brought it down in an arcing cut that sliced through the body of another from shoulder to hip.

Ephialtes reached for an ifrit with his bare hands. It laughed in disdain as it simply stood and waited for the giant to pass through it uselessly. Its chortling turned to surprised, strangled grunts as the giant's fist closed around its neck.

With his other hand, Ephialtes drew his silver sword. He slashed with it in the same motion and sliced the ifrit in two at the abdomen. He turned to face the others but stopped when he saw the sage.

Alice didn't bother to take aim at the remaining two ifrit. She simply pointed her gun and fired until she hit something. Many of her shots went wild, but only two needed to land. Seconds later, the last of the ifrit were melting into smoke at her feet.

They cast about, but there were no more to be seen. Altair spun to face Alice and ran to her. She met his embrace and pressed her face against his neck. After a moment, she remembered herself and pushed away.

Reluctantly, he let his arms drop, mindful of his sword. "You're alive!"

Alice nodded, a distant look in her eye. She returned the

pistol to its holster and drew another. "It wasn't far. I kept us safe until we could cross over."

She looked around, brow furrowed. "What happened? Where are the rest of us?"

"Oi! Here's one." Ephialtes toed at a rapidly melting cluster of fallen ifrit. The giant slapped at the side of something with the flat of his blade. Cries of fear faded into sounds of protest as one of the sila weakly sat up.

A female, the jinn rubbed at her temple and winced. Burning blood seeped from dozens of cuts and gashes. Recognizing the giant, she accepted his hand and let him ease her to her feet.

"Djamila?" said Ajdaha.

"Yes, lord," the sila replied weakly.

"Glad to have you with us!" he said. "Can you move?"

Djamila looked about the ruined cavern. The bodies of the ifrit were all but gone, the thick, black smoke overhead slowly dissipating as it found ventilation. Many of the fallen jinn were still smoldering, burning down to ash. The fewer nephilim corpses were badly mangled from the explosion. The battle that followed had reduced them all to unrecognizably tattered, bloody masses.

Her face fell where she recognized some of her fallen friends. With an effort of will, Djamila's features hardened and became impassive. She looked to Ajdaha, the press of her magic already mending her injuries.

"Well, I'm not staying here!" She pushed away from Ephialtes gently to stand on her own. Her legs soon wobbled, and she leaned against the wall for support. For a moment, Djamila looked as though she would fall, but she steadied herself by pressing her palms against the stone.

"Where are we going?" asked Alice. "Where's the Door?"

"There's no time." Altair tossed the katana toward the dragon. "We need to move!"

Ajdaha returned to human form, snatching the katana

out of the air and sheathing it smoothly before starting off after him at a jog. Most of the tunnels leading from their cavern weren't much bigger than the ifrit who used them, and some of them much smaller. With their ability to shift into smoke, if they had to, an ifrit could make do with a passage the size of a keyhole.

"Let me help you," Ajdaha told the sila as he put an arm under her shoulders. Djamila accepted the support gratefully, and the two of them followed after Altair. Ephialtes motioned to Alice to go before him with a quick flick of the tip of his sword. Keeping her pistol raised up in a safe direction, she nodded and took off after the rest.

"This is Tartarus," said the giant, keeping pace behind her, "the underworld of the ifrit. The tunnels are all ramping up, so I think we're headed for Abaddon."

"Aba-what?" she called back to him.

"Abaddon," Ephialtes repeated. "It's the ifrit name for the surface of this world."

Alice quickened her pace to catch up with Altair, as much out of fear as urgency. He glanced at the pistol in her hand and gave no objection to sharing the point position. The sage eyed his empty hands worriedly.

"How are you going to protect yourself?" she asked.

The jinn kept his eyes forward. "I hadn't given it much thought."

"Take this!" she said as she pushed her pistol into his hands. He held it gingerly, unsure of the device. Pausing their advance, she adjusted his grip.

"The safety's off. There're thirty bullets in there. Keep your finger off the trigger until you want to shoot something."

"Ok," said Altair, and the pistol went off in his hands. The gun's report startled them all to a standstill. The jinn looked over his shoulder, embarrassed, then down where the bullet had carved a deep furrow in their tunnel before burrowing out of sight through the rock.

"Sorry." He took his finger off the trigger and laid it on the guard instead. "What's the safety?"

Alice opened her mouth to reply, but angry shouting and howling could be heard faintly. There were echoes in those close passages, and she couldn't tell if it was wishful thinking they only came from behind. She shook her head and looked back to her golden son. "How much farther?"

"Just keep heading up," said Ajdaha. "Not much longer. You'll feel it when we get close."

They set off at a brisk jog. As they distanced themselves from the wreckage of their arrival, the usual features of Tartarus reasserted themselves. The ifrit Realm reminded Alice of an ant colony. Tunnels bored through solid rock, branching often. The all-too-frequent side passages left her nervously expecting dark, smoky hands to snatch at her at any moment.

"Aren't there any larger rooms anywhere?" she asked.

Altair nodded. "We're avoiding them. Ajdaha studied the local tunnel systems before we left Shambhala. His memory is nearly perfect."

"How's yours?" she asked.

"Imperfect," he admitted, "but he nagged the shit out of me before we left until I could at least recite the steps of our route."

Without breaking stride, the sage concentrated and extended her senses. They were moving quickly enough, she found it was easier if she closed her eyes. Otherwise, the dual streams of rapidly changing sensory information only left her feeling dizzy and sick.

Turning her attention ahead, Alice could discern the layout of the tunnels all around them. She whistled a soft tune, leveraging her magic to expand her awareness further. She could perceive where the ifrit were as black splotches in contrast to the burning points of light that were the jinn.

Alice opened her mind and whistled her imagery to

Ajdaha. *I think I know where we're going,* she thought, then highlighted a stretch of tunnel above them in her mind's eye. *Is this right?*

She heard the dragon's voice in her mind. *It is.*

Good, then keep close.

She felt Ajdaha's hesitation, but he relented when she turned and he saw the look of determination on Alice's face. Then, the sage drew a second pistol and shook her head at the guns in her hands. *This is such a bunch of hokey action movie bullshit.*

Her son's silent laughter echoed in her mind. Embarrassed, she muted her thoughts again and put her attention back on her whistling. Her clairvoyant knowledge of the tunnel network prepared her for what needed to be done.

Alice wasn't sure of the ways in which the ifrit were able to communicate with each other, but she could tell by their movements there was an active search for them. The denizens of Tartarus knew their tunnels intimately, and the ifrit were making good guesses as to where her group was going.

As they rounded a bend in their tunnel, Alice already had her gun pointed where it needed to be. She kept her head down and her eyes closed, whistling her magic as she shot a surprised ifrit in the face. She didn't break stride but ran right through the oily smoke of the corpse as it fell to ground and raised both her guns to cover an approaching cluster of side tunnels.

The next ifrit to emerge died instantly, an enchanted bullet leaving a strangely uniform, straight tunnel directly behind the place where its head had been. In the same breath, Alice fired her other gun toward another passage. The ifrit there tried to become discorporeal to evade the attack, but the sage's magic tore the black patch of smoke to tatters.

She sensed how the others behind her cautiously peered down the side tunnels as she sped past them. Alice didn't stop or attempt to share her headspace with them. Every second standing still was a second their enemies were moving. Letting her friends know her mind risked someone else seeing it, too. Trusting her friends to keep up, Alice kept her head down and her melody clear as she fired off another shot.

The bullet struck an empty space of tunnel and punched through the stone like paper. The shot didn't make sense until she had taken several more steps forward. At the mouth of a side tunnel, she pointed her gun without looking and fired again. An ifrit howled as its body disintegrated. The sage's first bullet had been a feint to prevent its advance, keeping it in place until she arrived.

They kept on like that, staying ahead of the main search efforts and picking off stray ifrit as they emerged. When they reached a point where their tunnel opened out into a chamber, a handful of ifrit were waiting, crouching mistily behind low rocks. The sage didn't hesitate and emptied both of her pistols into the waiting ambush.

The bullets sheared through stone and smoky flesh alike. The exchange was over before it started, and, in the momentary, hazy calm that followed, Alice stopped there to reload. She fumbled with the magazines, her hands shaking with adrenaline in the lull.

"Shit," she said as one of the precious stores of ammunition slipped through her fingers. Her deific hand snapped out to catch the magazine neatly. She smiled down at their perfection, and they stilled immediately, their divine nature overriding her human frailty.

Now reloading as if the movements were innate, Alice panned her attention about. As far as she could perceive, there were inbound ifrit. The closest would be on them in less than a minute. Many more would follow, and she could see their pursuers were gradually gaining as well as amassing. Looking up, Alice pointed at the ceiling with the barrel of a pistol.

"Ephialtes." She tapped a spot with her toe. "I need you

to come and stand right here."

The giant hesitated, first making sure Djamila could stand on her own. Altair pointed his pistol variously at several tunnels leading from the chamber and looked to Ajdaha uncertainly. The demigod moved to Alice's side and looked where she was pointing.

"We should keep moving, Alice," he said. "It's not safe to just push your way to the surface. For all we know, there may be a lake of lava right above us."

The sage shook her head. "Not a lake. It's a river. Ephialtes, your cloak. Everyone else, stay close."

Ajdaha frowned worriedly at the ceiling and then to his father, but neither said anything further. Holstering her pistols, Alice drew her concertina. She'd never touched one before, but her gifted hands worked the keys and bellows with uncanny precision. Laughing heartily, the giant slid his sword into the metal ring at his belt, then swept his cloak from his shoulders. Handing it to Djamila, he stretched in ecstatic relief and began to grow.

Ephialtes reached the ceiling in moments, braced his shoulders against the stone, and shoved. The chamber groaned, and then rocks tumbled down as the giant raised his hands and clawed with his fingers. Below, Alice stood between his feet and improvised a lively polka as she wove an aura of force about herself and her companions.

The sila screamed as the first boulder hammered down against the sage's shield. The magic flared brightly and sent it bouncing away. Altair laughed and let out an excited whoop as he put his arm around Djamila's shoulders to comfort her. Ajdaha stood quietly staring upward, his expression a mixture of horrified wonder.

The giant kept growing until his legs were the only part of him that was visible. A shout like thunder rang out, shaking their cavern, as Ephialtes reached the surface. Alice concentrated, her fingers a blur as they played over the keys, pouring energy into her shield until it was nearly opaque.

The irregular space around the giant's body brightened rapidly, and then lava poured down all around the giant's legs. Alice's shield flared even brighter as molten rock drizzled then gushed down onto them. For a time, the four of them could see nothing of the world, their little bubble of safety completely drowned in lava. Then, the flow began to rush down the tunnels, and the chamber emptied enough they could see above themselves again.

Laughing merrily, Ephialtes raised up one leg as he clambered out of his tunnel and onto the surface. The molten rock washed off his craggy skin like it was water. His other leg followed, and Alice had to close her eyes against the brilliance of Tartarus's sky.

Through the falling lava, a giant, red sun shone down. Alice redoubled her efforts, throwing herself into her song to repel the heat of it. Ephialtes knelt down and peered back the way he'd come and reached for Alice. His fingers were like massive stalagmites as they closed around her field of force.

Ephialtes lifted them effortlessly, dislodging another avalanche of rock to splash down in the lake of lava forming just below the surface. Alice could read understanding in the faces of her family. Their exit had made enough mess, no one would be following them that way any time soon.

Alice turned in place as she played, taking in the terrible sight of Abaddon. The great, red sun easily filled a quarter of the umber sky. Rivers of lava divided the rocky, black surface into irregular sections. She could see three active volcanos feeding them. The clouds above were patches of black soot that blotted out the sky wherever they reached. The heat-distorted air smelled of sulphur, constant winds scouring every surface with grit. Without her magic, the sage knew she would be dead within minutes in this environment.

"There!" called Ajdaha, pointing.

Alice followed his gesture, and, in the distance, she saw

a great lake of lava. It was broad enough its far shore could hardly be seen. In the center, there was a small island. The bit of land was oddly uniform, neatly level and cylindrical.

"That's the Door!" said Ajdaha, his voice ecstatic, his joy of discovery unflagging even then.

"Then let's move," said Altair. "That was an excellent roadblock you put up, Alice, but there will be more ifrit soon."

Ephialtes peered down at the sage and awaited her command. Alice stared down at the little island. She eyed the expanse of lava dubiously, then looked a question up at the giant. Ephialtes shrugged nonchalantly and gave her a massive thumbs-up.

"Shouldn't be a problem," he said.

"Alright then," said Alice. "Let's go."

Chapter 33:

AJDAHA WORKED QUICKLY, HIS golden fingers flashing in the red light of Abaddon. His eyes danced with the thrill of discovery. Any doubt or hesitation was scoured away by the demigod's delight in opening something secret.

Alice watched her son as he arranged his jinn fire just so. Soon, she would channel her power through the lines and vertices of the ritual pattern and open the Door to Urugal, Pazuzu's home and the center of his power. She was surprised to find she was calm despite it all, her hands occupied with playing the melody that kept her from being instantly burned to death.

Ephialtes could survive in the flows of lava that were a common occurrence across the surface of this world, but it was painful enough, he waited at the nearest shore. Beyond the scope of the sage's magic, he looked merely uncomfortable. With his knees drawn up to his chest and his arms wrapped around them, the giant resembled little more than a rocky hill.

Djamila stayed with Altair and the sage, Alice's sphere of force shielding them from harm as it rested on the surface of the molten rock all about them. Altair looked over Alice as she played and quirked an eyebrow at her quiet smile.

"What is it?" he asked her.

"This feels right," she said.

"This is what you were meant for," he agreed.

"It's funny," she said. "I never felt like I was really living because it wasn't *this*, you know?"

"I do," he said. "I've known you a long time, and I've never seen you keep yourself locked down like you were. In all your lives but this one, you didn't waste any time."

"What do you mean?" she asked.

Altair said, "I mean, before now, you've always made it so you knew yourself from birth. You've never had to hide your magic before, not from yourself."

Alice thought it over. The jinn's words left her feeling sad. She felt cheated knowing she'd spent decades of her life, the last one she was going to get, as a sort of failsafe against an enemy she hadn't even known existed.

"Seems like such a waste," she said, rueful.

Altair shook his head. "It's what you had to do."

"How can you be sure?" she challenged. "We still don't even know *why* we're doing this."

"We're doing this because Pazuzu will kill you if we don't," said the jinn, "and the fact that he's been trying hard to make that happen means we are headed the right way. You'll figure out the rest soon enough."

"How can you be sure?" she asked again.

Altair grinned. "Just because you don't know yourself very well yet doesn't mean you're not who you are."

Djamila smiled at that but said nothing. The sila was going through a series of motions and poses that reminded Alice of yoga. Apparently, they were supposed to help her focus her magic. The sage felt a pang of nostalgia for her Pilates class.

Catching the look, Alice asked her, "What is it?"

The sila said, "He's right. I'm here because of who you are." The smile faded from her face. "So were the others."

Alice fell quiet as she thought it over. Djamila was right. People had died to support her. Feeling melancholy that the first years of her life were spent in hiding suddenly seemed petty compared to their sacrifices. A somber mood settled over their little group, and no one spoke again while they waited for Ajdaha to finish his work.

Pazuzu's Place stank. As they passed through the Door from Abaddon and reality took shape again, it was the first thing about Urugal that came clear, the smell of blood and shit, sex and death, sickness and sweat. Breathing through the mouth only left a rich, oily sensation and the desire never to swallow again. As Alice's magic faded away, swirling lines and colors became distinct, and she realized the air was filled with screaming. The sage gazed upon the lair of Pazuzu and felt sick.

Their secret Door opened into a small recess overlooking a pit of bones. There were bodies scattered in, too. They ranged from recently dead, sometimes relatively intact corpses down to the cleanly white sticks that were all that remained of the long gone. Alice kept her wits about her as she swallowed back her gorge as she changed the concertina's tune to mute their presence.

"What is this place?" she asked softly, her hands all but forgotten as they went about their task.

Ajdaha's disgusted expression mirrored her own. "This is where the failed children and the dead mothers go. Not all of Pazuzu's offspring are viable, and he has no patience for them. Many more that survive their birth find their way here anyway."

Alice looked a question, and he answered, "Not strong enough to please their father.

"The mothers, too-" He grimaced. "-wear out over time,

and their bodies are taken here."

Alice watched insects and vermin as they ceaselessly feasted on the mass grave. Soon, each of the new bodies would be picked clean, indistinguishable from the rest of the bones. She forced herself to look away.

"How do you know so much about this Place?" she asked. "Is it in your notes somewhere? In your maps?"

Ajdaha replied, "In part. The specific layout, I didn't know before Salem and Eben were able to locate those maps, but a lot of it matches up with legend."

Alice cocked her head. "Legend?"

Altair nodded. "There're stories all over creation. The sort to scare young ones into being good. Urugal was even known to the ancients on earth, though poorly understood. Long ago, humans mistakenly thought it was just another name for Hell."

"They weren't far off," Ephialtes said as he shrugged his cloak off his shoulders so it hung down his back. He rested a hand on the pommel of his sword, the feel of it a comfort. Djamila kept quiet at the giant's side and scanned for threats.

The golden man nodded. "At Shambhala, it has been well established Urugal is a real Place, but only a few besides Pazuzu and his children have ever seen it."

"Sounds fascinating," said Alice. She couldn't quite keep an edge from her voice. She was eager to be done with Urugal, literal Hell or not. "Now, where do we go from here?"

Ajdaha panned his gaze around the area. The charnel pit dominated a cavern of black stone. A number of unmarked tunnels snaked away from the room. It looked much like Tartarus but colder. The thin seams of red light were absent, the space instead lit via sconces stuffed with bioluminescent fungi.

As the golden man got his bearings and headed toward one of the tunnels, Alice caught a rancid smell of excrement as she passed one of the lights. Looking closer, she saw the glowing mushrooms were growing out of wet hunks of feces. Feeling what she hoped were beetles crunching beneath her feet, Alice kept pace with her son.

Altair and Djamila fell in step behind them, and Ephialtes kept to the rear. The jinn held the gun Alice had given him carefully, as if it might discharge on its own. The sila kept her power focused at her fingertips, ready to lash out at short notice. The giant held his silver sword in an easy grip. Following suit, Ajdaha pulled his katana from its sheath. Alice was quietly envious, her hands longing for the feel of a pistol grip as they kept up their shrouding melody with the concertina.

Following their corridor, they passed from the pit of the broken ones into a realm of more vibrant abomination. As the walls of the passage opened out into a long room, ifrit, jinn, and all manner of nephilim were chained against the walls. They lay in ragged, filthy bedding, their chains glimmering with enchantments to keep them docile and weak.

Here and there, ifrit moved freely among the mothers of Pazuzu. They ignored the intermittent pleading and the cries of pain and fear. Those mothers were the minority. Most of them sat silently, their eyes empty, staring at nothing, idle hands patting listlessly against swelling bellies. To the willing, the ifrit passed out bowls of gruel made thick enough to be eaten with scooping fingers.

Once, Alice saw one of the shadowy creatures lean in to inspect an unmoving body. The mother looked elven, but her skin was darker than those she'd seen in Gaia's Place. As she watched, the jailor ifrit prodded at her with its claws. The ifrit pinched and pulled, even tore her skin until it was certain the nephilim was dead.

Flicking aside the ragged strip of dark skin with its jellied droplets of clotted blood, the ifrit stooped down closer to reach between the dead elf's legs. After a few moments, the shadowy creature raised up a small, unmoving body, jostling and bouncing it a little. When nothing happened, it jabbed the little form with a merciless claw. Even then, there was no response. Setting aside the tiny corpse, the creature worked the elf's body out of the restraints. Taking the body over its shoulder and clutching the stillborn to its chest, the ifrit passed close by Alice and her friends and headed toward the pit.

Another mother was screaming out her agony, with another jailor-midwife ifrit stooped before her in attendance. This one Alice recognized as a minotaur, her cries coming as a heavy lowing. The sage stopped there and watched with increasing, horrified certainty of what she was seeing as the ifrit worked.

The minotaur was at the end of her labor. With a final, wrenching heave, she fell back into her putrid bedding, and the ifrit called out triumphantly. Pinching an umbilical cord in half with its black claws, the monster held up a new, stolen life.

Reaching out with her senses, Alice could see the baby, a boy, was like his mother in many ways. The newborn had hooves and the head of a bull. In the world less than a minute, the infant looked like he was already trying to orient himself and get moving.

Where they differed was in that, where the mother was covered in a pelt of brown fur, the child's hide was a series of armored bands. Alice was reminded vaguely of an armadillo, but the baby's hide looked tough enough to stop a bullet. Her nerves tattered with disgust, the sage thought of her guns again and wondered if it would be right to simply start executing everything, just to stop all the suffering, or if she would simply be destroying in the act of preserving her own sanity. *Would it be mercy or just cleaning up?*

The exhausted minotaur mother did not protest or even look up at her midwife as the ifrit cradled the baby in its arms. Holding the child in an obscene parody of nurturance, the monster headed for another passage. Ajdaha waved them forward, and they followed after.

"We're in the inner spawning pits. This is where Pazuzu keeps his breeding stock with the greatest promise. He will want to see his new son," said Ajdaha softly. No one noticed them as they passed through the narrow spawning room. "This ifrit should take us to his court, or near enough."

Her fingers never faltering, Alice kept the four of them hidden as they passed into another chamber filled with mothers expecting, mothers dying, and mothers yet to be. Though many were humanoid, some looked like they were little more than animals, witless creatures with no understanding of what was happening. She wasn't certain whether that was better or worse.

"He impregnates *all* of them?" she asked, sickened and astonished. From what her son had said, it sounded as though these chambers were only Pazuzu's private reserve, yet she'd already seen dozens of captives. She shuddered despite herself as she tried to imagine how many more there must be for the monster to maintain his army.

"From what little information is available," said Ajdaha, katana held ready, "I understand it's an indirect procedure."

Altair, Ephialtes, and Djamila were close behind, each of them trying to look everywhere at once. If even one creature saw them, it would bring down Pazuzu's wrath on them in an instant. Wrinkling her nose in revulsion, Alice couldn't help but ask, "What the hell is that supposed to mean?"

The golden man shrugged and smiled weakly. "I have my guesses, but it's a mystery. We'll have to wait and see."

They crept along behind as the ifrit midwife passed from one chamber to another. The suffering was an unbroken trail of wailing mothers, dead bodies in chains, and stolen children. The midwives left with the babies and soon returned. Alice couldn't imagine—refused to imagine—what was happening to the young as they began their lives in Pazuzu's slave army.

Ajdaha put his hand on Alice's arm as their chosen ifrit made another turn. "That way leads to a nursery. The court is this way."

Alice wanted to ask the question, *A nursery?* She kept silent, knowing she didn't want the answer. She looked after the ifrit midwife despite herself as they headed their separate directions. She extended her senses, unable to bring herself to look away when she knew it meant leaving behind a helpless child. She stopped herself when she saw a shadowy room, filled with squat cages and the nightmarish sounds of screaming, cooing, newborn monsters. Withdrawing her senses and putting her attention fully on her music, Alice guiltily wished it was enough to drown out the awful noises of Pazuzu's nursery.

Ajdaha walked slowly and looked carefully, checking every step against the maps he'd committed to memory. Eventually, he led them down one of many nondescript passages, and, abruptly, they were out of the breeding pits. Alice looked around nervously as they found themselves at the edge of a massive chamber. At its center stood the raised throne of Pazuzu.

In the middle of a large dais, there was a great, gilded chair with red, velvet cushions. Beside it were two tables. At the first, attended by a pair of ifrit servants, the lord of Urugal was being coaxed to climax.

The lord of Gehenna was squat, layers of thick muscle sheathed beneath layers of dense fat. Stubby arms dangled awkwardly around his ponderous gut. Short, thick legs flexed and shuffled as they bore him up. Wide, watery eyes shone from skin like flaking, black ashes.

Pazuzu gripped the table as he climaxed, ropes of ejaculate dribbling and spurting from his thick, disproportionately stubby penis. The pale slime dripped down to ooze through shallow channels that headed toward the edge. One of the attending ifrit moved swiftly to position a large, silver basin beneath the table to catch his master's seed. The look on the creature's face was that of reverence, as if he were collecting mana fallen from the heavens.

Alice watched in stunned silence as Urugal's ancient master orgasmed continuously for several minutes. His attendants soon filled the basin and slid another into place. Immediately, they carried their prize to the work waiting at the other table.

The space was loaded with what looked like dozens of little, phallic-shaped decanters. The ifrit filled them quickly and then sealed each with a lick of their inky tongues that reacted with the contents to form a yellowed, crusted seal. By the time their lord had finished, the two of them had nearly bottled the entirety of their first silver receptacle. The second basin awaited them, nearly filled as well. Stepping back and stretching languidly, Pazuzu yawned, took a long drink from a proffered chalice, and then clapped his hands twice.

Immediately, another pair of ifrit materialized as if from nowhere, their smoky bodies seeming to grow from the shadows. From a dimly lit passage, another table emerged, laden with more of the strange decanters, and they wheeled it toward the dais. Alice looked on in distaste at the routine precision of it all as the first ifrit completed their task of packaging their master's precious seed and moved their laden table down a short ramp.

The two workstations passed each other without a word, the first vanishing down still another passage. As the fresh array of decanters were checked over, a pair of the attending ifrit turned to their master and began to massage his phallus. Alice looked on, sickened and incredulous, at the dispassionate, repetitive monotony of the act.

"He just does this *all* day?" Alice tasted bile at the back of her throat.

Ephialtes muttered, his voice thick with revulsion, "And that's how he keeps everyone pregnant."

Pazuzu paused, his erect member waving ponderously before him. Slowly, the ifrit lord turned to look directly at the giant. Alice realized too late her hands had fallen still. In her shock and disgust, she'd simply lost her focus, unable to do anything beyond stare, enraptured at that stage of atrocity. Now, Pazuzu looked back at her, and his eyes widened in recognition. Registering something was amiss, his attendants stopped in their work and followed their master's gaze.

Everyone there froze, then Pazuzu roared, "Get the sage! Kill her! Kill them all!"

Altair and Alice looked toward each other and spoke in unison, "Ah, shit!"

Half a dozen more ifrit materialized from the shadows and swept toward them. Ephialtes leapt forward immediately, his silver sword clenched in one massive fist. He swept it in an arc that cleaved through two of the hidden guards, killing the creatures instantly.

As the fallen ifrit melted into smoke, Ajdaha swept his katana down, cleaving another nearly in half before its body lost cohesion. Not wanting to risk hitting one of their allies, Altair stepped to the side and turned his pistol on Pazuzu himself. Shouting again and again for reinforcements, the ancient ifrit's form melted into smoke as he threw himself toward cover.

Djamila followed close behind the giant, her fire gathered around her hands. She didn't dare throw her orbs around in close quarters, instead striking out at an ifrit with her fist. The wraithlike creature dodged and hissed when her magic came close to its shadowy flesh.

Alice backpedaled as she dropped her concertina. Two ifrit were bearing down on her, reaching out to take her life. Snatching for a pistol, she tripped over the instrument in her very next step and tumbled backward with a wail of dismay.

She held up her hands uselessly, and her shout became a scream as the ifrit solidified. Towering over her, they reached for her throat with their wicked claws. She felt their cool skin against hers as she worked the pistol loose from where it had jammed awkwardly against her body. She made no effort to protect herself, knowing it would be useless. She would either get her gun or the ifrit would get her.

Before the black hands could close around her throat, the steady report of gunfire rang out. The ifrit above her screamed in pain and anger as the bullets tore holes through their bodies. The wounds were large enough to hold a fist without the knuckles touching the sides of the cavities. A moment later, the monsters were only so much drifting smoke.

Alice sat up. She squinted and coughed through the vaporous corpses. Altair was by her side in an instant to offer a hand. Thin, gray smoke drifted from the barrel of his pistol, to merge with the dark, oily fumes of the dead ifrit.

There was no way to hold their position. Ifrit were flying in from too many passageways to cover. It was only a handful to begin with, but the shouts of approaching guards were quickly growing louder. Taking the jinn's hand, the sage threw herself to her feet. She drew another gun from her tactical harness, worked the slide to chamber a bullet, and brought her pistols to bear on Pazuzu.

The ifrit lord had partially reformed, crouched behind his dais for cover. Alice didn't hesitate and began firing round after round toward her best guess at his position. Uncertain but determined, Altair followed suit.

Pazuzu's throne and collection table collapsed as the enchanted bullets scooped out massive furrows. Alice didn't let up the barrage for an instant. She thought of where all those little, filled decanters were going and what they would be used for if this creature wasn't stopped, and she let that focus her anger into something cold and lethal.

The decanting table and its many vessels exploded into clouds of slivered wood and pulverized crystal. The raised dais itself was soon cracked and cratered, the scent of burnt stone adding to the reek of Urugal. Behind it, Pazuzu was shouting in anger but also in pain. Alice felt her heart flutter and her gut relax. *He's hit! Now, did I get him, or is he just wounded?*

The sage's thoughts scattered again as more ifrit entered the throne room. Her divine hands moved swiftly enough to eject the magazine and load another before the first struck the ground. At her side, Altair was struggling to work the release mechanism for his own magazine. Without a word, she plucked the weapon from his hands and replaced it with the gun she'd readied.

Her hands danced, and the jinn's pistol was reloaded in a heartbeat. Raising it up, she sighted on the dais again while Ajdaha shouted and plunged his katana into the chest of still another ifrit. At last, the enchantments of the weapon could endure no more, and its light winked out. He dropped it without hesitation, and the useless blade fell through the cloud of the slain ifrit's body to clatter against the stony ground as the lord of Shambhala became a dragon.

His roars so loud Alice thought her eardrums would burst, Ajdaha opened his jaws wide and breathed a torrent of green flame onto a cluster of charging ifrit. The creatures collapsed screaming, the magic in the demigod's fire pulling their bodies apart.

"No!" Djamila screamed. Ifrit had taken her, one on each arm while another grasped at the sila's legs. She tried to strike them with the magic gathered around her fists, but they held her fast. Desperate, she tried to loose her own power against herself, tried to use the fiery core of her own body as a final weapon to destroy them all, but she couldn't move enough to manage it. Instead, twin orbs of fire and electricity sped off and struck uselessly against the walls as the ifrit made to fly off with their hostage.

Ephialtes shouted in dismay and reached for the sila, but there were too many ifrit on him to move. As they threw him back, the giant shouted in frustrated rage, snatched at his neck, and ripped Gaia's cloak from his body. The garment tore with a sound like thunder, and a hemorrhage of ruptured magic rushed out in a wave from him.

The force of the uncontrolled energy pushed everyone in the throne room back. Most were thrown from their feet, including Alice. Gasping on her back, the air knocked from her lungs, the sage saw the giant raise his silver sword as he grew to his full height, the intricate engraving of its enchantments catching the light so the name OTOS flashed across her vision.

As large as Pazuzu's throne room was, Ephialtes still had to stoop. His back and shoulders dug at the ceiling. Heavy rocks crashed down to shake the ground as he thrust the tip of his sword into the chest of a dazed ifrit, the sheer size of it enough to cut the creature nearly in half. Meanwhile, Altair had taken the form of a centaur in the chaos, his footing assured by way of having more feet to balance with.

Alice did a double take as it registered Altair's form had hands instead of hooves. The jinn's lower half looked less like a horse and more like the body of an elongated gorilla. Thick fingers gripped the stony floor, strong enough to press divots into the surface.

The giant took full advantage of the lull. He stomped and kicked at the ifrit as he swung his sword. All the while, Ajdaha swept around the room and breathed fire onto everything that moved.

Altair stayed by Alice's side. The jinn tried to make his shots count, and, though he missed as often as not, it was enough to keep Pazuzu pinned down. The ancient one was wise enough to know that, for all his power, a single lucky shot was all it would take to bring him to his end.

The sage ignored the chaos, extended her senses, and focused on the layout of the chamber. She noted the exits, withdrew her perception, and drew her ocarina as she hand-

ed off her pistol to Altair. The jinn took it with the large fore-
hand of his lower gorilla half while he continued to empty
his own toward the dais.

Alice knew they couldn't stay where they were and that
there was no way out. Raising the ocarina to her lips, she felt
the energy gather at her root and soul centers. As the melody
took shape, she felt the stone all about her. The sage's power
expanded to connect with her third eye and solar plexus.

She heard Pazuzu scream for her blood, saw him point
at her wildly, his watery eyes wide with anger but also fear.
All of the ifrit oriented on Alice at their lord's command.
They ignored her friends, though it cost many of their lives
as they rushed at her. The sage closed her eyes and played on.
Her consciousness reached out to feel at the structure of the
doorways around the chamber.

Ephialtes threw himself down before the charge, using
his body as a wall to protect her. Though prone, he slashed
with his great, silver sword. The weapon was slow and awkward without his footing, and ifrit threw themselves onto his
wrist, hanging tightly to weigh it down further.

Altair fired his last bullet, pulled the trigger several more
times, then threw the pistol in frustration. Seeing the ifrit
swarming over and around the giant, he became an ogre. Nowhere near as massive as Ephialtes, the jinn was still able to
throw some of the ifrit back before they could become incor-
poreal and pass through his fingers.

Ajdaha swept in, unable to breathe flame for fear of
harming his friends, and plowed into the fog of ifrit. His
long body swept some of them off Ephialtes, but the creatures were happy to latch onto his scales with probing claws
as the dragon came to ground. His roars joined the giant's as
black talons prised at his golden hide.

It was Djamila who finally held the ifrit at bay. Freed
from her would-be captors, the sila ran silently to Alice's side.
She muted herself and dodged around the flying bodies, re-

lying on the others to provide distractions and further openings to move forward. Dropping and skidding on her knees, she released her magic just as three ifrit closed on the sage.

Djamila poured her fiery soul into the spell, holding back nothing as her magic created a field of energy that shifted and flicked around the two of them like an open flame. The ifrit threw themselves at her barrier but were thrown back from the sila's shield. Relentless, the monsters pushed and piled against the warding spell, sacrificing their bodies to break it, but Djamila was committed. The sila kept emptying herself into the magic, shouting wordless pain and fury as she challenged the ifrit to break first.

At last, Alice's melody took shape. Tendrils of energy coalesced around the sage. They were nearly invisible, like conscious heat distortions. She reached out with them for the stone around every doorway to Pazuzu's court. Grasping it all with her will at once, Alice trilled on her ocarina and pulled the walls down.

Chapter 34:

ALL THE SHOUTS AND screams of battle were drowned out beneath the cacophony of falling rock. Alice pulled at the stone and felt it shift. The translucent feelers of her magic wormed their way into little cracks and forced them wider. All the while, some part of her screamed, *Stop! This is crazy! You're going to bury us all!* The sage ignored reason, telekinetically lifting the boulders she'd pulled loose and thrusting them into the exits to block the tunnels. She pulled the walls down on top of her barriers, trying to prevent passages of any size from reaching through.

Djamila knelt with her arms outstretched, faded to a shadow of herself, and fed her fire into her barrier. Snarling ifrit pushed against it but were thrown back again and again as it flashed and flared in response to their assault.

The giant, the dragon, and the jinn in his ogre form were obscured by the press of bodies around them. Dust and grit from sealing the great hall drifted and blew, mixing with the smoke of dead ifrit to add to the confusion, turning everything outside Djamila's shield into indistinct, tussling silhouettes.

Chris Rathburn

Alice hoped they were alive and reassured herself with grim truths, *All the ifrit would be coming for me by now if they were gone.* She tried but couldn't keep herself from her own thoughts. *If they were dead.* She'd moved a lot of rock, but she wasn't certain all passages were blocked. She desperately wanted to reach out with her senses and probe until she could be sure, but she knew there wasn't time. There was nothing for it than to keep going forward. Shifting her melody, Alice took control of the sila's shield.

Freed from the spell, Djamila collapsed instantly. She was dead before she reached the ground. The sila had poured out her fire until there wasn't enough left to sustain her being. Her body, already transparent, faded to nothing as her life force was exhausted. In the span of her dying breath, Djamila disappeared as if she never was.

Alice refined the magic with her will and her nimble fingers, her rapid tune reinforcing the fallen sila's barrier. It lost the look of a bonfire, instead taking on the appearance of a translucent dome of steady, white light as the spell strengthened and expanded outward. She could feel it as the flow of her magic shifted toward her heart and crown centers. Her love and memories of her friends made them stand out like beacons in her mind's eye.

The barrier pushed out steadily. It drove the ifrit before it, plowing them over and tumbling them where the creatures fought hardest to resist her. When the shield reached Altair, it parted where it touched his skin. Realizing his succor, the jinn threw himself deeper into the barrier. He called out in pain where ifrit claws dug into his body and tried to keep him from it. Then, he was through, taking his humanoid shape again as he fell weakly to his knees.

Ephialtes still clutched at his sword when the barrier reached him. The giant bellowed as he smashed it against his own body to crush the ifrit that swarmed over him, heedless of the chunks of stone he was breaking away from his own chest. With his other hand, he pulled at the limp form of the dragon and held him close as the protective light of Alice's spell washed over them to scour away the monsters.

With her friends safely inside, Alice kept expanding the barrier. The dome grew rapidly and pressed ifrit against the walls until they were forced to collapse into smoke or be crushed. In moments, the wreckage of Pazuzu's dais was within the light, and she stopped its growth.

It had been difficult, but the sage allowed one other besides her companions to enter into her ward. She'd relied on her rage, using that connection with the ifrit as she'd used her love for her friends to find them in the darkness. It made her feel sick, that sense of closeness with such a monster. She could feel his lust even then, as hungry to breed with her as kill her. She sensed his surprise as he realized the invasion into his consciousness just before shutting her out with his will.

Shaking with anger, ancient Pazuzu stood up from behind the ruins of his throne and faced her. Unable to speak while she played her ocarina, Alice reached out with her consciousness, modifying her music to open a bridge between their minds. Cursing out his displeasure in the sibilant language of the ifrit, he concentrated on resisting. At first, she thought he'd succeeded, but then she felt a shift, the barest sense his strength had begun to ebb.

The press of the sage's magic was inexorable, but the ifrit's strength was that of ages, and he knew more of magic than she ever would. Alice could feel his age, that he was something from before her soul had lived its first life. He used every bit of that knowledge then as he fought for the sovereignty of his mind. Nonetheless, she persisted.

The sage only kept playing while the monster struggled. Alice leveraged the raw power of what she was with the skill of her deific hands until Pazuzu's control wavered. His will shook with effort. The sensation of it reminded her of the trembling of overworked muscles trying to hold a difficult posture for too long. Her racing fingers trilled out a rapid melody in a response that pushed the magic forward like the swell of a great wave, and, at last, the demon's warding fell.

Pazuzu collapsed, the sage's invasion suddenly preventing him from using his own body. It was an odd sight, watching the ifrit drop limply to the broken stone rather than simply dissipating into smoke. His uncharacteristically solid body fell with a dull thud and the sharp clatter of shifting rocks. Alice pushed deeper.

She probed for a connection between their thoughts, revolted as she felt his consciousness squirming greasily in the grip of her will. Feeling like she was pressing her mouth against a filthy, clenching anus, Alice joined their minds.

Tell me what you know of your master! she thought.

I have had many masters, came his response, Pazuzu's thoughts oily and slick. Alice pushed aside the fear they would somehow taint her and ignored the laughter echoing through her mind as he sensed that fear.

No games, she replied. *You know who I'm talking about. The one who took the other sages. The one who wants me destroyed. Adam.*

Pazuzu hesitated at that. *You really don't know?*

The ifrit wrested back minor control of his body, enough to listlessly turn his head to face her again. He looked searchingly at Alice. When she didn't reply, his thick lips broke into a wide grin. Within the prison she'd made of his consciousness, Pazuzu cackled merrily.

You really don't know! he jeered. *Lifetimes spent pursuing him, and here you are, ignorant as a child.*

I knew enough to get to you! she spat at him.

The ancient ifrit laughed again at her anger. *But you don't know enough for him! You don't, or you wouldn't be here! You're trying to level the field, and you think this will matter, but the Master will realize his plan! All who oppose him will be swept aside in the new creation!*

Tell me what you can, and we will protect you. She expanded the telepathic connection so all within the barrier could perceive their exchange. *I promise you we will.*

The ifrit laughed again and said aloud, his voice deep and rasping, "No, my time is at an end. If I speak with you, the Master will make an end of me. If I hold my tongue, you will do it for him. I would rather die here, I think, in my home. Anything you could do will be a mercy compared to him."

Altair was still sitting on the stone floor, bleeding fire, too exhausted to stand. "Do it, Alice. We'll find the answers we need. We don't need this monster to tell us."

"It's useless," Ajdaha agreed. He was badly injured, but, with the fortitude of a demigod, his wounds were visibly closing. Soon, he would be healed. He said, "In his twisted way, Pazuzu is an honorable being. I have never heard any account or seen any record of him betraying a patron once a deal has been made. It's been his way for millennia."

Ephialtes sat quietly, his stony flesh chipped and battered. He said nothing but gently stirred a finger over the place where Djamila had fallen. Her fingers flying to keep up her song, Alice was uncertain how long she could keep it up before she made a mistake.

Then he has this last chance to make a change, she thought to them, already knowing it was futile. The feelings of revulsion were disorienting, fed from what she'd done to get there, what she was doing now, and what she knew must happen to be finished in Urugal. Despite herself, the sage despaired.

Before she could push past the emotions, Pazuzu took advantage of her faltering to make another press for control of his body. In an instant, he pulled a thick, black ring from his thumb. The ancient ifrit held it before his lips, ignoring them all as Alice's friends pushed themselves to their feet in alarm, and then he blew through it.

White smoke issued forth as the ring rapidly shrank until

it disappeared. When it was nothing more than pale wisps that drifted toward the ceiling, Alice felt Pazuzu's Place die. She didn't understand the mechanism of it but intuitively grasped the essence of what happened.

Just as Gaia had invested something of herself in Alice's hands, the ancient ifrit had formed Urugal using a portion of himself as its seed. Like the grit at the center of a pearl, she perceived through the shifting magical energies the Place had built up over time around that kernel of Pazuzu's power. Now, he had withdrawn that piece of himself, and the sage understood it had been more than a catalyst. Pazuzu had pulled out Urugal's heart.

The corpse of that Place began to crumble immediately. The ifrit, each of them a child of Pazuzu, looked about in horror as they, too, realized what was happening. The wraith-like creatures became smoke and flowed away from Alice's barrier. With dark eyes and writhing, probing fingers, they searched what remained of the great hall for an exit.

At first, it was futile. The children of Pazuzu wedged themselves into every crack and crevice they could find, but the sage had managed to seal the room well enough, dead ends were all there were. Soon after, however, new ways began opening as Urugal's collapse gained momentum. A shout of triumphant relief went up from one edge of the room as a deep crack opened and the call was quickly taken up by the desperate ifrit.

The ruins of Pazuzu's great hall emptied quickly. It looked like someone placed the mouth of a giant vacuum against the wall beyond their chamber and flipped it on, sucking out all the bad, black air. The smoky bodies of the ifrit swirled around each other as each fought against their brethren to free themselves. The Place was shaking, countless fissures in the stone becoming obvious to the unaided eye.

The ceiling was breaking apart above them. Slabs of black stone shook loose and tumbled down on top of Alice's barrier. Within their sanctuary, the crashing rocks and boulders were no louder than the patter of rain against a strong roof. The sage's fingers flew over the holes of her ocarina as she piped her music, a manic melody that harnessed an almost boundless but barely controlled magic. For all its ungainliness, her spell was enough. The ward fueled by the brute force of Alice's power turned each of the crushing boulders away.

Alice sent out her thoughts, *What have you done?! You're killing everyone! All your children?!*

Pazuzu only shrugged and smiled in satisfaction at the sage's disbelief. "It doesn't matter. My family had no purpose than to serve me. Most of them, that was. Now, it seems some have gone another way."

Ajdaha, fully healed, ignored the chaos beyond the warding and cocked his large head at the ifrit. "What do you mean, demon?"

The ifrit laughed. "I should have known it. Apparently, I have become lax in my old age. I have allowed some of my children to wander too far and to make too many of their own decisions. My leniency has become my undoing."

Altair looked to his son. "What is he talking about?"

Ephialtes was looking about, his eyes wild as the Place collapsed. "It doesn't matter! He's stalling! We need to get to a Door now!"

The dragon was watching the ifrit carefully. "He means he has people, probably his children, placed at Shambhala, but it seems at least one of them defected and told us of the hidden Door to Urugal."

Altair considered, then smiled. "Whoever our enemy is, the scum are falling over themselves to get on his good side. Looks like someone threw their father to the wolves for a promotion!"

"Lucky us," said Ephialtes, his heavy breath a hot wind that tugged at the smaller beings. "Now, let's go!"

Pazuzu held his stomach and laughed. "It's too late! The Doors were the first things to break! It looks as though my boy thought this through. You will all die!"

Altair cocked his head, then said, "Ah, hell! We were given a taste of the bait and ran right into the trap to get the rest of it!"

The dragon nodded. "The enemy must have known, if we put his back to a wall, with no other options, Pazuzu would destroy this Place."

"And with us in it," said Ephialtes.

No loose ends, Alice sent to them. *Tidy.*

"So, that's it?!" said Ephialtes. "We're doomed?!"

"Fucked," Ajdaha agreed. With that, the dragon pulled in a deep breath and held it. He reared up and glared down at Pazuzu. When the ifrit met his gaze, Ajdaha opened his mouth and blasted him with pale, emerald fire.

The flames washed around the ancient ifrit, but he shrugged them off. At first, it looked as if Pazuzu would simply ignore the fire, like it was only so many stray sparks. Ajdaha did not let up and kept bathing the ifrit in flame. Slow and grudging, the ancient demon's defenses weakened, little by little, until he ignited. Pazuzu died quickly after that, his squat body collapsing before his fat began to sizzle and melt. The dragon kept going, burning away at the monster until there was nothing left but thinning trails of black smoke to show he'd ever been.

When it was done, Ephialtes lowered himself to the ground. He sat with his legs crossed and gently laid down his sword over his knees. He stared at the section of scorched stone where Pazuzu had stood, watched the cracks appear there and spider web across the floor. Fear and worry left his face, replaced by a kind of peace.

"Otos." The giant looked down at the silver blade and ran a finger over its etching, "You are avenged, brother. I will be with you again soon, and we will celebrate together."

"Giving up?" said Altair. The jinn had walked over to Ajdaha and was patting his son's golden flank affectionately. The dragon, watching the Place collapse and looking as resigned as Ephialtes, looked to his father and nuzzled him with his muzzle.

Altair embraced his son, wrapping his arms as far as they would go around the dragon's snout. Then, the jinn looked to Alice, and the others all looked with him. The sage played her ocarina so quickly, her fingers were a blur. Around them, her warding barrier was shrinking away from the walls of Pazuzu's hall, becoming as small as it could be and still contain them all.

Alice wished she knew what she was doing as she played, but there was nothing for it other than to keep going and hope. In her mind's eye, she kept seeing images of old hands on the strings of a lyre. She couldn't see him clearly, but Alice felt Gregor somewhere in the back of her mind, picking out melodies with utter certainty. Taking comfort from the sense of that old German's warm heart, the sage opened herself to the memories of the life she'd lived before she was born and let them guide her.

She played for her friends, felt the energy of their lives within her sanctuary. She played for the hapless creatures caught in the death throes of Urugal. Monsters though they were, she knew at least a few of them would have gone their own way if one had been opened to them. She felt most for the mothers, trapped in their pitiful warrens, doomed to a life that began with most of them begging for death before their fate left them hollow, broken shells, fulfilling their base, reproductive function until their bodies failed them.

Alice played for the young children, born into slavery to a cold master who cared only to mold them into ugly, strong things to serve him. There might have been hope for at least some of them, if there had been time. Now, all she could do was let her prayers speak through her music, that their deaths be mercifully quick.

The sage played for Timothy and the people she'd left behind. Though she expected she'd never see her old friends or her family again, she hoped that, even though they had no way to know it, they might feel she was still out there somewhere, loving them and doing what she could to keep them safe. She hoped, wherever Timothy's soul had gone, he could see her then, and, if he could not forgive her, maybe he could understand.

At the last, Alice played for herself, though not out of some frantic, reflexive need to preserve her life. It wasn't that she had no fear of death. The real reason was an unshaking sense of responsibility that lay deeper than her own genes. Alice played because it was her duty. She was the last of the sages, and she knew, if she fell, there would be no one else left *to* play.

When Urugal broke apart, Alice was ready. Boulders the size of elephants crashed down on her sanctuary, but the magic held. The floors crumbled and fell away to reveal nothingness. The falling stones shrank away in the depths of the void, but her magic held them up. The walls collapsed and turned to dust. The vacuum of what lay beyond the Place sucked greedily at the cracking maze of twisting tunnels. A great wind whistled and roared past Alice's barrier like a hurricane, Urugal's dying breath. Alice played on, and her magic kept the air within her borders breathable.

Soon, there was nothing left of Urugal at all. Alice and her friends sat alone in her protective sphere of power. The blackness of empty space was all around them. It pulled at the sage's magic hungrily. It was almost a living thing, that great nothingness, and she felt something like resentment as they endured.

Then, the void itself began to collapse. It couldn't be seen with the unaided eye, and it made no sound, but, with her expanded senses, Alice felt the space beyond her barrier contracting. The formless borders of what had contained Urugal shrank inward like the Place was deflating.

Soon, the metaphysical space of that miniature world had become so small, it was little more than a tight, black skin around Alice's shielding spell. She played on, not daring to rest, Urugal's empty corpse trying to crush them all as it collapsed. The struggle went on until it seemed they would stay like that, Alice and her companions huddled together until death claimed them.

Ephialtes kept still, his head down and his eyes closed, his thoughts only of his lost brother. Altair kept his arms around the dragon's neck. His son quietly rested his massive chin over his father's shoulder. Alice felt a great swell of pride for their bravery and loyalty. She wanted nothing more than to lay down her ocarina and join with them in their final moments.

Then, the darkness split with a sound like a massive, rubber sheet being torn in half. All at once, the hellish brilliance of Abaddon was pouring into their enclosure. All of them startled and looked about wildly as the split widened and branched. More and more of the ifrit Realm shone through. The stability of its greater reality scrubbed away the cyst of Urugal and washed away the ephemeral dream of Pazuzu.

Finally, it was over. Pazuzu and his Place were gone, along with his mothers and so many of his children. The sage and her companions were floating in a sphere of translucent, white light over the lava fields of Abaddon.

Alice allowed herself to slow down, her lips and fingers raw with the effort she'd made. She could feel exhaustion rising up and knew she had little strength left. It was a fatigue like nothing she'd felt before, like she'd emptied out her very being. *I used so much magic,* she thought blearily. *Will I be like Djamila? When I stop playing, will there be anything left of me?*

The sage guided her sanctuary to a rare, low hill. It was

surrounded on all sides by a sluggish flow of molten rock, but it was safer than any of the plains. The next of the endless eruptions was unlikely to bury them there.

When they touched down, Alice felt her fingers falter. Her exhausted hands missed notes with increasing frequency, and her spell began to come apart. Soon, the barrier lost cohesion such that ribbons of energy pulled loose and drifted away.

The faults in her warding became gaps, and the sage felt the heat of Abaddon rising against her skin. She doubted she could survive on Tartarus' scorched, volcanic surface, but she was past caring. Her head drooped as the faltering notes became softer and weaker.

Alice could hear the others, but she couldn't make out what they were talking about. She didn't notice when the ocarina left her lips. Her hands drifted down gently to rest on her thighs. She sensed her sanctuary falling apart, but there was nothing to be done for it.

The sage felt herself fall to the ground, but it seemed slower than it should be. Weakly, she tried to look around to make sense of it. Altair's face was looking down at her, inches from her own, and she realized he had his arms around her, guiding her. She smiled up at the jinn, distant pricks of pain sounding from her cracked, bleeding lips. He smiled back and said something, but she couldn't hear it. Then, Alice closed her eyes and didn't open them again.

"Is she dead?"

Ephialtes crouched over Altair and Ajdaha like a doting mountain. The giant looked on concernedly as they attended to the sage. Neither the dragon nor the jinn were skilled with magic, but they pooled their power to protect her. The barrier of jinn fire they made was thin, but, if nothing else, it was enough to protect her from the worst of the heat.

Altair shook his head. "She's burnt out. Alice has been

getting stronger, but she doesn't know how to use her magic efficiently. She's been trading power to compensate for lack of skill, and it's caught up to her."

"How long until she's up again?" said Ephialtes. "Rested?"

The jinn shot a glance up at the giant and spat, "How should I know?!"

Ajdaha laid a hand on his father's forearm. Altair jerked his arm away but became aware of his anger. He took a breath and mastered it, then wiped at his eyes.

"I'm sorry, Ephialtes," he said. "It's just hard to see her like this."

"You've seen her like this before?" The giant looked hopeful.

Altair nodded and tried to keep the hitch from his voice. "Twice. Lifetimes ago. The first time, she didn't recover. The second, she did."

The jinn took a breath and let it out slowly, coaxing himself into acceptance. "The important thing is she doesn't look like she's getting any worse. She needs time, but I think she'll survive."

Altair looked over the sage. He refused to think in terms of hope. Alice was going to live, or she wasn't. As he'd always done, he intended to give her everything he had to care for her. Though it pained him, he pushed more of his fiery essence into his weak magic, daring the blasted plains of Abaddon to touch her.

"With those hands," said Ajdaha, sounding the most confident of the three of them, "she should be up again soon."

The dragon looked at the sage's deific hands. Curious, he reached out with his senses and felt for the pulse of Baalim power within their flesh. There was nothing.

"Wait . . ." said Ajdaha. The dragon closed his eyes and concentrated, tried again to perceive the touch of the divine, but still nothing. He opened his eyes again and looked to his father, the surety gone from his voice. "Something's wrong."

"What?!" said Altair, his outward calm broken again. The jinn closed his eyes and concentrated on the flow of energies around them. When he focused on Alice's hands, he felt it as well. Rather, he felt an absence that made his fiery blood run cold.

"What?" said Ephialtes. The giant had no skill at all with magic and could only watch and wait. His great hands clenched into fists, longing for this to be a problem he could solve with his sword.

"What is it?!" the giant boomed, unable to contain his fearful uncertainty.

"I'm not sure exactly," said Ajdaha, "but her hands have lost much of their power. I can still feel the quality of Baalim magic about them, but only faintly."

"Is it because she's tired?" asked the giant. "They'll come back with the rest of her, right?"

The jinn and the dragon exchanged a long, concerned look, then Altair said, "I don't think so. Something's changed."

Ephialtes' great brow furrowed with a sound like boulders shifting toward an avalanche, "What are you talking about? You're saying something's interfering with the power of a *god*? That's not possible, is it?!"

Ajdaha looked up at the giant. "I need more information to be sure, but there's only one thing I can think of that would have done this. It's possible Gaia may have been killed."

The giant's eyes widened until it looked as if they would pop from their sockets. "What could do *that*!? The Baalim are nearly invincible!"

"Nearly," the dragon agreed. "It doesn't matter now. There's nothing we can do for it."

Altair looked to his son and nodded. "We need to move her somewhere safe."

"We can't take her to Shambhala," said Ajdaha. "Not

until I know what's happening there. Pazuzu is gone, but, if we can believe what he said, his children have infiltrated the citadel. We don't know how long or how influential they've become."

"Do you believe it?" asked the giant.

Ajdaha nodded. "My guild controls the greatest collection of maps of all the Realms. I've been with them since the beginning. If someone had discovered a secret entrance to something like that, I would have been aware of it. My question isn't *whether,* but *why* someone decided it was time to drop that something in our laps.

Altair said, "It sounded like some of his kids went rogue on him."

"Then they'll be working more directly for the enemy now," said the dragon, "doing what they can to be useful enough to keep from being sacked themselves."

The giant scratched his head thoughtfully. "Do you think this enemy *wanted* Pazuzu dead? Was this part of the plan?"

"No way to know," said Altair. He looked to Ajdaha, inclining his head toward Alice's hands. "But I think we should stay away from the Baalim, as well. At least until we have a better sense of things. Do we have any options?"

The dragon nodded and extended a claw into the distance. "Actually, I know just the Place. If we move quickly, we can reach a safe enough Way before any ifrit have time to sort out what happened and come looking for us."

The three of them glanced about automatically at that. Though Pazuzu was dead, there was no way of telling how many of his children were still out there, and how many of those would remain loyal enough to their father's name to seek revenge. Besides that, none of them expected to be treated kindly by the denizens of Tartarus after the damage they'd caused and the lives lost trying to stop them.

With utmost care, Altair lifted Alice's inert body and laid it gently across the dragon's back. He climbed up to sit behind her, his attention devoted to maintaining the protective barrier that kept the Realm from killing her. Once they were settled, Ajdaha rose into the air with silken grace, taking care to do nothing to disturb the sage.

Ephialtes stood and stretched. His stony fingers seemed to scrape the sky. When the dragon had flown up to be level with his shoulder, he sheathed his silver sword and started forward, splashing through flows of lava as if they were nothing more than puddles. Within her little shelter of jinn fire, draped across the back of the dragon, Alice dreamt deeply of music and monsters.

Chapter 35: Epilogue

GAIA LOOKED OVER HER Place. The god smiled down at Elysium from the tallest branches of the world tree where she made her home. The god didn't bother with a palace or a castle or even a house. The tree simply wove its branches together as it suited her from moment to moment. Just then, she'd arranged an intricate, braided balcony. The railing was at the perfect height for her to bend slightly and rest her elbows as she enjoyed a peaceful moment.

Beneath her quiet bliss, she could sense all the little aspects of her self spread out through creation, tending to all manner of ends. Somewheres, she was speaking with her siblings, the Baalim. Elsewheres, she was meeting with all kinds of lesser creatures. Sometimes, it was answering prayers, but mostly she was simply doing as she had always done, shepherding creation along as best she could. Most days, keeping her own Place in order was enough.

For all she knew and saw, however, like all the Baalim, she was not truly omniscient. As a shadow fell over her, the god noticed too late she wasn't alone. For the first time in her long, long life, she was completely surprised. Gaia whirled around and called all her aspects and avatars back to her, wanting for their strength to handle whatever it was that had somehow come to her unawares.

Gaia felt the sword pierce her chest before she could see its wielder. She felt the cold metal slide through her body and push out the other side. The god gasped and clutched at the wound, cut her palms and fingers against the sharp metal. She felt a strange species of pain unlike anything she'd known before it.

A cowled figure stood before her. Black robes like shadows concealed their identity. One arm was extended, a black glove gripping the hilt of the weapon. The glove was covered in softly glowing runes that extended all the way back to the figure's elbow.

Gaia looked down at the sword and willed it away; nothing happened. Astonished, the god pushed at the blade with her will again to no avail. Somehow, it wouldn't allow her to make herself whole. Just as bizarre, she could feel her gathering power slow its rush back to this body, the core of her being, and begin to drift aimlessly through creation.

The god's eyes widened in disbelief as she realized what was happening. It shouldn't be, but, somehow, she was dying. The dark figure reached up with their free hand and pushed back the hood. Gaia's mouth opened as she laid eyes on the face of her assassin. A thin trail of shimmering blood trickled from the corner of her mouth. A single drop fell; a dove fluttered into being where it landed and swept away on outstretched wings.

"Adam?!" said Gaia. "But how?!"

The man was tall and thin beneath the flowing robes. Blue eyes glinted like ice beneath a tumbling mane of golden hair. He was much older now than the last time she'd seen him; for all his power, touches of gray had finally settled into his tresses. His features were fine; the beauteous angles left the man looking like he'd been carved by a master sculptor rather than having been born. Only traces of lines in his skin, well on their way to becoming wrinkles, betrayed the truth of his mortality.

"You've spread yourself thin these days, Ninhursag," said Adam. "It's made you *unfocused.*"

Her mind racing, the god could see his robes were just as much a masterwork as his weapon. Runework older than any written language devised by humans was stitched in patterns so intricate as to be nearly imperceptible to all but those who knew what they were looking for. Gaia knew where the man's Artifacts had come from in an instant but couldn't believe their creator would have actually *made* them.

Adam plucked at his robes. "You like these? They were a gift from a friend."

"I know what they are," Gaia choked, then spat out a mouthful of her shining blood. "I just never thought he— that *any* of the Baalim—would ever be so foolish."

"That's the problem with miracles," said Adam, his tone conciliatory. "They upset things until creation itself *begs* for balance. When you blessed the sage with your hands, the other Baalim knew something should be done. As the recipient of their blessing, I merely suggested the form it should take."

"You do *not* speak for all of them," said the dying god, "only one."

The man shrugged. "I'm not greedy. One miracle is enough to counter another. I am simply here for the sake of order, to restore the balance that you jeopardized."

Gaia scoffed, "Balance! As if it mattered to you! You serve only yourself!"

Adam said nothing but only smiled at her and basked in the god's radiance as it faded away. She coughed up another mouthful of luminous blood and asked him, "So, you've truly found it, eh? That bastard never would have risked helping you otherwise."

"Almost," said Adam. "I just need more time, and your

conspiring has managed to upset my schedule. You should be proud. I decided to risk a personal visit to ensure things were rebalanced."

The corner of the god's mouth quirked disdain at the word *visit*, but she was afraid. Beneath her pain, Gaia could sense there weren't any other aspects of herself anymore. Like any mortal, she was trapped in her one and only body. Singularity was a terrible sensation for her, nearly equal to the pain, but she didn't have the strength anymore to be anything more than that. Just the same, for all the power of the Artifact that had killed her, her lifeforce was not yet willing to disperse.

The god smirked and began to wheeze softly as her body failed her, bit by bit. "You're only here because you'd never dare let this sword out of your sight. And why talk about balance at all? You're here because you can't find *her*, and this was the best you could manage."

Adam said nothing, but she felt his grip on the sword tense. Her smile grew, and she said, "You know I can't really die. I will only rise again, and you will have accomplished nothing."

The man held up a finger. "Ah, but that's just it. Some*thing* will rise again. *It* will be much like you, with all your power, but *this*..."

Adam shook the sword in his hand, and Gaia cried out, unable to mask her pain, her flailing hands cut to tatters against the keen edge of the Artifact. The man sneered and twisted the blade, watching the god writhe helplessly before him. Beneath their coldness, his eyes danced with pride at his own power.

"... this specific incarnation of you will be just as dead as anything else that dies. When your essence draws itself back together, *that* Baalim will not be a patron to the last of the sages."

"But Alice isn't the l-" said Gaia, and then Adam ripped the sword from her chest. The Artifact pulled and tore at the

Baalim's essence as it came free, hungry to nest and break the god, as it was made to. The shock of it was beyond Gaia's strength to endure. Falling onto her hands and knees, she watched, even then in disbelief, as her lifeblood poured and pattered over the twining branches of the world tree.

Wherever it fell, life welled up. Clusters of flowers stood where her blood had splashed. Butterflies with wings like paintings fluttered up and away. Insects and little furry things brought into being only moments before scurried away from the conflict.

Taking the sword in both hands, Adam raised it high overhead before bringing the blade down in a sweeping arc. The god's head parted from her shoulders, and, in that instant, her form broke apart into countless pinpoints of golden light that drifted out into the sky to hang like little suns. The lights spread farther and farther apart, winking out one by one until none remained.

The man sheathed his sword deftly and turned to leave in the same motion. Reaching up, he pulled up his hood so his features were hidden within its depths. Before the first of Gaia's attendants could reach the landing, the man called Adam was gone.